Egypt's Sister

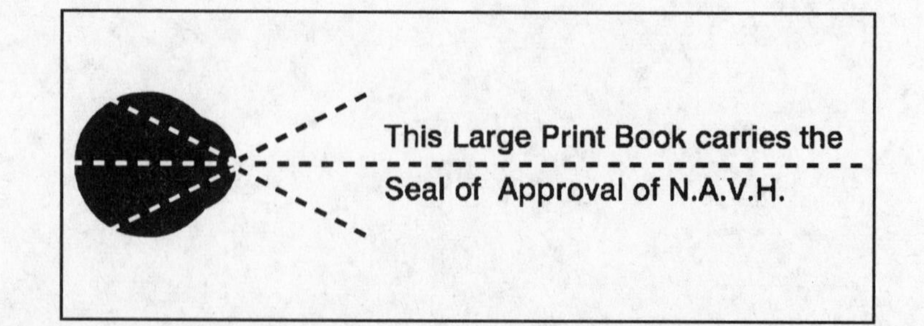
This Large Print Book carries the
Seal of Approval of N.A.V.H.

THE SILENT YEARS

EGYPT'S SISTER

A NOVEL OF CLEOPATRA

ANGELA HUNT

THORNDIKE PRESS
A part of Gale, a Cengage Company

Farmington Hills, Mich • San Francisco • New York • Waterville, Maine
Meriden, Conn • Mason, Ohio • Chicago

Thorndike Press, a part of Gale, a Cengage Company.

Thorndike Press® Large Print Christian Historical Fiction.
The text of this Large Print edition is unabridged.
Other aspects of the book may vary from the original edition.
Set in 16 pt. Plantin.

LIBRARY OF CONGRESS CATALOGING-IN-PUBLICATION DATA

Names: Hunt, Angela Elwell, 1957– author.
Title: Egypt's sister : a novel of Cleopatra / by Angela Hunt.
Description: Large print edition. | Waterville, Maine : Thorndike Press, a part of Gale, a Cengage Company, 2017. | Series: The silent years | Series: Thorndike Press large print Christian historical fiction
Identifiers: LCCN 2017022623| ISBN 9781432842031 (hardcover) | ISBN 143284203X (hardcover)
Subjects: LCSH: Life change events—Fiction. | Large type books. | GSAFD: Christian fiction. | Love stories.
Classification: LCC PS3558.U46747 E37 2017b | DDC 813/.54—dc23
LC record available at https://lccn.loc.gov/2017022623

Published in 2017 by arrangement with Bethany House Publishers, a division of Baker Publishing Group

Printed in the United States of America
1 2 3 4 5 6 7 21 20 19 18 17

In the Christian Bible, one turns the page after Malachi and finds Matthew as if only a few days fell between the activities of the prophet and the arrival of Jesus Christ. In reality, however, four hundred so-called "silent years" lie between the Old Testament and New, a time when God did not speak to Israel through His prophets. Yet despite the prophets' silence, God continued to work in His people, other nations, and the supernatural realm.

He led Israel through a time of testing that developed a sense of hope and a yearning for the promised Messiah.

He brought the four nations prophesied in Daniel's vision to international prominence: the Babylonians, the Persians, the Greeks, and the Romans. These powerful kingdoms spread their cultures throughout civilization and united the world by means of paved highways and international sailing routes.

God also prepared to fulfill His promise to the serpent in Eden: "I will put animosity between you and the woman, and between your descendant and her descendant; he will bruise your head, and you will bruise his heel" (Gen. 3:15).

For God never sleeps, and though He may not communicate as we expect Him to, He can always speak to a receptive heart.

Chapter One

Though I was as close as a shadow to many of the greatest men and women in human history, no historian ever recorded my name. Though I walked down marble hallways and dined regularly with princes and princesses, no one ever thought my presence significant. And though I influenced a woman who molded the hearts of formidable men, I am never mentioned in their biographies.

But I have a story.

My mother died the day she birthed me, but my weeping father took me from the midwife, then stepped onto the street and held me aloft, publicly acknowledging me as his daughter. A nurse chewed my food until I sprouted teeth, and a slave steadied my footsteps as I learned to walk. I lived in a palatial home only a short distance from the royal residence, so perhaps it was only natural that my father, known as "Daniel the scholar," regularly carried me to the palace where I played with other noble children. Only when I reached maturity did I realize that he did so not for my sake, but to benefit another child, one who could not leave the royal family at the end of the day. Her family called her Urbi, and I called her *friend.*

Out of all the honored foster siblings who were privileged to be the princess's playmates, Urbi loved me most. We came into the world only weeks apart, we grew at the same pace, and when we were old enough to learn, we sat before the same tutors, one of whom was my father. After class, we scampered through crowds of officials and hairless white-robed priests as we played tag in the royal gardens. In Urbi's chamber we played knucklebones and gave voices to terra-cotta dolls, then hid from the nursemaids until they cursed our mischievousness and sent for reinforcements. In the royal menagerie, we held hands and gazed at giraffes, bears, and snakes — one of them as long as a ship! — and felt ourselves small . . . but safe.

Only when the sun set did my father arrive at Urbi's chamber to take me home. Back in our house, my older brother Asher turned from his studies and looked at me with jealous scorn as I recounted the day's adventures. Father listened quietly while I babbled about exquisite gifts and strangers who spoke odd languages and flattened themselves on the ground when they chanced to meet us in the hallway.

"Why do they do that?" I asked.

Father ignored the question and offered advice: "You should watch, listen, and learn, Chava. Not every girl has the opportunities HaShem has given you."

Because I was young, I did not realize how fortunate I was. I did not know that few Jews had access to the royal palace, and I had no idea that hunger and deprivation existed. My life was a seemingly endless progression of games and fine meals; my biggest fear was that I might become ill and be unable to visit my best friend.

My heart yearned for frivolity, beautiful gowns, and polished jewelry from Urbi's treasure box. I could happily spend the day in her royal apartment, reveling in her massive collection of fine linen tunics and ornate headdresses . . . I was such a child.

If I had been wiser, I would have heeded my father's words. But as a mere girl I had no idea how swiftly life could change.

When Urbi and I were eleven years old, the

people cheered as her father the king sailed away. I did not understand why he left, and Father did not discuss it with me or my brother, but I could not help but hear the victorious shouts as his ship left the harbor.

Shortly after King Auletes's departure, Urbi's older sister Berenice decided that she wanted to be queen. Because she was female, and the people of Alexandria expected her to rule with a husband, she married — first, a Seleucid prince, who died mysteriously several days after the wedding, then a priest who seemed to please her better. As a young girl, I knew little about Berenice and cared nothing at all about her court. My only concern was for Urbi, who did not appear likely to ever become queen.

I was happy that Urbi was the second daughter and not a queen-in-waiting. Queens were busy and powerful and had no time for their friends. So long as Urbi remained a princess, we would be close.

We lived in beautiful Alexandria, a city of Greeks on Egypt's northern shore. Urbi's father had inherited the throne of Egypt from his brother, Ptolemy VIII, and that king had inherited from his father, and so on all the way back to Alexander the Great, the Greek founder of Alexandria and a god to the Alexandrians. Alexander's tomb stood in the center of the city, and kings from far away came to gaze upon his preserved corpse.

When I asked Father why so many of our neighbors lit candles for Alexander while we did not, Father told me that though Alexander had nearly united all the world's kingdoms, he could not defeat death, proving he was not a god and unworthy of having candles lit in his honor. "But consider Moses," he added. "Though Moses united the twelve tribes of Israel, a task *easily* as difficult as uniting the world's kingdoms, he was also unable to defeat death, proving that he was only a servant of HaShem, the one true God."

"And he does not need candles?"

Father smiled and ruffled my hair. "Correct, daughter."

The Greeks of Alexandria worshiped many gods, particularly Isis and Dionysus, the king's favorites. Isis, an ancient Egyptian goddess nearly always depicted with a sun disk on her head, was said to be the Mother of the Gods and wife to Osiris. Dionysus had not been an Egyptian god until Urbi's Greek forefathers landed on Alexandria's shores. With long, flowing hair and delicate features, Dionysus was the god of wine and the vineyard. The Ptolemies blended Dionysus with Osiris, expanding his power and influence everywhere but in the Jewish Quarter of Alexandria.

The people of our neighborhood worshiped one God alone, and He did not live in a marble house. We called him HaShem, Hebrew for *the name,* because His name was too holy to be used in conversation. Because HaShem was invisible, Father told me, we were never to bow before a graven image of any sort. We were different from the Greeks and Egyptians in that way, yet we, the sons and daughters of Abraham, had been chosen to bless the world.

"How?" I asked.

Father cleared his throat. "HaShem will show us when the time comes."

"But how will He show us?"

Father did not seem inclined to answer.

On every seventh day, at sundown we went to our synagogue to join with the community. A velvet-wrapped Torah scroll stood in a place of honor at the front of the room, and from where I sat with the women I would look at it and imagine the scribes who had pored over the parchments, copying the holy words of Scripture. Each time they had to write the holy name of God, Father said, the scribe would take a fresh reed, dip it into ink, and write the name.

Then he would toss that reed away and continue his copying.

When our rabbi stood, he would read from the Septuagint, a Greek translation of the Scriptures. Many in our community did not speak Hebrew, so if we were to understand HaShem's words, we had to hear them in the common tongue. Father told me and Asher that we should be proud to live in such a distinguished community, for the Septuagint had been translated in Alexandria. "Seventy-two translators, six from each of the twelve tribes, completed the Torah translation in seventy days," Father said, smiling. "Though I was not around to see it, the story is probably true. The rest of the writings were translated later."

Many of the men from our community carried on the tradition of Alexandrian scribes, for several were scholars like my father. When he was not teaching one of the royal children, he labored at his most precious work: a manuscript he called "The Twelve Testaments of the Patriarchs." In short, he studied the Scriptures and summarized what each of the tribes' patriarchs would say to his descendants were he given a chance. Often he would call me to sit with him and listen. He would read a paragraph, then squint over the top of the parchment to gauge my reaction.

"How is this?" he asked one afternoon. "And there I saw a thing again even as the former, after we had passed seventy days. And I saw seven men in white raiment saying to me, 'Arise, put on the robe of the priesthood, and the crown of righteousness, and the breastplate of understanding, and the garment of truth, and the diadem of faith, and the tiara of miracle, and the ephod of prophecy.' "

He lowered the parchment and narrowed his eyes. "Is the meaning clear?"

"Yes, Father."

"Can you guess who is speaking?"

I crinkled my nose. "Judah?"

"Who are the priests? The Levites. This is Levi."

Father went back to work while I tilted my head and considered the seven men in white raiment. "Father?"

"Yes, curious one?"

"How did the patriarchs know what HaShem wanted them to do? Did He speak to them through angels? Or did He speak to them in dreams, as He spoke to Joseph? Could He speak to me?"

"You and your questions." Father lowered the parchment in his hands as a wry but indulgent gleam appeared in his eyes. "And why would HaShem speak to a girl when He has not spoken through any prophet in nearly four hundred years?"

I felt myself flushing. "I do not know why He hasn't spoken. But He spoke to Samuel, and he was just a boy."

"So he was." Father stroked his beard, then smiled, restoring my confidence. "And who can say how HaShem will speak? Sometimes He speaks through the glory of the mountains or the power of the sea. He also speaks through the Torah, the writings, and the words of His prophets as recorded in the Tanakh."

I nodded.

"Sometimes He speaks through the voices of our leaders — like your father, the rabbi, or even a queen. For a king's heart is like a stream of water in the hand of Adonai; He directs it wherever He wants."

I nodded again.

"And sometimes" — Father's gaze focused on me — "He speaks in a small voice that pierces the heart and soul of a man . . . or even a child." A smile curved his mouth. "Have you any other questions for me?"

"Not yet." I slid from my stool and bounded away.

Who was I that HaShem should speak to

me? I was only a girl with no power or influence. But the more I thought about it, the more fascinated I grew with the possibility that Adonai *might* speak to me. Perhaps He would, if I listened carefully. . . .

When not with Urbi, I began to take my handmaid and go down to the sea, where we watched the waves crash as we listened for the voice of HaShem. And though I strained my ears, I did not hear Him.

I listened for Him in the rabbi's voice, in my father's teachings, and in the talk of the women who sat around me in the synagogue. But I did not hear Adonai.

Several months passed. We enjoyed the warm winds of spring and braced for the blazing breaths of summer. I spent my days with Urbi in the cool stone palace, and my evenings at home with Asher and my father.

One night, as one of our slaves lit the Shabbat candles, an unseasonably cool gust entered the room from the atrium's open roof. As the candles sputtered and Asher laughed, I lifted my eyes to the blue-black sky where a handful of diamond stars had already appeared.

Your friendship with the queen lies in my hands.

The voice came from nowhere, yet it engulfed me — behind me, before me, beneath me.

You will be with her on her happiest day and her last.

I shifted my attention to Asher, then to Father, expecting them to say something or rebuke whoever had dared interrupt our Shabbat meal. But they kept their eyes on the guttering candles, their mouths ruffling with good humor as the candles flickered and nearly went out.

And you, daughter of Israel, will know yourself, and you will bless her.

The flames straightened and took hold, brightening the gloom with golden light. Without acknowledging the voice and its message, Father began the Shabbat blessing: *"Barukh atah Adonai, Eloheinu, melekh ha-olam . . ."*

And I felt a tide of gooseflesh wash up each arm and crash at the nape of my neck.

In that moment, one thing became clear to me: my life was entwined with Urbi's, and HaShem intended for me to remain by her side always.

Chapter Two

Two days later I sought Urbi in her royal apartment. She squealed when she saw me, then grabbed my hand and led me into the innermost bedchamber where we could escape prying eyes. Though she had never said so, I had a feeling that Urbi suspected her sister the queen of positioning spies throughout the Royal Quarter of the city.

"I have important news," she said, crossing her legs and sitting on the silk-covered mattress.

I sat across from her and inhaled the delicious aroma of incense. Egyptians typically burned frankincense in the morning, myrrh in the afternoon, and kyphi at evening, but Urbi so loved the spicy-sweet scent of kyphi that she burned it continually.

"I have news, too."

"Me first." A dimple winked in her right cheek. "My father is finally coming home."

My mouth opened. This *was* news. If the

king was returning, Berenice was in trouble. She had been queen for nearly three years, but when the king returned . . .

"What — what will happen with your sister?"

Urbi lifted her shoulder in a casual shrug. "I do not know and I do not care. She should not have taken the throne while Father was away."

I tilted my head and nodded, silently acknowledging the truth.

"One day I may be queen," Urbi said, lifting her chin, "and you will be my lady-in-waiting. Together we will receive visitors, and if we like them, we will shower them with gifts. If we do not like them, or if they are stupid, we will have them executed."

I smiled, imagining myself behind Urbi's golden throne. "We will give banquets with so much food that we can feed the poor with the leftovers."

"Shall we have dancers for entertainment? Or wild animals?"

"Why not both?" I clapped, delighted by the possibility. "Tigers, perhaps. Ohh — *baby* tigers. They are adorable. And I would love to have an elephant."

"We could ride into the great hall on an elephant," Urbi said. "Can you imagine how people will stare?" She took a plum from her bedside table, then bit into it. "And what is your news?"

Suddenly shy, I took Urbi's free hand and leaned closer. "Two nights ago, HaShem spoke to me." I squeezed her fingers, waiting for her to shiver as I had when I heard the voice.

Her eyes flew up at me like a pair of frightened crows, then she pulled her hand away and playfully slapped my arm. "You should not tease me, Chava."

"I am not teasing. We were at dinner, and I heard a voice no one else seemed to hear. Best of all, He spoke to me about you."

Urbi gave me a quick, distracted glance and attempted a smile. "Did He say I would be beautiful? Did He say I would be *queen*?"

I deepened my smile. "HaShem said my friendship with the queen lay in His hands, and that we would be together on your happiest day and your last. And that I would bless you."

I grinned at her, thrilled to share such a wonderful foretelling, but Urbi's face did not reflect my joy.

"Your friendship with the queen," she repeated, her voice hollow. "What if He was talking about Berenice?"

I frowned. "Why would HaShem talk

about her? I have no friendship with her. I do not even know her."

"And you will be with me on my *last* day? You have just given me a reason to never see you again."

I stiffened, momentarily abashed. "I am sure HaShem did not mean it that way. You're not about to die."

"How do you know?" Her brow wrinkled as something moved in her eyes. "The Ptolemies have been known to kill their brothers and sisters. How do you know Berenice won't murder me?"

"Because . . ." I grasped for any reason available. "Because your father is coming home."

"He won't arrive for months. She has plenty of time to kill a princess."

I sat perfectly still, stunned by the taut expression on Urbi's face. She had never revealed this fear, but clearly she had often thought about the danger of being so close to the throne.

"I won't let anyone kill you." I straightened and propped my hands on my hips. "If I have to, I will sneak you out of the palace and you can live with us. No one would ever think to look for you in the Jewish Quarter."

Annoyance struggled with humor on her

face as she glared at me. “You are a foolish, naïve girl,” she said, bending her knees. “But I am glad I have you.” She hugged her knees and lowered her head, then abruptly lifted it. “My happiest day?” She arched a brow. “I wonder when that will be.”

“Perhaps when you marry,” I suggested. “Or when you have your first child.”

She leaned forward and peered through the open doorway, her eyes bright with speculation. “Wouldn’t it be tragic if my happiest day was also my last?” She lowered her gaze, her long lashes shuttering her eyes. “I wouldn’t be surprised if it were.”

“You cannot think that way, Urbi. I am sure you will have many, many happy days — and as your best friend, I plan to be there for all of them.”

“Swear to it?” She turned as her eyes searched mine. Then she caught my hand and peeled back my fingers, revealing my flat palm.

Breathing in the fragrance of incense, I stared at her, uncertain of her intentions.

“Forever friends,” she said, an odd, faintly eager look flashing in her eyes.

As I nodded, she pulled a short blade from the girdle at her waist and gripped my left wrist. I pulled back, but before I could break free she lifted the blade and swept it over my palm, slicing the skin from above my thumb to the end of the curving lifeline. I caught my breath as the blade stung my flesh, but I knew better than to cry out.

Then, imposing an admirable control on herself, Urbi opened her left hand and made the same cut on her own palm. She held it up as blood dripped from the red arc and stained the silk sheet beneath us.

"Forever friends," she repeated, pressing her bleeding cut to mine. She locked her fingers around my hand. "You are blood of my blood, and heart of my heart."

"Blood of my blood," I echoed. "Heart of my heart. Friends forever."

We sat without moving as our blood mingled, then she drew me close in a fierce embrace.

"If your father asks," she whispered, nodding at my blood-slicked hand, "tell him you cut yourself on one of my swords."

I opened my mouth to protest, but she was already off, hurrying away to recite for a tutor or pay a dutiful visit to her older sister.

I pulled a wide ribbon from my hair and wrapped it around my bleeding palm. Only then, after Urbi had gone, did I feel the pain.

Chapter Three

My feet tapped a jittery rhythm as my slave wound a length of hair around the heated *calamistrum,* a gift the king had brought from Rome.

"Hurry, Nuru — I cannot be late."

"I do not want to burn my fingers, my lady, or your neck. So if you would please hold still . . ."

I bit back my impatience and gripped the sides of the bench by my dressing table. Father might have already begun his lecture, and he would not appreciate his daughter rushing late into the room. If the royal children could make it to an appointment on time, he often reminded me, surely his fourteen-year-old daughter could.

Nuru smiled as a perfectly formed curl slipped off the narrow end of the calamistrum and dangled before my earlobe. "If you'll give me a moment to sew it to the other braids —"

"No time," I told her, leaving the bench to search for my sandals. "I must be away."

I found my braided sandals beneath the bed and slipped them on. Straightening, I ran my hand over the elaborate braids at the back of my head, then left the room, pausing only to check my image in the reflecting pool. Two ringlets danced in the breeze — Urbi would certainly tease me about those, but at least I looked presentable. My white chiton was spotless, and the blue himation artfully draped around my torso and over my shoulder. My nails had been scrubbed and my face washed. I looked as I should when entering the presence of royalty, so no one, not even Father, could upbraid me about anything but my tardiness.

I took a deep breath and signaled one of the slaves, who stood at the doorway. Understanding that I needed an escort, he joined me at once, and walked before me through the wide street that separated the Jewish Quarter of Alexandria from the Royal Quarter. He paused at the gate to the sprawling palace complex.

"I know the way from here."

Dismissing the slave, I spotted my friend Acis, one of the Egyptian guards, and waved. Acis lifted his chin, then moved to a side entrance, where he held the gate open long enough for me to slip through. I hurried down a path that led to the children's chambers. Only four royal children still lived in Alexandria — Urbi and Arsinoe, the youngest sister, as well as the two boys, Omari and Sefu. When one of them became king — *if* one of them ascended to the throne — he would take the name *Ptolemy,* inherited from the Greek general who had assumed control of Egypt after Alexander the Great's death.

I entered a building, turned a corner, and heard the baritone rumble of my father's voice. I waited a moment before tiptoeing into the chamber, hoping he had turned away from the door.

Fortune was with me. My father had indeed turned away, surrendering the room to Urbi, but she had not missed my entrance. Her brown eyes widened as I slid onto a settee, and an elegant brow lifted in unspoken rebuke.

"Master" — she turned to my father — "I seem to have lost my thought. Would you present my charge again?"

I glared at Urbi, then turned a smooth face to my father, who was frowning in my direction.

Urbi had not forgotten her topic; she

never forgot anything. She asked for guidance only because she wanted to direct my father's attention to my untimely arrival.

I waited, lips pressed together, until my father shifted his attention to Urbi, then I thrust my tongue toward her. Though her expression did not change, she placed her hand at her side and wagged a discreet finger in my direction.

My father bowed his head. "Princess, I charged you to debate a question of daily life. Is it more preferable to live in the country or in the city?"

Urbi inclined her head in a regal nod, then lifted her chin and addressed her audience — her tutor, her three siblings, her attendants, and me.

Schooled in the art of rhetoric and communicative gestures, she raised her left hand and swept it from right to left, gracefully including all of us listeners. "Life is pleasurable no matter where one lives, for what beauty does the grave hold? And the afterlife, though it may be sweet, is but a dream and cannot be adequately described. Life in the country is restful, for nights are filled with sounds of the wilderness and heralded by purple sunsets over the western mountains. Who can deny the majesty of the cliffs near the Valley of the Kings, or the beauty of the shimmering Nile during the inundation? But life in the city, Alexandria in particular, is equally grand. The city radiates with the greatness of its founder, the man buried at the city's heart, and no people in the world are as brave, resourceful, or as creative as Alexandrians. Where else do Greeks, Egyptians, Romans, and Jews dwell in harmony? Has any other city our lust for life? Has any other city a wonder like our library or our towering lighthouse? Has any other people such a thirst for the pursuit of knowledge? No. Though living in the country may be preferable to living in a small town, Alexandria provides life at its finest, more perfect than any man can imagine."

She lowered her head and placed her hand on her chest, signaling that she had finished.

My father stood. "Very good." His eyes glowed with quiet pride. "You could have added a few more gestures, however. Always remember that the hands can speak as powerfully as the mouth. Do we not use them to demand, promise, summon, dismiss, threaten, supplicate, express aversion or fear, question or deny? Considering what to say is not as important as considering how to say it."

Urbi dipped her head, acknowledging my

father's advice, then assumed her seat at the front of the room.

Father's eyes lit on me. "Chava. Perhaps you would present a eulogy for us."

I rose and folded my hands. "A eulogy for whom?"

"For —" he tilted his head, doubtless searching for a name that would not remind the royals of recent trials — "for Ptolemy. The first."

I took my time walking to the open space before the royal children's seats. I had not mastered Egyptian history and cared little about the man who had served Alexander and cheated the conqueror's son out of his rightful inheritance. But the first Ptolemy was the ancestor of these royal children, and Ptolemies had ruled Egypt for three hundred years. They built the city Alexander designed, so perhaps I could summon up a measure of respect.

Would that Father had asked me to give a eulogy for Simon, Joseph, or any of the patriarchs. *Those* I knew as well as I knew my father's face.

I walked to the center of the open space, straightened my spine, lifted my chin, and curled my hand into a discreet circle to avoid distracting my audience with what Father called my tendency to "accent phrases with flapping fingers and wild gesticulations."

"What can I say of Ptolemy?" I said, strengthening my voice so it reached the slaves in the back of the chamber. "What can I say of the man who was a schoolmate to Alexander the Great and followed him from the kingdom of Macedonia to conquer the world? Without Ptolemy's writings, we would have little knowledge of Alexander and his exploits. Without Ptolemy's cleverness in bringing Alexander's sarcophagus to Egypt, we would not have the founder of Alexandria entombed among us. Without Ptolemy's wisdom and foresight, we would not have an outstanding library that is envied by the world."

I glanced at my father, who had arched a brow. Immediately I realized that I had failed to emphasize a single point with a gesture, a severe oversight. How to distract him from my mistake?

I shifted to a Jewish perspective, an addition that would surely please him. "In Ptolemy, we see the fulfillment of what the prophet Daniel foretold to King Nebuchadnezzar of Babylon." I lifted my right hand high, like a prophet about to deliver a word of warning. "Nebuchadnezzar was the head of gold, ruler of the world. But after him another kingdom rose, the kingdom of the Medes and the Persians, the chest of silver. The Medo-Persians were defeated by the belly of bronze, the kingdom of the Greeks, and years before Alexander's birth, the prophet Daniel foreknew that Alexander's empire would not pass to his son, but would be divided to the four winds of heaven — four generals, one of whom was Ptolemy, whom we mourn today." With my closing words, I lifted both hands and gracefully crossed them over my chest as I bowed my head — a gesture, I hoped, of respect and reverent mourning. I held the pose until my father cleared his throat.

"Thank you, Chava. Princess — what did you think of Chava's eulogy?"

Urbi lifted her chin. "I approve it."

"*Why* do you approve it? How did you find her delivery?"

Urbi's dark gaze met mine. "Impactful." The corner of her painted mouth rose in the hint of a smile. "I was near tears at the end."

Father closed his eyes, then turned to Omari, Urbi's junior by eight years. "My prince — have you an opinion on Chava's eulogy?"

The boy, barely six years old, shrugged.

"You have no opinion?"

The prince glanced at me, then grinned. "She is very pretty."

"Thank you, Prince Omari."

The youngest royal son, adorable four-year-old Sefu, piped up. "I think she's pretty, too."

Father bowed his head. "Thank you, Prince Sefu."

Father turned to me, his mask of patient forbearance disappearing. "In spite of these royal compliments, you have disappointed me, Chava. Instead of telling us of Ptolemy's many accomplishments, you talked about prophecy, about his forefathers, and about the history of Alexander. It was not the best eulogy you could have improvised."

"I mentioned the library."

"But you did not mention the museum or Ptolemy's love of learning. You gave us little feeling for the man himself."

A line crept into the space between Father's brows as he looked from me to Urbi, then he shook his head. "I will never understand why HaShem makes one woman beautiful and another woman clever. But who am I to question His doing?"

He stood and bowed to the royal children. "That is all for today. I will meet you again tomorrow."

The two princes scampered away while

my father pulled his robe more tightly around him and slowly left the chamber.

After bathing and changing into a clean chiton, I smoothed a few stray hairs and went into the *triclinium,* where our slaves had prepared the table for the Shabbat meal. The light that usually flooded this room had dimmed, reminding me that the sun was balancing on the western horizon. Time was fleeting.

"Hurry," I reminded the kitchen slave as she set two challah loaves on the table. "The sun sets."

After covering the loaves with linen napkins, I lit a strip of papyrus in the kitchen cook fire and brought it to the table, lighting the candles. My father and Asher had reclined on their couches and watched in silence as I waved my hands over the candles to welcome the Sabbath.

I covered my eyes. *"Barukh atah Adonai, Eloheinu, melekh ha'olam, asher kidishanu b'mitz'votav v'tzivanu, l'had'lik neir shel Shabbat."* Blessed are you, Lord, our God, sovereign of the universe, who has sanctified us with His commandments and commanded us to light the lights of Shabbat.

Father and Asher replied in unison: "Amein."

Leaving the candles and challah on the table, I picked up my himation and draped it over my hair and shoulders, then followed Father and Asher out of the house. The synagogue was a short distance away, and already the street was crowded with neighbors on their way to the Sabbath meeting.

After greeting several of our friends outside the building, I slipped inside and found a seat among the women. An older woman whose name I couldn't remember squeezed my arm as she sat beside me. "And how is your father today?"

"He is well, thank you."

"I am eager to read his work. I am also eager to discuss my nephew with him." She crossed her spotted hands and chuckled. "Lavan is a fine young man and would make a good husband for you. How old are you now?"

I tried not to wince. "Fourteen."

"A pretty girl like you without a mother at this age —" The woman tapped her tongue against her teeth. "Do not worry, my child, we women of the community will watch over you. And we have all agreed that you and Lavan would make a good match."

I chewed my lower lip and glanced at the men's section, hoping to catch Asher's eye. He would help if I shot him a look of distress. If I behaved as if I were about to panic, he might even hurry me away from this place —

At that moment the rabbi stood and the room grew silent. The woman next to me pulled her veil over her head as we said opening prayers, and though she smiled and winked at me as we prayed, she did not speak again of her nephew.

We sang psalms, a young boy recited a passage from the Torah, and then the rabbi stood again. "I call for the elders," he said, lifting a folded material that looked like fine linen. "Take the four corners of this chuppah, and make it a tent of blessing."

I leaned forward, interested in this deviation from our usual service.

"And now," the rabbi called, smiling, "I ask all the wives and widows to come stand beneath this tent as we pray a blessing for you."

I gasped in pleased surprise as women around me stood and walked forward, many of them visibly moved by this unusual gesture. When they had gathered beneath the makeshift tent, the men began to pray, their heads bobbing as they lifted prayers to the God of Abraham, Isaac, and Jacob.

For an instant my heart ached to stand beneath that tent, to hear the voice of a husband begging heaven to shower me with blessings. But I did not want to be a wife, and why should I? HaShem had already told me that I would be a blessing to a queen, so I would need to remain at her side. From her happiest day to her last. Always.

I swiped away an embarrassing tear as the prayers ended and the women returned to their seats, their faces lit with an unearthly glow. I thought I managed to look content and happy, but the woman who had been sitting next to me handed me a linen square to wipe my eyes.

"You are ready," she whispered, nudging me with her elbow. "I will speak to your father soon."

Back at home, Asher and I settled onto our dining couches as Father lifted the linen napkins from the challah loaves and recited the blessing: *"Barukh atah Adonai, Eloheinu, melekh haolam hamotzi lechem min ha'aretz."* Blessed are you, Lord, our God, King of the Universe, who brings forth bread from the earth.

"Amein," Asher and I chorused.

The slaves brought in our meal as we passed the loaves and broke off pieces of bread.

"Your Latin teacher sent word — he is

sorry he could not come for dinner," Father said as he reclined on his couch. "He will come for your lesson on the first day of the week."

I declined the bowl of stewed pigeon with mulberries and reached for the salad instead. "I shall look forward to it, Father."

"Latin is easy," Asher said. "I am translating Homer's *Odyssey* as part of my lessons. Father says my Latin translation is very close to the original text."

"Good for you." My words dripped with sarcasm, a tone Father did not miss.

"*Shalom,* you two. I will not have you arguing on Shabbat."

I fingered a bowl of figs, then selected one and tore at the fibrous exterior with my teeth.

"How is the princess?" Father asked. "Has she been able to spend much time with her father since he returned?"

"Not much," I said, dropping the fig. "She wants to see him, but he is always surrounded by Romans."

"Urbi is a good student," Father said, dipping his fingers into the pigeon stew. "Though she will never be sought for her beauty, her charming personality more than compensates. None of the other royal children are as bright, and none of them speak as well. She even outshines her brothers, though they are still too young to demonstrate their full potential. One can only hope they will be given a chance to excel before —"

I lifted my head, silently reminding him that he had ventured dangerously close to a forbidden subject. Even at home, one did not talk about the Ptolemies' tendency to murder each other.

Mindful of the servants, I lowered my voice. "We should not follow these thoughts further."

Father's face flushed. "Indeed."

"I saw the king today," Asher remarked, grinning. "He was riding with an officer of the Roman Cavalry."

Father spat out a tiny bone. "Did this soldier have a name?"

"They call him Mark Antony. They say he personally commanded the troops who brought the king back from Rome."

I tilted my head, interested only because the story concerned Urbi. When Urbi's father had returned to Alexandria, one of his first acts had been to arrange a series of executions — of Berenice, her husband, and any high officials who supported his rebellious daughter's brief reign. Soldiers loyal to Berenice put up a brief fight, but the Roman legionaries made short work of them.

I had not yet found the courage to ask Urbi how she felt about the latest development in her family drama. She did not often speak about her siblings, and I did not dare question her about secrets she had closeted away. I was simply grateful that her father's absence seemed to compel her to seek me out. Perhaps I had already begun to bless her life.

Only once had Urbi touched on the subject of her executed sister. One day, as we strolled through the garden, she gripped my hand and squeezed it. "I am glad my father is home, for I love him dearly," she said, her tone deep with ferocity. "I liked my sister, but I shall not weep for Berenice. She chose a treacherous path, and her own actions sealed her fate."

I had nodded numbly, and only later did I fully understand what had happened. With that came the realization that after Berenice's death, Urbi stood first in line to inherit the throne of Egypt. My best friend had gone from lifelong princess to prospective queen, and I knew next to nothing about the responsibilities that awaited a ruler.

"Asher." Father's voice broke into my thoughts. "How goes your Torah study?"

My brother sucked at the inside of his cheek for a minute, his brows working. "It is . . . interesting."

"How so?"

Asher wiped his hand on his napkin and leaned forward on the table. "In the Torah, HaShem says He will come down upon Mount Sinai in the sight of all the people."

Father nodded. "And?"

"And Moses, Aaron, Nadab and Abihu, and seventy of the elders went up and saw the God of Israel . . . as they were eating and drinking."

Father nodded again. "As it is written."

"But how could they see Him, since HaShem is spirit? And does not the Torah say that Moses was not allowed to see HaShem, but only His reflected glory?"

Father smiled and stroked his beard. "What do the other Torah students say?"

Asher pressed his hands to the table, eager to explain. "Some say the writing is a metaphor, not meant to be interpreted literally."

Father arched a brow. "Continue."

"And others say that this is an occasion when HaShem cloaked himself in flesh, just as He did when he visited Abraham with two angels. That day, Adonai ate and drank with Abraham, so He must have appeared in some sort of body."

Father's smile deepened. "So it would seem."

"So then . . ." Asher tilted his brow and gave Father an uncertain look. "Someone suggested that if God was able to appear in a body, it must not need certain things."

"Such as?"

"Things that protect the body . . . like fingernails."

I laughed aloud. Father gave me a stern look, then directed his attention back to Asher. "Someone thinks HaShem has no fingernails?"

"In his physical form," Asher added. "Half of us think so." He tilted his head. "Why would He need to protect His fingers when He controls the universe? The other half believes that HaShem would want to look like His creation, so he *would* have fingernails, toenails, and sweat."

"Sweat." A corner of Father's mouth twisted upward. "In which group do you belong, Asher?"

Asher blew out a breath. "Fingernails."

"And why?"

"Because I think He would want to look like us. Abraham did not recognize Him at first, right? So He must have looked like an ordinary man, at least at first glance."

Father nodded slowly and studied his fingers as if seeing them for the first time. "One of HaShem's greatest gifts is the ability to reason," he finally said, lowering his hand. "But do not try to reason your way to understanding Adonai, for nothing is impossible with Him."

My stomach tightened when he turned to me. "Chava?"

"Father?"

"Tonight I met a young man at the synagogue, a wheat exporter. He inquired about you."

I swallowed hard. "About me?"

"Apparently," Father went on, the candles tossing his shadow onto the walls and ceiling, "some weeks ago he saw you strolling with your slave on the Canopic Way. He made inquiries, and his inquiries led him to our house."

I lowered my gaze. I might have been walking with Urbi, not Nuru, because my best friend loved to sneak out of the palace to mingle with ordinary people. But Father did not need to know that.

I glanced at Asher, who was staring at Father with unabashed curiosity. "Why would anyone ask about *her*?"

Father gave my brother a reproachful look. "Your sister is beautiful, and every young man — including you — needs a devout wife. He saw Chava, and he liked her."

I could no longer remain silent. "He doesn't even know me!"

"That can easily be remedied." Father smiled. "We could ask him to dinner. Or I could invite him to walk with us, or perhaps we could visit the library together."

I drew a deep breath, knowing that the time had come. I had carried my secret for months, but it was time Father knew the truth. "I am sorry, Father, but I am not going to marry. HaShem has a different purpose for me."

For a moment, Father's expression did not change, then my words fell into place. He stared until his eyes appeared to be in danger of dropping out of his face. "What did you say?"

"Father . . ." I leaned forward and pressed my hands together. "I have wanted to tell you this for some time, but I was afraid you wouldn't believe me. But why shouldn't you? You yourself taught me about how HaShem speaks to us."

Father showed his teeth in an expression that was not a smile. "Go on."

"One night, during the lighting of the Shabbat candles, HaShem spoke to me. He said my friendship with the queen was in

His hands, that I would be with her on her happiest day and her last, and that I would know myself and bless her. You see? That's why I cannot marry. I have always felt I was meant to be with her always, perhaps to be one of Urbi's attendants —"

"The girl is not a queen."

"She wasn't when HaShem spoke to me, but one day she will be. And she will need a trustworthy friend by her side."

Father blinked. "If HaShem wanted such a thing for you, He would speak to *me,* your father. And I have heard nothing from HaShem, except that a man should leave his mother and father and cleave to his wife. So it is time for you to find a husband."

"I do not want to marry!"

"You are fourteen, the age when a girl should be betrothed. I have not pressured you because I wanted you to continue your lessons. But you are a daughter of Israel, and you are old enough to find your husband and raise a family. If you marry Lavan or Japheth —"

"Japheth? The Latin teacher who did not come for dinner?"

"And what is wrong with marrying a teacher?" Father shook his head. "If you married him, you would have no worries. You would live in a nice home, you would never be hungry, and you could travel the world with your husband. You could visit Judea and worship in Jerusalem —"

I covered my face as understanding swamped me. My father always spoke of Jerusalem with an almost palpable longing, and apparently he thought Asher and I should long for Jerusalem, as well. Why should we? Why should anyone want to visit that dusty, blood-drenched city, especially when we had a Temple in Leontopolis, a perfectly fine Temple that had not been defiled by Syrians or Greeks or pretenders to the priesthood. . . .

Father's eagerness to get me out of the house hurt, but far more hurtful was his unwillingness to believe that HaShem had spoken to me. Why wouldn't He speak to a girl? Were women so far beneath men that Adonai had no use for them? Yet HaShem had worked through the little slave girl when He healed Naaman, the heathen with leprosy. And Adonai had used Deborah and Yael to kill an enemy of Israel.

"Excuse me —" I gulped back a sob — "but I must obey HaShem. And I am no longer hungry."

I dipped my head in a token nod of respect, then fled the room.

CHAPTER FOUR

Four years passed — four inundations, four seasons of planting, reaping, and harvest. The friendship between Urbi and I grew stronger, for we were no longer children, but young women, with all the energy and passion of those who are old enough to taste independence, yet young enough not to be burdened with responsibilities.

My father and I had established a temporary peace. Though he often made me feel like a loaf of bread that grew less desirable with every passing day, what could he say? He had introduced me to Urbi and allowed us to be together since our earliest years. He had told me that HaShem spoke to His people, so how could he deny what I had heard?

Father allowed me to live as I always had, although I knew his deepest prayer was that one day I would realize a yearning for something I would never find in the palace.

But there I found everything I could ever want.

Urbi and I made an odd pair in those days. Our tutors frequently commented on her intelligence and my beauty, never realizing that their words seemed to imply I was dull and Urbi plain. Nothing could be further from the truth. I was, after all, a scholar's daughter, and so learning came naturally to me. And while Urbi had no trouble passing as a plain slave when in disguise, when adorned in her finery, she was as striking a woman as I had ever seen.

"What does it matter what people think?" we asked each other. "Together, do we not make a perfect pair?"

Urbi's father insisted she learn about the Egypt that lay outside Alexandria, so together we studied the pharaohs, the gods, and the people who had created a most unique kingdom. We learned that because of the annual flood, Egypt was the most fertile and unique land in the world. Elsewhere, rivers flowed north to south, while the life-giving Nile flowed south to north. In other lands farmers tilled the land before they planted; in Egypt, farmers planted before they tilled. Egyptian men stayed home to weave while women sold goods at the market; but other men went to market and their women stayed home. "In Greece," one tutor added, "women do not leave the house at all, while in Rome, women are considered weak and feebleminded. But in Egypt, women conduct business, sell property, and raise families."

Urbi and I dismissed the rest of the world and considered Egypt the only land fit for human habitation. And Alexandria, we believed, was the most glorious city in existence.

"Of course, my tutor Polyphemus prefers Athens," Urbi said, laughing as she threaded her arm through mine one afternoon. "But he is Greek, and we Greeks are often blind to common sense."

I laughed and led her toward the skiff that would take us to Antirhodos Island, home to the building that held her new royal apartments. "Do you think we are blind to truth?" I asked. "We have our loyalties — to each other, and to our fathers. Sometimes I wonder if my attachments have caused me to judge other men and ideas unfairly."

"Ah, Chava, you are becoming philosophical with age. You never used to think of anything but pleasure."

"I am older now. And I have been studying philosophy for the past several months."

"It is the Greek influence — and believe

me, I know it well. You should go back to reading about your Hebrew patriarchs. They gave your thoughts a deliciously different flavor."

I shrugged her words away, though her suggestion made me uneasy. "I have always thought you and I were more similar than different. We have spent so much time together that we —"

"We could be joined at the hip, but you and I will always be different."

I stopped, stunned and surprised by her comment.

Urbi must have seen the dismay on my face. "Chava, please understand that I am grateful for our differences. What good would you be if you only told me what I wanted to hear? As it is, I can make no decisions without your discerning advice." She patted my hand, then stepped away and gestured to a slave near the dock. "You! Bring us fruit, bread, and cheese. At once."

As the man hurried away to do her bidding, I walked to the skiff, scattering a flock of ibises before dropping onto a pile of linen pillows near the bow. I inhaled a deep breath of sea air and pointed to a man approaching over the dock. "Is that one of your tutors?"

Urbi squinted. "That one teaches Troglodyte, a language that sounds like the screeching of bats." She sank onto pillows near me, then reached out to finger a fallen braid at my neck. "Is this a new style? My brothers seemed quite entranced with it."

I groaned, arranging the braid back into place. "I allowed Nuru to experiment. Yesterday I saw a woman on the street with hair styled something like this. She looked Roman."

"If it is from Rome . . . must it be better than what we have in Alexandria?" Urbi wore an inward look, as if she had asked the question of herself.

Any mention of Rome was apt to elicit a reflective response from her. I had learned that the people of Alexandria had forced her father from the city in our younger years because he overtaxed them to repay the Romans who sanctioned his kingship. Without the support of his people or his treasury, Auletes had been forced to beg influential Roman senators for money and support. Urbi was closer to the king than any of the royal children, and the thought of her proud father begging was enough to spark a fire in her eyes.

I left her question unanswered and stood when the tutor approached and knelt on the dock.

"I should leave you," I told her. "My Latin teacher will soon be at the house."

Urbi laughed. "You have not yet mastered that tongue?"

"My ear is not as quick as yours. Japheth keeps telling me I need more practice."

She gave me a sly smile. "Perhaps he is more concerned with marrying than teaching you."

"I doubt it — not when there are so many younger girls available. But Father insists that I speak to Japheth in Hebrew, then he complains that my Hebrew isn't good enough to be understood in Jerusalem."

"Are you planning a visit?"

"Not me. But Father dreams of it."

"Fathers." Urbi lifted a brow, then smiled. "Would you ever want to live outside Alexandria?" Honest curiosity flickered in her eyes.

I considered my answer. If I expressed even a slight desire to see some other part of the world, my impulsive friend might order a caravan or a ship to take us straightaway.

"I do not want to go anywhere." I reached over and squeezed her hand. "Wherever you are, blood of my blood, there am I as well."

Feeling restless after the Sabbath, on the

first day of the week I ordered Nuru to put on her sandals and accompany me on a walk. We crossed the colonnaded loggia outside our home, then zigzagged through the Jewish Quarter until we reached the Canopic Way, the broad avenue that transected the carefully designed city of Alexandria.

I inhaled deeply as the morning sun warmed my face. In terms of freedom, I was more fortunate than my best friend. Though Urbi and I both loved to explore the city, she could not wander as easily as I. On several occasions we had dressed her in a simple slave's tunic and a plain cloak so we could walk among the ordinary people and breathe in the scents of burning sacrifices at the temples, the stink of dead fish at the docks, and the acrid smell of dyes at the weaver's establishment. Not only did we enjoy observing the city's industry, we were also free to choose among dozens of entertainments — the bathhouse, library, museum, gymnasium, and over four hundred theaters. Actors and mimes who could not find work performed on the street, entertaining passersby before they held out gloved hands and hoped for a bronze coin or two.

I looked up and smiled at the scribbles of

clouds overhead. I longed for Urbi's company, but she had been spending her days with her ailing father. Until her father regained his health, Nuru would have to serve as my companion.

"My father does not understand me." I sighed as we walked. "Last night he spoke of marriage again — can you imagine? How can I remain at Urbi's side if I have to care for a husband? Father seems to think I should want a home and children, yet I would be perfectly content to spend the rest of my life as Urbi's servant. We are practically sisters, and the idea of tearing us apart . . . is unbearable."

I glanced at Nuru, but her face remained composed in a smooth and implacable mask.

"You may speak," I prodded, lifting my chiton as we approached a puddle.

"Your father only wants what is best for you, mistress. He worries about you."

Nuru's answer was safe and true, and the logic in it halted me in mid-step. Of course! Father was thinking like a protective parent. He thought I would need a husband to protect me, but I would not. Urbi was blood of my blood and heart of my heart, and no one would dare threaten me so long as I stood by her side. Urbi would one day be queen of the richest kingdom in the world, so I had nothing to fear — from anyone.

"Nuru, you are brilliant!" I squeezed her arm. "You have enlightened me. Tonight I will tell Father that he need not fear for me. If something happens to him, Urbi will invite me to live in the palace. I'll be perfectly safe there."

My slave's inscrutable gaze shifted to some commotion on the street. Irritation nipped at me, for only an untrained slave would let her attention stray from her mistress, but curiosity overtook my frustration. I looked down the road and saw that the relaxed pace of pedestrians on the Canopic Way had quickened. Like an undulating wave, news of some event was passing from group to group, leaving a ripple of agitation in its wake.

We did not have to wait long. I overheard the story from a man who turned to his companion with a look of surprised satisfaction on his features: "Auletes has gone to his fathers."

My throat went dry. I turned wide eyes upon Nuru, then a great exultation filled my chest nearly to bursting. Joy spurred my steps as I hurried toward the Royal Quarter. If the king was truly dead, my best friend had just become queen.

■ ■ ■ ■

With Nuru hurrying behind me, I went to the Royal Quarter and found the gates closed and heavily guarded. With no other choice, I walked home and told my father the news.

"You should remain here," he said, placing his hand on my shoulder. "Urbi will not have time for you now. She will be preparing a wedding."

"Whose?"

The thin line of his mouth clamped tight for a moment. "Her own. She will have to marry her brother."

I pressed my hand to my temple where a drum had begun to pound. "Why should Urbi have to wed her brother? Omari is an idiot."

Father loomed over me, his face a thundercloud of disapproval. "Mind your tongue, daughter! The palace has spies throughout Alexandria. Such a statement, falling upon the ear of someone in an exalted position, might result in your execution . . . mine and Asher's, too."

"But no one is more exalted than Urbi, and no one is closer to her than me."

Father lifted his hands in frustration.

"Today you say that. Tomorrow — who knows?"

Still stupefied, I pressed my lips together and crossed my arms.

"I know this sort of thing doesn't interest you," Father continued, locking his hands behind his back as he paced in the atrium, "but if you had been a better student of history, you might have gained an understanding of this matter. In Egypt, a queen rules by right of her royal birth, but the king rules by right of marriage. The right to the throne is passed down through the female, and whomever she marries wears the crown."

I frowned. "I do not see why Urbi cannot marry anyone she chooses. She shouldn't have to wed her stupid brother."

"She does if it was her father's wish. Her brother expects to rule Egypt, and Urbi would find it dangerous to thwart the desires of another Ptolemy, even if it is her little brother . . . because he has supporters." He lowered his voice to a conspiratorial whisper. "The younger the ruler, the more leeches he carries with him into the throne room. The child may not be dangerous, but the leeches are. Urbi must move carefully in the coming days."

"Still." I shook my head. "To marry her brother! I would rather marry a pig."

Father looked at me in patient amusement but did not remark on the insult to Asher.

"The royal family has been marrying their siblings ever since the first Ptolemy fabricated an ancestral link to the pharaohs. That is how they keep a grip on power. And if another relative threatens, they have never been shy about murdering their kin."

I sank onto a chair and struggled to understand. I felt like a child who had admired a lacy fabric for years, only to discover that it was not made of lace, but the sticky strands of a lethal spider's web.

"Omari may only be a boy of ten, but he has been groomed to wear a crown." Father seemed to calm as he watched my face. "He will agree to the marriage with his sister because he must in order to rule. But if she displeases him, or if she takes one step without his approval, he will depose her and marry his younger sister."

"Why is *she* the one at risk? Why couldn't she depose Omari and marry Sefu?"

Father tugged on his beard. "She could, I suppose. Those siblings will be engaged in a delicate balancing act, with their lives resting on the scale. Trust me on this, Chava. These matters are far more complicated than you realize."

"I — I have never had a reason to think

about these things. And Urbi never spoke of them." I looked at him as confusing thoughts whirled in my head. "How can this be? The Torah says a man who lies with his sister is cursed."

Father's brows lowered. "Egypt . . . does not heed the words of HaShem. So long as we live here, you will fare better if you keep quiet, live your life, and accept the way things are beyond the walls of our home. They are not *us.* We are not *them.*"

My heart broke in that moment — not because Egypt was such an upside-down place, but because Urbi must have carried this heavy knowledge for years. No wonder she had never spoken of finding a handsome husband! While I dreamed of a carefree life as her lady-in-waiting, Urbi had known that she would have to marry her spoiled younger brother. Even though she would be queen of a land where women enjoyed a rare level of independence, she would be the least free of all.

"I feel sorry for her," I whispered, more to myself than to my father.

But he heard and patted my hand as he clucked in sympathy. "Adonai's eyes saw you when you were unformed," he said, "and in His book are written the days that will be formed — when not one of them had come to be." He chuckled. "HaShem has written a story for you, and one for Urbi. They are very different stories."

"How do you know?" I asked. "HaShem has told me —"

"Urbi has been well prepared for the life HaShem has given her," he went on, his voice a soft rumble in the room. "Do not mention these things in her presence unless she broaches the subject. You must learn to think of her as two people, your friend and the ruler. Trust me, daughter — a great gulf will soon exist between Urbi and the woman you will bow before as queen."

As the sun sank behind the gleaming Temple of Isis, I slipped out of the house and ran toward the Royal Quarter. Father had gone to his room with a manuscript, and Nuru thought I had gone to bed. The doorman sat on a stool and nodded in sleep, so I crept past him and closed the front door slowly, not making a sound.

No matter what anyone said, I had to speak to my friend.

I hurried to the harbor and found the small gate that led to the docks. Without speaking, I stood before the guard and stared at him until he relented and stepped aside, allowing me access to the boats. He knew me — all the guards did — and he knew Urbi and I were as close as kin.

I climbed into a skiff, positioning myself in the middle of the bench, and gripped the oars. The guard gave me a sly smile and cast off the rope. I struggled to turn the boat toward the island. Finally I settled into a rhythm and worked the oars, rocking over a choppy sea until I reached the dock at the palace. A slave tied my boat to a pier, then helped me out of the rowboat. I walked between a series of matching red granite columns, each as tall as three men, and examined my stinging palms. I had worked up a set of blisters, and all but one had burst.

A guard stood at the ebony doors; I nodded and waited for him to admit me. After slipping inside the deserted antechamber with its marble-sheathed walls, I tiptoed over the tiles and moved silently past a life-size statue of Isis carrying a Canopic jar topped with a statuette of Osiris. A pair of polished granite sphinxes flanked the figure of Isis, and one of them featured the head of Urbi's late father.

A chill climbed the ladder of my spine as I crept past the sphinx. I couldn't help but feel that the dead king was watching from some outpost of the underworld.

Moving as silently as a ghost, I glided past the guards on duty, then entered Urbi's apartment. A heavy quiet filled these rooms, and her slaves respectfully lowered their eyes as I walked through the anteroom and gently tugged at the curtain that opened into Urbi's private inner chamber.

She was lying on her bed, curled into a ball, her back to me. I approached as quietly as I could and sat on the edge of the mattress. I touched her shoulder. "I am sorry," I said, modulating my words so they would not startle in the dense silence. "I know how you loved your father."

She turned, then sat up and threw her arms around me, her shoulders shaking with grief. "I am . . . so glad . . . you came," she whispered between sobs. "No one . . . no one else understands. Arsinoe and the boys think only of themselves, but I adored my father. He always did what was best for Egypt . . . and for me." Urbi released me, her tear-clotted lashes fluttering like butterfly wings. "At least . . . now they cannot hurt him. And he will no longer have to beg for their support."

I bent lower to meet her downcast gaze. "He was a good father. He made certain you would be ready to rule. You are prepared, and you are so clever, you will have no problems."

"I do not feel ready." She hiccupped a sob, then swiped tears from her cheek in a surprisingly youthful gesture. "I feel like a child who has lost her way."

"You know the way," I assured her. "And you are surrounded by people who love you. They will offer whatever help you need."

She released a slightly hysterical laugh. "I am surrounded by people who covet the throne. Even those who have no valid claim have gathered around to influence me and my brother."

"Omari?"

She nodded. "Since I am of age, there are fewer vultures around me, but a flock of them has already encircled Omari. They hover around him, ready to peck out his eyes. Ready to tear me to shreds."

I folded my hands and carefully stitched words together. "My father told me what must happen . . . how you must wed your brother. I am sorry I did not understand the situation sooner. I thought — I thought the ascension of a new queen would be a simple matter."

"Nothing is simple in Egypt." A mirthless smile twisted her mouth. "Yes, I will be married to my brother before I am crowned queen. They might as well marry me to Theodotus, Achillas, and Pothinus, for my brother does nothing without consulting that trio of raptors."

"If the tutor Theodotus dislikes you, it is because you preferred to be taught by my father, who is the better teacher," I said, managing a smile. "And the eunuch Pothinus dislikes you because he resents everyone because he is neither man nor woman. As for Achillas the captain —"

"That surly, sag-bellied lout has never forgiven my father for leaving him in Alexandria when he wanted to go to Rome," Urbi said. "So that is the state of affairs here. And I have no choice in the matter. In this, my father rules even from the grave."

"When everything is settled, you will feel better."

"Perhaps. But as for now" — her eyes glimmered with fresh tears, and her voice became husky — "I have lost my father. The scavengers have put distance between me and my brother. And I feel . . . bereft."

We sat in silence for a long moment, breathing in air thick with the heaviness of despair and the sweet scent of kyphi.

For the first time I had no idea how to comfort my best friend. My impulse was to recite a psalm or whisper a promise from Adonai, but Urbi might not appreciate assurances from a God she did not know. Still, I had to say something.

"I will lift up my eyes to the mountains," I began, "from where does my help come?
My help comes from Adonai,
Maker of heaven and earth.
He will not let your foot slip.
Your Keeper will not slumber.
Behold, the Keeper of Israel neither slumbers nor sleeps.
Adonai is your Keeper.
Adonai is your shadow at your right hand.
The sun will not strike you by day, nor the moon by night.
Adonai will protect you from all evil.
He will guard your life.
Adonai will watch over your coming and your going
From this time forth and forevermore."

Urbi closed her eyes as I recited the precious words of the psalmist, and she lay silent for a long moment after I had finished. Then she opened her eyes and managed a weak smile. "Thank you. And now I am weary."

"I will go so you can rest. But first, when will this wedding take place?"

Hugging her bent knees, Urbi seemed to

stare into a dark and uncertain future. "After my father is entombed. We will mourn for seventy days, then he will be laid to rest with the other Ptolemy kings. After the wedding, Omari and I will be seated on the throne."

I squeezed her shoulder. "You must send for me if you need to talk. I know nothing about matters of government, but I am always willing to listen."

She turned her face to mine, her eyes softening with seriousness. "At times, Chava, I think you and your father are the only people in Egypt I can completely trust."

"Really? Why?"

One corner of her mouth dipped in a wry smile. "You have never asked me for anything."

She clutched my hand for a moment, then released it and called for Charmion, one of her handmaids. I stood, bowing as I walked backward out of the royal bedchamber.

Chapter Five

Ten days after Alexandria buried the twelfth Macedonian Greek to call himself king of Egypt, all the noble families and leading figures of Alexandria gathered outside the Temple of Isis for the wedding of Cleopatra VII and Ptolemy XIII, known to me as Urbi and Omari.

I stood outside with my father and brother as Urbi climbed the stairs to the temple, her dark mane pulled back in the Grecian style, adorned with myriad braids and studded with pearls that had been skillfully sewn into her hair. She carried a bouquet of lotus blossoms, as befitted a virgin bride, and walked toward the wedding canopy, where her brother waited with a priest of Isis.

Charmion and Iras followed her, and behind them walked Apollodorus, a Sicilian mercenary Urbi had recently hired as a personal bodyguard. Even from where I stood, I could feel the broad-shouldered warrior's power to intimidate. When the man turned to scan the crowd, Asher stiffened. "Does Urbi really need such a brute at her side?"

"She no longer has her father to protect her," I replied, keeping my voice low. "Upon who else can she depend?"

"A thousand armed guards?" Asher said, lifting a brow. "Or are they only for show?"

"They are commanded by Achillas. And *he* is allied with Urbi's brother."

Father cast us a warning look, effectively stilling our tongues.

We followed the wedding party into the temple. The high ceiling drew my eyes to the painted hieroglyphs on the wall, but Father, who was clearly uncomfortable, kept his gaze lowered. I had no love for the sculpted images of false gods, but I could not stop stealing wayward glances at the candles, ornate altars, and gilded statues. At the front of the great hall, behind the wedding canopy, stood the goddess herself — a towering granite image that loomed over the crowd, her wide eyes staring at everything and nothing. On her head she wore the sun disk set between the horns of a cow, and in her hands she carried the ankh, the symbol of eternal life.

I shifted my attention to the bride and

groom, eighteen-year-old Urbi and ten-year-old Omari, whose head barely reached her shoulder.

"Does Urbi *want* to marry her brother?" Asher asked.

I sighed. "Would you want to marry me?"

"Then why is she doing it?"

Father hissed, silencing our whispers.

The high priest, a bald man dressed in spotless white, gestured for the bride and groom to extend their hands, then their feet. Omari obeyed, as did Urbi, and to symbolize the purity of their union the priest washed their limbs with fresh water from the life-giving Nile. After the cleansing, Iras stepped forward to offer a corn loaf. The bridegroom took it, broke off a piece, and offered it to Urbi as a visible pledge of support. Urbi held a bit of the bread between her lips to complete the ceremony, then turned away from her brother-groom.

I stood on tiptoe and craned my neck, trying to catch a glimpse of my friend's face. Had she resigned herself to this farce or was she still upset over her father's death? I desperately wanted to be with her, but Father had insisted that I stay away on such an important day. Still, of one thing I was certain: *this* was not the happiest day of her life.

As a priestess waved a stalk of pungent incense, the priest proclaimed that the royal couple would henceforth be known as *Neoi Philadelphia* or "new sibling-loving gods." As part of the final ritual, Theodotus of Chois, Omari's tutor-turned-advisor, gave the prince a jug of wine.

Omari placed the jug on the floor, then withdrew an oversized sword from a sheath at his belt. He swung the blade and slapped the jug, but the clay did not break. The young king cast a questioning look at Theodotus, who made a subtle gesture: *do it again.*

Again Omari swung, and this time the jug cracked, sending a trickle of red wine toward the newlyweds' feet.

With that, the wedding was concluded. The coronation, however, had only begun.

A proper coronation, Father explained as we walked home, might take up to a year, for the new king and queen would travel throughout Egypt, visiting all the major temples to present themselves to the people. "Some cities require special ceremonies," he said in the patient tone he adopted for complicated subjects. "In Thebes, for example, Urbi and Omari will meet the priests who care for the Buchis bull, which is revered in that city. Memphis will require the circumambulation of the White Walls. The new king and queen will walk in a procession around the city, accompanied by the gods and the priests. Since lifeless idols cannot move themselves, the stone gods will be carried by carts. . . ."

I bit my lip, my thoughts racing ahead of Father's explanation. Would Urbi invite me to accompany her on the journey? Many members of the royal household would go with her, and as her closest friend, I assumed she would want me by her side. And not only for her sake did I wish to join the caravan — I had always wanted to sail on the Nile, see the ancient pyramids, and marvel at the Valley of the Kings. Surely these were experiences we should share.

My father must have seen the light of hope in my eyes. "Do not count on traveling with her, daughter." Reproof lined his voice. "Your friend is now queen, and she has responsibilities you could never imagine. Give her time to find her footing. And do not be hurt if she is too busy to think of friendship in the weeks ahead."

"Chava could never go on such a trip." Asher scowled. "How could she keep Shabbat when surrounded by Gentiles? And how could she participate in rituals that involve false gods? She could not."

I shrugged away their concerns, certain that Urbi would make allowances for me as I had always made allowances for her. She would need company on the journey, and she would not want to talk to Omari or his counselors. She would want to talk to me.

Besides, HaShem had promised that I would bless her, and how could I do that if we were separated for an entire year?

So I waited, confident that Urbi would not forget her closest friend.

I waited patiently, and with every passing day I told myself that Urbi would soon send a message about my joining her on the journey south. I stood at the harbor and watched slaves load bundles of brilliant purple sailcloth, sure she would send an escort to fetch me. I had quietly packed a trunk and hidden it in my room, not wanting Father or Asher to see the visible evidence of my hope.

On the night before Urbi's leave-taking, I dreamed of boarding the ship and hearing Urbi say, "You could not have imagined I would be willing to leave you behind!"

Though Father advised against it, on the morning of the royal couple's departure, I bade Nuru accompany me to the harbor. At the largest dock, in a theatrical display, Queen Cleopatra and King Ptolemy XIII stepped out of ornate litters and approached the long, low royal galley. A line of guards kept us observers at bay, but I was close enough to see beards of seaweed on the pilings and slaves running up and down the deck. The purple sails rose and snapped overhead, then the mainsail unfurled and blocked out the sun.

Looking uncomfortable and awkward, Urbi and Omari stood on the dock and faced us, a noticeable space between them. Urbi's dark hair had been covered by a braided Egyptian wig, and on her head she wore the traditional double crown of Upper and Lower Egypt. Her brother wore the *nemes*, the striped headcloth with front panels falling onto his boyish chest. Both Urbi and Omari carried the crook and the flail, traditional symbols that served to tie this Greek pair to a long line of pharaohs who had risen from shepherds and nomads, the original occupants of the land.

The crowd cheered as the royal couple turned to board the ship. I tried to call Urbi's name, but my throat constricted on a sudden wave of emotion. She had not looked for me in the crowd. She had sent no messages during the days of preparation.

She had not even sent a letter explaining why she could not take me on the journey.

Had she forgotten me already?

I returned home with a heavy heart and sank onto a couch in lonely silence. Nuru retreated to the shadows.

I lifted my hand and idly traced the scar across my left palm. I wanted Urbi to be queen. I knew how keenly she felt the responsibility vacated by her father, and how hard she had prepared for her royal role. Despite being the second daughter, she had been born to be queen and would be a good ruler. When her father died, my heart had thrilled to know that Urbi would finally be able to fulfill her destiny.

On the other hand, if being queen meant she would rarely have time for me, how could I cope? I had always spent six days out of every seven with Urbi, and I knew her personality, her likes and dislikes, her habits and her quirks. I knew that she went barefoot in the palace and loved to read about her ancestors. I had seen her imitate a monkey's walk and I had watched her laugh until she cried. We had told each other stories, and we had asked a slave to judge who was best at burping. We had shared nearly everything two girls could share.

What was I to do without her? How was I

supposed to pass the time while she was away?

I could read, of course, but who would I talk to when I was weary of reading? With Urbi gone, I had no one to visit. The girls I knew from the synagogue were all married, most of them with babies. Father was probably hoping I would visit them and fall in love with domestic life. He might suggest that I try to learn a new language or brush up on my Hebrew . . . because he could always find an unmarried tutor who would be willing to teach his daughter.

I heard the front door open, followed by the sound of Father's slow steps. Keeping my head down, I braced for a rebuke — hadn't he warned me not to go to the harbor? Hadn't he said that Urbi's life would change? Hadn't he been hinting that I should focus on finding a good husband and establishing a home of my own?

I flinched when Father placed his hand on my shoulder. "I could use your help, daughter." He tugged on his beard as he smiled. "Would you read my work and mark any errors in the copy? I am afraid I am too familiar with the work to be a careful reader."

That afternoon he unrolled a scroll containing the first of his testaments of the patriarchs. I read the Greek slowly, beginning with the testament of Reuben, followed by the testament of Simeon. Father was a skilled writer, but even he made the occasional mistake. My heart lifted as I made a note of each error, grateful to know I was not the only imperfect member of the family.

After two weeks of reading about the patriarchs, Father called me into his library and asked me to sit. "I am beginning a new work," he said. "An exhaustive study of the recorded names of HaShem. I would like you to help me search the Tanakh and compile a list."

He tried to behave as though he did not care whether I agreed or not, but an almost imperceptible note of pleading filled his voice. He wanted my help, and as long as the work did not involve an unmarried man from the synagogue, I thought I might enjoy the effort.

"Where do we start?"

"Here." He unrolled an elaborate Torah scroll and pointed to the first book of the Pentateuch: *B'resheet.* Genesis.

"And what do I do?"

"Start reading. And when Adonai refers to himself as something other than *the name,* make a note of it on a separate parchment. Look here." He turned the scroll and pointed to a passage in Genesis. "*YHVH Yireh* means *YHVH will provide.* But the name refers not to daily needs, but to a substitutionary blood sacrifice. Adonai provided a ram to take the place of Abraham's son."

"So that should be the first name on my list?"

"Yes."

"Simple enough."

I took a sheet of parchment from a drawer, found a pen, and sat before the scroll, ready to read.

Reports about the new sibling-loving gods trickled into Alexandria. The noble families buzzed about the news, for though they had not loved their former king, they held high hopes for the brother-sister couple.

According to the first report, the people of Thebes had enthusiastically embraced Urbi and Omari. When the moon reached full, all the priests in Egypt converged on the city, where Cleopatra, "the Lady of the two Lands, the goddess who loves her father," boarded a boat carrying a new sacred bull — one with a white body and a black face — and sailed to his temple on the west bank of the Nile. She presided over the new bull's inauguration and oversaw the installation of the bull's recently deceased predecessor into the *Bucheum,* a cemetery for the mummified remains of sacred bulls.

In every report, we heard that the Egyptian people adored the queen because she revered their ancient customs and spoke to them in their own tongue. Apparently she charmed everyone who met her.

"The native people love and accept her," Father said one afternoon as he read a message from a friend, "and no wonder. She is the only Ptolemy who has ever mastered the native language."

Of course she was. Urbi spoke Greek, Aramaic, Latin, Ethiopian, Hebrew, Egyptian, and Troglodyte, and those were only the languages I knew about. She had never met a challenge she could not master.

I ignored the implicit rebuke of my linguistic laziness and pressed Father for more information. "Will she be returning soon?"

"She must still go to Memphis, where she will walk the White Walls and visit the Apis bull," he said, rewrapping the scroll around its spindle. He shook his head. "Is it any wonder our forefathers created a golden calf in the wilderness? How could they do otherwise, given the Egyptian fascination with bulls and cows?"

"About Urbi." I drew his attention back to the subject of my concern. "After Memphis, will she be coming back to Alexandria?"

Father shifted the focus of his gaze from some interior vision and looked at me. "I do not know, Chava, and perhaps you should not be so concerned about the queen's affairs. How are you coming with the names of HaShem? Have you finished a complete list yet?"

I sighed, recognizing his dismissal for what it was. "No, Father. I will get back to work . . . since I have nothing else to do with my life."

Urbi had been away six months when Father decided to host a sacred study in our home.

I had to admire his ingenuity — most studies of our sacred writings were held at the synagogue, but men and women were separated there, and my father had a particular reason for not wanting the men to be separated from *me.* So he announced that on the first day of every week, he would lead a group of young men in a discussion of the Five *Megillot,* or Scrolls, concentrating on the prophet Dani'el.

"Why Dani'el?" I asked.

"Why not?" He grinned at me and fingered his lush beard. "When one bears the name of a great prophet, why shouldn't he study the prophet's words?"

So on the first day of every week Urbi remained away, I prepared honey water and fresh fruit for the six or seven young men who entered our house, smiled at me, and sat on couches around the reflecting pool as they discussed Dani'el. I directed the slaves who served them, and I couldn't help but overhear. From time to time, as they posited points and counterpoints, I thought about Urbi, knowing that she would have loved to participate in the discussion. No matter the topic, she had never shied away from an argument, and being the only woman in the room would not have bothered her.

"From the going forth of the command for the answer and for the building of Jerusalem until the anointed one," one young man read from the Septuagint. "And who is the anointed one?"

Father lifted a brow. "The Hebrew word is *masiah,* a term that could refer to a priest or a king. Or, perhaps, a man who is both."

"Zerubbabel," one youth suggested. "Did he not return us to Temple worship after the exile?"

"Onias," another man countered. "Was he

not murdered for his righteousness? Dani'el writes that the anointed one will be destroyed."

"But the timing is wrong," another man said. "The command to rebuild the Temple came from Cyrus, did it not? That was five hundred thirty-nine years ago. Seventy-seven sevens have already passed, and we have seen no *masiah.*"

"The Word of HaShem does not lie," Father said. "So you have made a mistake. Cyrus sent men to rebuild the Temple, but the city was not built until much later. So perhaps we should consider the command to the prophet Ezra, which was given four hundred ninety-one years ago —"

"Seventy sevens," a student interrupted. "So where is our anointed one?"

"Chava."

I flinched as Father interrupted my eavesdropping. "Yes?"

"Some more fruit, please — the grapes, if you have them. Or figs."

"At once, Father."

And as I walked away, I heard his muted remark. "An obedient daughter becomes a dutiful wife."

I clenched my fists in frustration. Why would Father rather see me married than happy?

■ ■ ■ ■

Eleven months after Urbi's marriage to her brother, riders entered the city with news of the royal couple. The next day, Cleopatra VII and Ptolemy XIII would enter the city in a grand procession, and all of Alexandria was invited to watch.

I had hoped to meet Urbi before the grandiose royal welcome, but though my family was on a list of people granted permission to watch from a balcony of the great library, we would not be allowed to meet with the royals. "Only citizens will be allowed to greet the king and queen," we were told when a messenger arrived with our invitation to observe from the library. "And Jews are not citizens of Alexandria."

So we watched from a distance as the royal parade entered the city through the Sun Gate and progressed to the wide Canopic Way. The procession passed the Agora, the library and museum, and the Mausoleum of Alexander the Great. Lions and tigers in wheeled cages rolled over the gravel streets, eliciting applause and cries of wonder. I found myself at eye level with a pair of restless giraffes in a wagon. After the animals, a group of royal relatives and

Alexandrian officials strode over the streets, bristling with an unconscious awareness of their status. Behind them, on two white horses, rode Cleopatra and Ptolemy XIII, Egypt's king and queen.

Finally, Urbi had come home.

During her long absence, I had managed to convince myself that she did not write me before the journey because she knew my father would not want me to go. So she said nothing in an effort to keep from causing me pain.

But now that she was home, nothing would stand between us. We could be together again almost immediately, and she would tell me everything that had happened during our separation. We would talk for weeks, we would laugh, and she would share secrets that no one else in Alexandria could know. . .

I watched the parade turn at the eastern boundary of the Royal Quarter and head toward the palace.

As Father and I left the library and walked toward our neighborhood, I resisted a strong urge to break away and run to the dock where I could find a boat and row to Urbi's palace on Antirhodos Island. "I cannot wait to see her," I said, unable to control my enthusiasm.

"Not today." Father held up a warning finger. "She is certain to be exhausted from her journey. Let her rest for a week or two. Let her —"

"A *week* or two!"

"Urbi is no longer a girlhood friend, Chava. She is Cleopatra, queen of Egypt. Let her enjoy time away from curious onlookers and meddlesome priests. Even a queen needs time to rest. Especially one who has not known the blessing of a regular Shabbat."

"How can I call her *Cleopatra*? The name doesn't suit her."

"You must call her by her royal name, for that is who she is now. To call her anything else would be disrespectful."

I blew out a breath. I understood his point, but she would always be *Urbi* to me.

Though the idea of waiting taxed my patience, after six days a royal messenger appeared at our door. When admitted, he bowed before me and offered a scroll.

I broke the seal and read the note within. "Urbi invites me to dine with her," I told Father, looking up. "I am to go to the palace at sunset on the morrow."

A twitch of a smile broke through his beard. "Perhaps it is time you learned what life as a queen is like."

I made a face as soon as Father turned back to his work. Why should Urbi's life be so different? When we were children and the king went away, Urbi and I read manuscripts from the library, learned our lessons, and shopped in the marketplace. Queen Cleopatra might not be able to sneak out for shopping as we once did, but why should anything else change? The underlings who ran the government during her father's absence could run the government now. Egypt had been blessed with abundance, Father was fond of saying, and an *overabundance* of supervisors who told people what to do and how much tax to pay for doing it.

Being queen, I assured myself, meant that Urbi would give spectacular banquets and build amazing palaces. And, as always, she would want my help.

Chapter Six

I spent all day preparing for my first audience with Queen Cleopatra. As delight bubbled within me, I dressed in my finest chiton and adorned it with a silk himation on which a talented artist had painted peacocks in gold, blue, and green. I slipped gold loops through my earlobes while Nuru pulled my curly hair back, tied a ribbon around my head, and then tucked the length of my hair into the ribbon, resulting in a demure roll at the nape of my neck. This, she assured me, was the newest style of Alexandria's noble ladies. After having traveled so far into Egypt's primitive territories, I thought Cleopatra might enjoy being reminded that Alexandria was the most sophisticated and elegant city in the world.

I dressed carefully, running through a mental list of all the news I wanted to share with my friend. Though I had missed her terribly, my life had not been totally stagnant. I had made considerable progress on Father's manuscript about the names of HaShem. And on several occasions, Father had invited Yosef, son of Avraham the butcher, for dinner and a discussion about the prophecies of Dani'el. They talked until my ears hurt, and I knew Father had an ulterior motive.

After dinner, he would always ask, "Did you enjoy Yosef's company?"

"Yes, Father."

"Hasn't he a fine grasp of Dani'el's writings?"

"Very fine."

"A shame that he has not found himself a wife. Yet he has no desire to remain without one . . ."

At that point, I would quietly excuse myself and go to my room.

Why couldn't my father understand that I did not need to be concerned about my future? Why should I marry and subject myself to a man when my destiny lay with Cleopatra? Every day I saw the long scar on my palm, evidence of my commitment to her. Blood of my blood, heart of my heart. Urbi and I would always be part of each other.

As the sun began to sink toward the lighthouse, I draped my himation over my hair and shoulders and walked with our doorman to the gate at the royal dock. Several people stood there, all of them dressed in their best, but I assumed they were attending a function arranged by the boy king. His advisors were not at all shy about parading themselves before the public.

I walked up to the gate and searched for Acis, but the guards were not the friendly men who had been stationed at that post a year ago. They were Roman soldiers, and they did not know me.

"I am Chava, a friend of the queen's," I said. "She is expecting me."

The stern-faced guard who seemed to be in charge pulled out a parchment and checked the scrawling on the page. "You are having dinner with the queen?"

"Yes." I smiled in an overflow of relief. "My name is Chava, daughter of Daniel the scholar."

"Let her pass."

I went down to the docks and got into a boat, where a pair of slaves rowed me to the island palace. More than a dozen blazing torches lit the path, pushing at the darkness as I stepped onto the royal dock and walked between the granite pillars. No guards stood at the palace door, but when I turned toward the hallway that led to Cleopatra's private chambers, a slave pointed me in a different direction.

"Is the queen not dining in her chamber?" I asked.

"The queen dines in the great hall," he replied.

I sighed but kept walking until I reached a set of tall double doors. The slave opened them and allowed me access to the great hall.

A heavy scent of roses rolled over me the moment I crossed the threshold. The intricate mosaics that covered the floor in this luxurious chamber had been blanketed with several inches of rose petals, their fragrance almost overpowering as I waded through them. Braided garlands of roses swayed between the soaring columns supporting the painted ceiling, and rose oil sparkled in the perfumed lamps on the walls. In one corner, musicians played stringed instruments and patted small drums, enlivening the atmosphere with a cheerful melody. A trio of dancing girls swirled in the center of the chamber.

Dining couches, three per group, bracketed small tables, leaving the fourth side open for servants. The walls had been lined with the U-shaped seating arrangements, and a quick glance revealed that more than one hundred guests had been invited to dine in the hall.

My heart sank with disappointment. I had been hoping — indeed, I had been counting on — a private, relaxed conversation with my best friend, but this was not the setting for an intimate dinner. Would I have to share Urbi with dozens of others? The room had already filled with people — Jewish merchants, Egyptian priests, husbands and wives from Alexandria's first families. All of the other guests were older than Urbi and I, and they would not want to talk about the things I wanted to share.

When a servant saw me standing alone, he gestured to an empty couch. I walked over and sank onto the embroidered cushions, then leaned over and took a crusty loaf of bread from a basket. The table next to my couch had been set with gold dishes and jewel-encrusted tumblers. A silver platter held individual meat pies molded into the shape of swans, while a gold-veined pitcher held a ruby-colored wine.

"Welcome to the queen's dinner," I told myself. As others joined my group, I returned their greetings with an unenthusiastic smile.

I ate silently, eating whatever was offered

and speaking to no one. Why did Urbi invite me to this event? She knew I did not care for politics, nor did I have anything in common with the silk merchant who kept threatening to tickle my feet. The Egyptian priest across from me stared as if I were some species of rare insect, and the silk merchant's wife frowned every time I lifted my cup for more wine. I had never been more uncomfortable, and I made up my mind to tell Urbi so . . . whenever I saw her again.

I had just sampled a pomegranate-flavored stew when silence settled over the room, an absence of sound that had an almost physical density. I turned toward the head of the hall and saw Cleopatra step through a diaphanous curtain. Like the others, I gasped, for she had never looked more like a queen. She wore a simple white chiton with her hair held back with a white ribbon, the mark of a Ptolemy ruler. Over the tunic she wore a translucent mantle that shimmered in the lamplight. Long ropes of pearls dangled over her chest, and jeweled sandals graced her feet. She smiled around the room, then reclined on her couch, propping an elbow on the upholstered arm. Slaves appeared at her side, offering food and drink, but my friend only nibbled at the delicacies as she scanned the crowd.

I watched her like a sentinel. Though she nodded pleasantly at her guests, I thought I noticed a shadow behind her eyes and a hesitation in her smile. Why? She had enjoyed a successful victory tour. By all reports, she had been enthusiastically accepted by the Egyptians. So why did she appear less than perfectly happy?

A young man — Alexandrian, by the look of him — perched on the edge of my couch. "See how well she looks," he said, gesturing to the queen. "Have you ever seen her look better?"

I narrowed my eyes to see if I had missed something. "She has looked happier," I said, measuring my words, "but at least she appears relieved to be home."

The young man laughed, his beer-scented breath fanning my face. Clearly he had been in his cups long before arriving at the palace. The fragrance of roses was supposed to prevent intoxication, but this young man had arrived too late for the aromatic petals to do their work.

"Excuse me," I told him and pointed to a pretty young woman on the far side of the room. "But that girl keeps staring at you."

He blinked, thrust his face forward in concentration, and then stood to investigate the poor girl across the hall.

I blew out a breath, grateful to see him go.

I nibbled on a honey cake as the musicians played, the dancers twirled, and the servants walked among us with enough food to feed each guest for a week. A few people walked over to bow before the queen, and one or two were daring enough to speak to her. I leaned forward, hoping to pick up a word or two of their conversation, but the noise and the distance made it impossible to eavesdrop.

Should I go to her? Something in me insisted that this was not the place for our first meeting in over a year. We were close friends, but one did not station close friends across a crowded room. On the other hand, perhaps she had to observe some ritual or protocol I knew nothing about. Perhaps she had good reasons for not inviting me to a personal meeting, and if I did not approach her, I might hurt her as badly as she had already hurt me.

Finally I stood, walked to the queen's couch, and made a proper formal bow. When I straightened, Cleopatra smiled with something of her former warmth in her eyes. "Chava," she said, inclining her head in a regal gesture. She sighed. "How I have missed you."

"And I you." I attempted to match her smile in formality, then gave up and spilled the words in my heart: "Alexandria has been unreasonably boring since you left. I have been utterly lonely without you."

"But now I am home." She sat upright, and for an instant I thought she might invite me to sit by her side.

She did not. "How are your father and brother?"

"They are well."

"Has your father announced your betrothal yet?"

"No, but he keeps trying. The latest candidate is a scholar named Yosef."

"Is he handsome?"

I smiled. "He is not unattractive. And you — how do you find marriage to Omari?"

She lifted one shoulder in an elegant shrug. "It is a marriage in name only. He spends all his time with Pothinus, Achillas, and Theodotus. Fortunately, they keep the boy occupied while I attend to the work."

"Are you terribly busy? I had hoped —"

"Egypt never rests," she interrupted. "The Nile did not rise this year, so the land did not flood. The crops will not grow, and our people will go hungry. The priests are already complaining of shortages that prevent them from conducting their usual rituals. Robbers haunt the highways and waterways. The people will believe the gods have turned against me if the situation does not improve."

I blinked, stunned by the onslaught of information. "But surely they know that only a god can control the weather —"

"You forget," she said. "In Egypt, the king and queen are gods."

I stared at her as the concept twirled in my head. "They *truly* believe that? I thought it was tradition."

"Chava" — her tone did not sound pleasant — "read your history. Ask your father to explain it to you."

Her tone, which had been warm, chilled slightly, and the look she gave me brimmed with reproach. I lifted my chin, confused by her attitude, and only a reflexive respect for authority allowed me to step back and bow my head. "By your leave, I will return to my seat."

"It was good to see you." A conciliatory note filled her voice, and though I felt the tug of her eyes, I did not look up. She had to know I had taken offense . . . well, let her know. I would forgive her on the morrow.

"Good night, my queen." I bowed again, turned, and left the royal banquet.

■ ■ ■ ■

Later that night, after evening prayers had been said and the house lamps extinguished, I paused outside my room to ask Father what Urbi had meant. "She said something about the people blaming her if the river doesn't flood. But how could Urbi control the rise of the waters?"

Father paused and lifted his candle. "Chava" — weariness lined his voice — "how could you live so many years in Egypt and not understand the role of the pharaoh? The people consider him a god and believe their gods are responsible for the rise of the river. If the river does not flood, then the king has not done his job."

"But Urbi is neither pharaoh nor a god. She's just a girl."

Father's gaze darted toward the doorway, as if he feared others might be listening. "You are too familiar with the queen. But now that your friend sits on the throne, the Egyptians consider her more than human. Many of the Alexandrians adhere to this belief, as well. But she will never be like HaShem."

I frowned. "I have always thought most people worshiped the same God, though we call Him by different names. Urbi once told me that the god Ptah created the world by imagining it and giving utterance to his thoughts. Is this not the same way Adonai created the earth?"

"There may be very little difference between one story and another," Father answered. "But what little difference there is, is very important."

"What do you mean?"

His dark eyes searched my face as the silence stretched between us. "We know the world was created by HaShem, blessed be He. The Egyptians say the world was created by Ptah, the first of many gods. But there are *not* many gods: *Sh'ma, Yisra'el! Adonai Eloheinu, Adonai echad.*"

"Hear, Isra'el. Adonai our God, Adonai is one," I whispered.

Father nodded. "Amein."

I took a moment to absorb the reminder. I had never given much thought to the difference between HaShem and the gods of the Egyptians. We worshiped Adonai because we were descendants of Abraham, and we observed certain practices because we had received the Torah. Yet I had always thought that beneath our differences, Urbi and I held similar beliefs. Apparently the gap between us was wider than I realized.

We believed one God created the world with His voice.

She believed one god created the world with his voice, then created other gods, diluting his power, spreading out his duties until no one god was all-powerful. . . .

But what little difference there is, is very important.

I looked up at Father. "What will happen if famine comes? Will the people rise up against Cleopatra and Omari? Will they be in danger?"

He stroked his beard. "In generations past, the pharaoh who could not heal the land held an asp to his breast and gave his life to appease the gods. But that sort of sacrifice has not been practiced in generations. Cleopatra and her brother are more likely to pay homage to the gods at their temples and placate the priests. Your friend is well suited for the task of charming her people."

Father patted my shoulder. "Urbi was a good friend to you in your youth, but now she must assume responsibilities that would intimidate even an older man. She is a queen — a pharaoh, and the leader of her people — and she will need to concentrate on the tasks before her. She will walk a dangerous path, one filled with risks and traps set by her enemies. Always remain faithful to her, but do not expect to find Urbi when you visit the palace. No matter how dearly she cherishes your friendship, Cleopatra will have no room for girlish concerns."

I wanted to argue, but a note of finality in his voice left no doubt.

Father did not believe HaShem had spoken to me about Urbi. He did not believe I could be a friend of a queen. He did not take me seriously when I said I was meant to serve and bless her, and he did not want me to invest my life in a friend who might lead me away from Adonai.

So how could I respect and honor him while still believing HaShem's promise?

I blinked back a rush of stinging tears and slipped into my room where I could weep unobserved.

I was already drifting on the currents of sleep when I felt a hand on my shoulder. I startled awake, then lifted my head to see Urbi standing in a pool of moonlight streaming from my bedroom doorway.

"Urbi?" I mumbled, scarcely believing my eyes. "Am I dreaming?"

"Chava." She sat on the edge of my bed, and in the atrium beyond I glimpsed the bulky outlines of Roman guards. "I had to see you."

I sat up and wrapped my arms around my knees. "What's wrong?"

Urbi shook her head, then stared into the darkness. "My father warned me about this."

"About what?"

She spoke slowly, her eyes fixed on some ghostly memory from the past. "A ruler labors under a peculiar disadvantage — though he can protect himself from his enemies by arranging his friends about him, he has no one to protect him from his friends."

I blinked in confusion and touched her arm. "Surely you do not think you need protection from *me.*"

She smiled. "You are more sister than my siblings." She covered my hand with her own. "The friends I fear are allied with Omari. I thought the Regency Council was meant to advise my brother, but I have learned that those three men wish to be rid of me. Though my father's will expressly said Omari and I were to rule together, that threesome conspires to confound, depose, and kill me. They would murder me now if they could — they will probably try. I have had no champion other than my father, and now he is gone."

"You have me." I tightened my fingers around her arm. "And my father and brother would do anything for you."

She chuffed softly. "How can a family of Jews help an Egyptian queen? I need a warrior, a king with an army. I need someone with real power. A hero like Achilles or Heracles."

"Then why have you come to me? I have no power."

Urbi leaned closer, her eyes glittering like black diamonds. "I need you to be my eyes and ears. I need you to tell me when you hear rumors; I need you to discover the source of plots and conspiracies. We can no longer be carefree girls, but I will grant you freedom to roam throughout the palace compound. You will be free to go where I cannot. Come to me when you have news to report or give your news directly to Charmion, Iras, or Apollodorus — those three are completely loyal to me."

I was completely loyal — could she not see it? For a fleeting instant I wished I could be a slave, that she could own me even as she owned Charmion and Iras. Then she would not question my loyalty, and my father would not keep trying to marry me to some ardent prophecy student.

Holding her gaze, I nodded . . . and in that moment I forgave her all the hurts that had wounded me. How unfair I had been, chafing beneath her inattention when scheming men were intent on taking her life.

"Stay close," Urbi said, trapping me in a sudden fierce embrace. "Do not let time and distance come between us. Please."

"I will. I promise."

I held her for a long moment and assured myself that everything was as it should be. She had gone away for a while, but HaShem brought her safely back. Even though our carefree days were in the past, we would be bound in another, more significant way. Every day I would look out for Urbi's interests, and she would always know I was watching, listening, and caring. Implicit in HaShem's promise was a duty, and I intended to fulfill it.

"You look tired," she said. "I should go and let you get some rest."

The guards stirred the shadows as Urbi stood, and I knew several days might pass before I could speak to her again.

"One thing," I called, though I had no right to ask anything of a queen. "Do you promise to find me if you need me?"

A smile twisted the side of her wide mouth as she lifted her hand, marked by our vows to each other. "Blood of my blood, heart of my heart, I will always look for you."

Chapter Seven

Because it would have been inappropriate for me to go to the palace unescorted, during the following weeks I had Nuru accompany me to the throne room. On that first morning I dressed soberly and walked carefully, a sense of responsibility weighing on me like a cloak. Urbi had been deadly serious when she asked me to spy for her, and I would not let her down.

I waited until the doors of the great hall opened before slipping inside. Morning sunlight shone through the high windows of the long room, spangling the painted hieroglyphs and the tile floor. Gilded benches lined the walls, and I chose one near the center of the room. The legs had been fashioned to resemble a lion's, and lions' heads formed the front of the armrests. The bench was one of many, but the remaining seats were quickly filled by elder statesmen and white-robed priests.

Within a short period, so many people had entered the hall that Nuru and I lost all custody of our eyes and stared at the colorful assemblage. For generations of Ptolemies, offices and honors had been freely bestowed on Alexandrians who pleased the king. Auletes was gone, but his honorees remained, and they reminded me of peacocks as they strutted in the throne room, each attired in the colors of his station.

The highest honors were granted to the "Kinsmen of the King," whom the reigning king and queen addressed as "father" or "brother." They were allowed to wear the "splendor of the head band," a colored ribbon, and a gold brooch, which had been initially pinned on by the king himself.

Beneath the Kinsmen were the "First Friends" who wore purple robes and tended to pose themselves along the perimeter of the room so their plumage might be easily observed. Beneath the First Friends were the "Friends" who wore wide-brimmed felt hats and high-laced boots, many of them made of red leather.

I had observed these people on the streets of Alexandria, but never had I seen them assembled so thickly in one place. The effect was overwhelming, and for a moment I regretted choosing a plain ivory chiton — I might as well have been wearing wallpaper, so completely did I blend into the surroundings.

Before Urbi's midnight visit I would have been embarrassed to be among those who had nothing to do but sit and observe the court, but her tearful entreaty had filled me with courage. If anyone questioned my right to be in the hall, I would simply explain that I had come at the queen's request . . . and dare my questioner to challenge me again.

Finally, Urbi entered and sat on a golden chair mounted on an elevated platform. For the morning appearance she had chosen a beige sheath of Egyptian design, but she wore her hair in the Greek style, adorned with the simple white ribbon that signified a Ptolemy ruler. Large pearls hung from her earlobes and had also been sewn into the fabric of her gown. Her eyelids had been painted with glittering green malachite and heavily outlined with kohl. Little of my girlish friend remained in her appearance.

A long line of petitioners waited for an audience, so I opened my bag and pulled out a needle, thread, and a small piece of embroidery, determined to keep my fingers occupied while my mind absorbed everything I saw and heard.

The morning passed quietly enough, but

while a priest from Memphis was announcing the death of a bubastis bull, two messengers burst through the double doors and stalked forward with purposeful strides. The guards around the throne stepped forward and eyed the men with wary eyes, but the intruders knelt on the marble floor and presented Cleopatra with a scroll.

Cleopatra gestured toward Apollodorus, who took the scroll and read it. "Marcus Calpurnius Bibulous has sent his two sons to you," Apollodorus said. "He asks that his sons be allowed to address the Roman legionaries who came here in the service of your father. He requires their service in Syria, where he is gathering an army to repel invading Parthians."

Though Cleopatra's face remained composed, from the quick uptick of her shoulders I knew she was anxious about how to respond. One of her hands tightened on the armrest of her chair, and one foot tapped the floor in a quick rhythm. I knew nothing about Roman legionaries in Egypt, but the message had clearly made her nervous.

"You may speak to the legionaries," she told the two men. "You will find them camped outside the city. Present your case directly to them."

"Will the queen not order them to return

with us?" one of the men asked. "If you give the order —"

"They are Roman soldiers and Bibulous is a Roman governor," Cleopatra interrupted. "I will let the men choose whether or not to obey."

"Still, a royal command —"

"These men have lived seven years in Alexandria," Cleopatra continued. "They serve Rome by guarding Egypt's throne, Egypt's grain, and Egypt's port, but they are Rome's legionaries, and by Rome they are rightfully commanded. So speak to them if you must, but do not expect me to disservice Egypt by sending them away. That is my final word."

She nodded, dazzling the men with the brilliance of her smile. The two sons of Bibulous bowed again, then strode out as purposefully as they had entered. I watched them go and then shifted my attention back to the throne.

Cleopatra was listening to the Memphis priest, doubtless trying to focus on his words, but a small line between her brows told me that she was still thinking about the Romans' request . . . and she was still anxious.

I drew in a deep breath, comprehending for the first time what my father meant when he said Cleopatra had responsibilities I would never understand.

"Have you ever seen anything so charming?" Urbi smiled at me from her couch. "I discovered them in a little village near Memphis and commanded them to return with us. They will enliven many a dull day in our royal court."

I smiled and turned to the trio of singing dwarfs, who stood in the center of the queen's garden. Charmion and Iras stood beside Urbi, giggling every time she smiled, syncing their responses to their mistress's expressions. I felt my own smile freeze when I realized how organized — and *practiced* — their reactions were. Did every slave respond to her mistress so mindlessly?

I was trying to remember if Nuru behaved in the same way when a man approached the garden gate. Apollodorus, the ever-vigilant watchdog, went over to investigate. A moment later he approached Urbi, bending to whisper in her ear.

The relaxed curve of her mouth tightened. "I must see him now?"

"The situation is urgent, my lady."

The dwarfs continued to sing as she exhaled a breath and nodded.

Apollodorus allowed the man to enter the

garden, watching while he prostrated himself on the ground.

"Sorrowful news, my queen," the man whispered, not lifting his head. "The two sons of Bibulous have been murdered."

Cleopatra lifted her hand abruptly, cutting off the singing trio. Silence enveloped the garden, the wind catching the last bit of the melody and flinging it into eternity. Lines of concentration deepened along Cleopatra's brows and under her eyes.

Why? Because Bibulous was a Roman governor, and even I knew that Rome was best kept on the north side of the Great Sea. . . .

"Who has done such a thing?" Cleopatra leaned forward. "Rise, man, and answer!"

The guard reluctantly rose to one knee. "The legionaries killed them. The men do not want to leave Egypt. They consider it their home."

Cleopatra covered her lips with her fingers, and I knew she had to be desperate for guidance. But who could guide her? Apollodorus was a servant, not a politician, and Omari's advisors had only the boy-king's interests at heart.

She closed her eyes for a moment, then looked up and motioned for Apollodorus to come closer. He listened to her whispered command, straightened, saluted, and strode away.

What had she set in motion? I had no idea, and did not care to know.

I shifted on my couch and let out a sigh of relief, grateful I was not the daughter of a king. Urbi and I were only twenty, but she lived in a position where decisions could spread ripples that affected far more than one family. A realm where decisions, especially hasty ones, could have fatal consequences.

I did not envy her.

Wearing her face like a mask, Urbi calmly told the singers and slaves to leave us. When they had gone, she stood and walked toward me, then sank to the grass at my feet. "Chava," she said, pillowing her head on my couch, "take a guard and go home, for you must fetch your father. I have an urgent need for his wisdom."

I nodded at her command and left the garden as swiftly as my slippered feet could carry me.

By the time I returned to the palace with my father, the queen had retired to her private chambers. I found Urbi in the anteroom with her prime minister, a Greek called Protarchus. He stood as if planted on the marble tiles, his face a study in worry.

Urbi's visage remained smooth, but her lips curved in a smile when we entered.

"You cannot continue to ignore the situation," Protarchus was saying, his arms moving in the practiced motions of a professional orator. "The harvest is so bad that people are abandoning their villages and moving to the cities. But who will feed them there? Already the village of Tinteris has disappeared, its occupants unable to feed themselves or their herds. The people are unhappy —"

"Thank you, Prime Minister." Urbi dipped her chin in polite acknowledgment. "I am aware of the situation and will hear your report tomorrow. I must attend to another matter now, and I would hear from Daniel the scholar before anyone else."

The shadow of a frown passed over the prime minister's face as he watched my father genuflect before the queen. But what could he say? Protarchus bowed and backed away, then disappeared behind the heavy double doors.

"Welcome." Urbi stood to greet my father and gestured to a pair of chairs across from her couch. While she reclined, Father and I seated ourselves, grateful that she wasn't making us observe all the formalities that usually accompanied a royal audience.

Father pressed his hands together. "How may I serve you, my queen?"

Urbi rested an elbow on the armrest of her couch. "You gave me much advice when you were my tutor, and you listened while I framed arguments for situations I was unlikely to ever encounter. Now I am facing a situation that is terrifyingly real, and I find myself uncertain of how to proceed."

Father bowed his head. "You have but to ask, and I will do my best to advise you."

"I hoped you would say that." She straightened. "The situation is this: the Roman governor sent his sons to procure the services of the legionaries Gabinius left in Egypt when he escorted my father back to Alexandria. The soldiers do not want to leave, and they have murdered the governor's sons. I must do something, but . . . what?" She waved at the empty air. "If I do nothing, the governor may call on Rome for help — or even march on Alexandria. But if I punish the legionaries, the army may rebel. Though they enjoy living here, I daresay their loyalty lies with Rome, not with an untested queen. If the army revolts, the people of Alexandria may join them. They did not approve of my father's attempt to appease Rome, and the Alexandrians would welcome an opportunity to drive a wedge between me and the Roman army."

"But the people love you!" I interjected.

Both Father and Urbi looked at me as if I were a toddling child.

"The people are fickle," the queen said. "They are feathers, fluttering about with each change in the wind."

"They are sheep," Father added. "They follow the shepherd with the loudest voice." He turned his attention back to the queen. "A difficult situation."

"And that's not my only problem." Urbi leaned toward him and glanced at the door. "My brother's advisors are plotting against me. I have no proof, but they scurry away like frightened mice whenever I approach. This is not a good time to be a friendless queen."

My father fingered his beard, letting the silence stretch as he considered the queen's situation. I shifted my gaze from him to her, suddenly feeling as though they had left me behind. My father never dealt with armies or empires, but he knew history, and he did not seem at all daunted by the queen's situation.

As for Urbi . . . I did not understand how she could sleep at night. My father and my friend were obviously made of stronger stuff than I.

Father cleared his throat. "My lady, if you will allow me to speak frankly —"

Urbi nodded. "Please."

"Send some of your most trusted men to determine who committed the murders, then send the guilty men to the Roman governor." Remembering himself, he bowed his head. "Forgive me — I am not ordering you, I am stating what I would do in your situation."

"Understood," Urbi said. "What else?"

He pressed his lips together. "Regarding your brother — your father's will expressly stated that you should rule jointly with Omari, so it is as wrong for you to cast him off as it would be for him to do the same. Try to tolerate him and his Regency Council. Try to include him in your decision-making. I saw that you recently had a coin minted with your portrait — next time, place his image on one side, yours on the other. The people must see that you are trying to implement the stipulations of your father's will."

Urbi drew a deep breath. "Ruling with my brother is not easy, especially when he is ordered about by three fools who care only for their own ambitions."

"Yet those *fools*" — Father underlined the word — "are powerful, and your brother loves them because they spoil him. Be wary of them, especially the eunuch."

"And if co-ruling with my brother is not possible?" Urbi's brows arched. "What then?"

"Spread loyal people throughout the palace complex," Father advised. "Have your man Apollodorus cultivate friends among the guards so you can escape if they attempt to imprison you. If Omari's men move against you, you must flee to a safe place and rally support among the Egyptian people who love you. Then take the throne by force, if you must, but take it. Because you will be better for Egypt than your brother and the three misbegotten usurpers who feed him a steady stream of flattery.

"But know this," he went on, "even as you have found it difficult to share the throne with Omari, he will find it more difficult to share the throne with you. Your wit and intelligence outshine your brother's. He suffers in comparison, and he will not allow himself to look weak . . . and neither will his advisors. So he will move against you. It is only a matter of time."

Urbi arched an eyebrow in my direction, her way of telling me that I had a brilliant father. Then she stood, effectively ending our audience. "Thank you." She reached for my father's hands. "And if you pray to your God tonight, whisper a word for me."

Though Urbi never mentioned the matter to me, Father heard rumors that Pothinus had told the queen that the Romans were dismayed over how she handled the murder of Bibulous's sons, especially since she acted without input from Omari. The eunuch threatened to alert Rome of Cleopatra's "defiance of her father's will" unless she allowed her brother to be by her side whenever any royal business was conducted.

Ptolemy XIII began to take his place beside Cleopatra in the great hall, though the yawning space between their thrones seemed to represent the difference in their abilities.

For several weeks Father and I attended court six days out of every seven, silently observing Cleopatra's attempt to rule with her younger brother. From separate benches in the great hall we observed the queen and king, Cleopatra sitting erect and aloof while Omari slumped and giggled in his golden chair. The boy's three advisors whispered in his ear almost constantly, but the king's Regency Council did not speak to the queen unless absolutely necessary. Clearly, the threesome did not care to advance Cleopatra's interests. They did not know her as well as they knew Omari, and what they *did* know of her — that she was clear-eyed, level-headed, and quick-witted — frightened and intimidated them.

Once Omari and his retinue began to regularly appear at court, the atmosphere in the great hall changed completely. The quiet choirs and entertainments Urbi favored were replaced by jugglers, mimes, and grotesques from the neighboring temples. Animal trainers, with whips in one hand and jeweled leashes in the other, brought in jungle beasts that prowled over the marble tiles and rattled the candlestands with their roaring. I was among those who watched these spectacles with alarm, noting Urbi's seething frustration with her brother's antics.

When petitioners approached the throne, Omari settled frivolous issues with a word or a quick wave. Upon hearing about more important matters, he turned immediately to his advisors for their judgments. If Cleopatra tried to insert her opinion, four strident male voices drowned out her words.

More than once she looked at me after such an exchange and lifted her brow. I knew she was saying: *See what I must endure?*

Once I caught Urbi eyeing her brother with an expression of pure loathing on her face. Patience had never been one of her virtues. She tolerated her brother because Father had advised her to do so, but how long could she endure the boy king's ridiculous foolery and his advisors' self-serving ambitions?

I did not know. But even though I was naïve in the ways of politics, I sensed that the throne of Egypt wavered on a scale that would soon tip conclusively to one side or the other.

Chapter Eight

A few weeks later, just before the festival of Passover, Father and I were invited to dine privately with the queen. After spending so many hours watching Urbi deal with her brother and her many responsibilities, I had become resigned to not spending much time with my friend. But when the invitation to dinner arrived, hope bloomed anew. Perhaps she had found a way for us to remain close despite her demanding schedule.

"I do not blame her for wanting to get away from that circus in the throne room," Father said, a grim smile flashing in his beard as we prepared to leave the house. "You and I will seem dreadfully dull by comparison."

"I do not plan to be dull," I said, folding my arms. "I want to ask her what she thinks of the latest hair styles from Rome, about whether she will wear Greek or Egyptian fashion at the next festival, and if I can finally become her official lady-in-waiting."

Father sighed and led the way onto the street.

Urbi welcomed us with a warm smile and invited us to recline on the lushly upholstered couches in her private apartments. We nibbled from dozens of elaborate dishes, each laden with some delicacy I had never eaten. With quiet pleasure I noticed she had not served any shellfish or meat sitting in its own blood. She honored us even with her menu choices.

We talked of simple things — she asked about my brother, and I inquired after hers. We talked about the new moon festival and what we would wear. She asked about the synagogue where we worshiped; I remarked on the beauty of the moon rising over the Temple of Isis.

"I am so glad you have come," she said, her face glowing in the lamplight. "Chava, talking with you is such a wonderful distraction. When we are together, I forget all the things that are troubling me. If only I could forget them for more than a few hours."

She turned to my father. "Which is why I have invited you, Daniel. Once again, I find I must beg for your indulgence and ask for wisdom."

Father pressed his hand to his chest. "I

am always willing to serve you, my queen."

"Good. I have heard" — Urbi propped her elbow on her couch — "that the son of Gnaeus Pompeius Magnus is en route to Alexandria. I have also heard of civil war in Rome and would like to know your opinion of the situation. I must make certain of the truth but would rather not deal with this in the throne room. As you may have noticed, Omari and his advisors lack the diplomacy necessary to deal with foreign affairs, and I would not have my brother insert himself . . . unwisely."

As was his custom when pondering a matter, Father massaged the flesh beneath his beard. "I am not certain my information is current," he said, a note of apology in his voice, "but I know that Julius Caesar and Pompey have not been amicable since the death of Caesar's daughter, who married Pompey. The woman died giving birth to Pompey's child, and some say her death provided Caesar with an excuse for turning on his friend."

"Who turned on whom?" Urbi lifted a brow. "Pompey has always been a great friend to Egypt. He lent my father ships and money and troops so he could return and reclaim his authority from those who had forced him from Alexandria."

Father inclined his head. "I believe Pompey is a noble man. When he captured Jerusalem some years ago, he entered the Temple but did not intrude upon the Holy of Holies. He also left the Temple treasure alone, and such respect is but one mark of a noble man."

Urbi smiled. "Perhaps he had gold enough to satisfy."

Father matched her pleasant expression. "Perhaps."

"About the other man" — Urbi idly twirled a curl around her finger — "I have heard that Caesar is ambitious and would make himself king."

"Rome would never stand for another king and Caesar knows it," Father answered, his voice flat and final. "The Senate would not allow it. I have heard that Caesar wants the Senate to represent the people more equitably. He would add fresh blood to the old patrician senators and give voice to some of the plebeians and freedmen who have never been properly represented."

Urbi appeared to study her fingernails, then looked up. "In any case, I am inclined to be gracious to Pompey's son. He is coming to raise support for his father's army. Pompey has established a camp at Dyrrhachium, and they need supplies."

Father nodded. "You are to be commended for showing mercy to a man who showed mercy to your father. It is the right thing to do."

"I am glad you approve. I will send word to Pompey at once . . . quietly, of course. And thank you for your counsel. My father taught me that one must always be cautious when dealing with the lion that is Rome." The warmth of Urbi's smile echoed in her voice as she shifted her gaze to me. "You must find all this talk terribly dull, Chava. Would you like to speak of something more pleasant?"

I looked from her to my father and realized that the events of the last several months had created a gulf between us. Urbi had become a woman who spent her hours thinking about kings, wars, and feeding her hungry people. The most serious thing I had contemplated in the last few hours was what color himation to wear to dinner.

But I couldn't help who I was. And HaShem had given me a promise, so I would always be part of Urbi's life. If Adonai meant for me to be the queen's most entertaining distraction, then that is what I would be.

"If you are ready to talk about something other than wars and armies," I said, smiling, "tell me what you think about yellow hair. I hear that yellow-haired women are everywhere in Rome."

A contingent of royal guards and Egyptian dignitaries were waiting when Gnaeus Pompeius, son of the great Pompey, stepped off a ship in the Alexandrian harbor. Guarded by a select group of legionaries who had once served his father, court officials greeted Pompeius with great fanfare and led him to Cleopatra and Ptolemy XIII. The boy's advisors hovered around Omari's throne; Cleopatra sat to his right.

Father, Asher, and I stood among the fifty or so guests who had been invited to welcome the Roman consul's son. I had to rise on tiptoe to witness the unfolding drama, but because I had learned a little about what was happening in Rome, I would not have missed the historic meeting.

In a halting voice, Omari read a proclamation thanking Pompeius for his father's support of Auletes, the late king of Egypt. He then announced that Egypt would provide sixty ships and five hundred soldiers to aid Pompey's cause. Egypt would also send several tons of grain to feed the hungry legionaries at Dyrrhachium.

Gnaeus Pompeius bowed in gratitude, and

I caught Urbi's eye. She sent me a grim smile, acknowledging that her goals had been accomplished. But the worry line on her forehead convinced me that all had not gone well during the negotiation. What had her brother and his advisors done to cause my friend such worry?

After Pompey's son thanked the king and queen for their generous support, the assembly in the throne room moved into an adjoining chamber to feast with the Roman guests.

Along with Father and Asher, I followed the crowd. Abundant food and drink had been set out for Pompey and his retinue, and they wasted no time before dropping onto couches and feasting like men who'd spent a month gnawing on dried biscuits.

I stepped closer to Father, who had been mingling among the locals at the reception. Many of his acquaintances were wealthy traders who frequently traveled across the Great Sea. Their reports kept Father apprised of the current political climate, so he might have an idea about what troubled Urbi.

"Father?"

"Hmm?" He swallowed the honey wafer he'd been chewing and brushed crumbs from his beard. "You look worried, daughter."

"The queen appeared anxious — did you notice?"

He looked over at the couch where Cleopatra reclined, then sighed almost imperceptibly. "She does not appear to be enjoying herself."

"I cannot remember the last time Urbi did not enjoy herself at a party."

A smile quirked the corner of Father's mouth. "You know that the arrangement between Pompeius and Egypt was decided long before this morning."

"Of course. Urbi said she would arrange it quietly."

"What you witnessed today was pure theater. Not only was the matter concluded days ago, but word of Egypt's support has already reached the Roman Senate."

I frowned, unable to understand what any of this had to do with Cleopatra's unease.

"Several weeks ago," Father went on, "a large segment of the Senate fled with Pompey as Julius Caesar approached the city with his army. That segment camped at Thessalonica, where they recently passed a resolution to thank Egypt for its generous response to young Pompey's request. Furthermore, the Senate decreed that Pompey the elder should be appointed guardian of Cleopatra's brother."

The unexpected report whipped my breath away. "The Roman Senate . . . believes they have the authority to decide such things for *Egypt*?"

Father's eyes sparked with approval. "Now you begin to understand. Always look for the underlying message, Chava. In the politics of power, what a man says on the surface is rarely what he means."

I shook my head. "But how will this affect Cleopatra? *She* does not need a guardian. She is perfectly capable —"

"Correct," Father replied, keeping his voice low. "But Pompey will not consider her his equal, so she will be set aside. Pompey will come in, ostensibly to counsel Omari. But consider the words again, daughter. Cleopatra was not happy to hear of Rome's intervention, but who else will not welcome that message from the Senate?"

Nearly everyone, of course. But when I drew breath to voice my reply, a better answer surfaced: *Omari's advisors.* Those three bloodthirsty fleas would never surrender their exalted positions as counselors to the king. But how could three men resist the will of all-powerful Rome?

"In this," Father said, following my thought processes, "the advisors and the queen will be united. They will not want interference from Rome."

I lifted my head and looked at Urbi, understanding far more than I had when I'd arrived.

"I'll be home soon, Father." Standing outside the reception room, I rose to kiss Father's cheek, then tightened my grip on the bag that dangled at my waist. I had worked hard on the scroll inside and did not want to lose it.

"Chava." Father frowned. "You should leave with us. It is not proper for a young woman to wander about the palace unescorted —"

"I know these hallways as well as I know our house. I'll be right behind you, I promise."

I sent him and Asher away with a quick wave and then turned down the marble hallway that led to Cleopatra's apartments. The crowd from the reception had not completely dispersed, so people would be lined up at the dock, waiting for a skiff to row them across the harbor to the mainland. If Urbi wasn't too exhausted, we might have a little time to visit.

I smiled at the guard who always stood outside her door. "Is the queen available for me?"

The man narrowed his eyes at me, then stepped inside the chamber to inquire. A moment later he returned with Charmion, who inclined her head and gave me a brittle smile.

I tilted my head to study her. I was reasonably sure she returned my dislike and distrust in full measure, but I would never share these suspicions with the queen. My friend had more important matters on her mind.

"May I help you?" Charmion asked as the guard walked away.

"I wanted to speak to Urbi." I intentionally used the queen's family name to remind the slave that I was not some random person from the city.

She inclined her head. "The queen is resting. She was not feeling well, so the physician has given her something to help her sleep."

My hopes sank. I would not disturb Urbi if she felt unwell, but I wanted to share something —

"Please give her this." I opened my bag and placed the scroll in Charmion's hand. "It is a poem I wrote. I thought she might enjoy it."

Charmion held the scroll on her open hands. "I will tell her."

The slave slipped through the doorway, leaving me alone with the carved wooden door.

I sighed. Nothing to do, then, but join the others at the docks. I trudged down the hallway, realizing too late that I should have kept the scroll until I saw Urbi again. If she read it while we were together, I would be able to see her reaction — and I'd know if she liked it or if she only *pretended* to like it. Now I would never know, because Urbi had perfected the skill of accepting gifts with a pleasant, diplomatic expression.

The slaves had not yet lit the torches in the hallways, so I walked next to the wall and slid through shadows. My soft sandals padded noiselessly over the marble floors without a sound to mark my progress. Oh, what I would give to be a shadow on the wall in this place! I felt more at home in the palace than I did in my father's house, and HaShem had promised me that I would be Urbi's friend for a lifetime.

I was approaching a corner when I heard voices . . . whispering male voices that seemed oddly out of place in a hallway that led to the queen's chamber.

Instantly aware of my vulnerability, I leaned against the wall and hoped that whoever stood beyond the corner would pass and not see me. While I waited, heart pounding, I recognized the peculiar nasal quality of one speaker: the voice belonged to Achillas, commander of the royal guard.

"Tomorrow night," he said, his whisper creating a fist of fear in my stomach. "I have a company of loyal guards prepared to seize her. They will transport her to the port, where she will be taken on board and removed to Mauritania. Once we know she is safely away from Egypt, Pothinus will send word. But you have to open the gate for my men."

My blood ran cold, freezing me in place. Who could he intend to seize but Urbi? Achillas controlled the soldiers who were sworn to protect the royals, but few of them would disobey an order from their commander. And Pothinus! He had probably organized the entire plot. Once they had Cleopatra safely away from Alexandria, once they were sure they would not face insurmountable consequences, they would kill her. The Ptolemies had been murdering their relatives for generations, so why shouldn't they kill another one?

I waited, not daring to move a muscle,

until the voices ceased and the sound of footsteps faded away. I felt my way along the wall until I came to a carved niche, then nearly upset a vase of flowers as I stepped into the space. I hid behind the flowers and did not venture forth until a tall figure in a loincloth passed by. I knew the guard — he always stood at the queen's door. He must have slipped away to meet Achillas after he went to fetch Charmion.

You have to open the gate for my men . . .

I walked back the way I had come, cautiously navigating the darkness, keenly aware of the heavy thump beneath my breastbone. How would I explain my sudden reappearance? How could I remain cool beneath the gaze of the man I had just overheard plotting with Achillas?

I inhaled deeply to calm my racing heart, then drew a tight smile over my teeth. I approached the guard outside Urbi's door and gave him the most innocent look I could muster. "I have important news for the queen."

The guard looked at me as if I were some annoying species of insect. "Were you not sent away?"

"I have come back. I have to tell the queen . . . about news from Rome." I broadened my smile and fluttered my lashes, playing the naïve fool I had been for far too long. "She will want to see me, I know she will."

The guard frowned but opened the door and stepped inside. Not waiting for him to fetch Charmion, I followed, ignoring his cry as I strode through the anteroom and into Urbi's bedchamber, drawing the bed curtain with a quick flick of my wrist.

The queen had stretched out to sleep, and annoyance shone in her eyes when she lifted her head and saw me in the lamplight. "Chava," she said, her tone sharp, "have you forgotten where you are?"

I turned, trembling, and walked to the door where the traitorous guard stood, his sword drawn and his eyes blazing. "My queen," he said, his tone clipped, "what do you want me to do with her?"

Urbi sighed heavily, then waved a languid hand. "Leave her be."

My forearms pebbled with gooseflesh as I waited for him to step back and close the door.

"Chava," Urbi said and pushed herself into a sitting position, "if this is about your poem, we can talk about it later."

I fell to my knees by her bed. "Forget about the poem." Not knowing how far the plot had spread, I lowered my voice: "I heard them in the hallway. The guard at your door and Achillas. Tomorrow night the commander of the guards is going to order his men to take you away from Egypt. You must act without delay."

Disbelief flickered in Urbi's dark eyes, but she did not question me. Instead she sat up and rang a bell. Apollodorus appeared immediately, as if the bell had been connected to his arm.

Wearing only a linen kilt and brandishing a curved dagger, he bent toward the queen, his eyes flashing with alarm. "My lady?"

She placed her hand on my arm, acknowledging my support as she swung her legs off the bed. "We leave tonight. But we must go silently."

"Shall I alert the others?"

"Spread the word. Have our men meet us at the shoreline, not the dock. No torches."

I gaped at her. "You knew about this?"

She threw me a warning look. "Not when, but I knew it was coming, and so did your father. I saw them, like little mice, rubbing their hands as they plotted in corners."

Cleopatra pulled on a hooded robe and tugged on another cord. Charmion and Iras appeared, each carrying a loaded basket. "Time to go," Cleopatra told her slaves. "Take only what we need and pack the boat quickly. Apollodorus will alert our supporters. He has men ready to escort us out of the city."

Out of the city . . . away.

A boulder rose in my throat as the meaning of those words hit home. Urbi was leaving Alexandria again, perhaps forever this time. But HaShem had promised that I would be with her on her last day . . . Had that day come? Would she be caught and killed on her way out of the palace?

I caught her arm. "You must be careful, Urbi. They mean to kill you."

"I know."

Cleopatra moved to her desk and scooped up a pile of scrolls, then paused. With her free hand she reached out and traced the curve of my cheek. "I read your poem," she whispered, smiling. "I owe you so many things — years of friendship and love. But tonight I owe you my life."

"Let me go with you." I clasped her hand. "Surely it was meant to be. I could be useful on your journey —"

"You can be useful in Alexandria. Tell no one what has happened here tonight. Say nothing of your part in this, not even to your father. But stay close to him and learn as much as you can. I must have accurate reports if I am to defeat those who would destroy Egypt in their quest for personal power."

I would have protested again, but Urbi silenced me with the stern look of a queen. "I cannot let you come. Your father would not allow it, and I would not disrespect his wishes."

"But —"

"No." Her eyes flashed a warning. "But when you pray to your God, ask him to look with favor on Cleopatra, the unfortunate queen of Egypt. Now go home, and stay alert. I'll send a message if I can."

Reluctantly, I departed, choking on a knot of unshed tears.

Determined to keep the palace spies from knowing of my part in Cleopatra's abrupt departure, the next morning I dressed and went with Father to the throne room as usual. When the queen did not appear, with dozens of others I expressed shock. When I heard that Cleopatra could not be found in her apartments, I held my hand to my throat and did my best to look horrified. "Where has she gone?" I asked, wide-eyed. Tears sprang to my eyes in honest consternation when Achillas replied that no one knew.

Someone knew where she was — Apollodorus and Charmion and Iras, plus a few other loyal supporters — but I, her best friend, knew nothing.

I sat with Father and Asher as Omari and his counselors stormed and stewed, speaking in veiled terms no one else understood. Achillas fretted aloud, storming in and out of the great hall on the pretext of questioning the guards, and Pothinus was clearly discomfited, wringing his hands and occasionally venturing into hysterics. "How could we have lost her?" he kept asking. "What if she has gone to Pompey?"

Then Theodotus, who had always been the more pragmatic of the trio, pointed out that they had settled a thorny problem with very little difficulty. "We will have no more struggles with Cleopatra," he announced, publicly acknowledging that the sister-brother pair had not been amenable. "She has left Alexandria; perhaps she has left Egypt. Which can only mean that she has ignored her father's wishes and abdicated her position. As of today, Cleopatra is queen no more."

"I will not have her back!" Omari declared, energetically stomping his foot. "I do not need her to tell me what to do!"

"Of course not, mighty Pharaoh." Theodotus bowed low before his charge. "We will take care of things. Your advisory council will take care of everything."

A few days later, at dinner, Asher reported that Ptolemy XIII had issued a new *prostagma* or royal decree: no longer would grain be moved from Middle Egypt to Lower or Upper Egypt, but would be immediately dispatched to the port of Alexandria. Anyone who transgressed the new law would suffer confiscation and death, and anyone who divulged information about a transgressor would be richly rewarded.

Never had a decree about grain been so widely announced, nor had any decree concerning commerce warranted such a severe penalty. "They would kill someone for shipping grain to the hungry people of Upper Egypt?" I asked, baffled. "The famine is not so severe that Alexandria is starving . . ."

Father held up a finger. "What did I tell you about politics? This is political, you may be sure of it."

I bit my lip and struggled to remember. "What a politician says on the surface is rarely what he means —"

"Exactly. The famine is severe, but not so severe that we must condemn wheat exporters. This law is about Cleopatra. They want to starve her out."

I blinked. "Has she no food?"

"She must gather people to fight for her cause," Father explained. "Which means she has to feed an army. If she cannot, her supporters will leave. So her brother's advisors want to be sure Cleopatra has no access to grain."

I fell silent, absorbing the news. Urbi had an army. I did not know how she managed to raise one, but I wasn't surprised that she could.

By the time the spring windstorms had blown over Alexandria, we heard that Cleopatra had left Egypt. I thought Theodotus, Achillas, and Pothinus would relax their efforts to kill the queen, but they continued to wage war against Urbi, turning the nobles of Alexandria against her and rallying them in support of her brother. In the great hall of the palace, which I continued to visit with my father, Ptolemy XIII's Regency Council frequently proclaimed that Cleopatra was anti-Egypt and pro-Roman, citing her surrender of the murderous Gabinian soldiers as proof. They declared she was her father's daughter, because everyone knew the late king had been deeply involved with the Roman Senate.

Despite the council's bold attestations, my

father believed the treacherous trio betrayed Cleopatra for quite another reason. "She was never a pliable child," he told me, a gleam of pride in his eye, "and her spirit is still independent. She will not be ruled by them, so they want to be rid of her."

Like the rest of Cleopatra's supporters, I kept quiet and helped my father with his work. In everything I did, I kept an ear cocked for rumors about our queen. News trickled in slowly, reports coming to us through merchants and sailors who traveled the Nile and the Great Sea.

We learned that immediately after leaving the palace with a band of loyal slaves and soldiers, Cleopatra established a camp in the middle of the Egyptian desert. When it appeared her location had been discovered, she abandoned her camp in the dead of night and traveled to Ashkelon, a Philistine city located between Egypt and Palestine. The people of Ashkelon cheered her arrival, and Cleopatra charmed them so completely that they featured her image on a series of silver coins. Father obtained a set, which we proudly displayed on a table in the atrium.

While Cleopatra charmed the people of Ashkelon, the boy king's advisors fumed and made preparations for all-out war. Achillas assembled the army and marched them to the Egyptian border, waiting for an occasion when Cleopatra might leave the well-defended city and could be captured outside the walls. Omari and his advisors had already formally deposed Cleopatra, but they could not guarantee the boy king's position until she was dead and no longer a threat.

Though I could not be with my best friend, at night I lay in my bed, closed my eyes, and tried to imagine how she had spent her day. Were Iras and Charmion taking good care of her? Was Apollodorus standing guard outside her door? Was she worried about the future, and did she still fear for her life?

I prayed, begging Adonai to keep her safe from those who would do her harm. "I know she does not worship you," I would whisper, "but for my sake, will you guide her steps? Someday she will be a great queen, if you will preserve her life."

As I listened to rumors and watched the counselors manipulate the boy king, with increasing clarity I saw that these months, as painful as they were, had to be teaching Cleopatra lessons in commerce, diplomacy, and war. When she returned to Alexandria, she would be wiser and even better equipped to rule.

I said as much at dinner one night. Asher stopped eating and looked at me, surprise on his face. "How do you know she will make it back to Alexandria?"

Not wanting to risk an argument, I lowered my gaze and shrugged. "I know, and that is all."

"But *how* do you know?"

"I know because . . . it is not her time to die."

Asher snorted and went back to eating.

I knew because HaShem had given me a promise that had not yet been fulfilled.

I lifted my hand and studied the scar across my palm. It had paled over the years and seemed to parallel my lifeline. Would I spend my entire life waiting for Urbi to return?

While we waited to see which of the Ptolemy siblings would win the throne, Father continued to bring Yosef home for discussions about prophecy, particularly on Shabbat. While I oversaw the roasting of the lamb and the preparation of soft challah, I would hear them debating in the small room that served as Father's library.

"Dani'el said there would be seven weeks, and sixty-two weeks," Yosef shouted one afternoon. "And then the anointed one shall be destroyed."

"But who is the anointed one?" Father countered, his voice rising to match Yosef's. "The first seven has passed — seven sevens is forty-nine, and the reconstruction of Jerusalem took forty-nine years. Then we are to see four hundred thirty-four years, and we have not."

I ducked outside and went to the kitchen, where Nuru gave me a skeptical look. "Do you understand all the things your father is talking about?"

"No," I admitted freely as I lifted the clay lid on the stew pot. I inhaled a deep breath of aromatic steam. "That smells wonderful. I like the spices you have added."

"I think," Nuru said, her mouth quirking in a smile, "that you like this young man. You have never cared what we feed your brother."

"Yosef is nice," I admitted, "but his father is a butcher. We cannot have him going home and telling Avraham that we do not know how to roast a lamb properly."

When Father and Yosef had exhausted themselves with debating Dani'el's prophecy of seventy weeks, Yosef would slip out of the library and find me reading in the atrium. He would ask about my book, often surprising me with his knowledge of the text. Apparently he liked to read as much as I did and frequently spent time browsing Alexandria's famed library.

One afternoon he showed me a scroll containing the works of a young Latin poet named Publius Vergilius Maro, commonly known as Virgil. "Would you like me to read one?"

I smiled in anticipation. "Please."

With a well-modulated voice, he read the story of a barmaid called Syrisca, who yearned to leave the city and retreat to a pastoral setting. She set out a picnic and invited a young man to join her, then told him not to worry about the future, but to drink the wine and live for the day. . . .

When Yosef had finished, he lowered the scroll and looked at me almost shyly.

"You read beautifully," I told him, resting my head on my hand. "I like the poem. I have never been to a country setting like he describes."

"Nor I," Yosef said, "but Father tells me that there are well-watered lands outside Jerusalem. I hope to go there one day. I'd love to raise my children in a place where we could easily visit the Temple."

I lifted a brow at the mention of children. Was he planning to speak of marriage?

I stood in a clumsy effort to dissuade him.

"Thank you for the poem, Yosef. But I — I should see about dinner."

"Chava." He caught my hand, a bold move. "Do you . . . are you happy in my company?"

I sighed and looked away. What could I tell him? If I had not vowed to remain by Urbi's side, I could easily love the handsome youth before me. But I had built walls around my heart, strong defenses that could not be penetrated even by direct confrontation and lovely words.

"Yosef . . ." I forced a smile into my voice. "You are most charming, and I enjoy being with you. But I am not looking to marry now . . . nor in the foreseeable future. I hope you will understand."

Hurt flooded his eyes as he released my hand. I turned and walked quickly to the kitchen, to check on a roast that did not need tending. But what else could I do?

At sunset, I lit the Shabbat candles and held my hands over my eyes, feeling the pressure of Yosef's gaze upon me. I also knew that after dinner, Father would ask if Avraham the butcher should bring us a bridal contract.

I would have to reply that while I liked Yosef very much, I could not enter into a betrothal without first settling matters with

Urbi. "I pledged my friendship and support to her," I would tell him. "I am her eyes and ears in Alexandria. And I know you would not want me to dishonor one promise to enter into another one."

He would not argue with me, for how could he? The Torah had taught me to love and obey my father, but it had also taught me to be faithful to my vows. Any other father might have ordered me to marry Yosef, but my father could not order me to do anything that contradicted everything he had taught me.

So he would wait with the rest of us as Omari and Urbi played their dangerous game of cat and mouse.

Chapter Nine

The waiting game continued another year. During those months, Yosef continued to visit our home, Pompey chased Caesar, and Omari hounded Cleopatra, finally setting up camp across from the island of Mount Casius, where the queen and her army had established a base.

And I continued to pray for my friend's safety . . . even though a new friend had taken up residence in my heart.

Yosef, always kind and considerate, stopped debating prophecy with Father and spent most Sabbaths reading poetry with me. And while my will remained strongly committed to Urbi and HaShem's promise, my heart wondered what it would be like to live with Yosef, to dine with him every night, and to sleep in his bed. To have a son who looked like him, or a daughter with his dancing eyes . . .

Whenever my thoughts began to chase

these dreams, my stubborn will shut down my imaginings as quickly as possible. But as the days passed with no word from Urbi, my will grew steadily weaker.

Rome remained embroiled in civil war. Though at several junctures Caesar and his army appeared to be trapped, HaShem granted him grace.

But though Pompey also suffered numerous losses, he would not surrender. Because Egypt had been good to him, and because he had been named guardian of the boy king, the aging warrior gathered his wife and young children and set sail for Alexandria. The Gabinian legionaries, his former men, were still in Egypt, and Pompey envisioned them as the nucleus of his new army. He knew Egypt's great wealth could sustain him as he built up his forces and continued the fight against Caesar.

But life intervened. In late September, a small group of boats appeared near Omari's military encampment. He sent a small boat — a fishing vessel, nothing fine — to fetch Pompey. The boat was piloted by a three-man welcoming party: Achillas, Lucius Septimius, the current commander of the Gabinian contingent, and another Roman officer who had served under Pompey.

Pompey bade his wife and young children

good-bye and stepped into the vessel. As the four men neared the shore, Lucius Septimius drew a blade and viciously stabbed Pompey, then cut off his head. Egyptian battleships in the harbor fired on Pompey's ships, destroying several and killing one of Pompey's relatives.

Though the citizens of Alexandria despised Rome, no one cheered Pompey's death. The general had been a legend even in Egypt, and he had been known as a fair and reasonable man. Because he had spent his life being gracious and generous, he had approached Egypt expecting to be received in the same manner.

He had not expected betrayal from a boy king.

When Father brought the horrific news to our house, Asher and I sat in stunned silence for several moments. Then Father said Omari might have murdered Pompey in an effort to keep Caesar at bay. With his enemy dead, or so the king's advisors presumed, Caesar would come to Egypt in search of Pompey, view the dead man's corpse, and depart, having no reason to linger in the land of the pharaohs.

How wrong they were.

To pass the lonely days while Urbi was

away, I had taken to writing her long letters inked on slips of parchment that would never be wrapped around a spindle and delivered. Writing was not nearly as satisfying as talking to Urbi, but it did allow me to release all the swirling emotions and thoughts I experienced in her absence.

One afternoon I heard a knock at the door while I was composing a letter. Since Father and Asher were out, I kept writing, knowing the doorman would take a message from the visitor. But after a moment Nuru appeared in my doorway, a tentative smile on her face. "You have a visitor, mistress."

I lowered my pen. "Who would visit me?"

"Yosef."

I shook my head. "He has probably come to see Father. Send him on his way, and I'll tell —"

"He asked to see *you.*"

I bit my lower lip, then stood and brushed the wrinkles from my chiton. "I cannot imagine what he wants," I said, pausing to check my reflection in the looking brass. "He probably wants to tell me something about Asher. Or maybe he wants to know what Father might like as a gift. One never knows with young men —"

Nuru caught my shoulders, holding me still, and used her fingers to smooth a few hairs at my temple. She pinched my cheeks for a second, then smiled. "You look lovely. Go to him."

My pulse pounded as I walked to the vestibule and invited Yosef in.

Though he had been inside our home on dozens of occasions, he locked his hand behind his back and regarded the couch pillows as if they were works of art. "You have a lovely home, Chava."

"Yosef." When he turned to face me, I shook my head. "You are always welcome here. Father and Asher are at the synagogue, so what brings you today?"

He hit me with a sudden smile that made my heart lurch. "How like you to cut to the heart of the matter. In truth, I have come to see you."

I gestured to the couch as my heart warmed. When he sank onto the cushions, still smiling, I sat next to him and folded my hands. "Have you and Asher had some kind of quarrel? Or do you want to ask if Father has finally figured out the riddle of Dani'el's seventy weeks?"

He laughed softly as he looked at me, his eyes burning with the clear, hot light that gleams in the heart of a flame. "I came to speak to you," he said, watching me with an intense but guarded expression. "Your father insists that the time is not right, but I visit every week and on occasion I think I see the light of affection in your eyes. If it is affection, tell me truly — might it ripen into love? For I have prayed, and HaShem has led me to your door. No other woman in Alexandria is like you, Chava, and I will have no other to be my wife. So — will you consider a betrothal between us?"

I swallowed hard, feeling myself compressed into an ever-shrinking space between the weight of my conviction and my fondness for the ardent young man who sat beside me. I could not deny that I was attracted to Yosef. My pulse skittered alarmingly every time I heard his voice, and at dinner I often found myself studying his profile. His laughter wrapped me like a warm blanket, and I wanted to cheer whenever he won a point in a debate with my father. Yosef was a righteous man, handsome, strong, articulate, and bright, but I had promised to spend my life serving someone else.

Why would HaShem allow me to be attracted to a man I could not have?

"Yosef," I whispered, "I am not sure I can make you understand why I can't —"

"Have I displeased you in some way?"

"Never."

"Am I not clever enough? Being a scholar's daughter, I am sure you have high expectations —"

"Stop." I lifted my hand, scarred palm outward. "Therein lies the problem. I have *no* expectations of a husband, for I have promised my life to another."

A flicker of shock widened his eyes as panic, swiftly quelled, tightened his mouth. "I-I am sorry," he stammered. "Your father did not tell me —"

"I have not been promised in marriage," I said quickly. "But I have promised to be the queen's servant for as long as we live. When she returns, I will probably move to the palace to become her lady-in-waiting."

A frown flitted across his features. "*If* she returns," he said. "And if she does not, will you reconsider?" He caught my gaze. "For I will not marry anyone but you, Chava. I am certain of it."

"I wish you would not be so stubborn," I said, standing. "I am sure HaShem has a wife for you. You only have to find her."

"Look who is being stubborn now." He stood, too, and took advantage of the solitude to take my hands. "Consider all you will sacrifice if you commit to a life in the palace. You will not marry. You will cut yourself off from children, a blessing from

HaShem. You will be surrounded by strangers who worship false gods and who may expect you to worship them, too."

"The queen has never required me to —"

"You have never been a member of her household. You have been a free woman, but things will change if you live at the palace." He squeezed my hands as he leaned closer. "What do you want to do with your life, Chava? Why has HaShem placed you on this earth?"

The question stole my breath. No one had ever asked me such a question, and in all my study of philosophy, I had never considered my life in those terms.

"What — why, HaShem himself has told me what I will do. I will bless the queen. I will be with her on her happiest and last day."

Yosef's hands tightened on mine. "Can you not do those things married to me? Can you not do those things as a daughter of Israel?"

I blinked. I could, of course, but I had never imagined a life outside the palace. I had always envisioned myself clothed in silk garments and gold chains. In all my daydreams, I had never seen myself as a Jewish wife with children following in my wake. . . .

I shook my head. "No."

"Then know this." Yosef leaned so close that his breath fanned my cheek. "I am sure HaShem has a husband for you. When the time comes, you have only to look for me. I will marry no one else."

He released my hands and walked away. I sank slowly to the couch, my hands damp and my heart aching.

Four days after Pompey's murder, Caesar sailed into Alexandria's fair harbor with ten warships and over four thousand legionaries. Father and I watched from our balcony as a small boat bearing Ptolemy XIII's flag rowed out to meet him.

This time, I noticed, the king's advisors sent something grander than a fishing vessel.

"It is rumored that Omari has dispatched Theodotus with a gift for Caesar," Father said, his voice filled with dread.

"A gift?"

"Pompey's head."

We did not observe the encounter, but we heard about the aftermath. Ptolemy and his advisors had hoped to win favor with Caesar, but their so-called *gift* had the opposite effect. Caesar wept when he saw his friend's head, and though no one could say if those tears were heartfelt, his demand for justice was sincere enough.

The Roman consul came ashore wearing a white tunic and purple toga — not just dyed, but heavily embroidered with gold. "He comes in peace," Father said, "or he would have worn his armor. But he comes as a consul, for he wears the *toga picta,* a badge of high authority."

"How do you know these things?" I asked, surprised at my father's knowledge of Roman clothing.

He gave me a wry smile. "Daughter, you should read something besides poetry."

Twelve toga-wearing men surrounded Caesar — I had no idea who they were — and the attendant who walked closest to him carried a bundle of rods, one of which ended in an ax blade. When I asked Father what that was, he called it a *fasces,* a symbol of a magistrate's power and authority.

The sight unsettled me. Did Caesar intend to rule over us? He might have hoped to impress us with his fancy ax, but my fellow citizens — Egyptians, Greeks, and Jews alike — were offended by what we saw as a flagrant infringement of Egyptian independence.

Father, Asher, and I watched from the balcony as an angry mob surged toward

Caesar and his men. The Romans quickly retreated, but within days tents sprang up around the royal buildings Caesar's men had claimed for their barracks, and Alexandria's citizens rioted at every opportunity.

"Caesar clearly does not understand the people of our city," my father observed one afternoon, his hand falling protectively on my brother's shoulder. "Never has a city been more passionate and quick-tempered, and never have citizens been as eager to make their feelings known."

"Will he leave soon?" I asked, troubled by the sight of so many Roman ships in the harbor.

Father shook his head. "He could not leave if he wanted to. For the next few months the winds will be unfavorable, so the Roman will be anchored here until spring."

Omari, who had been encamped outside Mount Casius, returned to the palace. In an effort to persuade the Romans to be on their way, the boy king and his Regency Council arranged for substandard grain to be served to the legionaries and allowed only broken crockery to be used on royal tables, including the king's. The palace slaves were told that if Caesar asked what had happened to the gold and silver plates and utensils, they should reply that Cleopatra had absconded with everything of value.

When we realized that Caesar would not be leaving as abruptly as he had arrived, I began to hope that Urbi would return from exile. I knew she would not remain away from her beloved kingdom if an arbitrator would agree to settle the trouble between her and Omari. Although she had longed to enlist Pompey in her cause, she might be even more eager to recruit Caesar, who had left his wife in Rome and, if gossip could be trusted, had an especial appreciation for intelligent, attractive women.

Fourteen days after Caesar's arrival, I received a message from a slave who would not identify the scroll's sender. The message, penned in Aramaic instead of Koine Greek, told me to expect the delivery of a carpet within hours. The carpet had come a great distance, the sender warned, and should be handled with the greatest care. A Sicilian would meet me at the docks near the Necropic Gate to arrange delivery.

I lifted the scroll and studied the handwriting — was it Urbi's? She had always been so careful with her stylus, I could not tell if it was her hand. But the message had definitely come from someone close to her.

My pulse pounded in my throat as I summoned Nuru and told her we were going out. I draped my himation over my head like a cowl and led Nuru onto the street. We left the Jewish Quarter and walked down the Canopic Way, passing the great library, the Mausoleum of Alexander, and the Agora. I walked quickly, forcing Nuru to jog behind me, and we were both breathless when we reached the western part of the city. We crossed the bridge over the canal and reached the Necropic Gate, which opened to the port and the Necropolis where Alexandria buried its dead.

The sun had begun to color the western horizon as we waited for our unknown contact. Water slapped at the docks, sending sprays into the air, and a few boats bobbed on the surface and creaked their ropes. Nuru clung to my hand, her anxiety plainly visible. We had never been out this late, and we had never been in this part of the city without a male escort.

We walked along the docks until we met an old man, his face seamed by the sun and the passing of decades. When I asked if he had seen a Sicilian in the area, he pointed to a small vessel tied to the dock.

Nuru and I walked toward the boat. When we reached it, I called out, and almost immediately Apollodorus emerged from the shadows. Behind him, barely visible in the shadowy hold, I caught a glimpse of my much-missed friend.

I bit my lip, deliberately tamping down my exuberance. One of Omari's spies might be watching, even in this deserted place.

"How can I help you?" I asked, taking care to keep my voice steady.

Apollodorus nodded, his eyes urging caution, and glanced behind me before answering. "I cannot leave the parcel unprotected. But if you could hire a cart, or perhaps rent a donkey, I could arrange delivery tonight."

"I can do that." I stifled the urge to bow, then grabbed Nuru's arm and dragged her back over the dock.

Asher had a friend who rented pushcarts, and within the hour I had procured one. Nuru pulled it back to the port, then waited on shore while I hurried to the little boat.

I found Apollodorus on the deck, a dagger strapped to his waist.

"Behold, the cart awaits." Flushed with victory, I pointed to the conveyance. "Is there anything else I can do?"

"Yes." Apollodorus lowered his voice. "I hear Caesar sleeps on the grounds of the palace."

"He does. In a villa near the harbor."

"I would be recognized if I approached the guards. Could you deliver an item to the Roman? My lady says you are known to the guards, so your presence would not be unexpected."

I peered into the shadowy hold, hoping Urbi could hear me. "I can deliver anything you like. No one will think anything of it."

"If asked, you should say you are bringing a gift for Caesar. I will walk behind you, hooded like a slave."

Though every fiber of my being wanted to jump aboard that boat and find Urbi, I knew I could not risk exposing her. But I could help her reach Caesar.

Apollodorus's plan made sense, but I could not ignore the danger. If one of Omari's men discovered I was working with Cleopatra, my life would be in danger — and not only mine, but my entire family's. Since I was an unmarried woman, my father would be held responsible for anything I might do.

But Father would agree to do this himself, if given the opportunity. He knew Urbi would be a more capable ruler than her foolish, bloodthirsty brother.

I drew a deep breath and forbade myself to tremble. "Load your parcel into my cart," I told Apollodorus. "And let us be on our way before we lose the remaining daylight. Once darkness falls, we could be stopped and searched on the street."

Since we had a long walk ahead of us, I girded my courage about me and walked in front of Nuru and Apollodorus, who followed with his head lowered, dragging the handcart behind him. Though I was as jumpy as a cat — with good reason — part of me thrilled to be a part of such an endeavor. On that walk through Alexandria, I held a queen's life in my hands.

I tried to behave normally as we traversed the city, but every time someone turned to look at us, my heart nearly stopped beating. If Omari had heard rumors of her departure from Mount Casius, he might have planted spies throughout Alexandria. Was the man outside the theater squinting at me? The woman with the monkey — was she a lookout for the king? The three mimes performing across from the library — had they been positioned there to watch for Cleopatra?

My friend Acis stood at the entrance to the palace grounds, but beside him stood an unfamiliar legionary who had to be one of Caesar's men. "I am Chava, daughter of Daniel the scholar." I punctuated my words with a smile. "I bring a gift for your commander."

The legionary eyed the bulky bag on the cart. "What's in it?"

"A carpet from the East. Slaves have just taken it off the ship."

"I know this one," Acis said. "She and her father come to the palace often."

The legionary ignored Acis and walked the length of the cart, his sword in hand, and my pounding heart kept pace with his footsteps. Would he realize that the lumpy bag was the approximate length of Egypt's missing queen?

He pressed the tip of his sword to the bag as if to test its substance.

"Please!" My hand flew to my throat. "The weave is delicate. I could not present Caesar with a damaged rug."

"If the carpet is so delicate, how can anybody walk on it?" He prodded it again with the flat side of his blade.

Fortunately, the legionary's examination lasted only a moment. He returned to my side and met my smile in full measure. "Always a pleasure to serve a beautiful lady."

My face warmed with embarrassment. "May — may I ask where I may find Caesar?"

"You cannot go inside the gate. Leave the

bag here."

"Oh, I couldn't!" I swallowed hard. "Someone might be tempted to steal it, and I have been charged with seeing it safely into Caesar's hands."

The legionary hesitated, his eyes roving over me, then he gave me a lopsided smile. "You do not look dangerous. All right, take it in, but then you must leave at once. Caesar is staying in one of the villas by the harbor — the western one that sits off by itself. You'll see guards outside the door."

"Thank you."

I draped my himation back over my hair and strode forward, my heart resuming its normal pace only when I heard the reassuring creak of the cart behind me.

We walked slowly, taking care not to draw undue attention, and remained in the shadows as much as possible. The Ptolemies had built dozens of buildings on the palace grounds, for each ruler wanted something different from his predecessors. In addition, they had built small villas along the harbor for older children and visiting guests. Caesar, apparently, had taken one of these.

The sun had nearly vanished beneath the horizon when we stopped outside the westernmost villa, where a group of armored legionaries warmed themselves at a fire in an iron brazier. They faced the shoreline, where the surf rolled over the shallows and brushed the shore.

One of the guards stepped forward and jerked his chin toward the handcart. "What's in the wagon?"

I gave him my most beguiling smile. "I am daughter to Daniel the royal tutor, and I have brought a gift for Caesar."

"Caesar doesn't need a tutor."

"Please." I fluttered my lashes. "Is there some law against bestowing honor on a commander who has done so many mighty deeds?" I had no idea how many mighty deeds Caesar had done, but surely he had done *something* noteworthy.

The soldier glanced again at the bag on the cart, then shrugged. "Leave it here. We'll give it to him in the morning."

"Impossible. This gift is of great value, and a friend has charged me with delivering it directly into Caesar's hands. I can leave it with no one but him."

The man squinted at me. "Let me get this straight — you've come here on behalf of some tutor?"

"My father is a tutor. My *friend* asked me to deliver this gift."

"And who is this friend that we should heed his wishes?"

I hesitated. "Are you Caesar's man or the king's?"

He stiffened. "Caesar's."

"Then I will tell you — my friend is Cleopatra, Queen of Egypt."

From the corner of my eye, I saw Apollodorus's chest swell and his arms tighten. I did not know what he would have done if the guard had reacted with hostility, but Cleopatra's name proved powerful. The legionary motioned to his fellows, who opened the door to the villa and waited for us to carry the gift inside.

With great care and tenderness, Apollodorus lifted the burlap bag and placed it across his shoulder. Together we walked into the villa that had once belonged to Urbi's overly ambitious sister Berenice. A fountain splashed in the vestibule, but I led the way into the atrium. Around the reflecting pool I saw a desk, a trunk, and a triclinium of three cushioned couches. An older man — older even than my father — sat on a couch, a basket of scrolls at his side and a scroll in his hand.

At the sound of our approach, he lowered the scroll and eyed Apollodorus. "What is the meaning of this?"

"Please, sir." I stepped forward and bowed. "Cleopatra, Queen of Egypt, sends you a gift."

Caesar lifted both brows, then motioned us forward. "Your timing is odd, but" — he smiled — "you have aroused my curiosity."

Apollodorus gently lowered his burden to the tiled floor. He untied the string around the burlap bag and pulled the fabric away from the rolled carpet. Respectfully and with great gentleness, he gave the rug a push. The carpet began to move, unfurling under its own power. When it had finished, both Caesar and I were astonished beyond words. He was surprised to find Cleopatra sitting on the floor; I was amazed to see her sweaty, disheveled, and looking distinctly unlike herself.

But when she lifted her gaze and extended her hand for Apollodorus to help her up, no one could doubt that she was the noble daughter of many kings. I found myself bowing out of instinct. Her dignified demeanor demanded it.

"By all the gods —" Caesar began, blinking.

"That," Cleopatra interrupted, "is not the proper way to address a queen of Egypt."

Caesar released a brief grunt of surprise and lowered himself to one knee. It wasn't the most sincere genuflection I had ever seen, but Cleopatra smiled. Turning, she accepted the cloak Apollodorus offered, used it to wipe perspiration from her bosom and neck, then flicked her wrist toward the door. "Leave us," she said, and I knew she meant for me to go, as well.

Apollodorus and I backed out of the room, then joined Nuru outside the apartment. In full view of the guards, Apollodorus bowed to me, so unexpected a gesture that I felt my cheeks warm again.

"We owe you a debt, my lady," he said, a grim smile crossing his face.

"You owe me nothing," I answered. "Like you, I am determined to serve her."

Out of love. I did not speak the words, but in that moment I knew what I should have told Yosef when he asked to marry me. Why did I want to serve Cleopatra? Because I loved her, had always loved her. We were bound by love and a blood vow, and I could not abandon her any more than I could abandon my father or brother.

Though I would have given my favorite jewels to remain and hear about what had happened in Caesar's chamber, I could not stay, for darkness had fallen and Father would be worried. After saying my farewells, Nuru and I left the palace, parting with Apollodorus at the gate.

And as we hurried down the torch-lit

streets of the Jewish Quarter, my heart warmed to know I had finally been able to do something — perhaps something no one else could have done — for my most beloved friend.

Chapter Ten

Father lifted a brow when I refused the bowl of fruit Nuru had set out to break our fasts.

"You were out late last night," Father said, folding his hands over the soft rise of his belly. "You should not be in the streets after dark. They are not safe, particularly with so many soldiers in the city."

"Nuru was with me," I said, flushing. "And I couldn't help the time. I was on an important errand."

"What errand could be so important that you would risk your safety?"

"I was doing something for Urbi." I lowered my voice, as if it might drift onto the street and be overheard. "She came to the harbor late yesterday, and I helped Apollodorus smuggle her into the palace. We left her in Caesar's villa."

A dark look of foreboding settled over my father's face. He wiped his fingers on a napkin, then slowly stroked his beard. "The king will not be happy to hear that Cleopatra has returned."

"She has as much right to rule as he does."

"But he holds the reins of power, and he wants Cleopatra dead. If he finds her . . ." He shook his head, and his grim outlook sent a momentary shock through my system. Had I delivered Urbi into the hands of an enemy?

But I had to believe I'd done the right thing. "Cleopatra is clever. She will know how to win Caesar to her side."

Father sighed and reached for the bread. "I do not know Caesar, but I have heard he is a pragmatist, and a pragmatic man would not want to make trouble where none exists. At this moment the Alexandrian people support the boy king. The Egyptian army supports the king. So if Caesar is wise, he will support the king and keep the peace."

"Caesar may be wise, but Cleopatra is clever. She may find a way to convince him that she is best for Egypt."

Father's brows rose. "You give her too much credit."

"I give her what she deserves. Shall I fetch the coins from Ashkelon to remind you how charming she can be?"

"Caesar needs to side with the boy. This will keep Pothinus happy even though he hates the Romans. He is constantly telling the king that Romans are arrogant barbarians."

"Cleopatra may be wary of the Romans, but she does not hate them. Her father worked with them, and Urbi adored her father. What he did, she will do."

My father looked at me, an uncertain expression on his face. "She adored Auletes?"

"As I adore you, Abba."

"Then why won't you heed my wishes? You have supported your queen for years; you have kept your promises to her. It is time for you to move on — you are nearly past the age of marriage, and it is time to establish a family of your own. It would be good for you to have a husband and children, and Yosef is eager to marry you. HaShem has blessed you with beauty, health, and knowledge — why should you spend your life in the shadow of a childhood friend who has little time for you?"

I stared at him, bemused. As much as I wanted to obey and revere my father, I wanted even more to honor the promise HaShem had given me. Any girl could get married and have babies. Few girls could serve Cleopatra, and no free woman in Alexandria was as close to her as I.

"Father —" I stepped closer to him, as though being closer would bridge the rupture between us — "you taught me to love HaShem. You taught me to listen for His voice. So why won't you allow me to heed the prophecy HaShem spoke to me?"

He sighed. "You were such an impressionable child."

"You think I imagined it? If you can believe that Moshe obeyed HaShem and brought water from a rock, why cannot you believe that Adonai spoke to your daughter?"

He stared at me, and in those doubt-filled eyes I saw his unvoiced answer: *Because He has never spoken to me.*

A heavy feeling settled in my stomach as Father pushed away from the table. "I must see to your brother and the new Hebrew school. Asher is meeting me at the synagogue."

My heart contracted in anguish as I watched him go.

I had barely stepped through the palace gates before I heard the news. Acis left his post and pulled me aside, whispering that the king had been summoned to meet with Caesar that morning.

"The king strolled into Caesar's chamber

and found his sister already present," Acis said, his eyes widening. "And from the queen's demeanor and attitude it was clear she had been with Caesar for some time — possibly even overnight."

"What happened next?" I asked.

Acis looked around to make sure we weren't being overheard, then lowered his voice. "The king burst into tears and ran out of the villa, through the gates, and onto the city streets. In front of all the shopkeepers, he ripped the royal ribbon from his head and threw it on the ground, all the while screaming that Cleopatra had betrayed him."

The guard's wide mouth spread in a grin. "I could not believe what I was seeing. But the crowd supported the king and began to shout that Caesar had come to destroy the peace and put a puppet on the throne." Acis rested his hands on the heavy belt at his waist. "Over by the theaters, they're still shouting and throwing things."

I glanced at Nuru. "We missed all the excitement. If we'd only walked another block to the west —"

"I do not think you want to get in the middle of that rabble," Acis said. "Caesar's men went out and seized the king, then brought him back to his apartment. So now he sits in his chamber, waiting for Caesar to deal with him."

I bit my lip. "Is Caesar holding the king hostage?"

Acis grinned. "Depends on what you mean by *hostage.* But clearly, the boy's not going anywhere for a while."

I turned in a slow arc, surveying the many buildings of the sprawling palace complex. I did not know what to do. I could take my usual seat in the throne room, but it would probably remain empty since the king was confined to his quarters. I could slip into Cleopatra's old apartment and wait for her to arrive, if she ever did.

I could not imagine her staying with Caesar more than a few hours. He would have official work to do, and Cleopatra had spent months on the run. She would want to bathe, rest, and revel in her homecoming.

This time, I was certain, she would not run, but would remain in Alexandria. In Caesar she had found an ally, if even a temporary one, and I did not believe she would let him return to Rome until he had found a way to guarantee her safety.

My indecision vanished when I saw people rushing toward a spot near the southern boundary of the Royal Quarter. I followed them, and when I stopped to ask a woman what had happened, she said Caesar was about to give a public address.

Nuru and I joined a dense crowd and waited until the Roman consul appeared on a second-story balcony overlooking the long avenue that divided the Jewish area from the Royal Quarter. In a strong, slightly nasal voice, Caesar called for quiet, then held up a scroll and read what proved to be the late king's will. When he had finished, he lowered the scroll, handed it to an aide, and addressed the crowd with expressive gestures and thoughtful pauses.

My father would have approved of his oration.

"King Auletes clearly wished that his children Cleopatra VII and Ptolemy XIII live and rule together," Caesar said, his hands sweeping the air in grand gestures that would be visible from quite a distance. "Due to their youth and inexperience, they are to rule under Roman guardianship. This was the late king's wish, and it shall be honored."

Murmurs rippled over the gathering, but Caesar had not finished.

"Furthermore," he said, holding his right hand high, "I hereby bestow the island of Cyprus on Arsinoe, the youngest royal daughter, and Auletes's youngest son, hereafter known as Ptolemy XIV. They shall rule jointly according to the late king's wish."

A current of approval swept through the crowd. Auletes might have been disliked by the people of Alexandria, but he had assigned each of his children a role in the succeeding government.

"The people of Alexandria," Caesar continued, "have nothing to fear from Cleopatra, your queen, or Ptolemy XIII, your king. You have nothing to fear from Julius Caesar. I am here only to make certain that the terms of Auletes's will are fulfilled. To celebrate the reconciliation between these children of the late king, on the morrow we will hold a public banquet so that every citizen of Alexandria will know all is well in the house of Ptolemy."

With this, Caesar withdrew and disappeared inside the palace.

When it became clear that neither Cleopatra nor her brother would address the crowd, people began to wander away, most of them whispering about who would be invited to the banquet. I left, too, taking Nuru with me. Because Jews could not be citizens, I did not expect an invitation.

Caesar seemed a fair and honest man and

he had not exhibited favoritism toward Urbi or Omari. Rome had sent us an equitable arbitrator, and I had a promise from HaShem.

Surely the time of trouble had ended.

My breath caught in my lungs when a messenger delivered an invitation to our home. After reading it, I realized we had been invited to the reconciliation banquet only because Cleopatra wanted us to attend. She needed the support of every ally she could find.

Caesar held the banquet in the palace's great hall, and though the Roman was named as our host, I saw Cleopatra's influence in every detail. Despite the famine that had choked the land in recent years, bread and baked goods spilled from large baskets, while roasted birds, fish, and eels filled gold dishes on the serving tables. Urbi had thrown out the cracked tableware and unearthed the silver trays and gold cups. Honeyed fruit compotes dripped on tall stands scattered around the room, and wine flowed freely from gold pitchers. As hundreds of guests nibbled at the displays, Caesar sat on an elevated dais with Cleopatra at his right and Ptolemy XIII at his left.

I did not have an opportunity to speak to

the queen, but neither did anyone else. From her couch Urbi leaned toward Caesar and spoke only with him, and his answering smiles appeared genuine — apparently the great leader enjoyed my friend's company. The boy king, on the other hand, spoke to no one but sat glumly on his couch and stared at the guests as if he despised them all.

Father, Asher, and I kept mostly to ourselves and were careful to avoid unclean foods. Father greeted several Greek merchants, and although Asher pretended to be bored, more than once I caught him smiling at the merchants' fair daughters.

When Father left to go relieve himself, I turned to Asher. "Why do you look at them when you know it is impossible?"

Asher's eyes widened in feigned confusion. "What are you talking about?"

"You cannot marry a Greek girl. You may as well keep your eyes to yourself."

He grinned. "You would have me be blind?"

"I would have you be practical. The Jewish Quarter is filled with beautiful girls."

"But we're not in the Jewish Quarter, and no Jewish girls are here. And there's no harm in looking."

I would have made another retort, but the

sight of Father's distressed face distracted me. "What is it?" I asked, apprehension nipping the back of my neck as he rejoined us. "Is something wrong?"

He gave me a warning look, then pulled Asher and I so close there was barely a sliver of light between the three of us. "I happened to meet Caesar's barber," Father whispered. "I stopped him to ask about the Jewish settlements in Rome, but the man was clearly upset. When I asked if I could help, he said he'd overheard Pothinus and Achillas arguing. They mean to poison Caesar and kill the queen."

I clutched at his robe as my knees wobbled. "Are you certain?"

Father glanced around, a muscle quivering at his jaw. "I asked the same question of the barber, and he said he was not a man who would lie. He promised to speak to his master as soon as the banquet ends."

I turned toward the area where Caesar dined with Cleopatra and Ptolemy. "Is that enough time?"

Father blew out a breath. "I pray it is. I hope we can leave the matter in his hands, because I do not want to get involved in royal politics. I will not make an orphan of my children."

Asher put out a hand to steady our trembling father. "Caesar will not be surprised by this," Asher said. "I hear he sleeps at odd hours to thwart assassination attempts."

"Urbi does not always take such precautions," I answered. "She should be warned."

"We must leave her in Caesar's custody." Father pinned me in a no-nonsense stare. "You are not to go to her, Chava. You have already restored her to the palace; I will not have you get involved in matters that do not concern you."

"But they *do* concern me! HaShem has made me responsible for her."

"Really?" Father's exasperated question hung in the air for a moment, then he shook his head. "She belongs to Egypt now, and Egypt has been delivered into the care of Rome. You haven't the strength to resist either one."

Father caught my trembling hand and squeezed my fingers. "What you do not know, daughter, is that even now Achillas's army is marching to Alexandria. Caesar brought four thousand legionaries with him, but they are weary from their battles with Pompey. Achillas has five times as many men, and they will be fighting to defend their homeland. They are the stronger force, and they are likely to win."

I looked at the Roman commander, calmly

eating his dinner. "Does Caesar know this?"

"I am sure he does."

I stared at the people casually grazing through the great hall, most of them completely unaware that disaster was on its way. Caesar had brokered only a temporary peace. If Father was right, Achillas would soon defeat Caesar, and Ptolemy would —

"If they win" — I clutched at my father's robe — "what will happen to Urbi?"

Father shook his head. "If Caesar loses, or if he does not remain in Egypt, Omari's advisors will find some way to be rid of her. Two heads cannot wear one crown."

"I must go to her." I lifted my chin. "I am supposed to be with her on her last day."

"You will *not* go to her — because you cannot help, and I will not let you risk your life. Trust Adonai, Chava —"

"I *am* trusting Him! I trust what He told me!"

"Would Adonai tell you to disobey your father? He would not. Let HaShem prove His words, but you must obey me in this. Come along — we are going home."

For a moment I thought about wriggling free of his grasp and running, but I could never humiliate him in a public place. Such a display would embarrass Urbi, too, and I would never do anything to harm her cause.

Accepting Father's command was not easy, but as I looked over at the dais and saw the queen surrounded by powerful men, I realized Father was right. I could do nothing to save her now.

And so began what would later be called the Alexandrine War. When Achillas and his army marched into Alexandria a few days later, Caesar, Cleopatra, and Ptolemy became even more firmly sequestered in the palace.

Of particular concern to all three were the seventy-two royal Egyptian ships anchored in the harbor. Achillas wanted them, Caesar wanted to keep them from Achillas, and Cleopatra considered them rightfully hers.

Caesar proved to be the better tactician. His men rowed out from the palace harbor and grappled with the Egyptian fleet, overcoming their resistance. But since Caesar could not hope to hold the ships with so small an army, he ordered his men to set fire to the captured vessels. The flames, tossed and driven by the coastal winds, jumped to the quays and buildings off the Great Harbor. In the course of the blaze, a large number of manuscripts at the Library of Alexandria were destroyed.

Father tore his garments when he saw the

library burning — so much history, so many hours of scholarship! So many original parchments, works from Aristotle and Euclid, crumbling into ashes!

The Ptolemies had always been patrons of learning and the arts. They encouraged scholarship in many areas, particularly science, mathematics, and astronomy. Men came from around the world to study the original works in the Library of Alexandria. For years, every ship that entered the harbor was searched for manuscripts, and if a manuscript was considered a valuable asset to the library, it was copied before being returned to its owner. One of the Ptolemy kings had borrowed the original works of Aeschylus, Sophocles, and Euripides from Athens, only to return copies and keep the originals in the library.

From library manuscripts Urbi and I had learned about the equator and that the earth was a sphere revolving around the sun. We knew about the value of pi and the effect the moon had on our coastal tides. We had learned so many things — and so much was lost in that unfortunate fire.

Father took to his bed with grief over the loss. "Such folly," he moaned, beating his pillow. "How foolish to destroy priceless works for the sake of power and politics.

What will you do with us, Adonai? We are not worthy of the blessings you have given us."

As ashes rained down on the city, Caesar's legionaries enforced the walls around the palace and dug entrenchments, maintaining their defense without mounting an offense. The Roman, Father explained, would not provoke an attack for which he was not prepared.

But Achillas was not willing to surrender the power he'd held as Ptolemy's advisor. He recruited fighters from among the people, even enlisting slaves from wealthy residents of Alexandria. When Caesar sent two of his most experienced men to Achillas with a peace proposal, the ambitious advisor murdered the men without even bothering to read Caesar's letter.

Once Caesar learned of Pothinus's plot to kill him and Cleopatra, he had the advisor arrested and executed. When my father heard that others had also threatened the Roman leader, he remarked that Caesar's self-control was impressive. The Roman did not always retaliate against his enemies, but held a defensive position and tried to outmaneuver them.

Forbidden by Father to visit the palace — and, truth be told, I knew Caesar's guards would stop me at the gate — I had to content myself with imagining what Urbi's life had become. Ptolemy, Caesar, and Cleopatra were virtual prisoners behind those walls, each in his or her chamber, each frustrated with the others. Nor were those three alone — Ptolemy XIV, Cleopatra's youngest brother, and Arsinoe, her seventeen-year-old sister, were also confined in the palace complex.

I had not given much thought to the two younger royals until we learned that Arsinoe had escaped the palace with help from Ganymedes, a eunuch and her former tutor. Delighted by the girl's escape, the citizens of Alexandria promptly declared her queen. Arsinoe had proved to be exactly what they wanted — a Ptolemy who hated Rome and was clever enough to evade Romans who would force their will on her.

Arsinoe took her place beside Achillas, who kept skirmishing with Caesar's army, and together they planned to drive Caesar away. Once the Roman had gone, Arsinoe would marry one of her brothers and rule in Cleopatra's stead.

My blood chilled when I heard about their plan. Urbi once told me that she feared her siblings . . . and in that moment I understood why. Arsinoe could not reign unless

Cleopatra was dead, and apparently the younger girl was determined to make it so.

I fretted constantly about my friend. I wanted to write her, but how could I get a message through the blockade? And if my scroll was intercepted, would my family be cast as traitors?

During the months of unrest, Father urged Asher and I to keep quiet and trust in Adonai. I spent my days copying Father's *Testaments of the Patriarchs* and searching the Tanakh for the names of HaShem. Yosef still visited our home, but I was too anxious to listen to poetry, and too preoccupied to be good company.

One day, miracle of miracles, a slave boy appeared on our threshold and wordlessly offered me a scroll. I recognized Cleopatra's seal at once.

I unfurled the scroll and read:

Greetings, Chava!

How I wish you were with me! But I am content and secure, knowing my life is guaranteed because you are not here. For this reason, at least, I hope your God keeps his promises.

The days are long here, and I grow tired of waiting. But I am counting on Caesar not only for the defense of Egypt, but to help me restore Egypt to greatness. Rome's cavalier treatment of my father and grandfather broke their spirits, but I will not grovel before their Senate.

History has taught me that any ruler who fights against Rome will be destroyed, so I will not fight. I will cooperate, and by working with the Senate, I will restore Egypt's former glory.

As for Arsinoe — for I know you have heard of her plot by now — I have come to believe it is better to trust a Jewish friend than a Greek sister. As Euripides wrote, "One loyal friend is better than ten thousand relatives."

Urbi

I lowered the scroll and held it to my breast. I could not imagine what my friend was enduring, but her spirit seemed strong. Over the following weeks I received other messages, each of them affirming her fondness for me and her conviction that she would soon sit again upon the throne.

Only later did I discover that Urbi had not suffered from loneliness. In her last message to me, one written just after the conclusion of the war, she confessed that she was expecting Caesar's child.

■ ■ ■ ■

The war ended, finally, when Caesar's reinforcements arrived.

Months before, the Roman commander had yielded to the boy king's pleas and released Omari so he could lead his troops. Though Caesar would later record that the boy wept when they parted, the boy king became an enthusiastic military commander. But when Roman legionaries arrived on Egypt's eastern border — legions consisting of Asian, Syrian, Arabian, and Jewish soldiers — the tide turned in Caesar's favor.

Mithridates, commander of the Roman relief troops, discovered that Ptolemy and his generals had brought their fleet out of Alexandria and were about to confront him with a greatly superior army. He sent an urgent message to Caesar.

Leaving a small contingent at the palace to guard Cleopatra, Caesar and his men left Alexandria's harbor and appeared to be en route to meet Mithridates — but under cover of darkness, they doubled back and disembarked west of the city, then proceeded inland to meet the relief troops.

When the two units combined, the Romans easily routed the Egyptians, who retreated to their camp in confusion. The boy king tried to escape in an overloaded boat, but it capsized. Though his body was never found, most people assumed the king drowned in his heavy armor.

Arsinoe was captured and imprisoned. With the younger royals out of the picture, the war ended with a victory for Caesar and Cleopatra.

When Caesar returned to Alexandria, dozens of chastened city leaders brought statues of their gods to meet the victor at the gates. Caesar rode through the sea of stone and metal gods, then went straightway to the palace where Cleopatra waited.

As the city buzzed with news about the clever commanders who brought an end to the war, I was astonished to learn that Jewish soldiers had been among the relief troops assisting Caesar. After investigating the matter, my father explained that Antipater, a prominent figure at the court of Jerusalem, was directly responsible for the Jewish contingent. Antipater and his men had not only supplied Caesar's reinforcements with provisions on the journey to Egypt, but swept away the boy king's army after their arrival.

Father was delighted to discover that

Jerusalem's high priest, Hyrcanus II, had personally accompanied the relief troops on the journey from Judea.

"Why would he do that?" Asher asked. "The Jews in Jerusalem disapprove of our temple at Leontopolis. They want nothing to do with us."

"You are mistaken." Father wagged his finger. "We are all sons of Abraham, and we will always be united. They cannot ignore us, for the Jews of Alexandria are the largest Jewish community in the world."

"But we are Alexandria's most neglected community," Asher argued. "We are exempted from ordinary privileges. No Jew can even be a citizen."

Father placed his arm around Asher's broad shoulders. "Be grateful for what the Master of the universe has given us," he advised.

With the community we went to the synagogue and thanked HaShem for an end to the war. We also asked Adonai to bless Julius Caesar.

I thanked Adonai not only for peace, but for the freedom to return to ordinary life. I had spent very little time with Urbi since she became queen, but now that she ruled securely, I hoped we would once again be able to spend our days together.

Truth be told, I looked forward to serving her in a new way — I would provide an extra pair of loving arms for her baby.

I expected my father to be shocked by the report that our queen was expecting a child, but he accepted the news without comment. I expected him to rail against the queen's behavior, but years of living in Alexandria, where morality was as fluid as the sea, had tempered him. If I had been carrying a child, he would have pulled out his hair and worn sackcloth for weeks. But not so with the queen.

"We cannot expect those who do not know Adonai to live according to Adonai's word," he said, tugging at his beard as he looked from me to Asher. "Even so, Caesar is married to a lady in Rome."

"Not so," Asher said, looking from Father to me. "I heard he divorced the woman."

Father tilted his head. "Who can say? I know only what I hear from merchants and friends at the synagogue. But of this I am certain — if Cleopatra rules with Caesar at her side, the pairing will be good for Egypt."

"How can you say that?" I had been puzzling over the relationship between Caesar and Cleopatra for weeks. "He's old enough to be her father!"

Father's mouth quirked. "Age has nothing to do with attraction, and attraction has little to do with marriage. I do not know how they feel about each other, but I suspect they enjoy each other's company. If Cleopatra found the man repulsive, she would not be listening to his advice. From what I hear, she trusts him."

"I do not understand why they are still together," Asher said. "He is a Roman; she is Greek. The Romans and Greeks are said to despise each other."

Father smiled. "He is a brilliant man. She is an intelligent girl and able to speak to any topic he might broach. She has charmed men before, so I am not surprised she charmed this one."

"He won the war," I pointed out. "So why doesn't he go home?"

"I am sure he will, when he's ready."

"But . . . a baby!"

Father gave me a slow smile, tinged with wistfulness. "You might have a child, too, if you would consider marriage. Has Cleopatra's example not convinced you that happiness comes from investing your life in a family? Yosef is a fine young man —"

I sighed, weary of the familiar argument. "Indeed he is, but he is no more than a good friend because I have invested my life in a queen. My friendship with Urbi is part of HaShem's plan."

Father shook his head. "If you truly heard the voice of Adonai, daughter, I fear you have misunderstood His message. You should be like Rachel and Leah, fruitful and blessed . . ."

His words fell like the patter of a summer shower, easily dismissed. As soon as the defensive walls and barricades had been cleared from the palace compound, I planned to visit my friend and ask if I could live at the palace.

Chapter Eleven

When I was finally able to cross the threshold of Urbi's chamber again, I found my friend happy, heavily pregnant, and delirious with love. Her appearance, manner, and mien were so changed that for a moment I wondered if a demon had stolen her away and left some sort of changeling in the night.

"Chava!" Urbi embraced me and welcomed me into her bedchamber, then dropped rather ungracefully onto the bed. "Can you believe this?" She grinned at the protruding mound of her belly. "As Isis carried Horus, I am carrying Caesar's son." Tenderly, she stroked her stomach. "My father would be pleased. I have preserved Egypt for another generation."

"What do you mean, 'preserved Egypt'?" Frowning, I took a seat in a nearby chair. "You chose the right champion. Caesar saved Egypt."

"How little you know of life." Though she

smiled, her condescension stung. "Yes, Caesar won the war, and in Rome some senators are asking why Rome doesn't simply declare Egypt a province and place a governor in charge. But I saved Egypt because Caesar knows I can do a better job of managing the land than any Roman. I understand Egypt. I *am* Egypt. And I will preserve this throne for my son."

Who *was* this woman? I knew Urbi would change during the months we were apart, but I had not realized how different she would seem.

Somehow, I managed a smile. "I have something for you." I reached into the silk bag I carried and brought out a wooden box. "I wanted to show you how glad I am for your happiness. And how fervently I believe that we will always belong together."

Urbi sat up, her eyes sparkling. Like the girl I remembered so well, she reached eagerly for the box and lifted the lid. Inside, on a bed of black silk, lay a piece of driftwood that had been carved with words in Greek and Hebrew.

"Chava!" Throaty laughter bubbled up from her chest. "What is this? And how did you get it?"

"They are the names of HaShem." A flush warmed my face. "I had it carved by a craftsman."

Urbi ran her finger over the fine lettering. "One god has so many names?"

"He is many things," I said, leaning forward. I pointed to the outermost edge. "He is YHVH Nisi, our banner who protects us." I slid my finger to the next group of letters. "He is YHVH Ropheca, who heals our bodies and our souls. He is YHVH Tzva'ot, the Lord of armies, who gives us confidence and courage."

"Thank you; this is lovely." She placed the lid back on the box and set it to the side. "I will have to show it to Caesar when he dines with me tonight."

Ignoring another sting — after so many months apart, I had hoped to share dinner with her — I cast about for another subject. I leaned forward, ready to share my news about Yosef. But first I would hear her secrets. "Tell me . . . do you love Caesar? Truly?"

Urbi lifted both brows, then stretched out on the bed, her belly rising like an obstacle between us. "He is a fascinating man," she said, rolling onto her side and propping her head on her hand. "Intelligent, strong, and cunning. He has taught me so much over the past few months."

"You did not answer my question."

Her elongated brow arched. "What is love, Chava? When you can define it, perhaps I can give you an answer. Until then, am I grateful to Caesar for ridding Egypt of my murderous brother and his advisors? Yes. Am I in his debt for saving my life? Certainly. Am I grateful he is holding Arsinoe so she can no longer threaten my life? Indeed I am."

"Did you go to his bed willingly?" The words spilled out before I could stop them, but Cleopatra did not hesitate or blush.

"I did, and would do so again."

I lowered my head. "I did not mean to pry. I asked only because I care about —"

"You might try to care a little less. And believe me when I say that Caesar has been good to me. That's not to say I haven't been angry —" Her lower lip edged forward in a pronounced pout. "I was furious when he set my fleet afire and burned so many manuscripts in the library. So many priceless treasures, gone in one thoughtless act! But war always results in danger and destruction. In the end, we did not pay so great a price. And Egypt is finally mine."

"Even though you are now married to your youngest brother? I cannot imagine you married to little Sefu."

A dimple appeared in her cheek. "Ha! Yes,

even so. I shall do my best to keep him away from any would-be advisors. Except Caesar."

I grimaced as a sudden thought occurred to me. Of the five royal children, Urbi had always been the closest to her father. At fifty-two, Caesar was nearly Auletes's age. Had Urbi been driven into Caesar's arms because of a twisted wish to be reunited with her father?

"What is that face?" Urbi leaned closer, studying me. "What are you thinking?"

"When we were younger, you always knew what was on my mind."

She batted my words away. "We were children then, with thoughts of nothing but games."

"True enough. I was thinking — wondering — if you were attracted to Caesar because you miss your father. After all, they are about the same age . . ."

Urbi stiffened, her face flushing crimson. "If you are suggesting that my father and I —"

I gasped when I caught the meaning of her words. "I would never suggest such a thing. But if you miss your father, you might seek out an older man's comfort and advice."

"Caesar alone survived the sinking of his

ship, did you know that?" she snapped, her eyes sparking. "During a battle with enemy troops, he saw that his boat was about to founder. Wearing heavy armor, he jumped into the sea, clutching a number of important parchments. He would not let go of them even though he was swimming through a rain of arrows and spears. He traveled a considerable distance using only one arm!"

I had touched a nerve — or something even more sensitive. I lowered my head and reached out to my friend, palms open, eyes pleading. "Forgive me. I meant nothing evil. And I should not speak of such things, for I do not know the man."

"Indeed, you do not." Urbi lifted her chin and sniffed, then exhaled a deep breath. "Sit up, Chava, that posture is not becoming. I should have remembered that you lack the sort of cunning required to imply anything inappropriate."

I drew a breath to argue but then decided the better of it. She had quieted, and I would not risk rousing her temper again. I would not say anything about Yosef. And I would wait to ask her about permission to live at the palace.

"I should go." I gestured toward the door. "Father will be worried."

Urbi smiled. "I hope he is well?"

"He is. If he were here, he would offer you his congratulations and a blessing."

Her smile deepened. "Go in peace, blood of my blood. I will see you again soon."

The summons arrived just as I finished breaking my fast. The messenger left the scroll with the doorkeeper, and Nuru brought it to me.

"I am to go to the palace at once," I said, reading aloud.

Father tugged at his beard. "Am I expected to join you?"

"The queen asks for me alone."

Asher grinned. "I do not know how you get anything done. Now that she's back, she will be sending for you every day."

"That is how it should be." I stood and walked toward the reflecting pool in the atrium. I studied my reflection — the arrangement of my hair was not as elaborate as I would have liked, but Urbi had seen me looking worse. But one never knew when one might encounter Caesar.

I summoned Nuru and held out my arms while she draped a himation over my linen chiton and pinned it at the shoulder. After another quick glance in the pool to check the drape of the outer garment, I told Nuru to put on her heavy sandals and started for the door. Years of answering Urbi's summons had taught me that it was never a good idea to tarry if she expected me.

I found my friend in the innermost chamber of her apartment. She was still abed, one hand propped on her growing belly and the other holding her hair off her forehead. Despite the wide feathered fans plied by three slaves, the queen of Egypt was panting in the heat.

"Thank the gods you have come," she said, pushing herself up as I approached. "Quickly, sit. I have news for you."

My heart lifted as I sank to the edge of her bed. Despite our sharp exchange yesterday, apparently she had forgiven me. Her eyes glowed with excitement.

"You challenged me," she said, grinning as a slave propped pillows behind her back. "I kept thinking about the best way to thank you for your gift."

"You do not have to thank me," I insisted. "You honor me with your friendship. Your family has honored my family for years, and it is enough that I call you *friend* —"

"Words are not enough, not between blood sisters," Urbi insisted. "So I asked myself, what does Chava lack? You have a fine house, good horses, lovely clothes. You have a devoted slave, else I would send Nuru away and buy you a better one. You have scrolls and books. Then it hit me — you lack citizenship. I can make you a citizen of Alexandria. I can bestow citizenship upon your entire family."

I stared, caught in the grip of a curious, tingling shock. "I have never asked —"

"I know you haven't, and that's why I am so thrilled to do this. You, your father, and your brother — you shall all be citizens of Alexandria. When we are in famine and there are distributions, you and your family will now be able to receive grain from the storehouses of Egypt. You will be entitled to all the privileges of citizens, even though your people come from Judea. All you must do is worship at the Greek temples. Or —" she laughed — "worship with me at the Temple of Isis, it matters not. But because of your devotion and friendship to me, I stand ready to do this for you. I will change Jews into Greeks with a single command."

My throat squeezed so tight I could scarcely breathe. "Urbi, I cannot accept —"

"Do not be humble. You have been devoted; you deserve this good fortune."

"I am not being humble. But I cannot accept."

Her brows rose like the wings of startled

birds. "I know you were not expecting this, but consider what an honor this is for you! Your father and brother will never be flogged if arrested; your property can never be seized without cause. You need not confine yourselves to the Jewish Quarter — buy a house anywhere in Alexandria, if it pleases you."

"My queen . . ." I pressed my palms together and swallowed hard. "I am not unaware of the great honor you are bestowing on us. But my father, my brother, we cannot worship any god but the God of our fathers. We are and always will be the children of Abraham."

"Perhaps you could worship your god in our temples. Go to the temple of Zeus, say your prayers, make your sacrifices, and pray quietly to whatever god you like —"

"I could not. That place is filled with graven images. And HaShem forbids sacrifice on an altar dedicated to any other god."

Urbi shrank back, her hands returning to her belly. "I am not asking so much. Worship any god you please, but you cannot worship one god only. No one trusts people who refuse to live like others, and a citizen's behavior must not be suspect. All citizens of Alexandria worship at the temples, participate in the festivals, observe the feasts of the gods . . . why would you want to be different?"

"We cannot do these things. We will not do these things."

I kept my eyes down as I uttered the words, knowing she would not understand. In all our years of friendship, Urbi had ignored the greatest difference between us — my family's worship of HaShem, the invisible God who would not tolerate any other gods to be worshiped. Did she not understand that our beliefs about HaShem informed every aspect of our lives? Could she not comprehend that our faith was an elemental part of who we were?

A dart of guilt pierced my soul. Had I hidden the essence of my beliefs so completely that she could not see how different we really were?

Stiffening her spine, Urbi regarded me with the cold, impassive eyes of a sphinx. "You would refuse my gift?"

"Adonai demands that we worship no other gods. I must refuse, and so will my father. But we will never spurn your friendship."

"How can you be my friend when you would allow such an insignificant thing to come between us? I am a tolerant queen, an indulgent friend. I ask only that you be like everyone else and acknowledge the gods of our city." She looked at me, her brown eyes narrow and bright with fury. "If you would be a citizen of Alexandria, if you would be my lady-in-waiting and my friend —"

"Please." My voice broke as I choked on the word. "This thing you ask — it is not insignificant. We Jews are not like everyone else; we are unique. Yet HaShem has told me that our friendship . . ." My thoughts stuttered as I summoned the words from memory. "Our friendship lies in His hands."

Urbi's mouth twisted in a smirk. "Then let us leave it there."

"I will be with you on your happiest day . . . and your last."

"You want to be unique? Then go, and be as unique as you like." Cleopatra's complexion went a shade paler, but she did not falter. "You will soon know your god is false," she said, her voice soft with exasperation. "For my happiest day will be when I give birth to my son, and my last day . . . will not be today, though I will never see you again. Ever."

"Blood of my blood." Tears spilled from my eyes as I spread my hands in entreaty. "Heart of my heart. I will be your friend, your companion, and your servant, so long as you do not ask me to do things I cannot do. I am not Greek or Egyptian, and I must be true to the ways of my father and forefathers —"

"Get out."

She rose onto her knees and pointed to the door, her hand trembling. Slaves cleared a path, and I quaked as I slid off the bed and crouched on the floor. "Urbi, forgive me for insulting your graciousness. But surely you understand! Please, let us go back to the way we were as children. Let us return to being as simple as girls —"

"You must never speak my family name again," she said, her voice as cold as iron. "From this day forward, you will not come into my presence." She jerked her chin at a guard who had looked into the room. "You! Take her away."

I stood, took another anguished look at my childhood friend, then turned and left, my heart torn by grief and disbelief.

CHAPTER TWELVE

"Father?"

I found him in the library, poring over an unfurled manuscript.

He lifted his candle and blinked at me. "What troubles you, daughter?"

A sob rose in my throat, and I was powerless to tamp it down. It came out as a high hiccup, then I began to sob in earnest, shoulders shaking, tears flowing, nose running.

Father blinked again, then lowered the candle and drew me into the circle of his arms, awkwardly patting my shoulder as I wept.

"What brought this on?" he said, pulling away. He removed a square of linen from his sleeve and attempted to wipe my face.

I took the linen from him and sat on a nearby chair. "I cannot believe it, but Urbi and I have — we are no longer friends." My chin quivered at the memory of our encounter. "She meant to honor our family, but she asked the impossible, something I knew you could never do. So I refused her honor as gently as I could, but she went into a rage. She had a guard drag me out of her chamber."

Father leaned forward in a show of concern, but his expression remained calm. "Do you think she will calm down in a few days? This is not the first time you two have argued."

"This wasn't a girlish argument. This felt . . . serious."

Father sat at his desk and tented his hands over the soft pouch of his belly. "What honor did the queen offer?"

I wiped my eyes again and dabbed the end of my nose. "She wanted to give us citizenship, but stipulated that we would have to worship with other citizens from Alexandria. When I said we could never worship before a graven image, she became furious. I have never seen her so angry. I kept hoping she'd relent, but the more we talked, the more furious she became."

Father stroked his beard and stared at the open scroll as thought worked in his eyes. "You were right to answer as you did," he finally said, "and I am surprised she asked this of you. Citizenship would be a great gift, but perhaps we were not meant to be citizens here. Our home is Judea, our capital Jerusalem."

I barked a laugh. "Even though we have never been there?"

"Even though. Because it is the land HaShem chose for us. Because the Temple is there."

He leaned forward to pat my hand. "Do not worry, Chava. Women who are expecting a child often behave in ways that are completely foreign to their natures. The queen will calm down once her anger has abated. She probably has many things on her mind. She has to be on constant guard with Caesar, for at a moment's notice he could remove her and install a Roman governor. She might be worried about her baby — childbirth is dangerous for mother and child, as you well know. I am certain you will hear from Urbi before too many days have passed."

I sniffed. "Should I send her a message?"

"Don't stir the embers, but let the coals cool. I have heard that Caesar will soon be leaving, so give the queen time to adjust to his absence. Wait for her. In time, all will be made right. After all, did not HaShem tell you that this friendship was in His hands?"

He smiled, the creases at his eyes merging

into a solid line, and his comment elicited fresh tears. In that moment, at least, he had faith in HaShem's promise to me, and I desperately needed to know that someone else believed.

I propped my chin in my hand and studied Father's face as he returned to his work. The Alexandrian sun had leathered his skin, carving white lines on the wide forehead that always seemed to house dozens of profound thoughts, any one of which might be the answer to whatever problem bedeviled me.

The sound of pounding at the door disturbed the quiet of the library. "Who would be outside at this hour?" I rose. "Let me see where the doorman is —"

The pounding ceased, then I heard a scream followed by the slap of sandals on tile. Nuru came running into the library, her eyes wide as she whispered a warning. "Run, mistress! Run!"

I barely had time to look at Father before a half-dozen soldiers appeared — Roman legionaries, probably from Caesar's army. "We have orders to arrest three Jews: Daniel the scholar, and his children, Asher and Chava," the leader said, reading from a scroll. He lowered the parchment and narrowed his eyes. "Are you the residents of this dwelling?"

Father stood and gripped the edge of his tunic. "I am Daniel."

"You are under arrest. Gather what you will, but be quick about it."

"Nuru," I called, turning to her reflexively, "pack a basket for my —"

The guard cut me off. "Your slaves have been freed by order of the queen."

That news shocked me more than the announcement of our impending arrest. Anyone could be arrested and released, but freeing our slaves was . . . permanent.

Nuru's face went blank with shock. She staggered backward as the guard grabbed my arm. "Are you Chava?"

I winced at the strength of his grip. "I am."

"And where is —" he glanced at the scroll — "Asher?"

"I do not know."

Before I could say anything else, the guards grabbed Father and dragged both of us onto the street. Though my head filled with a jumble of confused pleas and protestations, one coherent thought rose to the top: Asher was not home. For the moment, at least, my brother would escape the queen's anger.

Chapter Thirteen

"Those who play with fire," Father once warned me, "are apt to be burnt."

The words came back to me on a tide of memory, rippling through my mind as scores of curious observers watched the legionaries drag us away from the marble steps of our home. Neighbors in the Jewish Quarter stopped and stared as we stumbled down the street, and more than one man called Father's name in consternation. I searched the crowd for Asher but did not see him. Like shameful criminals we were led past the synagogue and onto the wide Canopic Way, then through the gate at the city walls.

Finally we reached the Roman garrison. As a guard untied the ropes around our wrists, I prayed that someone would tell Asher what had happened and help him flee the city. Bad enough that Father had to suffer for my sake, I would not want Asher to be imprisoned as well.

Once my hands were free, a soldier pushed me toward a room and thrust me inside, then locked the door. At first I couldn't see in the near darkness, but when my eyes adjusted I saw three other women in the windowless chamber. Father had been taken somewhere else. I hoped he would remain in the same building. *Please, Adonai, keep him close.*

The women with whom I found myself said nothing to me but stared at me with faintly accusing eyes. Clothed in the plain tunics of common Egyptians, they wore their hair either in simple braids or hanging free, with no adornment at all. Dressed as I was, in a fine linen chiton and a costly silk himation, I felt uncomfortable and conspicuous.

Unable to stand the pressure of the women's eyes upon me, I stood facing the tiny window in the door, waiting for the guard to come tell me that the queen had ordered my release. I stood in that position for hours, then paced, ignoring the other women and trying to keep my chiton clean.

As the sun set and darkness thickened around me, I sat carefully on the floor with the wall at my back. Resolved to sleep sitting up, I closed my eyes, only to jerk awake every time my body listed and nearly surrendered to sleep.

I waited for relief that did not come.

By the time the sun had reached its zenith the following day, I had propped myself against the wall like the others, too weary to stand and too dirty to care about soiling my garments. That night I slept on the filthy floor, using my arms for a pillow and my thin himation for a blanket. Like the other women I relieved myself in a bucket and drank stale water from a communal ladle, grateful that the dim light in the room prevented the others from seeing the stains of humiliation on my face.

On the third afternoon, all four of us women were led out to face a magistrate. Egyptian justice was swift, and most punishments predetermined — common thieves were beaten, tomb robbers buried alive, and murderers executed. Since I did not know what charge had been laid against me, I had no idea what sort of punishment I might face.

The first woman had been arrested for stealing from her neighbor; the judge ordered the guards to beat her with a stick and send her home to her husband. The second prisoner had been accused of slandering the queen, but when no witness appeared to testify against her, the judge admonished her to mind her tongue and released her. The third woman, a common prostitute, stood accused of stealing from a customer. The magistrate ruled that she be released — after the guards had cut off her nose.

I covered my ears as a pair of guards held the harlot against the wall while another carried out the sentence. As my ears filled with the sound of frenzied screams, I imagined myself standing between a pair of guards while a third sharpened an ax to take off my head. Surely insulting the queen could not be answered by a light sentence.

I stood before the magistrate and lowered my gaze, bracing for whatever was to come. Would Cleopatra come here to testify against me? Surely not. She would never visit a garrison herself, so she would send word about my fate.

I fisted my hands when the magistrate's eyes focused on me. "Your case has not been decided." He gestured toward the door. "Back to the holding room with you."

"And my father? Please, sir, what of him?"

My question seemed to harden the magistrate's features, but he only pointed to the door. "We have not heard from the palace, so you and your father will remain here. Go!"

Not heard from the palace? What sort of game was Urbi playing?

As the guard led me back to my cell, I listened for the sound of familiar names. Father was here somewhere, and Asher might have been brought in. But though I strained to hear their voices, I heard nothing but the sound of rough laughter and belching as the legionaries took their ease at the end of the day.

By sunset on the third day, I had begun to believe that Cleopatra simply wanted to teach me a lesson. I had endured three full days in that dismal chamber without a change of clothing, a latrine, or my handmaid. I ate only when the Roman guards remembered to throw me a crust of bread or offer a bowl of gruel, and my hair had become a tangled mess.

She could not intend to leave me here forever. She had arranged for my father's and brother's arrest because she knew it would distress me to think of them suffering for my mistakes. But she respected my father, so at any moment we would receive a message from the palace, then we would be returned to our home.

As darkness filled my cell, I braced my

back against the wall and picked at my fingernails, which were now mere stubs. By the time the first watch ended, I had to face a cruel reality: the queen had not forgotten my offense, and she did not yet want to forgive me.

How could Father have been so wrong? He had predicted that Cleopatra would regain her composure and forget about my offense, but she had not. But maybe the command to imprison us hadn't come from Cleopatra, but from Caesar. Maybe the queen told Caesar that I'd called him an old man. Maybe such honest words were a crime in Rome, and I had committed a serious offense without even knowing it.

Perhaps I would sit here until Urbi took pity on me and ordered my release . . . or my execution. But surely she wouldn't execute my father. He had done nothing to offend her, and Alexandria had always prized its scholars. Surely she would release him, if only for the sake of his reputation.

I worried about Father. He was not a young man, and he had to feel physical discomfort more than I did. He always walked stiffly in the morning, even after sleeping on two feather mattresses. How was he walking after three nights on a brick floor?

On the fourth day, the sounds of cheering outside the garrison broke the monotony. I begged passing guards to give me the reason for celebration in the street, but they did not respond. Finally, one young guard stopped by my door. "They are celebrating Caesar's proclamation."

My pulse quickened. "What did he proclaim?"

The guard shrugged. "To reward the Jew soldiers who helped him win the war, he asked the queen to give full citizenship to all Jews in Alexandria." The legionary crossed his arms. "Oh — and she's going to build a new synagogue in the Jew Quarter. Nice for them, I guess, but I did not hear any news worth celebrating."

I listened to his report in astonished silence. Cleopatra was granting citizenship to Jews without forcing them to worship at the city's pagan temples? Why had she agreed to do those things for strangers when she refused the same freedom for me and my family?

The answer arrived on a wave of intuition: *Because Caesar had asked it of her.*

She did as he asked, for she needed him more than she needed me.

I slid down the wall until I hit the dirty floor. Though I had no idea what had transpired between Caesar and Cleopatra, I could easily imagine a logical scenario. After Urbi ordered my family to prison, Caesar might have come to her chamber at the end of the day. Over a glass of wine, she would have confided the details of our encounter — how I'd refused her offer because I could not worship any god save the God of my fathers. Caesar, fortified by the wine and pleased by the sight of his child in Cleopatra's belly, might have lifted her hand to his lips and said, "Why be so unforgiving, my dear? Grant citizenship to all the Jews, for we owe them a great debt. Require nothing from them, because they have already given their lives to our cause. We would not be sitting here if not for the Judeans who came to the aid of my legionaries."

And Urbi, always eager to please the man she loved, would have acceded to his request while Father and I sat in prison and Asher ran . . . only HaShem knew where.

Would she ever order our release? Or had she completely forgotten about us?

Caesar's proclamation gave me hope that we would be freed, because the entire city seemed caught up in a wave of magnanimity toward my people. But the day after the pronouncement, I overheard a soldier say that Caesar had sailed for Armenia, leaving three legions behind to guard the queen and keep the peace.

My shock yielded quickly to fury. How dare Cleopatra leave me and my father in prison for so long! Did all our years of friendship count for nothing? Or had she changed so much during our time apart that she no longer remembered our vow of friendship and our shared history?

That night I stretched out on the hard floor and begged Adonai to punish Urbi for her harshness. "I am here because I was being true to you, Adonai," I reminded HaShem. "I was being faithful to the worship of only one God, and now I find myself in prison! Punish Cleopatra for her spiteful action and compel her to release me and my father."

Two weeks later, I learned that Cleopatra had given birth to a boy. Invoking the titles of two great rulers, she named him Ptolemy Caesar.

"Ptolemy Caesar?" One of the guards spat the name with derision. "More like a little Caesar."

"Caesarion," another guard said, snickering. "A little Caesar to rule over us."

As the words drifted through the window in my door, I let my forehead fall against the rough wood. If Cleopatra had just given birth, her thoughts would be centered on her baby. They were nowhere near the forever friend who languished in prison.

Joseph, son of Jacob, was imprisoned for years under one of the ancient pharaohs, but during our more civilized time, only rarely did a prisoner remain in captivity for more than a few months. Those who remained in the garrison while awaiting trial fell under the supervision of the Roman garrison commander.

The commander of Caesar's remaining three legions was a man called Rufio. I met that officer after my first week of confinement and was immediately struck by the man's blank expression. Anything could have been going on beneath that immobile face, and later I heard two soldiers talking about the reason for his inscrutability: the man had once been a slave.

I had a feeling that Rufio did not know what to do with me and my father. I could not fault his uncertainty — I didn't have a rational explanation for our presence in prison, either.

"I have been waiting," he told me one afternoon when he paused at my door, "for some communication from the palace, but I have heard nothing."

"What of my father?" I asked, standing. "Is he well?"

Rufio grunted. "He is tolerable, but he has developed a cough."

"Please." I moved to the door and lifted my face to the window. "Will you fetch a doctor for him?"

I swallowed hard as another question lodged in my throat. I was desperate to know about Asher but did not want to remind this man that my brother's name had also been on the arrest warrant.

I drew a deep breath and looked through the small opening. "We have friends at the synagogue," I said, finding the commander's eyes. "I am surprised none of them have come to inquire about us. But perhaps one of them could find a physician for my father."

I studied the commander's face, searching for a sign of compassion, but saw nothing beyond an inscrutable expression.

"Please," I said again, lowering my gaze so the Roman would not see the tears in my eyes. "My father is not young, but he is a great scholar and teacher. HaShem will bless you if you care for him."

"What god is that? I have my pick of 'em around here."

"The God who sees and knows and is

above all."

Two days later, Rufio stopped by my cell again, but this time a guard opened the door. The commander stepped inside, startling me out of a shallow doze. Since I had no idea what his intentions were, I scurried to the back wall, determined to keep a measured distance between us.

Rufio gave me a quick head-to-toe glance, then cleared his throat. "Because I have heard nothing from the palace, I have written Caesar about the fortress prisoners. I hope to receive a reply within a few weeks."

I released a choked, desperate laugh. A few *weeks*? Even if the answer came by the swiftest boat in the Roman navy, it would take several months to hear from Armenia.

I lifted my chin, gathering my courage. "Were you able to find a physician for my father?"

"I am sorry," Rufio said, and something in his tone led me to believe he meant it. "I personally spoke to three physicians, but none of them were willing to come here. They know the risks of contagion are far greater than the odds of payment."

I closed my eyes, unwilling to let the Roman see the anguish that seared my soul.

"I have a brother," I said slowly. "Asher. Were your men able to find him?"

The commander's gaze shifted and thawed slightly. "We never found him. We are no longer looking."

I exhaled in relief. Had Asher left the city? I was fairly certain he'd been hidden by our friends in the Jewish Quarter. But if they had been afraid to be caught with him, they might have sent him south to fend for himself among the native Egyptians.

Rufio reached behind him for a torch, then brought it into my cell and held it aloft. The unexpected brightness caused me to look away, and even when my eyes had adjusted, I could do no more than squint at the man who stared at me, his eyes alive with calculation.

"Why are you here?" he finally asked. "Did you murder some nobleman? Did you steal from a wealthy merchant? Or from the queen herself?"

Looking away, I released a desperate laugh. "I am not certain of my crime," I confessed, "but the day before I was brought here, the queen was my best friend. We argued. And here I am."

Shock flickered over his face, then his features settled back into their natural stoic expression. Tucking one hand into his sword belt, he glanced around the filthy room that had become my home. "A lady should not be kept in such conditions," he said, meeting my gaze. "I will have this room cleaned and furnished for as long as you are here. Do you require anything in particular?"

Such unexpected largess . . . why? I shrugged to hide my confusion and studied the man's rugged face more closely. In his eyes I saw a look I had often seen in the eyes of other men.

I choked back a laugh. Urbi and I had often giggled about the effect of feminine beauty on the male species, but as I stood in that prison, my thoughts whirled in an odd mingling of gratitude and wariness. Wariness, because I knew what desire frequently led men to do, especially to unprotected women. Gratitude, though, for the soft concern I saw in the commander's expression.

"I want nothing more than what my father is given." I tucked a stray hank of hair behind my ear. "But water and towels for washing would be appreciated. And . . ."

"Yes?"

I pressed my lips together. "It may be my imagination, but sometimes I can smell something . . . delicious. Like meat on the fire."

Rufio snorted. "It is a boy with a cart. He has begun to sell meat pies outside the garrison."

"I do not suppose you could manage a meat pie for your prisoners every once in a while? My father and I are not accustomed to a diet of only gruel and bread."

The Roman made a noise deep in his throat, then turned and left, locking the door behind him. But by sunset, my little cell had been swept and furnished with a straw mattress, a blanket and pillow, a basin, a linen towel, and a pitcher of clean water.

And that night I found half a meat pie in my bowl. I hoped the other half had gone to my father.

As I bit into it, I asked HaShem to forgive me if the meat had come from an unclean animal. I had to eat, but if He would forgive this sin, I would eat only clean meats for the rest of my life. If He would arrange for our release, I would pray five times a day and do anything my father asked, including marrying Yosef, if that was what Adonai wanted. . . .

Later, I asked Adonai to bless the commander for his kindness, and prayed that either Cleopatra or Caesar would remember me and my father and have pity on us.

Chapter Fourteen

Days turned into weeks, and weeks into months. The Nile flooded and Egypt celebrated, indulging in song, dance, and feasting while the inundation covered the land. Summer ended, the life-giving waters receded, and the farmers planted. Cleopatra must have been pleased.

But no word came from the palace, and none from Caesar.

I grew weary of praying the same prayers. My pleas for Adonai's attention seemed to go no higher than the wooden ceiling. Grief pooled in my soul, a thick despondency I had never felt before. When my thoughts turned to the words of the Tanakh, I identified with Job, who suffered without explanation and yearned for death:

> "I am just worn out.
> By my life [I swear],
> I will never abandon my complaint;

I will speak out in my soul's bitterness.
I will say to God, 'Don't condemn me!
Tell me why you are contending with me.
Do you gain some advantage from
oppressing,
from spurning what your own hands made
. . . ?' "

I spent my days alone, with only Rufio for occasional company. Men and women prisoners were still brought to the garrison for trial, but rather than have the women disturb me, Rufio had them put in another room. I understood that he was trying to be kind, but after a while I yearned for the sound of other female voices.

I heard men at all hours of the day and night. In the hallway outside my door I heard them laughing, arguing, talking, whispering, ranting, and occasionally weeping. At least once a day, some guard would make his way to my door, press his eye to the square opening and stare in at me, calling out lewd encouragements and hoping for some sort of bawdy entertainment. I began to sit with my back to the door because I could not bear the touch of those intruding gazes.

With nothing to see in the dimness of my cell, my other senses became extraordinarily acute. I began to notice smells — the odor of my perspiration on my skin, the scent of rat urine on my mattress, the odor of sweaty men passing in the hallway. When Rufio brought in a meat pie — a luxury he probably bought with his own money — I could smell the aroma as soon as he crossed the threshold. And taste! I tasted the salt in the bread, the spice in the gravy, and sometimes I was certain I could taste the thin grass the cows had devoured before being butchered.

My fingertips also grew more sensitive. With my eyes closed, I could touch the wall and know if I was standing against the exterior wall or the cooler one that opened to a hallway in the garrison. My fingers could discern new straw from old and dirty linen from clean.

My chiton softened into rags, and only when I volunteered to help with the laundry did I find a way to get another one. Rufio looked at me in disbelief when I asked if I might help the slaves wash clothes, but after a moment of reflection, he allowed me that small bit of freedom. In truth, I did not mind helping, for the work of a laundress got me out of the garrison and into the sunlight. When the women came for the soiled laundry, a guard would clamp shackles around my ankles and lead me to the canal that skirted the city. There I basked in the sun while I helped a pair of Greek slaves scrub soldiers' tunics and cloaks until our fingers shriveled. Occasionally I would find a long tunic in the pile of dirty garments — probably belonging to some other prisoner or a harlot a soldier had smuggled into the garrison — and then I was able to switch my ragged garment for one not quite so tattered.

Laundry work also meant an opportunity to sit with other women. Though my guards forbade me to talk to them, no one could stop me from listening. While our guards stood on the bank of the canal watching for crocodiles, I worked a short distance away from the slave women and absorbed every word, particularly when they mentioned Cleopatra.

"I hear the queen is leaving soon," one woman said on a particularly fine fall day. "They need to sail before the winter winds blow."

I stopped scrubbing as my pulse quickened.

"What's so special in Rome?"

"She's taking her son to meet his father."

A vein of grief opened and welled within me. Cleopatra was leaving, and only HaShem knew how long she would be gone.

What more evidence did I need? My former friend had completely forgotten me. She would not spare a thought for me now that she was preparing for Rome, and she certainly would not think of me while she visited Caesar's country.

My father and I were finished. Despite my dreams, despite the promise HaShem had given me, I had become a laundry woman for the Roman army.

I picked up another tunic, gripped it in both hands, and furiously scrubbed the fabric against a broad stone. How could a woman call herself a forever friend and do such a thing? How could she abandon me and leave my father in prison? Caesar had been gracious and generous in victory, so why couldn't Cleopatra respond in like manner?

I stopped scrubbing as my emotions veered from anger to something far bleaker. I felt as if there were hands on my heart, slowly twisting the life from it.

How could HaShem be so cruel? Why had He taunted me with the hope of meaning something to a queen, and why had He promised that I would bless her? I had told her about His promise, I had testified to the power of Adonai, but now Cleopatra had good reason to laugh at me and my God.

I dropped the pile of wet fabric onto the stone and stood, my heart hardening as the love I once felt for Urbi turned into something that burned hotter and far more furiously.

As the weeks passed, I tried not to think about the travel preparations that were surely taking place at the palace.

By the time I heard trumpets from the parade escorting Cleopatra and her son to their ship, I had resolved I would never again think of my former friend with affection. I would close the door on my past and bury my memories. And if ever granted an opportunity to find my way back into the palace, I would take it and stand before Urbi with eyes blazing.

A week after Cleopatra left Alexandria, I looked up at the sound of metallic jangling outside my door. Rufio entered, but his face was missing its customary blankness. His eyes focused on me with unusual intensity.

"I have heard," he said, "from Caesar."

My heart leapt. "He wrote about me and my father?"

"Indirectly. Since the queen will be in Rome indefinitely, he directs me to empty this garrison of all royal prisoners."

I thought I might burst from a sudden

swell of happiness. “We’re finally to be freed?”

He shifted to avoid my gaze. “All prisoners are to be sold.”

The words hung in the heavy air, and for a moment I could not make sense of them. Sold? Only slaves were sold. Father and I were not slaves; we were people of status and wealth, people who mingled with nobility and royalty. Slaves, on the other hand, were barely human.

When the back of my head touched the stone wall, I realized how completely we had been debased. Not only had our status disappeared, but over the past year we had been imprisoned and forgotten. Caesar had almost certainly issued my father’s death warrant. Older slaves were not valued. When they became too weak to work, they were usually sold on the cheap or disposed of in some other way. . . .

A cry broke from my lips, followed by a sob. I buried my face in my hands and gave vent to my despair, not caring about the Roman only a few feet away.

“Do not weep,” Rufio said, and I heard the surprising sound of anguish in his voice. “This is not death. This is freedom . . . in a different guise.”

“You would call slavery *freedom*?” I looked

up at him, disbelieving. "How free did you feel when *you* were a slave?"

A muscle clenched at his jaw. "Life abounds with worse situations than slavery. Everything depends upon your master — a good master will allow you to purchase your freedom if you earn enough silver. You and your father are literate and will command a high price at the market. No one harms or abuses a slave who cost them dearly."

I trembled at the thought of being someone's property. If Father and I were sold at the slave market, what were the odds we would be sold together? We would be separated, and I would never see my father again. We had already lost Asher, but if we were to lose each other . . .

"This cannot be happening," I whispered, more to myself than to the Roman. "HaShem, what have we done to deserve this?"

I heard the wooden thump of the door closing and looked up to find the commander kneeling beside me. "Do not fear, Chava," he said, using my name for the first time in my memory. "I will purchase you and grant you manumission."

I stared at him in bewilderment. "Why would you do that?"

He looked at me with a perplexed expression, as if a question lay on his lips without the courage to ask it. Finally, he propped one arm on his bent knee and leaned closer. "I would free you . . . in the hope that you will become my wife when I retire from the army."

I blinked. Marry an ex-slave and a pagan Roman? I knew I was in no position to bargain, but still, the idea rankled. I had not promised myself to Yosef, but I had always thought that if Adonai gave me the freedom to marry, Yosef would be my husband.

And freeborn women of status did not marry ex-slaves, no matter how celebrated the men had become. While Rufio seemed pleasant and had treated me kindly, still . . . an ex-slave! And a pagan! Time and time again, HaShem had warned us not to marry idolaters. How could I join myself to a man who worshiped gods made of stone and wood?

And why would such a man want to marry me? I would have to be a fool not to notice that he liked looking at me, but why marry me? He knew nothing about me, not really. He had no idea who I was.

"Why would you want me for a wife?"

A slow smile spread across his face. "Does a man need a reason? I want you; let that be enough. Let me free you from this place.

Live with me until I am free to marry."

I should have refused; if I had been my old self I would have refused immediately. But I was no longer the girl I had been, and I had fewer options.

"And . . . when would that be?"

His smile diminished slightly. "Five years, but time does not matter. I will provide for you until we are married according to Roman law. We will sail to Rome and establish our home there."

I shuddered at the thought, and my dismay was not lost on him. "You do not like Rome?"

"I have never been there. But I cannot imagine any city as beautiful as Alexandria."

"Rome is not beautiful," he admitted. "It is brick, not marble, and most of the time it is crowded, dirty, and noisy. But if you do not like the city, we'll move to the country. The Senate has promised acreage to army veterans, and in the country we can raise goats and oxen and plant a vineyard. Would you like that better?"

Would I like the country better than slavery? Who wouldn't?

But I was not born for the country any more than I was born to be a slave.

"I appreciate your kindness," I said, carefully choosing my words, "but I cannot leave my father behind. If I am free, I must do all I can to secure his freedom. He did nothing to deserve prison, and he deserves slavery even less."

Rufio drew a deep breath through his teeth. "Even a commander cannot afford to buy two slaves."

"I wouldn't expect you to. But my father is a scholar — a very learned man — and one of his friends might be able to redeem him. Please, have some of your men spread the word among the Jewish community. Tell them Daniel the scholar will be sold at the slave market, so he must be redeemed."

Rufio nodded. "I can ask . . . but if no one comes forward, you will have to let your father meet his fate."

"How can I do that?"

"You walk away." For an instant his eyes hardened. "You say good-bye to the things and the people you loved, and you surrender to the fates. They take you where they will, and you make the best of your situation. Your father will do the same, trust me."

"My father will trust in HaShem."

Rufio did not reply but examined my face with considerable concentration. He might have wanted to ask if I would trust in HaShem, too, but how could I? HaShem had made me a promise and not kept it. He had led me to believe certain things were possible and then dashed my dreams. For over a year I had been praying for our release, watering my pillow with tears, begging the God of Abraham, Isaac, and Jacob to hear and answer my prayers.

And HaShem had not.

I wanted to be free.

I wanted freedom to walk into the palace and let the queen see me standing tall, unbroken and resolute. "You know you were wrong to insist that the Jews worship at Alexandria's temples," I would declare. "That's why you gave them citizenship without that requirement. You treated me unjustly after I had pledged my life to you."

I closed my eyes and tried to imagine her response, but I could not. After so many months in this windowless room, I could barely picture her face.

"Chava," Rufio said, his voice a low rumble that was both powerful and gentle, "I can protect you from slavery if you will promise to become my wife."

"So be it," I whispered, my voice broken. "Let it be so."

I woke in darkness and listened to the sounds of legionaries shuffling outside my door. As the golden stream of torchlight faded to the faint gray of daylight, the guards changed positions and the halls quieted.

Then Rufio's face appeared at my door. "The time has arrived," he said, his voice gruff above the jangle of his keys. "Your father is coming."

I sat up, smoothed my sweat-stained tunic, and combed my hair with my fingers. I despaired at the thought of meeting Father in such a ragged condition, but it couldn't be helped.

I shivered as I approached the door. I should have been calm and confident of Rufio's promise, but I dreaded looking Father in the eye knowing he might not be set free.

The door swung open, and Rufio waved me forward. I stepped out, then turned toward the commander as a sudden thought struck. "How do I know" — I leaned toward him — "that you will keep your promise?"

In answer, he pulled a dagger from his belt and offered me the hilt. "Plunge this into my heart now if you do not believe I am a man of my word," he said, his gaze moving into mine. "By Jupiter's stone, I will set you free, even if it takes every denarius I have earned in service."

I did not take the dagger, but stepped

back. An instant later, a pair of guards brought Father into the vestibule, and my heart thumped so heavily I thought it might burst. A guard stood ready to clamp shackles around my wrists and ankles, but Rufio held up a restraining hand, allowing Father and I to embrace for an all-too-fleeting moment.

"Now step aside," Rufio commanded, and Father and I reluctantly parted. Standing at a distance, able to examine my beloved parent for the first time in over a year, I gasped at the change in his appearance. His beard had grown longer and gone gray; his broad face had narrowed, and his eyes seemed to peer out like animals in a cave. The arms he extended for shackles trembled, and his shoulders bent forward at an awkward angle.

The man was a ghost of the father I had known, but the smile he gave me was more warming than the Alexandrian sun.

"Are you well?" I asked in a low voice.

I strained to hear his hoarse reply: "Naked I came from my mother's womb . . . and naked I will return. Adonai gave; Adonai took; blessed be the name of Adonai."

Adonai gave, Adonai took . . . and Adonai promised. Who would hold Adonai accountable?

"He does not complain," a soldier behind me said. "If anything, these hardships have made him more focused on HaShem."

I startled to realize the guard was Jewish. Then I remembered — some of the relief forces from Judea had remained in Alexandria.

"It is an injustice," I said, careful not to raise my voice to a level that would attract unwanted attention. "And it is all my fault. I brought this trouble on us."

My father jerked his head in my direction. "No, Chava. This is from the hand of Adonai."

"This?" My sharp answer earned a scornful glance from the legionary at my left, so I reined in my temper. "Why would Adonai do this to faithful people?"

Father's shoulder lifted in an eloquent shrug. "Perhaps . . ." He paused to release a cough. "Perhaps we were not faithful enough."

And as we followed the legionaries out of the garrison, Father quoted words from the Pentateuch:

"See now that I, I am He!
There are no other gods beside Me.
I bring death and give life,
I have wounded, but I will heal,

and none can rescue from My hand."

As the chinking of our chains punctuated our steps to the slave market, one phrase kept repeating itself in my ears: *I have wounded, but I will heal.*

May it be so.

The swollen orb the Egyptians knew as Ra was dangling like a burning plum in the west when I spotted a man moving cautiously among the enclosures at the auction yard. He wore the long, untrimmed beard of a Jew, and when he came closer I grabbed my father's tunic. "Father, wake up! Is that not a friend from the synagogue?"

Father opened his eyes and blinked, then peered in the direction of my pointing finger. "Who?"

"It is Avraham the butcher," I answered, my spirits rising at the sight of Yosef's father. "What is he doing here?"

Father pulled himself upright and stared through the woven iron bands that formed a cage around us. He did not call out, but waited until Avraham looked in his direction, then he gave his old friend a discreet wave.

Relief melted Avraham's stern face as he quickened his step and hurried forward.

"Daniel! Chava! I had hoped to find you here." He took Father's hands through a gap in the iron weave and lowered his forehead to meet Father's. "When Asher told us they had taken you and Chava away, I couldn't believe it. But two of your slaves came to our house and told us what had happened."

"Is Asher with you now?" Father asked.

Avraham shook his head. "We hid him a few days, but we knew the legionaries would keep looking. So we sent him away with Yosef."

Yosef was with Asher? "Where are they?" Unable to resist, I stepped up and met the older man's gaze. "Please tell me if they are safe."

"They are." Avraham's eyes softened as he smiled. "My Yosef and your brother are in Jerusalem. I have received messages from them, so I know they are well."

Father closed his eyes. "Praise be to Adonai. I have been so worried —"

"Asher asks about both of you in every message," Avraham went on, shifting his attention to my father. "So I have been paying a boy to sell fried meat pies outside the garrison. He has kept his eyes and ears open, and this morning he told me you had been taken to the slave market. I came as soon as I could."

"Thank you, Avraham." My father clasped the older man's gnarled hands. "Though I do not know what will happen tomorrow, your news has brought comfort and encouraged our faith. Knowing that Asher lives, and that he is in Jerusalem, gives us great peace."

I closed my eyes, suddenly aware of just how relieved I was — not only for Asher, but for Yosef, as well. Why on earth had I refused him when he declared his desire to marry me? If I had not been so caught up in my pretension to royal grandeur, I might have recognized happiness when it was staring me in the face.

"I wish I could free both of you at the auction tomorrow." Avraham hung his head for a moment, then looked up, tears shining in his eyes. "But I will pray. I will ask HaShem to keep you safe and strong until your family is reunited."

Chapter Fifteen

The bright morning shot a shaft of sunlight through the iron weave of our holding pen, startling me into wakefulness. Like animals, Father and I had spent the night in a cage with two small children — *Gauls,* someone called them. Last night a slave girl had slid a cup of water through the bars. The four of us shared it, but in other nearby enclosures the first to grab the cup greedily devoured all, creating fierce squabbles among the occupants. The only pens that remained quiet were those with inhabitants who were too sick or too exhausted to fight.

I forced myself up from the ground and pushed hair out of my eyes. Beyond the slave market, people had already begun to move about, setting up tents and tables to sell their slave-oriented wares: cheap tunics, matching costumes for litter bearers, papyrus sandals, wooden bowls, leather whips. Soon this area would be swarming with well-dressed Alexandrians who would carefully pick their way through the less desirable population as they sought fine foods, exotic animals, and capable slaves.

Urbi and I used to shop the market together, occasionally pausing to stare at the unfortunates who waited to be sold. I always felt slightly sick after viewing humans in cages, and I certainly never imagined that one day I might be one of them.

Father and I had been fortunate to remain at the garrison until yesterday. Some of our fellow captives looked as though they had spent days broiling in the sun.

I turned back to where Father lay curled on the ground, a piece of thin fabric shielding his face. He had crossed his arms over his chest, a posture that reminded me far too much of death. "Father." I gently prodded his shoulder. "Are you awake?"

His hand rose to pull the fabric from his face. He smiled. "I am now."

"Sorry," I said with a grimace. "Go back to sleep."

"I have an eternity to sleep." With difficulty he rose to a sitting position, bent his legs and lowered his forehead to his knees. *"Sh'ma Yisra'el, Adonai Eloheinu, Adonai echad,"* he began, and continued to say his prayers.

I felt a stab of guilt as I looked at the two children, both of them wide-eyed. Did they understand what he was doing? They probably did not speak Greek, let alone Hebrew. I had never been terribly fluent in Hebrew, though Urbi was. How ironic that she would be able to understand some of Father's writings better than I.

His writings . . . what had become of them? Had one of the slaves collected and preserved his manuscripts, or had they been tossed out when someone else took possession of our home?

My throat ached with regret. Perhaps I never should have become close to Urbi. In the beginning, I should have realized that royalty could not mix with common people. Someone should have explained that Urbi could hurt me as many times as she wished, but the first time I hurt her, our relationship would end and I would pay a painful price.

When Father finished praying, we sat in silence and listened to a concert of sounds, all of them different from what we had heard at the garrison. From somewhere outside the city wall came the mournful call of a jackal; from the crowd, laughter and the slap of sandals; from farther away, the steady crash of the tide against stone pilings.

"Do you think about her?" Father asked. "Do you ever ask yourself why she abandoned you?"

"Every day," I whispered. "And every day I ask HaShem to grant me an opportunity to stand before her again."

"Are you thinking of vengeance?" His eyes filled with disappointment. "Because if you are —"

"What vengeance can I take against a queen? I only want her to see . . . and know that she could not destroy me."

Father stared blankly at the merchants' tables in the distance. "Urbi is queen now, just as HaShem told you she would be."

I blew out a breath. "Apparently I was wrong about HaShem."

Father gave me an enigmatic smile, then tilted his head. "I have had time to think, daughter. I have come to believe that I was jealous. I wondered why HaShem would speak to you, a mere child, and not to me."

I stared at him.

"Over the past few months, I realized something." A shade of wistfulness stole into his expression. "I had been so busy working, writing, studying, that I had forgotten how to listen to HaShem's voice. But listening came naturally to you. Perhaps it always will."

He extended his wavering hand until it covered mine. "I am sorry, daughter. I was wrong to doubt you."

"Maybe you weren't." I swallowed, forcing down the bitterness that filled my throat every time I thought about my foolishness. "I went around telling everyone — even Urbi — what I thought HaShem had told me, and none of it has come to pass."

"She is queen."

"But that is all! I am not with her, she doesn't care about me, and there's no way I can bless her. I no longer *want* to bless her. If she were here now, I would curse her."

"Hush." Father patted my hand and glanced around, probably terrified that someone would overhear my rant. His gaze roved over the other cages, where men, women, and children stood or squatted and waited for their lives to change. "At the garrison, I heard you speaking to the commander."

I froze, suddenly at a loss for words. How could I tell my father that Rufio could only afford to buy one slave? "The commander," I finally said, finding my voice. "He sent a man to ask if someone from the community could purchase your freedom, too."

"Does he love you?"

"He doesn't even know me. I think he longs for the sound of a woman's voice."

Father chuffed softly. "I can understand that."

"I think he ought to buy you, not me —"

Father released such an abrupt laugh that the effort triggered another round of coughing. I leaned toward him, wanting to help, but he held up his hand and turned until his coughing had quieted.

"Daughter," he said, wrapping his frail hand around mine, "do not be foolish. What would the commander want with an aging man on his way to the grave? Let him buy you, let him free you, and do not forget to thank HaShem for His provision."

I remained silent, grateful that Father hadn't heard all the details of my conversation with Rufio. I could not imagine any situation in which he would approve of my marriage to a heathen.

As the horizon shimmered in a heat haze, the auctioneer's men opened our cages and led out the captives.

I had visited auctions where the traders took great care with the men and women for sale — men were bathed and their bare chests polished with oils; women were groomed and displayed in undergarments to show off their natural attractiveness. But the only preparation this auction master made was to powder our feet with chalk dust. Even I knew the dust was intended to warn buyers that we were first-timers, and first-timers had a tendency to be intractable and eager to run.

As I listened to the first several auctions, I realized that his sales reflected a lack of effort. I had seen adult male slaves sell for as much as five hundred drachmas and females for as much as six thousand, but the first few males at this auction sold for less than three hundred.

Gripping the metal weave of our cage, I watched a tall, stately woman reluctantly submit to the auctioneer's demands to remove her clothing so buyers could better see what they were purchasing. I averted my eyes, unwilling to participate in the humiliation of another human being. What had that lady done to deserve a place here?

A moment later I watched in horrified silence as a guard led a mother and her toddling child to the auction platform. The auctioneer cut the fabric ties at the woman's shoulders, allowing her tunic to fall and expose her milk-swollen breasts. I had never felt such sympathy for a slave, but my heart twisted as I watched the poor woman struggle to hide herself and shelter her little one.

"A fertile young woman from Gaul," the auctioneer called. "Doesn't speak Greek, but understands most gestures. Has been a housemaid in Rome, sent to market because the baby caused her to become slack in her duties. Potential wet nurse here. Make a good offer and I'll throw in the child for only two hundred denarii."

I pressed my hands over my ears at the cacophony of voices. Was this what Nuru endured before she joined our household? She had been Father's birthday gift when I reached thirteen years. I had never considered Nuru's life before she came to me, but if it had been anything like this —

The door to our cage swung open. I helped Father to his feet, then we led the two children onto the hot sand and stared at a line of guards intended to intimidate. We edged forward and moved up a series of wooden steps until we stood on a platform before a sea of expectant faces.

I looked away, afraid I might spot someone I knew. What if one of my childhood friends was shopping for a new handmaid? What if one of the palace officials stood in the crowd? Despite my forlorn appearance, I could still be recognized, and I would rather die than have anyone realize the depths to which I'd descended.

Then I remembered Rufio, my only hope, and lifted my head to search for him. Though he had promised to buy only me, I hoped he had found a way to purchase my father, as well. Father would be a credit to any household and might prove extremely useful as an amanuensis or scribe.

The auctioneer grabbed Father's sleeve, pulled him over, and consulted a card. "Great bargain here! Older male, educated, speaks Koine Greek, Hebrew, Latin, and Aramaic. Reads and writes. Was a teacher of rhetoric to the royal family."

A murmur rippled through the crowd, and several faces lit with interest.

"We will start the bidding at five hundred drachmas. You'll never find a tutor for less."

"So much?" a man called. "He's a breath away from the grave!"

"He only needs a little fattening up." The grinning auctioneer wiped sweat from his neck. "So come on — who'll make the first bid? Do I hear five hundred?"

I searched frantically for Rufio and finally spotted him at the edge of the crowd. He was clutching a purse and shouldering his way through the onlookers, vying for a good position.

"Six hundred!"

"Six-fifty!"

I stared at Rufio. Why wasn't he bidding?

"Seven hundred!

"Eight! Eight hundred drachmas."

"Sold! For eight hundred drachmas. To the man with the red hat."

I swallowed a hysterical sob as the auctioneer's men led Father down the stairs. I searched for a man with a red hat but caught only a glimpse of him as he made his way to the government official who recorded the sales.

I felt more alone than ever.

I lifted my head again and saw Rufio. He now stood only a few feet from the front of the platform. Soon this nightmare would be over, and once I was free I would find my father and arrange for his manumission. After all, we still owned a house and furnishings, and property in Alexandria was valuable. . . .

I palmed tears from my face, straightened my spine, and raised my chin. Clothing myself in the dignity Urbi and I used to imitate when we pretended to be queens, I walked to the center of the platform and narrowed my gaze against the sunlit horizon.

"Ah," the auctioneer called, his voice taking on an oily tone, "the best of this lot.

Young female of childbearing age, educated. Can read, write, and sing. Has been trained in the courtly arts such as dancing and playing the lute. Tall and graceful. Look beneath the dirt and you'll find a true beauty. Use her to increase your slave stock or keep her for your pleasure. Let's start the bidding at four thousand drachmas."

I had hoped to maintain my aloof perspective, but a wave of anxiety swamped me at the mention of such a large sum. My eyes sought and found Rufio's. He stood as erect as a pillar amid the surging shoppers. When our gazes crossed, his jaw clenched and he lifted his hand. "Four thousand drachmas!"

"Ho!" the auctioneer crowed. "The commander thinks to buy himself a slave. I did not know Rome paid its men so well!"

Did they? I closed my eyes and tried to do the math. I had heard that the average soldier earned 255 Roman denarii each year they served in the army, and a denarius was more or less equal to a Greek drachma. So if Rufio never spent a single sestertii, in twenty years he would earn — I suddenly wished I'd paid more attention to mathematics — 5,100 denarii. As a commander, he might earn a bit more, but he hadn't always been a commander, and surely he had spent some of his wages on things like meat pies —

"Forty-five hundred!" From a tall bald man at the back of the crowd.

"Five thousand!" Rufio called out.

I closed my eyes and prayed for the auction to end.

"Six thousand, and not a copper more!"

My eyes flew open as an unfamiliar voice entered the fray. A swarthy little man stood in the center of the mob, surrounded on two sides by burly seamen. The man squinted at me and grinned, then waved a bag that sagged with the weight of coin. "I am ready to pay."

"Sold for six thousand drachmas!" The auctioneer brought his hand down on empty air and the deal was done.

I glanced at Rufio, who stared into space with defeat on his features. He had kept his word, but he'd been outspent.

"Who?" I asked one of the men who stepped forward to wrap my wrists with rope. "The man who won the auction — who is he?"

The man grinned, exposing a gap where two front teeth should have been. "Lucky you. Your new owner is Lippio the Greek."

"Does he live here? In Alexandria?"

"He's a sailor. Buys Egyptian slaves cheap, resells 'em in Rome. Doesn't usually buy 'spensive slaves like you, though." The man pulled me down the steps, then pushed me toward a stand where several other bound slaves waited. "Gods go with you, girl. You'll be headed for Rome as soon as the winds turn."

Chapter Sixteen

During my carefree childhood, I spent hours with Urbi on the palace balcony, watching exotic ships sail into the harbor and imagining the treasures that filled their holds. In those days the words *slave ship* had flowed from my tongue as easily as *merchant ship* or *warship,* but I had no idea what a slave ship looked like beneath its scrubbed wooden decks.

With my ankles shackled and my hands imprisoned by an unmoving iron brace, I was added to a line of slaves who shuffled over the dock and stepped onto the deck of a Greek slave ship. Sailors herded us like cattle, driving us down a ramp and into a dark hold where we were told to lie on racks made of wide planks. Flat on our backs, with another rack only five fingers away from the ends of our noses, each of us had one hand chained to a wooden support. The other hand remained free — to feed ourselves with stale bread, to scratch, or to lift our garment so we might relieve ourselves without rolling out of the rack. With great dismay I realized that we would not be allowed to move about until the ship arrived at its destination.

After we were shackled into place, we were left alone in the dimly lit hold. Fresh air entered through narrow windows high on the wall, but only when the wind blew across the body of the ship.

I had braced myself for confinement and primitive conditions, but I had not imagined the sounds — weeping, cursing, moaning from the sick. Women sobbed over babies they would never see again. Men cursed the slavers, the Greeks, the Egyptians, the gods.

Then the torture of lying still.

Movement could be painful at times, yet lying in a constricted space was more excruciating than I would have believed. Our close confinement not only tortured our muscles, skin, and bones, but it also tormented our minds. By turning my head all the way to the right, I could see other racks along the opposite wall, though nothing of the occupants except shadowed forms and bare feet. Turning my head to the left, I saw the ship's wooden beams.

Forced to stare at the rack above me, I

could not help but feel that we had been buried alive. I could not roll onto my side without banging my hip against the rack above. I could not turn over. I could not lift my head high enough to see my feet.

My chest tightened until I could barely breathe.

Sleep brought the only respite from our ordeal, and in dreams I found myself running, rolling downhill, twirling outdoors, and lying facedown on grass with my nose pressed into yielding, fragrant earth. Then the painful cramp of a leg muscle would force me to wake and weep in frustrated agony. My only consolation was the knowledge that Father remained in Alexandria and Asher was safe in Jerusalem.

We endured two days of stifling restraint before the ship even left port. From a lifetime of living in Alexandria, I knew the currents were tricky and fair winds necessary for a successful voyage, but each morning I railed against our captain for not either releasing us or sailing away. Each day at sea meant one less day on the rack, and if he refused to leave the harbor, he prolonged our ordeal indefinitely.

When we could not sleep, we found solace in conversation, a sure antidote to the isolation that permeated the crowded hold. I learned that the woman above me was a Greek called Effie. She had been born a slave and had twice crossed the Great Sea. "It is not so bad," she told me, a note of compassion in her voice. "With the boards close together like this, at least no man will be climbin' on top of you in the middle of the night. And the voyage isn't a long one. Once we start movin', Rome is only a month away from Alexandria, and Alexandria is only two or three weeks from Rome."

"That . . . makes no sense."

She chuckled. "The winds, love. They blow faster when a ship is heading home. A captain cannot sail directly to Rome, but must head east and north to use the winds. And we have to put into port each night to pick up foodstuffs — no room for storage aboard these boats. Then, finally, we'll pull into port at Puteoli."

Still, a month at sea? I couldn't bear the thought.

I was dozing in a heat-induced haze when I felt the timbers shiver beneath me. I opened my eyes to the groaning of rope and wood, and felt my stomach drop as waves slapped against boards only a short distance from my head. With the sensation of movement came renewed cries and curses, but finally the sounds faded and we rode the swells of the sea in a dense silence.

I kept telling myself my situation was a mistake HaShem would soon rectify. If Father could accept both good and bad from the hand of Adonai, so could I, but the bad had gone on long enough. Soon HaShem would end this horror, return me to Alexandria, and allow me to rescue my father.

I dreamed of revenge, although I had no idea how to take it. While I thirsted for justice, I was powerless to employ anyone in my cause.

Our ship sailed steadily, zigzagging across the Great Sea according to the whims of the wind.

Effie said she'd been allowed to remain with her mother until she reached the age of five years — after that, she was sold to a merchant who needed helpers for his cook. Effie learned to cook and clean in that Roman house, and would still be there had the master not died and bequeathed his possessions to a brother who already had a cook. So Effie was sold to a trader, who transported her to Alexandria, where she was purchased by a Greek magistrate who reported directly to the palace. "He was important," she said, her voice brimming with pride. "We frequently had guests who had waited on the royal children, and who had worked for their father before that."

I said little as I listened to her stories. When she asked about my history, I gave her the simple truth: I was the daughter of a Jewish scholar. We ran afoul of a powerful person, so we had been arrested, forgotten, and sold as slaves. "My father is in Alexandria and my brother in Judea," I said, the words sounding unreal even as I spoke them. "But one day I am going to find my family and avenge our losses."

"Ah, dear." Effie clicked her tongue in sympathy. "If only it were that easy. But what did you do to get in such trouble?"

I released a cynical laugh. "I refused a gift."

"Oh." She laughed as well. "You should have known better than to commit such folly. As a slave, you will be offered no gifts unless your mistress is about to throw something out. You will also have no opinions worth discussing. So mind your words and learn to swallow your thoughts before they reach your lips. Your *dominus* and *domina* have no time for anyone but themselves, and sometimes their children."

Dominus and *domina.* Master and mistress.

I thought of Nuru, who had been my slave for so many years. I passed hours in her company every day, but had I ever asked for her opinion? Had I ever asked if she *wanted* to go shopping? If she felt like walking along the docks? If she was tired or ill or lonely?

Of course not. One did not converse with slaves, thank them, or mind their feelings any more than we minded the feelings of stray dogs on the city streets. And while one might converse with a stray dog, we did not expect it to answer. While we might occasionally throw a dog a bone, we did not do so every day because we did not want it to *expect* such rewards. . . .

I closed my eyes against a sudden wave of dizziness.

"Never look a master in the face," Effie was saying when I opened my eyes. "And never contradict them."

"Even if they're mistaken?"

"They're never mistaken, dear. They're Romans." She laughed. "We are always in the room, working a fan, standing guard — we slaves are everywhere. In your master's house you might hear and see things that will make you want to run and hide, but you must see and hear them without reaction. Gossip about your master only if you are prepared to lose your tongue. Some say that a mute slave is the only kind worth having, so guard your tongue if you want to keep it."

"What about . . . ?" I hesitated to ask the question that had been haunting me. "What if the master *uses* his female slaves?"

"I take your meaning," Effie said, her tone low. "I heard once about a slave who was beaten every day because the master's wife was jealous — apparently the man spent more time sleeping with the slave than with his wife. No one ever protested the beatings because it was the wife's right to handle such matters in her household. And though I did not get a look at your face, I can tell from your voice that you are a gentle thing — probably pretty, too. So be careful. Don't make the domina jealous, and do not make the dominus angry. They have every right to do with you as they please."

"What . . . what if a slave has a child?"

"Well, yes, of course that happens. If a baby is born to a slave, she will lay it before the dominus. If he picks it up, he is acknowledging that it is his, so the child becomes his slave. If he ignores the baby, a woman can keep it and try to feed it without any help from the dominus, or she can leave it outside. She will consider it an offering to the gods — happens all the time. But better by far is to get rid of the baby before it is born."

"That . . . is possible?"

"Jump," she said. "Seven times, so your heels touch your buttocks. The baby will be unable to remain inside you. Or drink a tea of juniper berries or giant fennel. Better still, if you want to prevent a child in the first place, tie a cat liver to your left foot when your master comes to you."

I focused on Effie's advice, memorizing her words and heeding her warnings. I was entering a new world, and until I met Effie, I had been completely unprepared.

I had spent my youth in a glorious excess of freedom, and I had no idea how to function as a slave. I had lessons to learn, but this time I would be a good student. Because I fully intended to survive.

"You'd best resign yourself to Roman ways," Effie said. "Life there is not so bad. There's always something to see and some scandal turning heads among the nobility. Everybody watches everyone else, and no two days are alike. If you get a good master, you can live a good life in Rome."

"And if I do not get a good master?"

"If you get a swag-bellied barnacle, you could always kill him." Effie hesitated, then dropped her free hand so I could see it.

"Don't do that," she said, wagging her finger. "You would not live long afterward. So pray to your gods. If you absolutely cannot endure, you can always run away. Some slaves make it to freedom . . . but you have to know what you are doing before you start running. Better by far to be a loyal servant, earn your master's favor, and buy your freedom, or pray that your master will include your manumission in his will. Happens more often than you might think. Might as well happen to you."

When the ship put into port at the end of each day, a seaman would come below the deck and toss a stale biscuit and a bit of dried fish to each of us — the only food we would receive until the next port. After we had eaten, other sailors would come down with buckets of seawater, which they tossed onto us in an effort to clear our plank beds of rat droppings, urine, and excrement. As we neared the end of our voyage, only a couple of stalwart men came below because the stench and putrid air of the hold made the chore intolerable for all but the most determined seamen.

At night, the upper deck quieted, and the only sounds that reached my ears came from creaking timbers, scurrying rats, and moaning captives. To block out the horrific sounds coming from where I lay, I stared at the wooden planks above me and tried to focus on the occasional voices that drifted downward. Most of the seamen spoke Aramaic, and as a child I had learned the language along with Urbi.

One night I overheard the captain speaking to one of his mates. According to rumors he had heard, Cleopatra was living in Caesar's country villa on the west bank of the Tiber River. People said Caesar was keeping the queen out of the crowded city partly because it was rough, and partly because the populace had not been happy to hear that Caesar's mistress would be living in the same city as Calpurnia, his wife — or ex-wife, depending on who reported the news.

The report surprised me. I had imagined that Cleopatra would be warmly welcomed in Rome — after all, hadn't she promised to feed the Romans from the abundance of Egypt's grain? Hadn't she done all she could to assist Pompey and Caesar?

Although I heard the seamen laughing about Caesar's lovers in foreign lands, not one of them spoke approvingly of his relationship with Cleopatra. The child, apparently, was the chief reason for their disapproval. They seemed to believe that her son was likely to be advanced as Rome's next king — and the Romans would not tolerate a king.

"But what if Caesar has no such plans?" one seaman asked. "He has no sons, so is it not natural that he would want to celebrate the boy?"

"Not until we know what sort of magic the Egyptian woman used on him," another countered. "And how can he be sure the child is his? She might have lain with a servant and attempted to pass the boy off as a Roman."

Another man scoffed. "Caesar is no fool. He would not be so easily duped."

"Are you certain? Then why did he not side with the young king who held the city when Caesar arrived? The wisest course would have been to secure the kingdom under Ptolemy, execute the troublesome queen, and keep Egypt under his thumb with the boy as king. But instead Caesar wages war, requires reinforcements, and spills rivers of Roman blood in order to put that woman on the throne. The man has been bewitched."

"By what power?"

"Egyptian magic." The first man's voice softened to a hushed tone. "Have you not heard of their ancient gods? They have power far beyond that of Jupiter and Mars. Their priests are more powerful than ours, everyone knows it. This Egyptian woman calls herself Isis, a goddess. She has enchanted Caesar and enticed him with powers of her bed and body. That's why the woman is in Rome. Caesar wants to declare himself king and install her at his side. He's determined to destroy the republic."

Their arguments, which I found silly and ignorant, did touch upon some thoughts I had considered myself. Could Cleopatra have fallen in love with Caesar? When I last saw her, she certainly seemed enamored of him, but she was far too devoted to Egypt to lose her head and heart to a Roman. Urbi knew Egypt would never accept Caesar as a co-ruler unless they were married, so bedding him and producing a son was a natural first step. What did it matter that Cleopatra and Caesar had not been united in a Roman marriage? Cleopatra was the law in Egypt. If she wanted Caesar at her side, she would have him there.

Besides . . . anyone who saw the look in Cleopatra's eye when she spoke of Caesar would know that she cared for him enough to give him a son. She had also given her people what they craved most — a ruling couple, descended from royalty, a pair of divinities. Cleopatra and Caesar. And an heir to continue the dynasty into the future.

I closed my eyes, painfully aware that even in my chains and misery, Cleopatra's shadow followed me.

After several days at sea, my throat grew parched and my skin tender. My bowels turned to liquid, and I could not eat. I whispered entreaties for water, but the sailor who came below with a ladle and bucket did not give me enough to cool the scorching fever that had begun to distort my thinking. My ears filled with a ringing sound, and the noises around me dulled, as though my head were stuffed with cotton.

I refused the hard biscuit and salted fish. Sleep, when I found it at all, was fitful and imparted no rest. I drifted in and out of consciousness, imagining myself back in the prison, in the palace, and at home in my own soft bed.

I dreamed I was home, working in Father's library, writing out the names of HaShem. But the only name I could write was *YHVH Rophecha,* the healer.

I am Adonai, your healer. The voice filled my ears until I could hear nothing else. I recognized it as the voice that had promised

I would bless Urbi. But how? If Adonai had broken that promise, why was He talking to me again? After all the prayers in which I accused Him of deserting me, why would He speak to me at all? And why was He promising to heal me when I was about to die?

"I am YHVH Rophecha, Adonai, your healer."

The God who heals body and soul. The God who could repair my body *and* keep the promise I thought He'd forgotten.

"All right," I told Him, resigned to my fate. "You do not forget. I understand."

I do not know how long I drifted in and out of consciousness, but one morning I woke and noticed that the air smelled different. "What is that?" I forced words over my thick tongue. "Where are we?"

"There you are," Effie answered, her voice heavy with relief. "I was afraid we had lost you. One of the deckhands came below, and he paused by our rack. Knowing he'd throw you overboard if he thought you were dead, I told him you were sleeping, but I do not think he believed me. A good thing I finally convinced him or you'd have awakened in the sea."

I blinked as the planks above my head slowly came into focus. "Thank you," I murmured. "I feel . . . better. I . . . must have had a fever."

"Aye. I could tell that much. You were talking and making no sense."

"Talking? What did I say?"

She chuckled. "You talked about someone called Urbi, and someone called Yosef. And once I thought you were crying."

Maybe I was. I could not think about Yosef without wanting to weep. Or Father. Or Asher.

I closed my eyes. "What *is* that smell? Something's different."

Effie snorted. "I do not know how you can smell anything but filth, but I am guessing you are smelling earth. I heard one of the hands call that they'd seen land. We'll soon be anchoring, and not a moment too soon. Time to get off this ship of pain."

I drifted away again, but when I woke, a scruffy sailor was unlocking the manacle on my wrist. Too weak to respond, I said nothing as the iron bracelet fell away and a gruff voice told me to "roll out and stand."

I rolled over but crumpled like thin parchment when I attempted to put weight on my legs. Effie managed the drop better than I, and she supported me as I struggled to stand. For the first time in weeks, I glanced at my body — I was covered in grime, insect bites, and a violent rash. I suspected that the areas I couldn't see looked far worse.

We waited, clinging to the racks for support, until the man had unlocked all the captives. Then we were herded up a ramp and onto the upper deck. I had to lower my head and shield my eyes from the blinding sun, but with Effie's help I shuffled forward and tried not to lose my balance. Behind me, I noticed several slaves were so emaciated that they had to be carried out on stretchers. If not for Effie's help, I would have been among them.

"I pity them," Effie said, pulling me forward as if to put a great distance between us and the weaker ones. "They will be thrown into cages and left to die. Unless they can find the strength to stand for an auction, they will be tossed out like garbage."

I shuddered at the inhumanity of our situation. Had this sort of thing been going on forever? Hard to imagine that such squalor, filth, and cruelty could exist only a few feet from my home. If this sort of thing was common in Alexandria, why had I never seen it? Why had no one approached Cleopatra about the manhandling of slaves? Men were creations of HaShem, made in His image. No one, not even the poorest of the poor, deserved to be treated worse than animals.

After disembarking, we were doused with buckets of water and given cursory examinations. One man *tsk*ed as he held up my arm, now bone-thin, but his pity did not prevent him from looping a rope around my waist and tying me to Effie. When all of the surviving slaves had been tied in a single line, we were led away from the docks to a slave market much like the one in Alexandria.

This time I was in far worse condition: sick, barely able to stand, barefoot, and filthy. My long hair was matted, and my face felt like bone beneath my fingertips. Any trace of beauty I might have once possessed had been obliterated by illness and dirt.

The observers at this slave auction were not well-dressed noblemen or scholars, but common men who wore short tunics and woven grass sandals. Without being told, I knew I was looking at the lowest of slave traders, those who could only afford to purchase the weakest slaves.

Like me.

In this place, only slaves in good health and muscle tone stood on the auction block. The rest of us were arranged in groups of three and four, the weakest of us dispersed so that every group had at least one slave with little life left.

I barely listened as the slave master called out lot numbers and took bids. I kept my head down and lifted my gaze only long enough to see I'd been grouped with an old man, a fierce-looking woman, and a girl of about ten years. Her wide eyes met mine, seeking solace, but I had no smile to give her.

When the bidding had concluded, the four of us were roped together and led to a wagon hitched to a team of oxen. We climbed in, urged to hurry by an overseer who kept flicking a switch over our backs.

Effie, who was making her way to the auction block, called farewell as the overseer climbed onto the wagon bench and cracked his whip. "Farewell," she called in Greek. "Looks like you are going to the country. Enjoy the fresh air!"

Did she think I would ever enjoy anything again? She had more faith than I.

I slumped against a bale of straw and closed my eyes. I knew nothing about the country, nothing about planting or harvesting, and I had never lived outside a modern city. Life as I had known it was finished.

Wrapping my arms around myself, I curled into a ball and tried to sleep.

Chapter Seventeen

I woke in a hut built of rough mud bricks. Weathered branches formed the roof over my head, dried leaves still clinging to the limbs that rustled with every breath of the wind. The odor of manure flooded my nostrils, mixed with the acrid smell of smoke, but I found the combination strangely pleasant compared to the stink of the slave ship.

I watched as a stout woman kneeled beside a cook fire in the center of the room. Smoke rose through a round opening in the ceiling, and what did not rise curled and crept down the back wall where I saw the girl who had been with me in the wagon.

"Ah, there you are." The beginning of a smile tipped the corners of the stout woman's mouth. "Glad you woke up. I wasn't sure you were going to make it."

With an effort, I pushed myself up into a sitting position. I had been lying on a pile of rags and cast-off tunics, with a rough piece of burlap serving as a blanket. "Where am I?"

The woman left the fire and sat on a low stool next to me. "You're on the Octavii estate. We grow food for the market and provide them with a good living."

"And . . . who are you?"

The woman grinned, exposing a mouthful of brown teeth. "The *vilica,* charged with seeing to the health of all the slaves kept on the farm. I had my doubts about you when the wagon pulled up."

The word was new to me. "Vilica . . . you are a healer?"

She chuckled. "The vilica is the wife of the *vilicus,* the overseer. I oversee the women's work, but mostly I oversee the overseer."

She turned back to the fire, where a fragrant stew or something bubbled in a cauldron. "I am stirring a pottage that will set you to rights and put a little flesh on your bones. I'll have you on your feet in no time."

My stomach growled in anticipation. I tried to sit a little straighter but winced at the touch of the rough burlap against my skin.

The woman gave me a sympathetic look.

"You've got a case of sores on your backside — comes from rubbin' against the ship's planks. But I have already applied salve, and you'll —"

"Be on my feet in no time," I murmured, finishing her thought. I looked at the child, who hadn't said a word but watched me with large gray eyes. "And who are *you*?" I asked.

The girl did not reply, but her eyes widened and something that might have been a smile lifted the corners of her mouth.

"We do not know what to call her," the woman said. "She doesn't speak."

"Not at all?"

"Not a word in any language." The older woman sucked at the inside of her cheek a moment. "I was afraid someone had cut out her tongue, but it is still there. So maybe she will talk, someday."

"You ought to call her something," I said, staring at the child. Her golden hair had once been cut, perhaps even shaved off. But now a growth as long as my first two knuckles stood out from her head, reminding me of Isis with her sun-disk crown.

"Moria?" I suggested, looking at the girl. Again, no answer, but the muscles in her cheeks flexed.

"Triton thinks she was dropped on her

head," the woman said. "An imbecile."

I frowned. "And Triton is — ?"

"My man," the woman said. "The one who brought you from the port, and overseer of this farm."

I nodded, remembering the deeply tanned face behind the whip. "And the others who came with me?"

"They're here. The old Egyptian probably won't last through the winter, but the woman is strong. We call her Kepe. She's been given o'r to the pigs."

A thrill of fear rippled up my spine. "You fed her to *pigs*?"

The woman stared. "What do you think we are? I ordered her to *feed* the pigs. What's in your head, girl?"

I blew out a breath. "I am . . . not from the country."

"Aye. No worries. You'll get used to things around here."

"Did Kepe say where she was from?"

The stout woman waved her ladle at me. "*That* one has no tongue. She must have said the wrong thing to the wrong person at the wrong time."

I swallowed to combat a rising wave of nausea. Given the horrible conditions at the slave yard, I should not have been surprised at the condition of my companions. I should no longer be surprised at anything.

I leaned against the wall and closed my eyes. I could almost go to sleep, trusting myself to the care of this woman, who seemed the kindliest soul I had met since leaving Egypt. And she spoke Aramaic, a language in which I was competent.

I opened one eye. "What can you tell me about this place?"

" 'Tis a farm." The woman shrugged. "We grow grapes and olives mostly, for the fruit, wine, and oil. We grow the vines and trees, tend and harvest them. We women stomp on the grapes until they are juiced. The men handle everything else, along with the transport to market. The family's not especially wealthy, but they're counted among the nobility in Rome."

"Don't they live here?"

"Why would they?" The woman flashed her brown smile. "Sometimes they visit in the summer, but most of the time they live in Rome. More to do there, I suppose, than sit around watching grapes grow."

I closed my eyes again. "And you are the vilica. Do you have a name?"

"Aren't you full of questions?" She clucked her teeth, and when her stool creaked my eyes flew open. I found her standing beside me, the large wooden ladle in her hand. "Now open your mouth, dearie, and have a cupful of this. It'll settle your stomach and ease you back into eatin' regular. No more dirty water and stale biscuit for you."

When I had dutifully taken a few sips, she nodded her approval. "Name is Berdine," she said, thumbing a dribble from my chin. "Do you have a name?"

I drew a breath to answer, then hesitated. Should I reveal that I was Jewish? I had heard that Romans did not harass Jews, so perhaps my heritage would not matter. Effie had told me that her previous owners did not even inquire about her background. "Oh, they're proud to say they have a Greek tutor or Greek physician," she said, "but did anyone ever ask where I was born or who my parents were? No. They only care about things that make them look clever."

"My name is Chava," I said, aware that I was hearing my name for the first time in weeks.

The woman smiled again. "Not a very common name around here. All right, Chava. Now eat." She offered the ladle again, and her gaze met mine as I sipped. "Where'd you come from, then? You're not from Gaul — we get lots of slaves from Gaul and Judea, but you do not speak like a woman from one of those untamed regions."

"I came from Alexandria," I said after I'd swallowed another mouthful. "My family . . . fell upon hard times, and my father and I were sold into slavery. A trader brought me to Rome."

"I know the type," Berdine said. "Brutal men who care nothing for their cargo, only about earning a few denarii. But do not worry — I'll get you back on your feet, and the vilicus will put you to work." Her eyes narrowed. "From Alexandria, you say? Home to the great library?"

"What remains of it. It was damaged in the recent war."

Berdine sighed. "I can only imagine such riches. Our mistress adores reading; she is always talking about the library and all the knowledge stored there. I have always wanted to read. In my younger days I was nurse to a young master and mistress who had a Greek tutor. I would listen as he taught them the alphabet and how to recognize letters." Her expression grew wistful. "Whenever he caught me listening, though, he chased me away. Said it wasn't right for a slave to bother with reading and writing. But *he* was a slave, same as me. And my dominus had a Greek slave for his physician, and he read long manuscripts all the time."

I leaned forward to better study her. Berdine looked to be in her late forties and did not appear slow-witted. "I could teach you," I said. "My father was a tutor, so I know I could teach you to read and write."

"You could be a tutor? By all the gods." Her eyes widened as her mouth rounded to the shape of an omicron. She lowered her ladle. "If you can read, you shouldn't be in the fields. Domina will want you to work in the villa, or maybe even at the house in Rome."

Despite the disappointment on her face, my spirits lifted. "In Rome? Near the port?"

"Of course, where else would it be?"

My mind raced. I'd need a boat to carry me home. Any work I could get in Rome would be better than working out in the country.

"What kind of work might she want?"

"Hard to say," Berdine said, turning back to her pot. "But she has frequent need of a scribe. And someone to keep accounts. There's plenty of work to be done with figures. Or, given your looks, she might want you to warm her son's bed. But do not worry about such things — for now, your job is to rest and get well. Time enough later to find your place in the household."

I closed my eyes against a sudden rush of tears. How could I make her understand that my place could never be among the slaves?

"There now," she said, turning back to me. "Time enough to sort all that out. Right now you need to rest and regain your strength. So sleep, little one, and let my potions do their work. You'll feel better in a few days."

I nodded, yielding to her entreaties, but the rough caress of a burlap blanket did nothing to put me at ease.

After several days under Berdine's care, I grew strong enough to leave my sickbed. Berdine suggested that I learn my way around the orchard and vineyard as I strengthened myself with daily walks. "The women here work as hard as the men," she said and settled a kettle onto the fire, "and if you do not do your fair share, Triton will sell you to the next trader who passes by."

The thought of standing for another auction made my stomach sway, so I determined to regain my strength as quickly as possible. I also wanted to explore every hidey-hole and bramble on the estate. If I ever needed to hide, I'd have to know where

I could safely conceal myself.

Barabell, a slave from Gaul, waddled under the weight of her unborn baby as she gave me a perfunctory tour in elementary Greek. Pointing to a simple villa of plastered stone, she said, "There is villa for Domina. She comes not much."

"So I have heard."

Barabell pressed her hand to the small of her back and moved forward. Behind the house, next to a small vegetable garden, we found the animal pens. "Pigs and sheep," she said, flapping her hand at two separate enclosures. "Pigs for eating. Romans like pigs. The sheep for cutting hair. Romans like wool."

Though I did not eat pork, I had owned dozens of woolen garments, yet I had never seen a living pig or sheep except at a distance. I counted at least twenty pigs in the pen, most of them happily wallowing in mud or rooting around in the dirt, and about the same number of sheep. The sheep were messy, their long hair caked with mud and broken twigs.

"Cletus care for animals." Barabell pointed to a man with short, curly hair. He gave me a narrow-eyed look that seemed to pluck at my tunic, so I turned away.

"There." Barabell gestured toward an area

filled with what appeared to be mounds of clay. "Hives for bees. Do not steal honey. Triton flog, then sell to mines. No one wants to work in mines."

I silently absorbed the warning and said little as Barabell continued. "Well," she said, pointing to a round circle of rocks, "and barn — keep hay and food for animals."

She stopped and regarded me with a weary look, then propped a hand on her swollen belly. "Each day, eat one meal. Each year, one tunic. Old tunic to Berdine, she make blankets. If you run, you be caught and marked." She held up one finger, blew on it, then touched it to her cheek and made a hissing sound.

"Branded?" I whispered.

"Yes. And wear iron collar always. No escape here."

She looked across the field, and I saw that she could have been a lovely woman. Strands of copper-colored hair had slipped from the knot at her neck and pasted themselves to her rosy cheeks. Large green eyes dominated her face, and her features, while smudged with grime, were as delicate as any noblewoman's.

I prodded her when she fell silent. "Anything else I should know?"

She gave me a sidelong look. "You not talk

like slave. But you obey like slave. You must."

I nodded in rueful acceptance, at least for the moment. "You need not worry about me."

Her upper lip curled. "You have fancy talk. Let us see fancy work."

When Triton told me that my first job would be to help Berdine, I imagined the work would be easy — after all, slaves only ate once a day, so only one small meal had to be prepared. Then I learned that Berdine did far more than cook.

Aware that I was unaccustomed to hard labor, Berdine did not demand much of me in those first few days. She allowed me to follow her around the property and become familiar with the tasks associated with each area. She also urged me to learn the names of the other slaves.

Berdine kept saying the farm was not large, yet it seemed huge to me, with most of the land being devoted to the vineyard and olive grove. I never thought I would find beauty in country property, but the surrounding fields were a colored quilt, each square painted in a different hue. I had grown up with the blue of Alexandria's sky and the white of her stone buildings, but on the farm I was surrounded by earthy browns and the emerald and gold of trees, vines, crops, and grasses. Though Egypt greened with life after the inundation, for most of the year the land around Alexandria was arid and brown with little variation.

Fortunately, Berdine said, the grapevines and olive trees required little of us except during the harvest when every slave pitched in to help. "On harvest days," she assured me, "we will all be too tired to eat."

Triton kept us busy doing the work that kept us alive. When he returned from the market with grain — from Egypt, I realized with wry satisfaction — Berdine and I had to grind it, mix it, and bake it into the rough loaves we ate every day. Vegetables from the garden supplemented our meager diet, and unless one of the men caught a rabbit or several pigeons, rarely were we offered meat. When one of the sheep died from a mysterious illness, I hoped we might boil the carcass and have mutton for dinner, but Triton declared the meat unsafe and ordered the animal burned.

Each sunrise we stepped out of our mud huts and reported to the vilicus. I counted fifteen slaves on the farm — not a huge number, but enough to keep the place running.

Berdine told me our domina owned another villa in the country, a home the family visited far more often. "It is their place for relaxation and pleasure," she said, grimacing as she turned the stone mill that ground our grain. "And Domina keeps more slaves there — many more. There are slaves to tend the gardens and fish ponds, slaves to clean the lake, gardeners, bird keepers, gamekeepers, and fish minders. The house is large, so they bring slaves from the city — the doorkeeper and the keepers of the kitchen and bedchambers. The master has his *ornator* to dress him, his *tonsor* to shave him, and his *calceator* to care for his feet. The mistress brings her dresser and hairdresser, plus a woman to draw her bath. The children also have slaves, and they travel with the family in their own litters, carried by a matched set of Cappadocian slaves in uniforms." She chuckled. "Dominus even has a *nomenclature* who walks with him and tells him the name of anyone he cannot remember."

"You mentioned a dominus," I said, "yet you refer to Domina as if she runs the farm."

Berdine nodded. "Domina is a widow who married again, but the farm is hers, as is the country villa. So yes, we have a dominus and domina, but we answer mostly to her."

"And the dominus?"

"We stay out of his way." She smiled. "He is a good man, but quiet. I think he stays out of Domina's way, too."

I used the scoop to collect the ground grain and poured it into a bowl. "How do you know so much about the city house?"

A dimple appeared in her cheek. "I was a cook in the *familia urbana,*" she said. "Then the vilicus asked me if I wanted to be in charge of the women at the farm, and of course I said yes . . . because I had come to love Triton, you see, and he was going to the farm." Even at her age, a blush brightened her cheeks when she spoke of her lover. "So we came to the farm and have been here ten years."

"Is our domina a good mistress?"

Berdine nodded as she sprinkled more grain over the mill. "She is a kind woman and a good mother to her son and daughter. I enjoy being left alone to work, because sometimes I can almost pretend Triton and I are free." She gave me a guilty smile. "On other days, I wish Domina came here more often so she could see what we need. Sometimes I think she forgets about us. And on a farm, the slaves should not be left unprotected."

"Unprotected from what?"

"Raiders. Thieves." She gestured, directing me to pour the ground grain into a clay pot and cover it with a lid. "Triton would fight to defend this place, and perhaps Cletus, but if a group of raiders came here with villainy on their minds, how would we defend ourselves? Sometimes I worry. And then I wish Domina gave us more of her attention."

I listened intently, eager to learn all I could about the place. If I were to get back to my family, I would have to escape. I had never been particularly brave or an eager risk-taker, but since my life had taken a sharp turn into unexpected territory, perhaps it was time to change.

I had already begun to formulate a plan. To get back to Alexandria, I would have to reach Rome and secure passage on a ship. I had no idea how it could be done, but I knew I had to try.

Though I proved clumsy with a shearing blade and was terrified of the huge pigs, I demonstrated my worth to Triton and Berdine the morning I picked up a spinning wheel. Apparently none of the other women were skilled at spinning, but I'd watched Nuru spin by the hour, and the technique wasn't complicated. Besides, sitting in one place reminded me of all the afternoons I had listened to Urbi's tutors with embroidery in my hands. "I am good at sitting still," I told Berdine, "and I am good with thread. Let me spin, and I promise you won't be disappointed."

Doubt glimmered in her eyes, but when she stopped working at midday to see how I was doing, she found a ball of tightly spun thread, a good morning's effort. She unwound a length and rolled it between her fingers, then grunted in satisfaction. " 'Tis a bit rough for fine sewing," she said, "but you are bound to improve. And you cannot be worse than the other girls."

I felt my shoulders relax. For days I had been trying to demonstrate some skill that would earn the others' respect. If I proved useless on this farm, I might be sold and transported even farther away. This place, rough as it was, seemed safe enough. The men kept their distance, though Cletus looked at me from time to time in a way that lifted the hair at the back of my neck. Berdine and Triton were in a *contubernium,* or unofficial marriage, and so were Barabell and Darby. Each of the couples lived in their own home, leaving the rest of the men in one hut and we women in another.

Whenever I looked at the couples — Berdine and Triton or Barabell and Darby — I thought slavery might be more bearable if one had a companion. At night, I soothed myself to sleep by imagining that the soft sounds of breathing belonged not to several women, but to a beloved man. The formless shadow beside me always wore Yosef's face.

After proving myself capable of producing something of worth, I set out to learn about the area around the farm. I learned that the property lay near the city of Neapolis, south of Rome and just north of a seaside resort called Pompeii. By listening to the men talk about the market at Neapolis, I calculated that it would take a day to walk to that city, and another seven days to reach Rome — provided all went well. The Via Appia ran along the coast, so the journey would be smooth as long as I did not run into soldiers, bandits, or slave hunters.

My escape would be easier, I realized, if I had someone with me. We could not only keep each other company, but one could stand watch while the other slept. We might even do a bit of role playing, if we could manage it. With the proper garments, we could pretend to be a noblewoman and her slave, or a mother and daughter, and avoid looking like two runaways. But which of my fellow slaves would want to risk the danger of failure?

At midday, when we gathered outside Berdine's hut to receive our bread and a bowl of whatever garden vegetable she had boiled, I studied the other women and wondered if any of them might be persuaded to run for Rome. Barabell would not — with her baby due at any time, she was in no condition to escape, plus she seemed truly attached to Darby. "They are mates," Berdine had told me, "in all ways but legal. Domina could sell either of them if she wanted, but she's not likely to as long as they're breeding. That baby could be another pair of hands to work the farm, and more hands are always welcome."

"Babies would be more welcome if they came without another mouth to feed," Triton groused, but Berdine ignored him.

"I am looking forward to having a babe around the place," she said. "It has been a while."

Doreen, a tall red-haired Gaul who spoke little Greek or Aramaic, might be persuaded to run away, but I wasn't sure I'd be able to communicate the finer points of a successful escape. We couldn't simply take off; we would have to be wily and clever. Could she pass as anything but a slave? I doubted it.

Melleta, a Greek woman, handled everything to do with the vines. Every day she went into the vineyard and studied the rows of plants, running her hands along the twisted branches and adjusting the wooden supports as she looked for signs of leaf roll or beetles. Berdine said Melleta had worked in the vineyard since childhood, and she knew every vine by heart. I had thought she might be convinced to escape the farm, but after watching her work the vines, I doubted she would leave the plants that had become her life's work.

Lesley was the shepherdess, and she seemed as devoted to the sheep as Melleta was to the vineyard. Vara was not attached to any of the men, yet her eyes followed Alroy every time we all gathered together. From the flush on her cheeks I surmised that if she hadn't yet attempted to lie with him, she soon would. Even slaves grew lonely at night.

Kepe, who had arrived with me and now worked with the pigs, was minus a tongue and a little unsound in the mind. I wasn't sure she could be calmed enough to pass for a typical traveler on the Via Appia.

The girl who had arrived with me did not survive the first month. She refused to eat, rejected our attempts to comfort her, and wasted away before our eyes. She never spoke, though she cried out often during the night, and three weeks after our arrival we found her lifeless in her bed. Minos buried her in a small slave cemetery outside the vineyard.

Minos wore his history on his face — his cheek had been branded with the letter *F,* for *fugitīvus,* and he wore the infamous iron collar around his neck, advertising to one and all that he had tried to run . . . and failed. He wore his attitude on his face as well, and with one glance I understood that he did not take to slavery as easily as some. Some slaves, like Melleta and Vara, had been born into captivity and accepted slavery as their station in life.

But the Gauls had been forced into slavery when the Romans invaded their land and defeated their army. With hundreds of others, Barabell and Darby had been tied up and roped together, then torn from their dead and driven southward into Roman territories. They were slaves because they had been conquered, and fierce resentment simmered beneath the surface of their faces.

I waited for someone at the farm to ask how I had become a slave, but aside from Berdine's gentle questioning when I first arrived, none of the others seemed curious about my background. None of them was especially friendly, either, and none of them appeared to think much of my abilities when I mended the harvesting nets or attempted to help Kepe catch an escaped pig.

And I did not blame them. As I lay in the women's mud hut and stared at the twig ceiling above my head, I looked over the winding length of my life and realized that I had never excelled at anything except being beautiful and spoiled.

Barabell went into labor on a cool spring day as we were preparing to mend the harvest nets. We had just spread the nets beneath a shady tree when she cried out and bent over. When she stood erect, clutching her belly, I could see that the bottom of her tunic was spattered and wet.

"Sorry," she called, her face flushed. "I know . . . bad time."

"Her waters have broken," Berdine announced, eyeing the evidence. "I'll take her back to the huts. Chava, bring the others back for dinner at midday."

Berdine, whose eyes were focused on the mound of Barabell's belly, tried to step over the huge net but caught her foot in the weave and fell, face-first, to the ground. Barabell gasped and I ran over to help the older woman. “Let me aid you,” I said, slipping my arm around her waist.

Berdine slapped my arm away. “Don’t make a fuss.” She tried to stand, but the moment she put weight on her right foot, she groaned and staggered forward. “Can’t . . . walk,” she hissed between clenched teeth. “My ankle . . .”

I looked at her leg, where the ankle was growing thicker before my eyes. “Let me call one of the men, someone who can carry you.”

“The men are needed here.” She glanced around again, then reluctantly focused on me. “Chava, take Barabell and help her. Triton can carry me home at the end of the day.”

“But you are injured! You need to put your leg up —”

“I need to help with the mending,” she said, sliding off the olive nets. “Go on now. Get Barabell to the hut and stay with her till the baby comes.”

I gaped in astonishment, my hand flying to my pounding heart, but another cry from Barabell urged me forward. I caught her arm and walked her down the path that led back to the huts.

“I think big baby,” Barabell muttered

between gasps as we walked. "This not easy birth."

"I am sure it will be fine." I smiled as though childbearing were as easy as belching. "Babies come every day."

"Women die every day," Barabell said. "You help with birthing before?"

"No — but I have seen one."

I had, but only from a distance, and only because Urbi and I hid behind a curtain in her mother's bedchamber. We had been present when the youngest Ptolemy was born, but all I could remember was the pregnant queen clutching an amulet and squatting while a white-robed priestess of Taweret uttered incantations and waved a censer.

When we reached Barabell's hut, she asked for water, so I ran to the well. I filled a bucket, grabbed some woolen rags from the laundry shed, and hurried back to the hut. Barabell was pacing, her chest damp with sweat and her tunic sticking to her back.

"Have you had a baby before?" I asked, trying to make conversation.

She released a low, painful groan, then glared at me from beneath hanks of sweat-drenched hair. "Yes."

I smiled and looked around, then realized

too late that I had not seen any young children on the farm. If Barabell had given birth before, the child was no longer with her.

I pressed my lips together and resolved to remain quiet.

Barabell groaned again, and I searched my memory for lessons on childbirth. Father once mentioned the love between a man and woman, but his descriptions had been cloaked in metaphor. The older women at the synagogue might have taught me if I'd been betrothed, but that had never happened. Urbi and I had gossiped and giggled about how babies came to be, but Urbi had abandoned me by the time she prepared for her first child.

In all my reading, if only I had read a manuscript on the art of love and childbearing . . .

"Is there anything," I asked Barabell, "you would like to talk about while we wait?"

"Ngggggggggad!" Barabell screamed as another pain struck. Then she glared at me and told me to keep quiet.

The labor continued throughout the afternoon, a relentless series of pacing and moaning and gritting of teeth. At midday I went to have a bowl of pottage and brought some to Barabell. She took one look at it and shook her head as though the food were offensive, then went back to pacing.

Finally, as the sun balanced on the western horizon, Barabell sank to her knees and pressed her hands to the earthen floor. "Baby coming," she said, the tense lines on her face deepening into crevices. "Catch."

Catch? I looked at her, crouching on all fours, and decided that a human baby must arrive in a similar fashion as a piglet or a lamb.

Trembling with uncertainty, I lifted the back of her tunic and crouched behind her, holding out my hands. Barabell groaned, the space between her legs widened in a rush of blood and fluid, and a blue baby dropped headfirst into the world and landed in my arms.

I gasped, astounded and overjoyed even as I struggled to hold on to the slippery infant. "A boy," I whispered, finally securing him by cupping his head in my palm. "You have a son!"

Barabell nodded toward a ball of spun wool on the floor. "Tie knot in cord, cut by knot."

I set the child on a blanket and wrapped the wool around the cord. I struggled to tie the knot, however, because I could not find a blade to cut the string. "How do I cut the — ?"

"By Jupiter's navel, must I do?" Barabell groaned as another mass followed the baby, a cloud of membranes and fluid that seemed to pulse in the dimming light. With a great deal of exasperation, Barabell rose to her knees, grabbed the cord, and cut it with her teeth. Then she picked up her silent child, placed her lips upon his mouth and nose, and sucked fluid from his nostrils, spitting onto the floor between efforts.

Almost immediately, the pale baby pinkened, opened his mouth, and let out a mewling cry. "Shhh," Barabell said, wrapping the child in the blanket. "You safe. Welcome."

I hugged my bent knees, caught up in the wonder of childbirth. Only when I tasted the salt of tears on my lips did I realize that I was crying . . . not only because I was awed, but because Urbi had also experienced this miracle and I had not been there to share it with her.

The next afternoon, Berdine ordered me to go to the market with Minos. Eager to travel beyond the farm, I took an extra moment to braid my hair in what I hoped was a current style. I had not been away from the property since my arrival, and I wanted to see more of the surrounding countryside. Not even the thought of riding with sullen, scarred Minos could dampen my anticipation for the journey.

"Take an empty basket," Berdine said as I came out of my hut. "And watch carefully while Minos bargains. You are more fluent in Aramaic than he is, so speak up if you can get a better price."

I nodded, then grabbed two supports on the wagon and hoisted myself onto the bench that served as a driver's seat. The back of the wagon was crowded with jars of olive oil, spools of spun wool, and pots of honey. Two stout oxen, borrowed from a neighboring estate, had been harnessed to pull the load.

Minos emerged from his hut, tightened the strings of his sandals, and glared up at me, his eyes glittering above the *F* on his cheek. "I do not need help on this trip," he said, speaking his native Greek.

"Then I apologize for my presence," I said, folding my hands. "But the vilica asked me to come, and I have to obey her, no?"

He scowled, loosened the rope belt at his waist, and pulled himself up. The hair on his burly arm brushed against my bare skin, and I found myself leaning sideward in an effort to put more space between us. He was so malodorous and *male . . .*

Minos cracked the whip and lashed the oxen's hindquarters. The animals lifted their heads and began to move over the rutted path.

I did not look back, but kept my eyes focused ahead. The road we traveled on was not easy to navigate, and we jounced and rattled over it until we finally reached the paving stones of the Via Appia. I sighed in relief when we turned onto the pavement, and Minos gave me a sidelong glance as he guided the oxen northward.

"You're not from Greece," he said, settling the whip beneath a meaty thigh. "But not from Gaul, either."

"No." I parted my lips, trying to breathe through my mouth. The man had particularly bad breath, probably from a rotting tooth.

"Where you from, then?"

I glanced at him, then decided to give him the truth. "Alexandria," I said. "In Egypt."

He frowned, staring at the road ahead. "Egypt? You do not look like a Gyp."

"Egypt is populated by many different groups," I said, settling the hem of my tunic so it covered my sandaled feet. "Greeks, Egyptians, Jews, and even Romans. Alexandria was founded by Alexander the Great." I nodded at my companion. "He was one of your people. You should be proud."

"No," Minos said. "Alexander was a Macedonian. I am an Athenian."

I shrugged. "Greece is Greece."

Minos shook his head. "Would you call yourself Egyptian?"

I tilted my head, considering. "Yes and no. We Alexandrians are nothing like the Egyptians who live along the Nile."

Minos shrugged. "You see? Macedonian is not Athenian."

We rode in silence for a while, saying nothing even when we passed a family walking on the road. They stepped off the pavement at our approach, and though most of them watched us with sullen faces, one or two looked at our wagon with frank longing.

I was shocked by their expressions — they envied *us*? We had a wagon and oxen, but we did not own them, nor did we own ourselves. That family appeared to be *free,* yet they coveted our wagon.

I shifted my position to study the slope of Minos's cheek, marred forever by a branding iron. He had once wanted to be free.

"Tell me about your escape," I said, looking directly at him.

To my surprise, he answered with a smile. "I knew it," he said, his grin deepening. "You show up, you talk in fancy language, you walk with mincing steps. I tell Triton you will run when you can. He says no, you are too smart, but I told him you will. You will run, yes?"

His expression, so frank and encouraging, elicited a nod of agreement from me. But I had scarcely finished nodding when his face darkened like a thundercloud. "You are a fool!" he roared, startling a flock of roosting birds in an overhanging tree. "Where would you run? You came from a boat, so you have no friends in Rome and no stranger will shelter a runaway slave. You are nothing but property belonging to Domina. If you would suffer as little as possible, work hard and strive to please your mistress. That is all you can do. That is the best you can do. And if you do this, you may find some unexpected happiness. Domina may reward you, give you a husband, or allow you to keep your child. She may allow you to run a business or sell on your own. But you will deserve none of these things if you try to run. If you are not killed in the attempt, you will be branded forever and never trusted again."

I leaned away from the flow of angry

words. "I-I haven't done anything —"

"Better to not try. What gods do you worship?"

The question caught me off guard. "What?"

"Venus? Isis? Jupiter? Whatever gods you serve, you should make a sacrifice and swear you will never entertain such foolish thoughts again."

His hands, I noticed with some surprise, trembled on the reins, as if the passion behind his words had shaken him to the core.

"All right," I said, not willing to provoke him further. "I will not be foolish . . . though I do not understand why it should matter to you."

"You do not understand?"

"I do not."

"You do not understand because you are new and have not been in the city. The slaves are so many, we are so strong, the Romans are afraid of us. We outnumber them, see? We could rise up and kill our masters in their beds, so they quake in terror while they sleep. They have made laws — if any slave kills his master or a member of his family, all the slaves in the household will die as well as the guilty man. And if any slave escapes, all slaves are punished. If you are foolish, all of us pay the price."

Somehow I found the courage to ask: "What price?"

Again he glared at me, and for a moment I feared he would kill me for asking a stupid question. Better that I should be dead than the entire slave population.

"Whatever the dominus wills. Maybe we do not eat for three days. Maybe we are all flogged. Maybe we find our children sold. And you? You who run? You cannot escape. If you try, you must live on the run while slave hunters search for you. Your master will offer a reward for your return, and when you are found, you are not only branded and collared, but you are tortured as an example to others. You are pretty now, but you would be pretty no more. Trust me."

I shriveled before his scalding anger, and when he had turned his gaze back to the oxen, tears sprang to my eyes. I did not weep out of fear or anxiety, but out of despair. If I could not run, how could I cope? I could not live this life.

"Do not cry," Minos said after a while, his voice softer than it had been. "You are not happy, I can see. Everyone sees. But if you cannot be happy, there are other ways to escape."

I sniffed. "What ways?"

He shrugged. "Some die by their own hands, especially warriors who will not serve those who defeated them. They jump from cliffs or open a vein. Some have eaten burning coals. These are the ones who say death is better than slavery."

I recoiled from the thought of suicide. "My God would not approve of self-murder. I could never do that."

Minos slapped the reins. "You are not the only highborn person to be enslaved. Many brave warriors have walked the path you walk. You are not the only one to suffer hardship on account of the Romans."

"The Romans did not make me a slave, it was —" I bit my tongue.

"Who?"

"My best friend."

Minos barked a laugh, then snorted. "Does not matter. You should not despair. Sacrifice to your god, pray that you can make yourself valuable to Domina. If you bring in money, you can buy your freedom. You do not have to remain in slavery forever."

A sprig of hope sprouted someplace deep in my chest. "A slave can earn money?"

Minos gave me the look he would have given a child who asked silly questions. "You perform a service. You are paid. You have

money."
"What sort of slave is paid for his labor?"
The man shrugged. "Artist, painter, sculptor, doctor, midwife, tutor —"
"Midwife?" I clutched at his sleeve. "They pay midwives?"
He nodded. "Yes, sometimes more than doctor, especially if woman and baby both live."
I pressed my fist to my chest. A good reason to learn the art of midwifery. I may not have known much when I helped Barabell, but any trade could be learned.
If I could become skilled and deliver many babies, I could earn enough money to buy my freedom and return to Alexandria. I could walk into the great hall and stand before Cleopatra with my head held high. She'd have to look at me and realize I was strong enough to succeed without her.
And HaShem was a God who kept His promises.

Chapter Eighteen

I do not know how I managed to doze in that wagon, but I did. As Minos cursed at the oxen and navigated broken paving stones, I dreamt of Egypt, the royal palace, and Cleopatra's chamber. Urbi and I were playing with clay dolls when I heard the mewling of a newborn. I cocked my head, searching for the source of the sound. "Is that your baby brother?"

Urbi tipped her head back and laughed, then a rough voice spoke from her lips: "Shut up your squallin'!"

Startled, my eyes flew open. I was not in the palace; I was riding in a wagon, my head resting against a support post. The crude command had come from Minos, who remained next to me in a cloud of stink, but the crying came from *behind* me, amid the baskets and honeypots.

I turned, rose up on one knee, and peered into the back of the wagon. "Is that a baby?"

"Sit," Minos barked. "We're nearing the city."

"But it is a baby!"

"Sit down, will you?"

I shot him a scornful look, then climbed into the wagon bed where I found a lidded basket. I lifted the lid. There, like Moshe in the bulrushes, lay a baby. Barabell's little boy.

"Hush now." I lifted the baby out of the basket and held him against my chest, fumbling with the wet wrappings in the bottom of the basket. "What is the meaning of this?" I called to Minos. "Have you stolen this child?"

He hesitated before growling his reply. "The baby is broken. Berdine says to get rid of it."

"What do you mean, 'broken'? I caught this baby myself. He's perfect."

Minos shook his head. "Look at the boy's back."

Confused, I held the child against my shoulder and pulled the swaddling cloths away from the baby's skin. The dimpled pink buttocks appeared perfectly normal, but in the center of the child's back I saw a red spot not much bigger than my thumbnail. "Oh . . . what is that, little one?"

I crossed my legs and turned the baby

over, resting his chest against my thigh. I examined his ruched flesh and saw that the pale skin had not completely covered his backbone — as if HaShem had run out of flesh when forming the child.

"He has a wound, so what of it?" I lifted my voice so Minos would hear. "Can't we cover it with a dressing until it heals?"

Minos hunched forward and did not answer.

"Minos! Surely this child can get well."

"Berdine has seen this before. She says the child will sicken and die, so best to be rid of it now."

"But the wound isn't very big. Perhaps I could sew the edges of the skin together —"

"Berdine says no!"

I turned the baby over and stared in horror at the little boy's perfect face. He squinted against the hot sun and sucked two of his fingers, desperately seeking nourishment . . .

Guilt assaulted me — had I done something wrong when I delivered the baby? Had his skin caught on my hands, on a fingernail, on something nearby? If I had injured Barabell's son, she might never forgive me. I might never forgive myself.

"Sometimes a baby is born like this, sometimes even worse," Minos went on, tossing the words over his shoulder.

"Are you sure? That babies can be born like this?"

He shrugged. "Berdine says so."

"And did she tell Barabell she was sending the baby away?"

Minos tossed a sour look over his shoulder. "Would *you* tell?"

With a groan I held the baby close to my body. He began to cry again, lustily this time, and the longer I patted his back, the louder he screamed.

"He thinks you are going to feed him," Minos said, apparently understanding more about babies than I did. "Put him back, let him sleep."

I obeyed, wrapping the baby in his swaddling cloths and settling him in the basket. I did not cover him with the lid, but draped a linen square over the top to block the sun.

"Have you done this before?" I asked while climbing back onto the bench. "Taken babies away?"

He gave me a guilty glance. "Only broken ones. Most of the time, women keep babies until they are weaned. Then they are taken to house of the Dominus or sold at the slave market."

I nodded, slowly comprehending why there were no young children on the farm.

"And if they are sick? Or . . . broken?"

He cracked his whip, startling the plodding oxen. "Some leave them out in the woods for the wolves. Some leave them by a cistern, hoping a poor farmer will pick the child up. And some take them to a Temple of Juno or Venus, where a priestess might raise the child . . . or consecrate it to the god's service. Those live in the temple."

I did not know which option horrified me more. Abandoning a child to the woods or to a pagan priest? Giving it to a poor family seemed merciful by comparison.

"What do you intend to do with this child?"

He looked away. "I have not decided."

"And what of Barabell? What will she do when she comes home and finds her baby missing?"

"She will keep her mouth shut," he snapped, glaring at me. "Which is what you should be doing. This is not your business."

I stiffened. "I will not keep silent. I want to find the child a proper home."

"A proper home?" He held out his hand, indicating the woods around us. "Tell me where that is."

"I do not know, but I will not allow you to leave it where it might be in danger, killed, or offered as a sacrifice to some pagan god."

We rode on, and the baby in the basket grew more fitful. The little boy was probably starving, but I had no milk or water to give him.

But on the road ahead, walking with a group, I spied a young pair — a girl about my age, perhaps a little younger, and a young man. From the way they walked together I discerned that they were coupled, so perhaps they had thought about children.

As we passed the travelers, I turned to Minos. "Stop the wagon."

His dark brows slanted in a frown.

"Please. I need to relieve myself."

He sighed but pulled on the reins until the oxen stopped. "Be quick about it."

I climbed into the back of the wagon. While Minos protested, I scooped the baby out of the basket and jumped to the road. I strode toward the group of travelers, ignoring the three older people and heading straight for the young couple.

"Please," I said, holding out the baby, "will you care for this child?"

The girl reached for the baby immediately, but the young man stepped in front of her, then peered at the child in my arms.

"Boy or girl?" he asked, his voice gruff.

"Boy," I answered.

After lifting the swaddling cloths to make sure I spoke the truth, the young man took the infant and handed it to the young woman.

I gave them a quick nod, then hurried back to the wagon. Minos shook his head when he saw my empty arms. "Who has the baby?"

"It is not your concern," I replied, keeping my voice light. "You were told to be rid of the child, and the baby is gone. So your job is done."

"Did you tell them the child is broken?"

I pressed my lips together as my conscience nipped at me. "Perhaps they will know how to heal him. Or they can take the child to a physician."

Minos scowled but said nothing else as he cracked the whip.

Neapolis had been built on a promontory that jutted into the bay of Naples. Nearly as Greek as Alexandria, the city prided itself on its artistic sensibilities, for statues of Hercules, Venus, and Zeus adorned nearly every street corner. Even the name of the city testified to its Greek beginnings, as *nea* meant *new,* and a *polis* was a Greek city-state.

As Minos navigated the narrow streets, I

noticed several elegant villas, some high on the slope of an imposing mountain to the west. Arched aqueducts led from the mountain to the city, and a central plaza offered public baths, a theater, and a large temple. The city square was spacious, relatively clean, and undoubtedly far more beautiful than overcrowded Rome. Long strings of laurel leaves decorated the façade of public buildings, probably to commemorate some festival to a Roman god.

The marketplace was not so beautiful — no matter how artfully the merchants attempted to display their wares, visitors who stood downwind could not escape the odor of animal waste. The sounds of clucking chickens, barking dogs, and lowing cattle filled the air, and after riding past the slave market, I could not erase the images of emaciated captives from my mind.

"The wagon can stay here." Minos pulled up to a shed in an alley, then jumped out of the wagon and stalked away — in search of a merchant, I presumed. I climbed down to stretch my legs. I certainly had no desire to wander about in this part of the city.

Yet despite my memories and initial revulsion, I found myself wandering back to the slave market. I stood at the fringe of the curious crowd, not wanting to venture too close to the people waiting in chains. Some appeared to be family groups; others had the look of defeated soldiers. One cage held nothing but women, and from their bored expressions I suspected they had worked as prostitutes in some foreign town. Even as free women, they had sold themselves every day.

Two years before, in the days when Urbi and I had disguised ourselves and wandered in and out of the merchant booths, we had seen such women and wondered why they would lower themselves to that sort of life. Now, older and wiser, I understood how life could change in a moment. Things that would have been unthinkable became possible, even necessary, merely to survive.

I turned away from the pitiful captives and walked through the market, eyeing vegetables, fine linens, scented candles, dishes, lamps, painted jugs and vases. The goods became finer and more expensive the farther I walked. I turned a corner and found myself in a booth that sold scrolls, dozens and dozens of them. They were neatly written on sheets of papyrus and tied with leather straps. A king's collection of fine stories and human wisdom, neatly stacked on spools in wooden cubicles.

The owner of the booth took my measure

with one swift glance, and I braced for his rebuke. But instead of chasing me away, he came forward. "Does your mistress read?" he asked, his fingertips tripping over several scrolls on a table. "Would she like a new copy of Homer's *Odyssey*? We have a fine collection of Egyptian love poems."

A sudden thought startled me. "Have you a work on midwifery? Anything about the birth of babies?"

The merchant tilted his head, then snapped his fingers. "Over here," he said, stepping back to pull a heavy scroll from a stack. "All the latest information assembled from experts in the field: Pliny the Elder, Celsus, and Galen."

I took the scroll and held it on my palm, admiring its heft. "How much?"

"One sestertius."

A valuable work, but I had no money. I could not even sit and read for a while, for the hawk-eyed merchant was intent on the sale and waiting for my response.

I scanned the marketplace and saw Minos standing on the base of a fountain across the square, shading his eyes as he looked for me. "I will return," I told the merchant, placing the scroll in his hands.

I hurried across the crowded square.

"Where were you?" Minos demanded. "I

have finished the trading."

"One sestertius." I held out my hand. "I have to buy a manuscript."

He blinked. "Oh ho, has the princess been shopping? You think I have a sestertius to give you?"

I refused to be intimidated by his bluster. "I know you do."

"Berdine will sell me if I do not bring back a full amount."

"Berdine will applaud you for making a sound investment. She sent me to help you, right?"

"But you helped not at all with the trading."

"I am helping now, guaranteeing a way to line your mistress's purse. So give me one of those coins and be quick about it."

With an abrupt grunt, Minos dropped a sestertius into my hand. I hurried back to the merchant.

With the scroll safely wrapped in silk and tucked beneath my arm, I set out for the wagon. Rather than cut through the crowded plaza, I took a few moments to savor my treasure and slowly retraced my steps. I strolled past the booth with scented oils and silk fabrics, past the fine linens and embroidered himations. I quickened my pace as I neared the stockyard and shied away when a pack of snarling dogs spilled from an alley as they fought over some bloody prize.

As several men chased the dogs away, I clutched the scroll and lifted my hand to get Minos's attention. My hand sank, however, when I stepped on something and looked down . . . and glimpsed a bit of swaddling cloth, stained with urine and blood.

I froze as the wings of foreboding brushed my spirit. When I could move again, I looked up and scanned the crowd, then spotted the travelers we had met on the road. Three older people and a young couple . . . but the woman was no longer carrying an infant.

I strode toward them, horror and indignation lighting a fire beneath my feet.

"What happened?" I asked when I reached the couple. They stared at me, eyes wide and blank. I looked from the woman to the young man, then repeated the question in Latin, "What happened to the baby?"

The man pointed to one of the older men. I glanced over my shoulder, ready to confront him, and saw that his face was set in resolute lines. He might have been poor, but he was still the *paterfamilias,* and in his home, his word would be law until the day he died.

"He took the child," the young man said. "Didn't want to feed it."

"So what did he do with it?"

The young man did not answer, and his woman refused to meet my gaze. I whirled around to face the older man. "Did you give the child to someone else?" I demanded. "Will you tell me so I can be sure the baby has a proper home?"

The old man pushed me. "Go away, slave."

"Where is that baby?"

When the girl began to weep, I should have realized. But defiance had lit a flame in the older man, and he stepped close enough for me to feel his hot breath as he . . . barked.

The bloodstained cloth. The alley. The frenzied pack.

My knees crumpled as the world spun around me. I fell in the dust, and someone kicked me once, twice, three times — then I heard Minos roar.

I opened my eyes as he waded into the fracas and stood over me. "This woman belongs to the Octavii family," he said, his huge arms flexing. "Strike her again and you will pay damages!"

A wave of muttering enveloped me, then

the crowd shuffled away. I waited, expecting compassion from my fellow slave, but Minos leaned down and none too gently hauled me to my feet. "What were you thinking?" he scolded, his eyes narrowing as he gripped the back of my tunic. "You could have brought dishonor upon Domina!"

"And what is the penalty for *that*?" I glared at him and struggled to stand upright. "I have never even *met* Domina. Why should I care about her?"

Surprise siphoned the blood from Minos's face. "Why? Because she holds your life in her hands. If she hears of this — and you would be surprised how quickly word travels — your life may be forfeit. Mine, too, for letting you out of my sight."

Ignoring him, I picked up my scroll and strode toward the wagon. I had tried to do something good — something that ought to have resulted in good — yet my efforts had resulted in barbarity.

What sort of world was this?

Though Minos tried to distract me with talk of loading the wagon and traveling back to the farm, I couldn't shake the horror of what had happened to Barabell's baby. A burning rock of guilt had lodged in the pit of my stomach, and it wasn't going away, no matter what Minos said. If I hadn't given the baby to that couple . . . would it still be alive? Minos insisted the child was destined to die no matter what, but I couldn't agree with him. HaShem was the giver of life, and His gifts should be respected.

I looked around the marketplace at Neapolis, my vision gloomily colored with the memory of that sweet little boy. Minos was loading bags of cow manure when a distant group of men and women lifted their hands and began to wail. One of the men, a cloth merchant, pulled a length of material from beneath his counter and proceeded to hang black bunting over the stacks of bright fabrics.

An approaching man, one who wore a toga over his tunic, called to the merchant in Latin: "What has happened?"

I leaned forward, as did everyone else in the vicinity.

"A horrible thing," the merchant answered, turning. "Caesar has been murdered! Killed by a group of conspirators who called themselves *liberatores*!"

The announcement was followed by gasps, anguished cries, and exclamations of dismay in several different languages. Yet Minos did not seem much affected, and at length he met my troubled gaze. "Caesar meant something to you?" he asked, his tone casual. "You look as though you have lost your father."

Still reeling in shock, I shook my head. "He was not my father."

"But you knew about him, even down in Egypt."

I drew a deep breath. "I met the man. We might have been friends . . . if my life had not changed."

Minos did not press for an explanation, but climbed into the wagon and picked up the reins.

As the sun lowered toward the Great Sea, Minos snapped the whip and urged the oxen homeward. I suppose we could not have avoided hearing the report — bad news, my father always said, flew around the world while good news was still putting on its sandals. We passed a few torch-lit litters as we traveled north. Even after sunset, the story of Caesar's death spurred wealthy senators and patricians to hurry home from their leisure villas to discover how the world was about to change. In those litters I caught glimpses of Roman matrons with undone free-flowing hair, pale faces, and black tunics. Men on horseback passed us, their faces dark with the beginning of beards that would grow until the mourning period for Caesar had passed.

When we stopped at a well to stretch our legs and water the oxen, we learned further details. A pair of men, each wearing the toga that symbolized Roman citizenship, stood outside the adjoining tavern and spoke without bothering to lower their voices. "They burned him in the Roman forum," one man said, clutching the edge of his toga. "Mark Antony stirred the crowd into a riot with his eulogy."

"What do you think will happen to the Senate?" the other man asked.

The first man shrugged. "Time will tell. But Caesar named his great-nephew, Gaius Octavian, as his heir."

"And that Egyptian woman?"

"Gone. Left Rome as quickly as she could."

My flesh contracted at the mention of Cleopatra. Even here, I could not be rid of her shadow.

Minos waited until we had ridden some distance before he asked me for a translation of the men's conversation. When I told him what I'd heard, his brows constricted.

"What?" I asked. "You have heard of this Gaius Octavian?"

One corner of Minos's mouth twisted. "I know the name," he said, smiling. "He is

Domina's son."

I stared at him. "I do not understand."

"He is a boy no longer," Minos said and shook his head. "But Gaius Octavian will likely be our master someday. But now . . . he is Caesar's heir." He chuckled. "Imagine that."

I fell silent. I sensed a pattern in this development, an omen or sign that had an important meaning. I sensed it, I could almost feel it, yet the details eluded me.

Was it possible? Could it be that even in this, HaShem was ordering my life? That He was watching even now? *El Ro'i, the God who keeps watch. The God who sees.*

I did not see how it could be so, yet the feeling persisted: HaShem's eyes were upon me.

Chapter Nineteen

When Minos and I returned to the farm, I expected Barabell to meet us in tears. But she did not, nor did she mention her baby when I saw her at dinner the next day. Either she had resigned herself to losing the infant or she had already lost so many that she had grown accustomed to having her children taken away.

Darby, father of the child, sat at dinner with his head lowered, refusing to look at anyone throughout the meal.

But when we set to work the next day, Barabell went about her work with a stony face that showed no emotion. If not for her red and swollen eyes, I would not have known that she was suffering.

And I did not tell her what happened to her child in Neapolis.

Late that morning, I pulled Berdine aside and showed her the scroll I purchased at the market.

"You bought something?" she said, her brows rising nearly as high as her widow's peak. "Who gave you permission to spend Domina's coin?"

"You charged me with making sure Minos made good bargains," I said. "If I read this and learn the art of midwifery, I can save the lives of Domina's slaves and earn money for her. I understand a good midwife can be well paid."

She looked at me, her eyes narrowing as she studied my countenance. "Yes," she finally said, "you are right. I am not sure how busy you will be out here on the farm, but you will likely be called on enough to give you some practice."

"I want your help, too," I said, catching her arm. "I know you have delivered babies here —"

Berdine cackled as if I had just told a joke. "I am no midwife. I deliver babies because there is no one else to do it."

"But you know things. Surely you can teach me what you know."

"I can do that in the time it takes to blink an eye. But you won't know nearly enough. Sometimes the mother cannot push the baby out, and sometimes the baby chokes on the wee rope."

"What do you do then?"

All traces of humor vanished from Berdine's lined face. "You watch them die. Sometimes the mother, sometimes the baby, sometimes both." She crossed her arms and scuffed the ground with her sandal, then lifted her head and looked at me. "Barabell has lost two babies at birth, and I was of no help either time."

"I am sorry."

"Well." Together we stood and listened to the sounds of the woods — the whisper of wind in the olive trees, the churr of insects, and the rumble of male voices coming from the men's hut.

"Maybe you will do us some good as a midwife," she finally said. "When I tell Domina, I will say you are smart, so you will do her honor. But —" she pointed to the scroll, partially unfurled on the table — "are you sure you can read that? It looks like chicken scratching to me."

I smiled. "It is written in Greek, the language of Alexandria. I will have no trouble with it."

"Just keep up with your work," Berdine said, moving away. "If you must read, do it at night. You can use a lamp."

Content to know that I had begun to make my way home, I went to work with a lighter heart. I spun wool, helped Lesley feed the sheep, and dumped old food into the pigs' trough. I helped wash clothes, mend tunics, and gave Berdine a hand in the kitchen when necessary. And at night, when everyone else had gone to bed, I went back to the tables where we ate, lit a lamp, and read until my eyelids were too heavy to remain open.

Though the farm kept all of us busy, I thirsted for news of the outside world. At home, either Urbi or Father had informed me about what was happening in the world; I knew nearly as much about international affairs as I did about my neighbors in the Jewish Quarter. But on the farm, passing travelers were our only source of news.

I asked Berdine if she had heard anything else about Caesar's death, but Minos and I knew more than she did. Because she had been born in the city, Berdine also missed hearing news of the world, yet in her younger years she had gleaned her news from Rome itself. In the city, she told me, even those who could not read could learn of noteworthy events by studying the pictures scratched or painted onto public walls. "It is all there," she said. "Who is in love with who, who is selling her body, who has the best bread in town, and who is the worst swindler. Of course, some of the images are crude, and others only make sense if you know the people involved."

In April, at the Festival of Ludi Ceriales — an eight-day festival dedicated to Ceres, goddess of the harvest — Triton visited Domina at her country pleasure villa and returned with a report that gave all of us much to consider.

Cleopatra had been in Rome, he told us at dinner, when republicans in the Senate murdered Caesar. These killers accused Caesar of aspiring to tyranny and planning to establish a monarchy, but most of them were old men who did not favor Caesar's egalitarian approach to government. Instead of welcoming foreigners and individuals from the lower classes to the Senate as Caesar wished, they wanted to reserve the upper echelons of government for those who had been born from noble parents and therefore deserved to rule. "As if," Triton added, "the gods had declared power as their birthright."

"Tell me," I asked, edging carefully into the conversation, "what you heard about Cleopatra."

Triton replied that the Egyptian queen began to prepare for her journey home as soon as she heard of Caesar's murder. "No one could blame her," Triton said, passing a bowl of greens to Berdine, "for some accused her of being among those who planned Caesar's death. But when Caesar's will was read, he left her nothing. He left the house and grounds where she had been living to the people of Rome, and gave seventy-five drachmas to every male Roman citizen. And he named Domina's son as his heir."

"If he loved the Egyptian woman, why would he not mention her in his will?" Berdine asked.

"Because Egypt is the richest land in the world," I answered as I stirred my stew. "What could Caesar leave a woman who has everything?"

Several curious faces swiveled toward me as I spoke, but they returned to Berdine when she rapped for attention. "Given Octavian's new situation, will Domina make changes?" she asked. "Here, with us?"

Triton shrugged. "Who can say? She may leave us alone, for she has more pressing matters to consider right away. The gods are clearly angry. A thunderstorm followed Caesar's funeral, and for a week after his death, a burning star streaked the nighttime sky. When the heavens finally stilled, the Egyptian queen got into her ship and sailed back to her homeland. Apparently she was done with Caesar and Rome."

As the other slaves murmured among themselves, awed by Triton's stories of the rich and powerful, I rested my chin in my hand and closed my eyes. Did the entire world see Urbi as an evil seductress? She was neither a temptress nor a power monger. All she had ever wanted was to be the queen her father raised her to be, but how could she explain herself to Romans who sought a scapegoat for the murder of their beloved leader?

"There is more." Triton lowered his voice to a whisper. "The noble Cicero claims that Cleopatra was carrying a second child for Caesar when she sailed for Egypt . . . and this one was conceived on Roman soil. Cicero worries she will try to disrupt the transfer of power to Caesar's heir. If this foreign queen has another son, Gaius Octavian will lose the authority he would command as Caesar's legal son."

Prickles of unease lifted the hair at the back of my neck. Cleopatra, pregnant again? I thought of the many times we had pretended our clay dolls were babies. We had named them, given them personalities, and promised that we would never abandon them as our mothers had abandoned us.

Urbi and I were now twenty-six, and only

one of us had held her baby in her arms.

One chilly afternoon, as the sun was sliding toward twilight, Triton built a fire in the clearing outside our huts. We had all put in a long day, and the thought of spending a few minutes around the fire brought a little cheer to our hearts. Kepe and I were the first to claim places by the fireside, and within a few minutes we were joined by Vara, Alroy, and Meletta, who joked about her arthritic knees as she sank to a log behind the others in the circle.

Not everyone wanted to be social. Minos took one look at the comfortable gathering, grunted, and walked straight into the men's hut, presumably to go to bed. Cletus lingered a moment before withdrawing into the shadows, where he leaned against a tree and watched the women. Doreen came close to the fire, held up her hands, and then proceeded to show us a dance from her homeland. Vara and Meletta started clapping, and the more they clapped, the better Doreen danced, the hem of her tunic flaring outward as she twirled in the firelight, her coppery hair tinged with highlights from the fire.

I sat with the others and smiled, grateful that even we slaves were able to find moments of joy in our lives. While the farm demanded a lot from us, Triton and Berdine were reasonable overseers, perhaps because they worked as hard as we did. Domina left us alone for the most part, and so long as the farm turned a profit, she would probably continue to do so.

"YHVH Ro'i," I whispered, remembering the Hebrew for yet another name of HaShem. *"YHVH my Shepherd, the one who keeps and protects."* He had certainly kept me through every circumstance.

Triton approached the campfire, his wide mouth stretched into a rare grin. "Tum, can you sing us one of the songs of Egypt?"

The old man, who rarely spoke, lifted his head and looked at me. I understood at once — Triton had asked the question in Latin, and Tum probably spoke only Egyptian or Aramaic.

I translated Triton's request into Aramaic while the old man listened, his face impassive. When I had finished, he looked at Triton, and for a moment I thought he would refuse. Then, with a dignity we rarely saw in the country, Tum stood, thrust back his shoulders, and lifted his arms as he began to sing. His voice was parchment-thin and reedy, the tune quavery and unpredictable, but when he finished, Tum lowered his arms and saluted us with a smart dip of his chin.

We broke into spontaneous applause, and I marveled at the mystery of the little Egyptian man. What had he been before he came here? Where had he lived in Egypt?

I would never get a chance to ask. Before our clapping stopped, a blade flew through the air and struck the old man's bare chest. Tum looked down, his eyes widening when he saw the handle protruding from his breastbone. Then he looked at me and crumpled beside the fire.

Triton, Darby, and Alroy sprang to their feet, and the rest of us spun around to see a band of five men at the edge of our gathering. Dressed in the rough tunics of Roman soldiers, the men wore no armor, but carried knives, swords, and spears. Unlike the typical Roman soldier, they were not clean-shaven, but scruffy, and the eyes with which they stared at us were bold and brazen.

"We are hungry." The apparent leader stepped forward, his eyes roving around the circle of seated women as he drew his sword. "And we are tired. You will feed us, pleasure us, and let us rest here. If you do not complain, we will allow the rest of you to live. If you resist, you will be joining your friend over there." He jerked his chin toward the spot where Tum lay motionless.

"We have nothing to give you," Triton said, standing. His chest seemed to swell as a warning cloud settled over his features. "This is the Octavii farm, and the family keeps nothing of value here."

"I wouldn't say that." A second intruder emphasized his remark by spitting toward Triton's feet. "I see women. I see tables. If we looked around a bit, I am sure we could find a jug of ale and some food."

"You will not touch our women," Triton said, taking another step forward. "They belong to a noble Roman family. If you abuse them, you are abusing the property of —"

An owl hooted, and reflexively I glanced up to the trees. In that same instant, a spear flew across the fire and struck Triton's chest, knocking him backward and pinning him to a tree.

I gasped but was unable to draw enough air into my lungs to push a scream past my throat. Doreen shrieked and took off running while another of the intruders went into the woods after her.

As color drained from Triton's face, he reached for Berdine and made a noise that sounded like several languages jumbled together. She hurried to his side, her arms reaching up to cradle his face.

"Now," the leader said, "perhaps one of you ladies can fetch us some dinner?"

At the mention of food, Berdine seemed to collect herself. She turned and lowered her head. "Go!" she shouted, her voice hoarse. "Run!"

Like the others, I sprang to my feet and fled.

The owl.

Running. Straining to see in the darkness, leaping over shadows, falling on my knees, running again.

Sweating, despite the chill of the night.

Screams in the distance. Shouts and curses.

A flash of Triton's surprised face; Berdine's insistent plea: "Run!"

I was. Running. Running. Couldn't breathe.

I dashed into the vineyard, where the aging vines had formed living walls. I crouched behind them and crawled in the dirt, seeking out a hollow where I could hide myself.

Another scream echoed from the clearing.

I spotted an opening in the vines and squirmed into position, ducking my head beneath a gnarled vine, forcing my knees to my forehead, tucking my feet out of sight.

Thick clouds blanketed the moon as I took deep breaths, trying to calm my heart.

A sudden memory — hiding in Urbi's garden in a similar position, trying to calm my breath lest I burst out in laughter.

My blood banged in my ears; the rhythmic beat kept time with my frantic panting.

All was quiet. Breathe.

A dead branch snapped. The clouds parted, and a stream of moonlight fell on my tunic, turning it silver. A beacon.

I closed my eyes. *Please do not let him see me, please do not let him see me, please do not let him see me, please —*

My eyes flew open as a dried leaf crunched. A foot appeared just beyond a sheltering branch, close enough for me to count the taut stitches in the leather between the intruder's toes.

I bit my lower lip until I tasted blood. The sandaled foot moved away.

Overcome by relief, I slipped into oblivion.

I woke in the dirt, felt gritty soil on my fingertips, and gasped as horrific memories came rushing back. I rolled onto my side, nearly choking on the bolus of vomit that rose in my throat, and crawled out of the muddy depression where I'd hidden.

Despair rose inside me like a fountain,

sending rivulets of agony in every direction. Branches scraped my cheeks and twigs snapped beneath my palms as I crawled, afraid to stand lest I be spotted by the enemy. I heard a soft tapping of blown rain, the wind whistling through the cypress trees, and somewhere, women keening.

I drew a deep breath and realized the attackers were gone. The women would not mourn unless they were.

Slowly, I stood and walked out of the vineyard, back to the huts.

I hesitated at the edge of the clearing and looked around. I saw Tum lying where he had fallen. Triton, dead now, pinned to the tree, his arms ending abruptly at the wrist. Behind our vilicus, Alroy, tied to another tree and disemboweled. Vara lay still at his feet, her skin a pale shade of blue.

Were all of the others dead? Had I imagined the sounds of grief?

I crept backward, sank to the earth, and curled into a ball. *HaShem, God of Israel, are you seeing this?*

"Operam! Nunc ergo veni foras!"

The commanding voice woke me, and I felt grateful for the authority in it. I crawled back to the tree line, then lifted my head to see a unit of Roman soldiers, fully armed and uniformed. The captain stood at the embers of our fire, his sword drawn and his face a mask of distaste.

Slowly I stood, bracing myself on a nearby tree as my legs trembled beneath my weight.

One of the soldiers saw me and nudged the commander, then pointed in my direction.

The captain's features softened. "Come out, woman, and tell us what happened here."

I glanced left and right. Surely I wasn't the only one who survived the night. The others were probably hiding or had run for their lives.

I took a few steps forward. "Outlaws," I said, struggling to find the right Latin words amid the jumbled thoughts in my head. "They wore military tunics, no armor. But they had weapons."

"What did they want?"

I lowered my gaze. "Everything. They took . . . anything they could get."

The captain came closer and pointed to a tree stump near the fire circle. "Sit."

I sat.

"Now . . ." The captain squatted before me, and for the first time I could clearly see his face. "Who is your master?"

"We belong — this farm belongs — to

Atia, mother to Gaius Octavian Caesar."

The captain shot a sharp glance to his second in command, then turned back to me. "And how many slaves lived here?"

"Fourteen. Twenty pigs. Twenty-five sheep. Two dogs. A cat." I shivered. "The others must be hiding."

The captain stood and looked into the woods. "Dead or alive, we'll find them."

By the end of the day, the Roman soldiers had completed their work. Five out of the fourteen slaves were dead: Triton, Vara, Alroy, Tum, and Kepe. One of the pigs had been slaughtered, and one of the lambs was missing, probably carried away. Doreen was also missing.

"Could be anywhere," the captain said, speaking to those of us who remained. We had gathered around the cold fire, taking warmth from one another. "She might have fallen off a cliff or drowned in a lake. She might still be running."

"Or they might have taken her," Berdine said, her eyes hard. "Men like that —"

"We will send a message to your domina," the captain promised. "In the meantime, take care of each other and get back to work when you can. Your mistress will expect you to continue with your duties."

I stared at him, too numb and astounded to voice my horror. Continue with our duties? As if nothing had happened?

I looked around, examining the others for visible signs of damage. Berdine's cheek bore a bruise the size of a man's fist, plus she had lost her husband. Cletus's tunic was torn and dotted with burrs, so I suspected he had run through the woods and escaped most of the trouble. Barabell was untouched, but she clung desperately to Darby, leading me to believe that the outlaws had gotten the best of both Gauls.

Minos had a swollen eye, a cracked lip, and a gash in his upper arm — he had not run. He had fought and been beaten. Lesley was both bruised and disheveled, her tunic torn, and I was fairly certain she had been violated. Meletta, the old woman, appeared to be untouched. I later learned that she had run to the olive grove and climbed a tree. The intruders never found her.

"We will be going now," the Roman captain said, picking up his helmet. "Your mistress will be in touch."

He turned, and his men with him, and began the long walk down the avenue that led to the Via Appia. I watched them go, feeling as though someone had just pulled a warm blanket from my frozen body, leaving me alone to shiver in the dark.

Berdine stood and faced us. “As your vilica,” she said, her voice cracking, “I would urge you to sleep. Tomorrow I will tend to your wounds, and we will go on. The captain —” she paused to draw a deeper breath — “the captain said that group has been terrorizing small farms for miles around, but they will be caught. They will not bother us again.”

A smile flickered over her lips, a smile that might have been the bravest effort I had witnessed in hours.

Swallowing the sob that rose in my throat, I stood, embraced Berdine, then walked slowly to my hut.

And as I lay on my collection of piled rags, I pressed my hand over my face and remembered *YHVH Nisi, YHVH my banner, the God who protects.* I had escaped physical harm, but I would never forget the horrors I had seen. Yet even though I was a slave, the lowest of the low, I had a defender even greater than the men who had come to our aid: *YHVH Makah, the one who smites and punishes sin.*

Powerful knowledge, but it brought little comfort in those moments. I pulled a worn sheet over my shoulders in an effort to stop my shivering, and yearned for Yosef.

■ ■ ■ ■

We buried our dead and tended our wounds. Our domina did not come to the farm, but sent a parcel of food, wine, and new tunics, as if those items could assuage the pain we had endured.

Over the next several weeks, we accustomed ourselves to new roles, as the work of maintaining a farm could not be ignored. Minos took over Triton's role as vilicus, and Lesley tended the pigs Kepe had left behind. We all worked a little harder and spoke little about the attack.

Grief hung over the farm for months. A heavy sky, pregnant with unshed rain, drooped over the earth and blocked the sun. Later, scribes would record that the sun did not show its face during the year after Caesar's death. Berdine declared that the gods were mourning Caesar, but I wondered if HaShem was mourning the loss of Cleopatra's second child. For no word came of a second birth, and no second son of Caesar's was ever acknowledged.

By the time we marked the anniversary of Caesar's death, I realized that Urbi must have lost her second baby. And despite my anger toward my former friend, I could not rejoice in her sorrow.

With Triton gone, Berdine reached out to me for friendship. Though she was an unsophisticated, earthy woman, she hungered for stories of wealthy people, fine cities, and distant queens. I did not tell her about growing up in the royal palace because I did not think she would believe me. Even if she had, I decided it was not wise to reveal my relationship with a queen who was unpopular in Rome.

But because Berdine hungered for tales of life more exotic than what she had known, I told her about Alexandria's wide streets, the wealth of marble statues, the many exotic obelisks, and the brilliant ships in the harbor. I described rich dinners in noblemen's houses and dining off plates of gold and drinking from tankards of fine silver. I described our coins, most decorated with images of the queen, and smiled when Berdine said she had heard everything worth hearing about the mysterious Cleopatra who bewitched the mighty Caesar.

I suppose my stories were the only entertainment Berdine had, but somehow she learned to trust me. I would say we became good friends.

"How far away," I asked her one day, "is Rome?"

She lifted a ragged gray brow. "By foot or horse?"

"Foot."

She shrugged. "Seven or eight days. Domina usually takes ten days when she comes, but of course the family travels by litter with their slaves. They stay with friends on the journey and make a party of it, spending as much time at dinner and drink as traveling on the road."

"Are they coming any time soon?"

"Domina will come when she is able," Berdine said. "They always spend the festival days of Lemuria at their country estate, and sometimes stop here to examine the orchard and vineyard. So we — those of us who are left — must be at our best."

"They come *here* when Rome fills with festival goers?"

"Domina doesn't care for bloody sports, and the days of Lemuria are filled with gladiatorial contests. She told me that once she saw a herd of elephants killed in an event sponsored by Pompey. The animals seemed human to her, and she never got over it. She will not go to the arena again, if she can help it."

I shuddered at the thought of the gladiatorial arena. Egypt had not yet caught the blood fever that seemed to infect so many

Romans. While horse racing and animal fighting were popular among the Egyptians, gladiatorial contests had not yet become commonplace in Alexandria.

I hoped they never would.

Once things settled down at the farm, I returned to my study of midwifery. Reading not only took my mind away from dark memories, it also renewed my hope. Every night, while my little oil lamp poured a stream of weak light over the scroll on the table, I read about pregnancy, childbirth, and pregnancy prevention.

To discover if a woman was pregnant, the scroll advised, the midwife should keep emmer wheat and barley seeds moistened with the woman's urine. If the seeds sprouted, she was pregnant.

A woman who had trouble getting pregnant should go to bed with a clove of garlic between her thighs. If she woke with garlic on her breath, all the channels were open and she would be able to conceive.

Pliny the Elder wrote that boys were delivered more easily than girls, and I noted the truth of his words, for Barabell's baby had not involved a great deal of fuss or bother.

For more difficult labors, Pliny said, fumigations with the fat from hyena loins would produce immediate delivery. Also, placing the right foot of a hyena on the woman would result in an easy delivery, but placing the left foot in the same spot would cause death.

I made a note in the margin — *tie a string around the hyena's right foot to avoid mistakes.* But where would I find a hyena in the city?

A drink sprinkled with powdered sow's dung would relieve labor pains, as would sow's milk mixed with honey wine.

Fortunately, we had plenty of sows, so obtaining the required dung or milk wouldn't be a problem in the country. But would they be available in Rome? Finding honey wine might prove difficult in the country, but should be easily procurable in the city.

Delivery could be eased by drinking goose semen mixed with water, or the liquids that flow from a weasel's uterus through its genitals.

Since I had no idea how to obtain either of those items, I read on.

The root of vervain in water, Scordotis in hydromel, and dittany leaves were recommended for the lying-in woman. Amulets and other objects were also considered efficacious. To withdraw the infant, a midwife should obtain the afterbirth of a canine bitch, make sure it had not touched the ground, and place it on the woman's thighs. Or tie a snake's slough to the woman's thigh, but be sure to remove it immediately after delivery of the child.

A vulture's feather might be placed under the woman's feet to aid delivery. A sneeze would relieve difficult labor. And drinking hedge mustard in tepid wine on an empty stomach would also ease labor pains.

Earthworms taken in raisin wine, Pliney insisted, would bring away the placenta.

I looked at the list of recommended treatments and scratched through anything I knew nothing about. I also slashed through amulets, for they were far too much like graven images for my comfort. I wasn't sure where to find a snake's shed skin or a dog's afterbirth, but if I did find them, I could always preserve them in a clay pot.

"A suitable person for midwife," the author concluded, "will be literate, able to keep her wits about her, possessed of a good memory, a hard worker, respectable and not unduly handicapped, sound of limb, robust, and endowed with long, slim fingers and short nails at her fingertips. She should be of sympathetic disposition and keep her hands soft so as not to cause discomfort to mother or child. She should also be free of superstition so as not to overlook some beneficial measure on account of a dream or omen."

After reading the summary, I felt certain I would be a good midwife. Surely a woman who used common sense and followed the principles of the Torah would be more effective than one who surrounded herself with pagan idols and amulets. I would be a simple midwife, relying on cleanliness and HaShem's design of the body. After all, who would better know how to care for a mother and child than the God who designed procreation?

All I needed now was practice . . . and several heavily pregnant women.

Chapter Twenty

The sound of an approaching drumbeat pulled me to the doorway of the women's hut. Anticipating our mistress's arrival, Berdine had given each of us a clean tunic, then she had plaited my hair and sewn the plaits so they draped in loops around my head. Her attempt at hairdressing was a far cry from the fashionable arrangements Nuru used to create for me, but I thanked Berdine for her trouble.

"I am hoping Domina likes you," Berdine said, her generous nature shining on her face. "I do not know which god sent you to us, but you do not need to be picking grapes when you could be delivering babies or teaching someone to read. I am going to introduce you to Domina at exactly the right moment."

I leaned against the doorframe and watched from the shadows as a pair of horsemen came into view, followed by two slaves beating drums. After the drummers, three gilded litters arrived, surrounded by a large company of slaves. The first litter held a tall, thin youth in a white toga, whom I assumed was Gaius Octavian Caesar. The second litter carried Atia, our domina and mother to our master. The last was occupied by a young woman, whom I assumed to be Octavia, sister to Gaius Octavian. As the family members stepped out of their litters and approached the villa, I shrank back into the women's hut. Young Gaius had the appearance of one who noticed everything, and I did not want to be spotted before Berdine could make proper introductions.

I tried to remain quiet and calm, but I was hoping that her plan worked. Why should I risk my life trying to escape when my mistress might transport me to Rome? Berdine's plan was far better than mine, and I looked forward to meeting the woman who could change my future in a moment.

After arranging for the family's refreshment and rest, Berdine came to the hut and grabbed my hand. "Here," she said, handing me a pole with wide feathers at the end. "Domina has just complained about the heat. You know what to do."

I turned the fan and smothered a smile. As a youngster, I had sat beneath dozens of similar fans, though I had never held one. Nevertheless, I followed Berdine into the villa and silently moved to a position behind Domina, who was reclining on a couch. Carefully, I moved the fan back and forth in a constant rhythm.

"Oh, that's much better." The woman adjusted the front of her dress and smoothed her throat. "Thank you, Berdine, for seeing to my comfort." She glanced upward, her dark eyes fixing on me. "I do not recognize this one."

"Domina." Berdine bent forward at the waist. "Chava has been with us over a year."

"So long?" The woman looked up, her eyes vacant and distracted. "Where was she acquired?"

"Triton arranged for the delivery of more slaves after the Gaulish woman died. But this one, my lady, is not suited for the farm."

Domina's features hardened in a stare of disapproval. "Is she rebellious? I could have her whipped —"

"No, not rebellious. Indeed, she is quite agreeable. Furthermore, she has been educated. She reads and writes. She is studying to be a midwife."

The noblewoman shuddered. "I simply do not understand why anyone would want to perform such work. The girl must be Greek."

"She comes from Egypt, my lady. From Alexandria."

"Have her present herself."

I lifted a brow, amused that the woman would not simply look up at me. But I lowered my fan, walked around the couch, and stood before her.

"Why has the air stopped moving? This room is stifling."

Quickly, another slave stepped forward to take the fan.

When the mistress pinned me in a long, silent scrutiny, I lowered myself to the floor and bowed.

"Lift your head, girl."

I did as I was told.

The mistress squinted at me. "You speak Greek?"

"Yes, Domina. And Aramaic, Hebrew, and Latin."

"You read and write these tongues?"

I nodded.

"Speak, girl. Do not be impertinent."

"Yes, Domina."

"Read this." She pulled a small scroll from her sleeve and handed it to me. I bowed as I accepted it, then lifted the seal and read the words: "My dear Atia: May the gods continue to favor you! We have missed you at our dinners, and would appreciate it if you would grace us with your presence again. Could you —"

"Enough." The woman held out her hand, and I returned the scroll.

"Have you ever taught children?"

"I have not, but I believe I could. Yet I would rather practice midwifery."

I had spoken honestly, openly — as I would have responded in Alexandria if someone had asked the question of me. But I had not answered as a slave.

The woman stiffened as if I had struck her. "Do you think I care what you would rather do?"

"Please, Domina." Berdine stepped forward, her head low. "She has been studying hard; I am sure she spoke out of enthusiasm. She will serve you well in whatever capacity you choose. She is a clever girl, obedient and honest."

The woman shot me a penetrating look, then nodded at Berdine. "One thing is certain — we will not waste such a lovely thing out here in the wilds. When we pass this way on our return from the country, we will pick her up and take her to Rome. Now, girl — take the fan and keep the air moving before I expire."

As I resumed my place, the mistress smiled at Berdine. "I will see that extra sestertii is added to your wages this year. You have served us well."

I worried that Atia would forget her promise to return for me, so my nerves were strung as tight as a bowstring when the family caravan appeared on the road. After looking out of her litter to make sure I found a place in line, Atia uttered words that made my heart tremble: "Good. You will deliver my daughter's baby."

Octavia was pregnant?

Now I walked, shivering, toward the first real test of all I had learned in my study of midwifery. My mind vibrated with a thousand possibilities — I could make a mistake and kill the mother. I could kill the child, or I could kill them both. And this would not be just any mother and child, but relatives of Gaius Octavian Caesar, one of the men whose name carried great authority in Rome.

The Octavii family did not travel lightly. I was one of many in a parade of slaves whose titles ranged from butler to kitchen slaves. The *anteambulones* went before the procession to clear the way for the family's litters, and half a dozen maids followed Atia's conveyance, carrying incidentals she might want on the journey: wraps, feathered fans, and fabric sunshades. Next came a pair of horses hitched to a cart that carried the family's trunks and supplies, and finally, oiled and armored gladiators, matched pairs that walked at the beginning and end of the procession to provide a show of strength.

We traveled for days, and though I would have gladly asked questions of the slaves who traveled with me, few of them seemed kindly disposed toward a newcomer. Those who did speak above a whisper were shushed by others, so we trudged silently northward, forcing other travelers from the road as our procession made its way to the city of seven hills.

From what I had heard of Rome's greatness, I expected to see another Alexandria rise from the hills in gleaming splendor. But the city that opened before me was nothing like my home. Rome had no seacoast, only the Tiber — a winding, muddy river that marked the city's northern border. The streets were scarcely wide enough for a wagon, and serpentine, turning and twisting without warning.

As we made our way to Palatine Hill where the Octavii family resided, we passed by tall buildings. The lower apartments were storefronts selling various goods, but evidence of renters — laundry, flower boxes, and balconies — appeared on higher stories. Wooden shutters framed the windows, and in several of those openings I spied men and women who looked down and pointed to our procession as we passed. These poorly constructed *insulate* housed dozens of families. I shuddered as we walked by, realizing that a single wayward spark could enflame one of these structures and consume every occupant within minutes.

Palatine Hill, I later learned, had been built on ancient ruins that reportedly stretched back to the time of Romulus and Remus, the founders of Rome. According to the story, the two infants, sons of Mars, had been abandoned on the flooded Tiber and washed up at the foot of the Palatine. There they were discovered by a she-wolf who nursed them until they were able to fend for themselves.

I expected to see expansive homes of gleaming white limestone like those in Alexandria, but the houses of Rome were plain in comparison. The buildings seemed pathetically similar, brick structures finished in stucco and offering no windows except on the upper stories. I saw no gardens, no statuary, no fountains, and no sparkling colors to entice the eye. If grandeur resided in Rome, it must live on the *inside* of the buildings.

We stopped outside a home that appeared larger than most. A mosaic path led from the street to the front door, yet other than a few potted palms, the open courtyard was unfurnished. The family members climbed from their litters. Amid a chorus of complaints about the length of the journey, they approached the carved front door. A slave opened it, bowed, and waited outside until they had all entered.

Once the family was inside, the slaves seemed to slump in relief. Relaxed chatter filled the air like birdsong as the gladiators dismounted and walked their horses around the house, presumably to a stable. Several female slaves sat on the raised walkway along the side of the street and examined their blistered feet while others pulled baskets and trunks from the wagon.

I stood alone and wondered if any of the other slaves would speak to me. A couple of them had hissed when I stepped out of formation on the journey, but none of them had proven as friendly as the slaves on the farm.

Finally, a dignified man in a white tunic approached. "You." He pointed to me.

"Speak Latin?"

He had addressed me in Aramaic, so I understood him easily. "Yes, but I am more fluent in Greek."

"I am Helios. Come with me."

We walked up to the house, where he opened the door. *"Vestibule,"* he said, pointing to the space between the door and the street. "And this is the *ostium.*" He pointed to the doorway.

I nodded. Mosaic tiles covered the wide threshold, where someone had arranged light-colored tiles in the word *Salve.* Welcome. Above the doorway, embedded in the transom, tiles spelled *Nihil intret malī.* No evil may enter. I hoped the saying would prove true.

Glancing around, I saw an older man sitting on a stool against the wall. "Doorman," Helios said. Above the doorman's head, the wall had been decorated with a mosaic featuring a chained dog. Across the bottom, Latin letters spelled *Cave Canem!* Beware of the dog!

"Is there a dog?" I asked.

He smiled for the first time. "Not anymore."

He peered into the next room, then held up his hand, warning me to wait. Looking over his shoulder, I saw Atia and Octavia conversing in an open doorway. When they went their separate ways, Helios motioned me forward. "We never walk through a room when a member of the family occupies it," he said. "Walk around the house if you must, but never appear before the mistress unless you are summoned. Domina believes that slaves should do their work without being seen."

"A fine trick," I muttered.

Helios shot me a stern look. "You will learn how we do things here," he said, "but it will take time. I am trying to make things easier for you."

"Sorry." I offered a small smile. "Forgive me."

He led the way into the atrium, a room that reminded me of home. The large rectangular chamber featured a reflecting pool in the center. Above the pool, the ceiling opened to the sky, allowing light and air into the space. To the right and left I saw doorways leading into smaller rooms. I turned to my right, almost expecting to see my father at work on a manuscript.

"The atrium," Helios said, spreading his hands. "These smaller rooms are for dining, reading, or sleeping. Beyond the atrium" — he pointed to a wider doorway at the rear of the house — "is the peristylium, which features the garden and kitchen. You'll spend most of your time there, unless someone in the family calls for you."

I nodded. "My home in Alexandria was similar. We preferred light colors, though, and not so much . . . red."

Helios grunted. "As much as I would love to discuss color palettes with you, I have no time for such foolishness. Let me introduce you to the man who really runs this house."

Already I had realized that urban slaves operated in an entirely different pecking order than those on the farm. At the top, Helios explained, was our mistress's assistant, the amanuensis who wrote her letters and attended to her schedule. He was an educated Greek called Amphion.

We found the man in the garden, where he was choosing linens from a basket. When he had finished, he looked at me. "And this is?"

I dipped my head in a polite bow. "Chava."

Peering down his nose, Amphion took my measure in one glance and seemed to find me lacking. "Helios," he asked, a note of exasperation in his voice, "where did we find this one?"

"On the farm."

"That might explain the dirt under her nails. Go at once, girl —"

"Amphion?" Domina's voice startled all of us. Coming into the garden, Atia pulled her veil from her hair and released a tinkle of laughter. "Be kind to that one — she reads, writes, and delivers babies. She is going to deliver Octavia; then we can hire her out as a midwife."

"She is literate?" Amphion looked to Domina, but she had already wandered away. When he frowned, I intuited that he did not want anyone encroaching upon his responsibilities.

"If it please you —" I began, keeping my gaze lowered.

"Silence." He cut me off with a stern look. "You will not speak unless directly addressed. You will not look up unless asked a direct question. And you will never, ever, look your mistress or a superior slave in the eye. Do you understand?"

"I apologize." I kept my head down. "But until this moment, I did not know one slave could be superior to another. Are we not all property and owned by the same woman?"

Silence simmered between the three of us for a moment, then Helios laughed, breaking the tension. "She has a point," he said. "Just because one slave has more responsibility than another does not make him a free man."

Amphion's scowl deepened. "Go with Helios," he said, jerking his head toward a room at the back of the house. "He will set you to work."

Helios took me to the kitchen, where the cook was choosing vegetables from a boy who struggled beneath the weight of a produce basket.

Helios tilted his head. "Do you cook?"

"Not well."

"What *do* you do?"

"I can spin wool and embroider," I told him. "I read, write, and speak Greek, Aramaic, Latin, and a bit of Egyptian. And I have studied midwifery."

He nodded, scratched his head, and gestured for me to turn around. I did, moving slowly, and when I had finished, he clicked his tongue against his teeth. "First, we get something to fatten you up," he said, his voice heavy with weariness. "Then we scrub the dirt from the back of your neck and give you a decent tunic. When you are fit to be seen, we will ask Domina how you should spend your days. But know this — in this house, the slaves are always well-groomed and clean. Any slave who does not keep herself tidy will be sent to the farm or the slave market."

He pulled a folded square of linen from a

shelf in the kitchen, then gave me a small loaf of bread and pointed the way to the bathhouse.

Helios was not jesting when he said he would have someone scrub the dirt from the back of my neck. I had just settled into the steaming bath when another slave entered the room and smiled at me. "The butler sent me," she said, kneeling at the side of the pool. "He said I am to scrub your skin until it is pink."

I instinctively recoiled when she picked up an instrument that looked like a blade.

"This is a strigil." She held up the instrument for my examination. "Do not worry, it is not sharp enough to cut. It is used for scraping dirt off your skin."

Relaxing slightly, I lifted my hair from the nape of my neck and settled on the stone seat in the pool. "I am Chava."

"I am Sabina."

"How long have you been here?"

The girl shrugged. "Five years? Six? This" — she waved a hand to indicate the bathhouse — "is my domain. I keep the water hot, the towels clean, and a strigil at hand."

She dipped the blade in the warm water and began scraping it over my neck. "I have a rinse to clean your hair, and a brush to scrub beneath your nails."

I peered at her from beneath the fringe of my damp hair. "I can clean myself, you know."

"Next time you will," she answered. "But this time, we will make certain you meet Helios's standards. He is meticulous, that one."

Gradually, I relaxed as she scrubbed my skin and worked a pumice stone over the soles of my feet. I could almost close my eyes and pretend I was home, where Nuru had performed these duties for me.

Sabina kept up a steady stream of chatter as she scrubbed, probably to ease my nervousness. I learned that she liked her work, that she had come from another household where she had been required to look after children, and she liked her new position better. In the course of talking about the other slaves, she mentioned one name more than once.

"And who is this Duran," I asked, giving her a sly smile, "that you should mention him in every other sentence?"

A flush rose from her neckline and colored her cheeks. "Is it so obvious? He works in the stable and I adore him."

I smiled, amused by the thought of love flourishing in even dire circumstances.

"Does this Duran return your adoration?"

"He does." A smile trembled over her lips. "We are hoping to earn our freedom so we can marry. But even if that day never comes, it is enough that we are together now."

I made a small sound of agreement because I did not know what else to say.

"Have you ever been in love?" Sabina asked.

"I might have been," I admitted. "My father was always bringing young men to the house — bright and handsome. I always felt I was meant to be something other than a wife, but one man —"

"His name?"

I smiled, recalling Yosef's face. "His name does not matter, but he said he would always wait for me." My smile faded. "I do not believe he is still waiting. Even love's patience has a limit."

Sabina crouched beside me, her eyes filling with pity. "You must open your heart to someone else. Love is everywhere."

"Even for a slave?"

"Why should slaves not know love?" Her words were convicting, but she spoke them gently. "It would be easier if I did not love Duran, but then what joy would I find in this life? Because I love him, and I know he loves me, I love being part of this household.

I love being where he is, and I would follow him anywhere. And who can say? Perhaps you will find someone to love among the slaves in this house."

"But —" I stopped when a man in a slave's tunic entered the bathhouse. He halted at the threshold, his eyes roving over my submerged body, and the smile he gave me was nothing less than lecherous.

"Thanatos!" Sabina snapped. "You should not be in here."

"I smell of horse," he said, turning his head to sniff beneath his hairy arm. "The mistress has sent for me, but she will have me whipped if she catches a whiff of the animals."

"Wait outside," Sabina commanded.

I froze as images from the farm flitted through my mind. The men who attacked us had been brutes like this one, and they had smelled of animals and sweat and feral living. A man like this one had almost caught me —

"Chava?"

Shivering, I closed the curtain on my dark memories and met Sabina's gaze. "Yes?"

"He is gone."

I looked behind her and saw only empty space. Only then did I feel my shoulders slump and realize how tense I had been.

"Who was that?" I asked.

Sabina sighed. "Thanatos, the stable master. He is a crude sort."

"I am surprised Domina would keep a slave like that. Or that Helios would let him into the house."

"He usually confines himself to the barn," Sabina said. "But he has always made me uneasy. He is always staring at the girls, and once he tried to — well, it is a good thing Helios interrupted when he did." She stopped scraping and looked at me. "We slaves have no legal recourse if we are ill-used. Most masters do not want to hear about our troubles. I have heard of girls becoming pregnant and then being sold because their masters thought a big belly spoiled their beauty."

I looked away as my face burned. I had heard Urbi dismiss slaves for the same reason, and at the time I thought her reasons sound.

"Stay clear of that one," Sabina said, scraping my skin again. "And do not ever think you can snatch a nap in the barn. Better to curl up on the hard kitchen floor than to let your guard down near Thanatos."

She swished the strigil in the water, then picked up a sponge, dipped it in a basin of cool water, and dribbled it over my shoulders.

"If all the male slaves were as gallant as Duran, this would be a perfect place." She stood and picked up a folded piece of linen, unfolded it, and held it up.

I stepped out of the pool and into the large square, wrapping the linen around me. "What would you do if Domina sold Duran?"

Sabina shrugged. "Why should I worry about that until it happens? That would spoil all the joy I feel today." She pulled a clean tunic from a basket. "Here," she said, handing me the white garment. "Sometimes Domina will want you to wear something more festive, but we wear these tunics every day."

When I had pulled the linen tunic over my head, she nodded, tied a rope belt around my waist, then ran her fingers through my tangled hair. "You will do very well here," she said, smiling, "if you learn to relax and enjoy the place. Others have not been nearly as fortunate."

Chapter Twenty-One

That was how I came to find myself living in the seat of worldly power. As HaShem would have it, a great deal of that authority emanated from a home in which I was one of forty slaves who served five people.

The eldest member of the household was Lucius Marcius Phillipus, an aristocrat who claimed descent from the royal line of Macedon, the same line that had produced Alexander the Great and Cleopatra. Lucius spent his days meeting with visitors who called on him for political favors and expert opinions. As Atia's second husband, he had little to do with her adult children who sprang from a different marriage. Unfortunately, he died not long after I joined the household.

After Lucius's death, Atia became the authority in our home. Our domina was fond of reminding visitors that she was descended from the Julii clan, whose members traced their lineage to the years before the founding of Rome. She was also great-niece to the late Julius Caesar, and mother to Caesar's heir, Gaius Octavius.

Octavia, Atia's daughter, had married Gaius Claudius Marcellus, another man who seemed content to let his wife handle the family affairs. Gaius Marcellus was at least twenty-five years older than his bride, who expected their first child around the turn of the year. Though I suppose Octavia and her husband could have set up their own household, they preferred to live with Atia — perhaps because Atia's house was large and elegant, or perhaps Octavia wished to remain close to her mother and brother. In any case, Atia and her grown children were as close as a fingernail is to the quick.

Nineteen-year-old Gaius Octavius was Atia's son and, due to Caesar's bequest, arguably the wealthiest man in Rome. When he began to call himself Gaius Julius Caesar Octavian, he could also boast of wielding the republic's most powerful name. While he was of average height, slender and physically unimpressive, I found him to be reasonable, studious, and admirably cautious.

As I worked in Rome, I learned lessons I would never have learned in Alexandria. At home, I had been sheltered and spoiled by my association with Cleopatra. I had lacked for nothing, and whatever I wanted appeared simply because I asked for it.

But in Rome I learned practical lessons. From my fellow slaves I learned how to work hard, please a master, and value freedom. The Romans took their slaves for granted as I once had, but hours of eavesdropping in out-of-the-way corners alerted me to the tumultuous state of the world beyond my master's home. The nobility tended to forget that slaves had eyes, ears, minds, and opinions.

In those days Rome was not yet an empire, but the Roman republic was on its deathbed and gasping.

While slaves like Sabina seemed content to keep their heads down and do their work, I had been reared in a place where politics mattered a great deal. As I went about my daily duties — cleaning, serving wine, whatever I was asked to do — I could not ignore comments and whispers exchanged by family members. Through Atia, her husband, and her children, I learned what was happening outside the Octavii family.

Since Caesar's death, Octavian and Mark Antony had been involved in a struggle for power. Power required arms, and Octavian had won three thousand legionaries to his side by promising each man two thousand sestertii, more than twice their usual pay. When the Senate refused to make the payment, Octavian marched eight legions, cavalry, and auxiliary soldiers into Rome. Worried that his mother and sister might be taken hostage by Antony's forces, he had his family go into hiding — with their favorite slaves to care for them, of course. I remained with others at the house, to wait and watch the drama unfold.

When Octavian led his army into the city, the cheering citizenry elected him to supreme governance of the republic. He met Atia and Octavia at the Temple of Vesta, where he kissed them and made a sacrifice to the gods. A vulture swooped down and appeared to endorse his sacrifice, and the people took it as a sign that young Octavian had not only inherited Caesar's name and fortune, but also his power.

After attending her son's celebration, Atia came home, ate a light supper, and went to bed. When her handmaid went in to wake her the next morning, she found our mistress dead.

A steady stream of visitors came to the house to pay their respects. The women came with undone hair, the men with unshaven faces. The guests gathered in the atrium, where Atia had been laid next to the reflecting pool, and bent to kiss her cold lips.

The crowd quieted for the reading of the will. I was about to leave the room, figuring Domina's will held nothing to interest me, when Sabina plucked my sleeve and shook her head.

I stepped closer. "Why stay?"

"Because," she whispered, "many a woman's will has freed her slaves. I hope our mistress will do the same."

Could it be?

Scarcely able to breathe, I stood in the shadow of a column and dared not look at the executor who held a scroll in his hand.

"To her daughter Octavia, Atia leaves the country villa, all her jewelry, and her clothing. To Gaius Caesar Octavian, Atia leaves her farm, her house, the wax masks of her ancestors, and her slaves, knowing he will have need of well-trained servants in his household.

"And to Helios, the slave who ran her household for more years than Atia cared to recall, she bestows manumission."

A murmur ran through the room as onlookers turned to congratulate the faithful slave. Helios bowed his head and struck his breast, a gesture of aggrieved happiness. Atia had freed one slave, but not me.

I looked at Sabina and tried to summon a smile. "Apparently we are to serve Octavian."

"At least we are not likely to go hungry."

"That all depends," I replied, knowing that the richest men were often stingy. "Time will tell."

While I waited for HaShem to open the door for my return home, I paid careful attention to events unfolding around me. I knew nothing about Roman politics when I arrived in the city, but was eyewitness to astounding developments after the death of Julius Caesar.

Not long after my arrival, the Senate voted that a Commission of Three for the Ordering of the State would be established for five years. One of those three was Atia's son Octavian. Together with Marcus Antonius, commonly known as Mark Antony, and Marcus Aemilius Lepidus, the three men formed the Second Triumvirate — a triad of rulers to replace Caesar.

The Senate granted enormous power to the Triumvirate. Not only could the three men repeal and make laws, they also carved up the sprawling Roman Empire, each man assuming responsibility for a specific territory. Antony took Gaul, Lepidus took *Gallia Transalpina* and the two Spains, and Octavian accepted oversight of Africa, Arminia, and Sicily.

One evening I stood in a corner and waited for orders as Octavia and her husband reclined on couches in the atrium. Octavia's belly was expanding, so I kept a careful eye on her.

Yet Octavia was not thinking of her baby, but of her brother. "Why would they assign Africa to Octavian?" she said. "Nothing important ever happens in Africa."

"You are mistaken," her husband corrected. "Egypt and Cleopatra are Africa, and without Cleopatra's grain, Rome would starve. Your brother has been given greater power than you realize."

A thrill raced through me at the mention of my old friend. Perhaps Octavian would go to Egypt and take slaves with him . . .

The Triumvirate had problems they discussed only in private, usually in Octavian's study. As I served honey water and melon wafers to these important guests, the three discussed how they could raise the funds needed to finance their war against Brutus and Cassius, two murderers of Caesar who were still at large. Brutus and Cassius, the members of the Triumvirate agreed, would have to be defeated to keep republican opposition at bay.

After a thoughtful lull, Octavian leaned forward. "I have an answer — and there is precedent for it."

"Robbing the rich?" Antony jested.

Octavian did not smile. "A proscription. Lucius Cornelius Sulla organized one forty years ago. He not only eliminated his political opponents, he amassed a fortune from their confiscated estates."

Antony propped his chin on his fist. "Are you suggesting that we kill our enemies outright? And claim their property?"

Octavian nodded soberly. "In the name of Rome."

"The idea is fraught with risk," Lepidus said. "Organized murder?"

"Legal murder," Octavian answered. "And I myself am of two minds about it. The nobility will not like it, for our enemies are noblemen. But the common people will cheer us, especially when we point out that many of the dead were among those who plotted the death of Caesar."

"If there is legal precedent," Antony said, "and if it is for the good of the Republic, who can stop us?"

I stood like a pillar near the doorway, my eyes lowered and my lips compressed as the three men drew up a list of their enemies. The group grew ever more excited as the candles burned lower.

I had never heard of a proscription, but I knew my father would not have approved. This was not like the cleansing of the land when the Israelites entered Canaan, for the Canaanites had committed abominable practices and the land needed to be cleansed of their sin. As far as I could tell, many of the men on the proscription list had committed no crimes; they were on the list only because they were wealthy or because they had voiced an opinion critical of Antony, Lepidus, or Octavian. Since the Romans had gods who behaved like people, these three men took it upon themselves to behave like gods, deciding who lived and who died.

Since Rome had no organized force to carry out proscribed killings, nor a prison to incarcerate those who were marked for death, the proscription would be an open invitation to murder one's neighbor and be rewarded for it.

That night I prayed that HaShem would somehow speak to my master and show him that such killing was nothing less than premeditated murder.

But if HaShem spoke to Octavian, he did not listen.

Within hours of the list's publication, Roman streets ran with blood. Friends turned upon friends, fathers turned on their sons. Within moments, cherished wives became impoverished widows.

Dominus did not speak of the horrifying murders conceived beneath his roof, yet he enthusiastically approved. More than once I saw his face light with inspiration, then he jotted a name on a scroll, sealed it, and had one of the slave boys deliver it to Mark Antony, keeper of the proscription list.

For the next several weeks, horror and dread hung over Rome like a miasma. Former wives, disgruntled children, and creditors were the first to attack, but any privateer in hope of quick money could search for patricians in hiding and earn a fortune. Noblemen murdered each other in every conceivable fashion, then decapitated their victims in order to present evidence for the reward.

The slaves around me buzzed with stories: wealthy Romans were fleeing the city, abandoning their expensive togas in favor of simple tunics and rough mantles. Entire families slogged through the filthy sewers, breathing through their mouths as they held hands and hurried toward the country where they hoped to live in anonymity. Others climbed into the soot-covered rafters of their homes, baking beneath the sun's heat as looters ransacked the house in search of its occupants or their treasures.

As many as three hundred senators were murdered — among them Cicero, a leading Senate spokesman — and up to two thousand equites. In short, all those who had supported the concept of a self-governing Roman republic were eliminated.

One story in particular chilled me: One republican nobleman went into hiding when he discovered his name on the evolving proscription list. His wife, Turia, took all her gold and jewelry and sent it to her husband so he could afford to feed himself in hiding.

When the proscription ended several weeks later, Octavian pardoned Turia's husband. But Lepidus, who was in charge of affairs in the city of Rome, refused to acknowledge Octavian's decision. Turia went to Lepidus, prostrated herself before him, and asked him to recognize her husband's pardon. He did not extend his hand in mercy and lift her up, but had her dragged away and flogged.

My master, Octavian, was not at all

pleased when he heard the news. The other slaves seemed not to care about Dominus's political fate, but I knew our destinies were tied up in his. Though the Triumvirate came through the proscription united, I spotted cracks in the façade.

And I told myself that no people on earth were more scheming and bloodthirsty than the Romans.

I kept thinking of something I had once read from Euripides: *"Those whom God wishes to destroy, he first makes mad."*

Chapter Twenty-Two

The hour I had dreaded finally arrived.

Two weeks after the conclusion of the Saturnalia festival, an insistent shaking of my shoulder woke me from a deep sleep. Sabina crouched next to me, her eyes huge and glistening in the lamplight. "Come!" she hissed, pinching my arm to bring me fully awake. "Octavia has begun her travail."

I sat up, pulled my hair back and tied it with a leather strip, then slipped into a clean tunic and searched for the basket I had filled with materials. I nodded at Sabina and followed her to the bedroom Octavia had been using. Her elderly husband, Gaius Marcellus, sat on a chair beside the bed, his face pale in the dim light.

"Bring more lamps," I told Sabina, "and a basin of clean water."

I walked to the old statesman, who seemed bewildered to find himself amid so many women. "Would you rather wait in the garden, sir? There's a lovely moon in the sky."

He took my none-too-subtle hint and pulled himself out of the chair. "You will call me when my son arrives?"

"Or your daughter." I stepped aside to let him pass.

I lingered a moment in the doorway. "HaShem, author of life and children," I whispered, closing my eyes, "guide my hands tonight." In a flash that was barely comprehendible, a name came to me: *YHVH Tzva'ot, YHVH of angel armies.* Armies that inspired confidence.

When I opened my eyes, Octavian stood before me, clad only in a light robe. "Chava," he said, his eyes gleaming black and dangerous in the lamplight, "my mother took you off the farm because you assured her you could deliver a baby. But know this — if you have lied, or if any harm comes to my sister or her child, I will have you beaten to death."

He spoke in a clear and calm voice, meaning every word. My stomach tightened further as Octavian stepped back and nodded. "Now do your work."

YHVH Tzva'ot, may your angel armies assist me tonight.

I turned to Sabina and took the basin she

held. "Now," I told her, my voice trembling, "I need you to wake Amphion and ask about the stool I had the carpenter build. When you have found it, bring it here."

"A stool?"

"Amphion will know. I need it."

While Sabina hurried away, I nodded at Octavian, then turned to my patient. Octavia was a healthy young woman, neither malnourished nor obese, and should have a normal delivery. She was dozing, one hand on her bare belly and the other tucked beneath her pillow. She did not seem to suffer from any of the emotional excesses that might cause a difficult delivery. Grief, joy, fear, anger, or extreme indulgence, I had read, could make things difficult for mother and midwife alike.

I took my supplies from my bag and arranged them next to the water basin: a small container of clean olive oil, soft sea sponges, squares of wool, swaddling cloths, a pillow, a sharp blade, and a bit of woolen string. One pregnant mother. One midwife. One birthing stool on the way.

I blew out a breath and sat to observe my patient. Dominus paced outside the doorway, though I tried to ignore him as I took deep breaths to calm my pounding heart. I was beginning to think we had responded to a false report when Octavia opened her eyes, bit her lip, and screamed through clenched teeth.

"Shhh," I said, rising to help her. "Breathe deeply. When the pain comes, purse your lips and pant like a dog. You will be fine."

She obeyed, but her gaze kept flicking at my face as she panted. When the pain had passed, she relaxed and looked directly at me. "Who are you?"

"Chava. Your mother brought me from the farm, remember?"

"Vaguely." She narrowed her eyes. "Are you *certain* you know what you are doing?"

I forced a smile. "With help from my God, I know I can do this."

A wry grimace crossed her face. "I am not so sure of my god — even though I sacrificed a goat to her yesterday."

Octavia rose onto her elbows to brace for another pain as Sabina appeared in the doorway. "Amphion says your stool did not arrive."

I felt my stomach drop. "What?"

Everything I had learned — everything I knew — depended on having a proper birthing stool. I had ordered a stool exactly like the one pictured in the scroll. It would have armrests for the mother to grasp during delivery. It would have a sturdy back against which the mother would press her hips in order to push. The front of the seat would feature a crescent-shaped cutout through which the baby would be delivered. I would have assistants stand at the back and sides of the stool in order to keep the chair from moving.

How could I properly deliver a baby without a stool? I had caught Barabell's baby, but Barabell was a slave, and she had positioned herself like a cow. Octavia, on the other hand, was a highborn lady and not about to get on the floor. I had been brought to Rome to provide her with the best possible birthing experience. . . .

I closed my eyes. What would Urbi do? She would smile and pretend she had always meant for the situation to unfold this way. Then she would work her magic and charm everyone in the room.

"Sabina." I pasted on a reassuring smile. "I would like you to find a clean cloth and soak it in the warm olive oil. Then go find another slave, someone Octavia knows and trusts, and bring her back with you."

Sabina hurried away while I stood in the doorway and watched her go. I felt as though I stood at a crossroad, one path leading to midwifery and home, the other leading to a lifetime of slavery. Both paths held risks and dangers.

I could call for Octavian, tell him I'd been wrong to mislead him, and urge him to send for an experienced midwife. He'd be angry and he might have me beaten, but he wouldn't kill me.

Or I could turn and go to Octavia, comfort her, and trust in the God of angel armies.

I drew a deep breath and turned toward my mistress's bed.

Six hours later, Octavia was no closer to delivering her child. She was no longer drowsy or relaxed, but suffering in the grip of regular pains and terrified that something had gone wrong. Furthermore, for the last several minutes I had been able to see the child — but not his head. Instead I saw pale-blue flesh, a smooth section of what looked like a baby's bottom.

"Something's wrong," I mouthed to Sabina while Marcellus held his wife's hand and chanted prayers to Juno Lucina. "The head is supposed to be the first thing to appear. Instead, I see hind parts."

"Then pull it out," Sabina said, staring past me at the weeping woman. "Our mistress suffers."

I grabbed a linen square and wiped perspiration from my forehead. The baby had to come out, that much was certain. But how? I had wanted to use a birthing stool; barring that, the ideal position was to have the woman lean against another person. Marcellus might possibly support his wife, and if not, Sabina would oblige. But this baby was not behaving like the other I had handled. This infant was upside down and appeared to be stuck at the mouth of the womb.

I lifted the lid off the crock of olive oil and poured a generous amount into my palm. "Mistress," I said, offering Octavia an unsteady smile, "I am going to pull your baby out. Master, would you sit behind your wife and hold her as she labors?"

Marcellus gave me the wide-eyed look of a man who has just been asked to stand on his head. "I will not."

"Sabina?"

Nodding reluctantly, Sabina climbed onto the hard mattress and positioned herself between Octavia and the wall.

"Mistress Octavia, please take Sabina's hands and squeeze as often and as hard as you like. I am going to begin now."

I moved the lamp closer to the bed, then slid two oiled fingers between the baby's leg and the flesh that held him captive. I could see the child's buttocks and part of its thighs, but all movement had stopped. As Octavia screamed, I placed my left hand beneath the little body and turned him so that his back faced the ceiling. Then I slid one of my oiled fingers under his little leg, pushed upward slightly, and freed it from the womb.

The leg dangled freely, and the resulting movement elicited a shift in the baby's body, bringing down the other leg, as well. Elated by this progress, I patted the little body and considered how I should proceed. The arms would have to be freed, but how? I bit my lip, then turned the body until the child's back — completely covered by skin, thanks be to HaShem — faced the wall. I slid an oiled finger beneath the flesh of the womb and felt the little arm. As Octavia groaned, I hooked it with my finger, then gently but firmly pulled it toward me. An arm appeared, with a hand and five tiny digits. Smiling, I turned the slippery body again and repeated the procedure. A second arm soon dangled in the empty space.

Now . . . the shoulders and head. If I did not get this right, the child might die. Might already have died as I dithered in indecision.

I again turned the baby so that his back faced the ceiling. With my right hand supporting his belly and the other on his back, I slid the fingers of my oiled right hand into the birth canal and stopped when I felt the tip of a nose. I spread my fingers, taking care not to touch the child's eyes, then used both hands to pull, changing the angle when I felt resistance. In one smooth movement, the mother's body yielded and the infant slipped out. I lifted a perfectly formed baby boy and held him up for his parents to see.

I placed the child on a pillow, then used a rough towel to swipe a layer of mucus from his face. Almost immediately the baby began to cry, and Octavia's cries of distress became sobs of joy.

I used a sea sponge to clean the newborn with warm water, then swaddled him tightly and gave him to his mother. And then, weak with relief and humbly grateful, I looked at Marcellus . . . and saw nothing but approval and pleasure in his dark eyes.

Somehow I had successfully handled a difficult birth and needed neither hyena nor amulet to do it.

Only Adonai.

After I proved myself to Dominus, he told Amphion that I could be hired out as a midwife. Rome was so densely populated that I could have kept busy no matter who my master was, but because I belonged to Gaius Octavian Caesar, nine or ten wealthy pregnant women attempted to hire me every week. Amphion decided which babies I would deliver and demanded a high price for my services.

When I explained Shabbat to him, he was considerate enough to reserve one day in seven when I would be free from working as a midwife, though I would still be expected to serve in the household. "I cannot have the other slaves considering you an exception," he said, jotting notes to himself. "But one day of rest will be good for you. We would not want you to be so overtaxed that you make a fatal mistake."

Like thousands of other slaves, I surrendered the idea of escaping. Running away might have been possible in the country where one could hide in ditches and caves, but it would be nearly impossible in Rome, for clothing marked the man and woman on the city streets. A man's toga, or lack of it, left no question as to his status, and a respectable matron could easily be identified by her *stola,* a garment that covered her inner tunic and fell to the floor. When a woman went out in public, her stola commanded respect: men made way for her in the streets, and she was always given a place at the theater or at public games. Prostitutes, women condemned for adultery, and slaves were forbidden to wear the stola. A slave caught masquerading in a stolen stola would surely be put to death.

Roman Sumptuary Laws decreed that only male citizens be allowed to wear togas, so those without a toga over their tunic were either slaves or freedmen. Prepubescent boys wore a white toga with a purple border, but once they reached seventeen they donned the all-white *toga virilis.* Men in mourning or disgrace wore dark-colored togas, while the highest-ranking officers of the Senate wore the purple-and-gold-embroidered *toga picta.* Senators and sons of senators were allowed the privilege of the *lotus clavus,* a broad purple stripe on the tunic, while equestrians — tax collectors, bankers, builders, and other wealthy businessmen — wore tunics with a slightly narrower stripe.

The laws had been purposefully engineered so that anyone could read anyone else's social status with one glance, and anyone who dressed above his or her station was severely punished. Watchful eyes constantly probed the crowds, noting and judging, and for every man who was too self-absorbed to care about the milling throng, there were ten others who would sell their children if it meant collecting a bounty for reporting a lawbreaker.

I was amazed when Amphion explained the Sumptuary Laws that governed banquets, festivals, and private spending. Banquets were limited to a certain number of guests, and expenses had to be kept below a certain amount, depending on the festival. Coming from Alexandria, where every party was lavish and every banquet an overflowing feast, I thought the Romans tightfisted in comparison. But it was all done, Amphion explained, to keep the classes in their proper place. "You cannot have an equestrian outspending a senator," he said, "even though he may have the money. Everyone else would overspend to keep up with the equestrian's example, and then we'd have impoverished senators." He shook his head. "Chaos would result. Utter chaos."

So I committed myself to the task of working for my freedom. Each morning I reported to Amphion, who gave me my assignment. If a summons came at any other time, he found me and reported that a woman had gone into labor.

One morning, about six months after the successful delivery of Octavia's son, Amphion smiled as he gave me directions to the home of a wealthy patrician family. "They are paying twenty-five denarii for your services," he said, his mouth curving in a one-sided smile. "Congratulations. Not even a scribe earns as much for a single day's work."

"Twenty-five denarii . . ." I closed my eyes and translated denarii into drachmas. "That is quite a lot."

Amphion nodded. "If you were free, you could live well on that wage."

A surge of happiness flowed through me. "Good. I will earn my freedom quickly."

Amphion held up a warning finger. "Do not be hasty. Were you bought at a great price?"

Happiness surged again. "I was bought for practically nothing. I was sick and purchased in a lot from a slave ship. They could not have paid much for me."

"But your purchase price is only part of the equation. You must consider your present worth as well. You are a slave who brings in twenty-five denarii each time you go out the door. You are literate, you are lovely, and your patients shower you with favor. You also belong to Octavian Caesar, so your status has a certain weight. To purchase your freedom, you will need a great deal more than you realize."

Disappointment struck like a blow to my stomach. I caught my breath, reluctantly adjusting to this sudden shift in perspective. A moment ago I had been certain I would be on my way to Egypt within a few months, but my journey might yet be years away.

I swallowed hard as grief shredded my heart. "I had better get to work."

"Good thinking."

I lifted my chin, squared my shoulders, and again asked Amphion how to find the address where I was needed.

Chapter Twenty-Three

"Amphion, may I ask a question?"

The old man lifted his head and stared as if surprised I could speak. "Yes?"

"I am so pleased that I work steadily for you. It occurred to me I could support you better and handle more women if I had an assistant."

"You need help?" Amphion released a sharp laugh. "You seemed perfectly capable when you delivered Octavia's son."

"Thank you. But if I could train another slave — Sabina, for instance — she could deliver a child at one woman's home while I delivered at another. And if either of us had difficulty, we could call on the other for assistance."

Amphion looked at me through half-closed eyelids, then stared at the wall, thought working in his eyes. "And you could both earn . . . mmm." He faced me again. "When would you like to train her? How long would it take?"

"Not so long. Sabina does not read, so I would have to teach her everything I have learned, but after ten deliveries or so, she ought to have a good understanding —"

"Make it five deliveries," Amphion said, smiling. "Teach her quickly so she can begin to earn sooner."

I folded my hands in gratitude, then went in search of Sabina.

I found her in the bathhouse, tending the fire that heated the water. "It is settled," I told her. "You will go with me on my next five deliveries. Then you will begin to work by yourself."

"Chava! Thank you!" She squeezed my arms, then clapped her hands to her face. "You are so clever and so kind to do this for me. Not only will I be freed from this bathhouse, I will be able to buy my freedom and marry Duran. And I'll have a skill, so I can earn a living to help support us."

"In time," I said, lifting a warning finger, "for there is much to learn. I will read my midwifery book to you whenever we can get away. I want you to be fully prepared in case something goes wrong."

She grinned and threw her arms around me for a quick hug. "What could possibly go wrong? The gods are smiling on me!"

■ ■ ■ ■

As I hurried from my master's house to a waiting pregnant woman, I could almost forget I was a slave. Indeed, if I had worn something other than a simple slave's tunic, a passerby might think I was a member of an outstanding family. I walked with a slave boy who carried my birthing chair. On hot days, Amphion sent an additional slave with a parasol to shade me from the sun, reasoning that it wouldn't do for me to arrive hot and sweaty from exertion. And when I lifted a newborn in my hands and accepted praise and thanks from the happy mother and her attendants, I blushed with pleasure, realizing I was exercising a gift HaShem had graciously given me. A gift and a skill I could employ anywhere, at any time, no matter what my status.

On other occasions, however, when I remained in Dominus's home, Amphion would call on me to serve guests, rub the master's feet or scrub the stepping-stones that led from the curb to the front door. On those days I felt very much like property.

At least I was not alone. Sabina was often required to assist me with various duties, so when we were not dispensing wine, offering platters of fruit, or fanning guests, we would retreat into the shadows and talk about midwifery.

One night Amphion called for me, looked me over with a critical eye, and gave me a gown of sheer material. "Wear this when you serve tonight," he said, his tone clipped. "Dominus is entertaining a group of friends."

I had only to hold up the garment and peer through it to realize what sort of entertainment Dominus had requested. "Are these men expected to stay — ?"

"Not your place to ask questions," Amphion snapped. "Now go make yourself appealing. Dominus will not want his guests to be disappointed."

I sighed heavily, then went downstairs to the slaves' rooms to change into the diaphanous garment. Sabina had already changed, and when she stepped out from behind a stack of boxes, the blush on her cheeks spoke volumes.

"Have you had to do this sort of entertaining before?" I asked, pulling my regular tunic over my head.

She ran her fingers over her hair, smoothing it. "Our master is not much given to pleasures of the flesh, so he does not entertain like this often. His mother, while she lived, much preferred to be the center of attention, so she would never dress us this way. But this is Rome, where it is considered manly to pursue fleshly pleasures." She pulled her long hair back, tied it with a leather strip, and turned to face me. "How do I look?"

I blew out a breath. I had seen such sheer garments in Egypt, where the ancients saw nothing wrong with displaying the female form.

I gave her a reluctant nod. "Dominus will be pleased."

The gathering was not as large as I had expected. Octavian had invited his sister and her elderly husband, along with his two closest comrades, Marcus Vipsanius Agrippa and Gaius Cilnius Maecenas. Dinner had been served in the peristylium, and afterward the five of them lounged on couches around the atrium's reflecting pool.

Maecenas, who was witty and talkative throughout the dinner, was clearly taken with Sabina, as he often called her to his side and held her close as she poured his wine.

Deducing that Dominus had asked for me and Sabina so he could impress the two single men, I let Sabina work Maecenas's side of the room while I stood near Agrippa.

That young man remained quiet and did not touch me, though I often felt the pressure of his gaze.

The quintet talked of many things — young Marcellus, Octavia's growing toddler; Mark Antony's decision to name Herod and his brother Phasael as tetrarchs in Judea; and Antony's decision to winter at Alexandria with Cleopatra.

Small prickles of unease nipped the back of my neck at the mention of Cleopatra's name. Though I would never forget her, the hard work of midwifery, coupled with the task of training Sabina, had freed me from obsessing over Urbi. But no matter where I went, I could not escape my childhood friend. She was with me in that warm atrium, her charms evident even though she was far away. . . .

Octavia's eyes crinkled at the corners as she lifted her cup. "They say Antony is quite smitten with her."

"The people of Tarsus are still talking about the banquet she threw for him," Octavian said.

"Banquet?" Maecenas looked from Octavian to his wife. "What banquet?"

Octavia smiled. "Twelve banquet rooms," she said. "Thirty-six couches, glimmering with embroidered tapestries. Tableware set with semiprecious stones, rose petals knee-deep. And above their heads, a lace of lights strung through the tree branches."

Agrippa frowned. "How did she manage — ?"

Octavia continued as if she hadn't heard him. "And the woman herself — draped in jewels, dangling earrings, and a plea to excuse her appearance; she had dressed in a hurry and would do better next time." Octavia snorted softly. "The woman simply knocked him off his feet."

Octavian lifted his cup for me to refill. "No doubt she has a flair for the dramatic."

I barely suppressed a smile. If he only knew the extent of Urbi's talents.

"I heard," Maecenas said, "she allowed Antony and his guests to take all the furnishings after the meal. Every man present carried away couches, tapestries, litters, horses, and Ethiopian slaves."

I pressed my lips together, imagining how the slaves would have been dressed. They were probably wearing less than I.

"Antony tried to reciprocate by giving a feast for Cleopatra," Octavia went on, smiling at her husband. "But he was completely unable to compete. So he poked fun at himself, describing his banquet as 'meager and rustic.' Instead of being offended,

Cleopatra laughed at him as he had laughed at himself. When he was coarse, so was she; when he belched, so did she."

"Really!" Maecenas gaped.

"Then she introduced Antony to her son, her co-ruler. Ptolemy XV. The so-called son of Caesar."

I tilted my head, confused by what I had heard. Ptolemy XIV was her co-ruler as far as I knew; she had married young Sefu after Omari died in the Alexandrine War. So Caesarion could not be her co-regent . . .

"At least this one has a good chance of surviving," Marcellus said. "The first died during the war, and they say she poisoned the second a few months after Caesar's death. All to make way for her son, of course."

My arm began to tremble so violently that I turned and rested the heavy pitcher on a pedestal. Cleopatra poisoned Sefu? She who used to tell me that she feared being murdered by her siblings? I did not want to believe it, but I felt the truth like the solid stone beneath my feet. In order to advance her agenda, Cleopatra would not hesitate to kill her brother, and poison was a quiet way to commit the deed.

I should have realized what she would do. She could have but one co-regent. Once she decided that Caesarion should share her throne, sweet Sefu was doomed.

In the curve of my back, a single drop of perspiration navigated the course of my spine. Cleopatra could be warm, charming, bright, and lovely — until her purposes were thwarted. Then, as coolly as any of her royal ancestors, she could destroy even a friend.

A shiver spread over my shoulders as I remembered something Urbi once told me. "A ruler labors under a peculiar disadvantage," she had said. "Though he can protect himself from his enemies by arranging his friends about him, he has no one to protect him from his friends."

Urbi had gotten it wrong. Her friends needed someone to protect them from *her.*

"Cleopatra has a —" I snapped my mouth shut, unable to believe I had actually begun to speak my thoughts. A slave did not speak while serving her master, and she did not join in conversations with guests.

Maecenas's brows rose. "Did that one say something?"

I backed away, hiding my face in shadow.

"Did she?" Dominus stood and grabbed my arm. "Slave, did you speak?"

"I am sorry, Dominus." I lowered my gaze. "The words . . . slipped out."

"You spoke as if you knew something

about Cleopatra." Octavia leaned toward me, her eyes bright with curiosity. "Finish your thought. If you've heard a rumor, I am sure we would all like to hear it." She smiled a bright smile, yet I couldn't tell if she was being friendly or merely toying with me.

I glanced at Dominus, Octavia, and Agrippa, in whose eyes I saw nothing but kind concern. "I grew up in Alexandria," I said, my gaze flitting over the circle of faces to measure their reactions to my words. "I knew Cleopatra."

"Well, of course you did." Maecenas shook his head as if I were an idiot. "The entire country knew their future queen, surely."

"She was not a queen in those days," I continued as something like pride slipped into my voice. "She was my friend. And she has always had a changeable nature . . . and a gift for measuring people, no matter what language they speak or what status they hold. She is a chameleon."

I glanced around the circle again, wondering if I'd said too much, but Octavian and his guests were looking at each other, their eyes sending silent signals I could not discern. Were they inwardly laughing? Would I be punished later?

"Thank you," Dominus finally said, dismissing me with a quick bend of two upraised fingers. "We will send for you when we have an urgent need for insight into the minds of other royal leaders."

Flushing, I backed out of the room, then walked quickly to the kitchen, where I lowered my pitcher and pressed my lips together. Thanatos stood near the back wall, stealing leftovers from the dinner trays, and his brows rose when he saw me. "Serving Dominus's guests tonight?"

"I was," I answered, realizing that not only had I paraded myself before Romans, now I was providing a show for a fellow slave. "But I am done. I am going to change —"

"I wouldn't," Thanatos said, idly popping a fig into his mouth. "Until the master's guests have departed."

I turned as Amphion entered. His brows lifted when he saw me. "You left the master?"

"He sent me away."

"Do not go far. He has two male guests, and he had me prepare two rooms. I have a feeling you will be summoned again."

I was waiting in the shadowed hallway when I heard Dominus bid his guests goodnight. Octavia and Marcellus departed for their new home, but Maecenas and Agrippa were invited to stay in guest chambers. "I hope you rest well," Octavian called as they went into their rooms.

I turned, about to head back to the kitchen when I heard footsteps behind me. "Slave."

I froze. "Dominus?"

"Agrippa has asked for you. He is in the second chamber."

I drew a deep breath. "Shall I . . . would he like to hear music?"

A smile slid into Dominus's voice. "You'll have to ask him."

With my heart in my throat, I left my master and walked slowly toward the room where Agrippa waited.

I argued with myself as I walked to Agrippa's room. By some miracle of HaShem's grace, I had never been forced to lie with a man. Yet I knew what my master considered me — a profitable slave, an attractive creature to be used for men's pleasure and service. Perhaps I was naïve to think I could avoid the situation looming in that guest room.

To further complicate the situation, Agrippa was not the sort of man who repulsed me. He had been coming to the master's house long enough for me to know he was not from a noble family. He and Octavian had become friends when they met at school, and their friendship seemed to be based on knowledge, trust, and mutual acceptance. I did not think Agrippa a bad person, and if he insisted on taking me to his bed, I would not think of him as evil for behaving like thousands of other Roman men.

But what would I think of myself? And if Yosef knew what I was doing, what would he think of me?

Perhaps I was foolish to think of Yosef. He had probably found a wife in Jerusalem and settled down to raise a family. I was only a distant memory, so he wasn't thinking of me at all.

I reminded myself that Agrippa was not a Jew. He was as Roman as Caesar, and as a Roman he worshiped a host of gods and goddesses, he offered sacrifices to graven images, and he considered marriage little more than convenient arrangement. The Romans considered sex one of many sensual pleasures; they did not look at it as the cleaving of two souls that had become one in marriage. I could still hear my father's voice in my ear: "The physical union of a man and woman is HaShem's illustration of unity, and its blessing is new life. Always treat it with reverence, and always revere the husband Adonai brings you."

HaShem had not brought me a husband, nor had He given me a man who could understand what I had been taught about love and marriage. So what was I to do?

I could ignore my master's order and go to my own bed, but on the morrow I would be flogged within an inch of my life. Even worse, I would lose my master's trust. He could send me back to the farm, forbid me from practicing midwifery, or sell me to someone far more brutal.

And I would never see my family again.

I released a sigh as I knocked on the door of the guest room. When I heard "Enter," I placed my hand on the latch and went in.

Agrippa was sitting on the edge of the couch, a smile playing at the corners of his mouth. "I was about to untie my sandals," he said, indicating his intricately laced shoes. "I suppose you'll want to do that?"

Was that all he needed? I sank to the floor and reached for the laces, desperately hoping he only wanted someone to help him prepare for bed.

"I have noticed you before," he said, his voice warm in the room. "Octavian tells me you are a midwife."

I kept my eyes lowered as I undid the leather laces. "That's right."

"You were by far the loveliest girl in the

room tonight. Perhaps the loveliest girl I have seen in all of Rome."

When I pulled the last shoe from his foot, he stood and held out his arms. For an instant I thought he meant to embrace me, then I realized he was waiting for assistance with his toga. I hurried forward and lifted the toga from his tunic, preserving the intricate folds as I draped it over the back of a chair.

Agrippa came toward me again, his gaze dropping from my eyes to my shoulders.

I closed my eyes, knowing what was expected of me. A good slave, an obedient slave, would offer herself to her master's guest, allowing him to do whatever he wanted, for she was only a thing, a commodity, a possession offered by a generous master. Any other slave in the house, male or female, would have freely done so, knowing that to refuse meant a whipping or even worse.

But I —

"I am not like the other slaves." The words spilled out of my mouth before I could stop them.

"Really? How so?" Agrippa's hand was on my shoulder, his fingers tugging at the brooch that supported my gown.

"I am . . . precious to my father." I did

not know where the words came from; I had never spoken or thought them before that moment. But when I looked up into Agrippa's face, I saw traces of mild confusion, accompanied by a suggestion of humor at his mouth. "You have a father?"

"Everyone has a father, but mine taught me about the acts of love and marriage, and this is not what they are meant to be."

He withdrew his hand, then stretched out on the couch, bending his elbow and propping his head on his hand as he smiled. "This should be entertaining. Will you show me what they are meant to be?"

"I will tell you, if you like."

"A slow start, but we are making progress. May I have your name?"

"Chava."

He tried the word out on his tongue. "I asked Octavian to send you to me because I was hoping for an evening's entertainment . . . mostly because you are beautiful and I wanted to look at you. If we are not going to couple, will you at least talk?"

I stared at him, astounded. "You want me to talk?"

"I know you can. You proved it this evening."

My cheeks burned at the memory. "That was a mistake. But Dominus was speaking about a friend."

Agrippa's smile widened into a grin. "Already I can tell your story is not at all like the stories of other slaves. You were not brought to Rome as spoils of war, were you?"

I shook my head.

"And you were not enslaved as a child, because you speak like an educated woman. You are refined, which is highly unusual for a slave so lovely. Most beautiful slaves are used up by the time they reach your age."

I swallowed hard. "I would not have you think I am naïve. I am not."

"I believe you. So tell me your story. I would very much like to hear it."

I tilted my head to study him better. His face was broad, unlike Octavian's narrow visage, and his eyes were a mingling of blue and green, so his ancestors might have hailed from Gaul or some other northern land. His hair was the color of light-brown sand and clipped short, like most soldiers'. His smile was even, with good teeth. He was not a big man, like some brutish warriors, but tall enough that I looked up to catch his gaze, and slender enough that I could slip my arms around him. Intelligence snapped in his eyes, and already I had seen that he was a man who could put his desires aside in pursuit of something more valuable. Finally, he was not so aware of the social gulf between us that he would refuse to have an actual conversation with a slave.

"You are judging me," he said. "Do I meet with your approval?"

My face heated with embarrassment. "It is not my place to judge you. Besides, I thought you wanted to hear my story."

"I beg your pardon. Please." He tipped his head in my direction. "Tell me everything."

I perched on the edge of the chair, careful not to sit on his intricately folded toga. "I was born —"

"Not like that," he interrupted. "Sit on the couch where you can relax. Talk to me as anyone would."

I lifted a brow, then slowly moved to the couch and sat at the end, near his feet. Then I began sharing the history of my life. One moment slid seamlessly into the next, one episode followed another, until the candles guttered and my voice had grown hoarse.

I stopped talking and listened for noises in the night. A Shabbat stillness reigned in the house, with only the distant sound of Maecenas's snoring to disturb it.

"I am so sorry." I slid off the couch and moved to the door, my head bowed. "You wanted entertainment and all I have done is bore you."

"You have not." Agrippa sat up, his eyes seeking mine. "And I will not send you away at this hour, when anything could happen on your way to the basement. You must stay with me tonight."

"But —"

"Wait." He stood, picked up his toga, and shook out the folds. He then wrapped me in the rectangle, cocooning me in its soft warmth. "There. Be warm. Be safe."

Stretching out on the couch, he slid to the far edge of the cushion and patted the empty space beside him. "I am a sound sleeper, and I am tired. On my honor, I will not disturb your rest."

As if to prove his point, he lowered his head to his outstretched arm and closed his eyes. I wavered, studying his face, which seemed durable and boyish in the lamplight. I was on the verge of fleeing to the slaves' quarters when I remembered Thanatos, who had been lurking in the kitchen earlier. Agrippa was right — at this hour, I would not want to run into anyone, not even one of my fellow slaves.

I lay down beside him, wrapped up like Urbi in Caesar's carpet. I was drifting on a tide of exhaustion when I felt his hand on my waist. I stiffened as my eyes flew open, but he did not move again. After a moment, his breathing deepened and the candle sputtered out, thrusting us into darkness.

I closed my eyes and relaxed, and after a while I felt nothing but his arm around me, keeping me safe.

Life settled into a routine. Octavian, my master, remained in his mother's house, and I regularly left that house to deliver the babies of Roman wives. Our master was rarely at home, however — he, Lepidus, and Mark Antony kept themselves busy running the Roman republic, so Amphion ran the household. He never complained about my midwifery, though, because now two midwives brought in a steady income.

Every week or two I would stop by the amanuensis's desk. "How much more?" I would ask. "How much do I need to buy my freedom?"

Amphion would sigh in exasperation, flip through a few pages of his ledger, and look up at me. "Years," he'd say, one corner of his mouth drooping. "So get to work."

Even with the excitement that accompanied every birth, life might have become predictable if not for Agrippa, who had become Octavian's chief friend and second in command. What Octavian envisioned, Agrippa carried out, and even from my lowly position I saw what a talented and capable man Agrippa was. If not for his humble and obscure origins, he might have been Rome's first citizen, but I found his devotion to Octavian admirable. The relationship between Agrippa and Octavian reminded me of Urbi and myself before Urbi turned into a queen who would stop at nothing to advance her own ambitions.

A friendship of sorts had formed between me and Agrippa the night he summoned me to his room, though both of us knew it could never be publicly declared. Romans barely acknowledged household slaves, and only held meaningful conversations with trusted handmaids or personal servants. Octavian rarely spoke directly to me, and neither did Agrippa while in Octavian's presence.

But whenever he visited the house and saw me, a simple quirk of his brow let me know he had noticed me; a twitch of an uplifted finger meant he wanted to speak to me. I would go to the garden and sit in a sheltered niche, or I would linger in the shadows of the library, pretending to peruse the family's scrolls or dust the death masks of their noble ancestors.

Did I think of Yosef in those days? Yes, at first. But as the months passed, I found it increasingly easy to believe that he had forgotten me and married another. I wished him every happiness HaShem could provide, even as I yearned for another meaningful friendship.

One afternoon I caught a flicker of Agrippa's signal and went to the library, where he joined me after a few moments. He stood so close I could smell incense on his clothing, and my heart thudded when he smiled down on me.

"I have some news that might interest you," he said.

I could not imagine what he meant. "News?"

"Of Cleopatra. As you might know, her sister Arsinoe has been held at the Temple of Artemis in Ephesus, upon the orders of Julius Caesar."

"I did not know." I closed my eyes and tried to remember the last time I'd heard Arsinoe's name. It had been during the Alexandrine War, when she had proclaimed herself queen in Cleopatra's absence. "It has been years since I've thought of her."

"Caesar brought her to Rome, where she rode as a prisoner in his triumph." Agrippa's face darkened. "The people of Rome did not enjoy the sight of a young girl in chains. Caesar's mistake. Too many of the people felt sorry for her."

I shook my head. "They should have withheld their pity. Arsinoe was conniving and ambitious."

"All the same, she and the priest of that temple have been kept in Ephesus until now. Mark Antony has just ordered that she be removed from the temple and executed on the steps."

My hand flew to my throat. "Is this — ?"

"We know it is Cleopatra's doing. Arsinoe has been plotting against her sister all these years, even having the high priest proclaim her queen. Cleopatra begged Antony to release the priest, and he did. But now Cleopatra has no more siblings. She rules with her son, Caesarion, as her co-regent, and Antony as her lover."

I sank to a chair, stunned but not surprised.

"We hear," Agrippa went on, "that Cleopatra spoils Antony, allowing him to indulge himself in sports and the diversions of a man of leisure. They have made a pact — they call themselves the Inimitable Livers."

I made a face. "Livers?"

"Apparently they intend to live with — how was it termed? — 'an extravagance of expenditure beyond measure or belief.' "

I drew in a deep breath and released it slowly. Extravagance was a Ptolemy trait, and Urbi reveled in her heritage. But what must the staid Romans think of such a free-spending queen?

"We hear that she plays dice with him, drinks with him, hunts with him," Agrippa went on. "They say he goes out among the populace, and she accompanies him, disguised as a serving maiden."

I nodded, remembering how Urbi and I had done the same thing on the Canopic Way.

"Can these reports be true?" Agrippa asked. "They sound so . . . unbelievable."

"If she is not allowing him to leave her side, she doesn't trust him," I said. "As to whether or not they're believable . . . yes, Cleopatra would do those things. She would do anything to please the man who can help her save Egypt."

A line appeared between Agrippa's brows. "Rome is not at war with Egypt."

"But . . ." I hesitated, torn between Urbi's interests and my own. If I said too much, would I be giving the Romans an advantage? On the other hand, did Urbi deserve to have her secrets protected? "Cleopatra is aware that Rome could remove her at any time," I finally said. "So she will love Mark Antony; she will please and humor him. She would do anything for him . . . because of Egypt."

Agrippa leaned back. "So Antony might stay in Egypt for the foreseeable future."

"If Cleopatra has her way, she will keep him as long as possible."

Agrippa stared thoughtfully at the wall of death masks, then turned. "Is she really so beautiful?"

"She is really so . . . fascinating."

My heart twisted at the thought of my friend. I did not allow myself to think of her often, but Agrippa had asked, and my mind had conjured her up, as real and vital as she had always been.

"I will see her again," I whispered, daring to speak only because I had learned to trust Agrippa. "HaShem gave me that promise."

Agrippa caught my shoulders, pressed a kiss to my forehead, and released me. "Maybe you will," he said, retreating. "One never knows what will happen tomorrow."

I stepped onto the street, then nodded at the men who had brought torches to escort me safely to Palatine Hill. I had just delivered my second set of twins, and though the labor was long, once the first baby arrived, the second followed soon after. The mother was overjoyed by the double blessing, and the father's disappointment over having a girl had been eased by the arrival of a son moments later.

Walking between my two escorts, I gripped my basket of supplies and stepped carefully over the paving stones, not wanting to turn an ankle in the darkness. A cloudless sky had painted the buildings to my right and left with a thin wash of moonlight, accented by the occasional spill of lamplight from the edges of a shuttered window. I did not enjoy walking the streets of Rome at night — trouble always seemed to stir in darkness, and amid the uneven staircases, shadowed doorways, and shuttered shops, men tended to forget their better natures. Even at this late hour, the city vibrated with noise — an angry voice, a screaming woman, the wail of frightened children. Rats skulked in the shadows, and stray dogs splashed through the sewers in search of food. And always, always, the scent of sewage, rotting fruit, and the occasional corpse dumped into the street.

I looked up in gratitude when we reached the house of Gaius Octavian Caesar.

"I believe this is your master's house?" one of my escorts asked.

"Yes. Tomorrow I'll send a message as to

where the birthing chair should be delivered." I moved toward the door. *"Bona noctem."*

The doorman had been sleeping beneath the BEWARE OF DOG mosaic, but he woke at the sound of the door closing. He gazed at me, eyes wide, then realized who I was. *"Salve,"* he said, greeting me. He leaned back against the wall and nodded, probably eager to get back to sleep.

But I needed to ask a question. "Has Sabina returned?"

We had both departed that morning, heading for two separate homes. Her prospective mother was pregnant with her fourth child, so she wasn't expecting a protracted delivery.

The doorman's brow furrowed as he shook his head.

"Are you sure? I would have thought —"

"No," the man interrupted. "Now be off with you."

I stepped back and eyed him, wondering if he'd made a mistake. I had been gone all day and half the night, so something must have gone wrong with Sabina. If she were struggling, I might be able to help her.

"What was the address?" I asked the doorman, who had already lowered his eyelids. "Where did Sabina go?"

The doorman's dark eyes bored into mine. "Can you not see I am trying to sleep?"

"I thought it was your duty to guard the door."

"For the dominus, not for the likes of you!"

My mood veered sharply to anger. "Would you like me to tell Dominus that you refused to help one of the midwives? Our women give him a great deal of money for our services. I would hate for him to hear that you refused to cooperate when we needed your help."

His face paled, all but a pair of deep splotches over his cheekbones, as though someone had slapped him twice. "The home of Harpocrates the blacksmith, on Aventine Hill." He spat the words.

I hesitated. The area surrounding Aventine Hill was rough and poor. The towering insulae held dozens of families, and Sabina could be working in any one of the many apartments.

"Have you no clearer direction?" I asked. "Or tell me who escorted Sabina to the Aventine — perhaps he will take me there, as well."

The doorman's face twisted in a leering smile. "Duran took her. If she's not back, maybe we should ask *him* where she is."

"Where is Duran? In the men's quarters?"

"I do not know. And I wouldn't advise you going down there at this hour."

The doorman had a point. I stepped back and bit my lip, weighing the risks of the streets versus the risk of the men in the basement. Thanatos might be in there, and the man was still watching me, taking every opportunity to make rude remarks or crude gestures. . . .

Perhaps I could walk a short distance. I might encounter Sabina on the street, and we could keep each other company on the walk home.

"I am going to find her." I leaned closer to hiss in the doorman's face. "And I will be back."

Years of traversing Alexandria with only Nuru by my side had taught me to walk quickly, avoid other people, and behave as though I knew exactly where I was going. Since I had no one to accompany me, I grabbed a blanket from my bag and draped it over my head like a hood, allowing the rest of the fabric to hang over my shoulders and down my back. My simple tunic, the uniform of a slave, might actually draw less attention than if I'd been dressed like a Roman matron, with tunic and stola.

I strode quickly down Palatine Hill and past the Circus Maximus, then along the street that led to the Aventine. I looked out from beneath my hood, searching for any sign of a slave between escorts, but all I saw were groups of men, occasional clutches of legionaries in search of a tavern, and a couple of scrawny children. A line of white-robed priestesses walked the street, murmuring some incantation, but they made me uneasy, so I hurried past them.

I stood at the base of the Aventine and looked at the insulae, several of them rising four and five stories high. Lights glowed through the shutters, and the sounds of humankind echoed in the darkness. Tatters of clouds hung like rags above the rooftops of the buildings, and stiff clothing swung on laundry lines stretched from window to window.

I lifted my chin and girded myself with courage. If I were ever going to find the home of Harpocrates the blacksmith, I'd have to ask someone for direction. Which meant I'd have to approach someone, and I had not seen anyone who looked even slightly approachable.

I had started climbing the hill when I realized I should look for signs of a forge. A blacksmith used a fire and tools and usually had a bucket for cooling hot metal. Most of the insulae had businesses or shops on the first floor, so if I found a building with a forge, I would narrow my choices considerably.

I kept moving. I walked past a butcher shop, a brothel, a shop that sold idols. A weaver, a sculptor — and there, a forge. *Custom-designed swords and blades,* the sign proclaimed in Latin. *Tools for your country estate.*

I stepped back and looked up. No lights shone on the fourth floor; only a solitary light gleamed on the third. But the second floor, just up the wooden staircase, blazed with light.

I gripped the stair railing and climbed the first six steps, then turned at a small landing — and froze. At the top of the stairs, exposed to the night, lay Sabina, her throat cut and her eyes open. One step down, just beyond Sabina's lifeless hand, lay a newborn baby.

A scream rose in my throat, but I choked it down. What good would screaming do? It would only attract attention, which would result in more screaming, and people taking sides, and before I knew it I'd be injured or dead like Sabina, and I would have no answers. I lowered my head into my hand as words flooded my head: *YHVH Makeh,* YHVH smites. He punishes sin.

When I could move again, I rushed up the stairs and reached the baby. I picked it up and turned it over in my hands. A little boy, perfectly formed, but blue, colored by the night and the lack of life in his little body. The cord had been properly cut and tied, his face had been cleaned, yet here he was . . .

And Sabina?

I groaned as I sank to the steps beside her. I did not bother to feel for the pulse of life at her neck; her blank eyes told me she was gone. She still wore her tunic. Her hair was pinned back, her face splashed with flecks of dried blood.

A tear trickled down my cheek, and I slapped it away. This was not right. Though I did not know details, I knew Sabina's patient had not done this. A woman who had just delivered a child was not likely to spring up and cut the midwife's throat. That meant the husband or lover or someone else in the house had committed this murder. Someone who had not been pleased with the outcome of Sabina's work.

A compliant slave, one born to the life, would not have done what I did next, but my feet were accustomed to freedom. I climbed the remaining steps and pounded on the door. I heard movement from within, then stood with both hands on my hips.

A hulking man opened the door, his face red, his tunic splashed with blood.

"What have you done?" I shouted, pointing to the two corpses on his stairs. "You will be held accountable for this!"

I was thinking of his accountability before HaShem, Master of the universe and defender of the poor and helpless, but he was clearly thinking of something else. Though his eyes flared when I began to shout, by the time I finished he had turned and moved away. "A moment," he called, leaving me to blink in the lamplight and wonder what he could possibly be doing.

He returned with a bag in his hand — a bag of coin, I realized, when I heard metals clinking against one another.

"I did not know," he said, lowering his head, "that the slave belonged to Octavian Caesar. I reacted in anger when the babe was born dead, and afterward I learned to whom the slave belonged. Take this to him with my apologies. If he desires more, have him send word, and I will pay."

He closed the door, leaving me speechless and holding a bag of blood money.

■ ■ ■ ■

By the time I woke the next morning, the full story had spread throughout the area and reached our household. Sabina had delivered a beautiful baby boy to the blacksmith's wife, already mother to three girls, but the cord had wrapped around his neck during delivery. The father burst into the birthing room as Sabina worked on the stillborn child, trying to encourage him to breathe. The man yanked Sabina away from the infant, cut her throat, and dragged her out of the house so swiftly no one could intervene. His hysterical wife screamed that the midwife belonged to Gaius Octavian Caesar, so by the time I arrived, the blacksmith was prepared to pay.

I gave the money to the doorman when I came in and then went straight to bed. After hearing the missing details from another slave, I went to the room where Dominus was working and rapped on the door. "Enter."

Still dazed, I gave my report of what had happened and gestured to the bag of coins on his desk. "I see you have already received recompense for Sabina's life."

"Yes. Thank you for bringing it to me." A

smile flashed briefly over his lips. "A lesser slave would have taken the money and run, but she wouldn't have gotten far."

I blinked at him. A woman would have to be a fool to run with so much coin — she'd be beaten and robbed before daybreak.

I drew a deep breath. "If you have any questions for me —"

"None," he said, returning to the parchments on his desk.

I thought — hoped — he might remark on Sabina's courage and valuable work, but he seemed to have already forgotten the matter.

"Sir —" I hesitated, carefully choosing my words — "should we not send someone to pick up her body? She should be cared for and buried —"

"She was a slave, not a person of significance." Octavian shuffled through the pages on his desk. "She has probably been thrown into the Tiber by now, so you need not concern yourself."

"Will you take no action against the man who killed her?"

"Why should I? He has paid his debt."

He looked up, a smile lighting his face. "That reminds me — you will be the first to hear my news. I am getting married."

"Sir?"

"A lovely lady called Scribonia. We will have the wedding here, within the month. Send Amphion to me, will you? I expect we have a lot of work to do."

He waved me away with a flick of his fingers, so I left him, reminded once again of how unimportant slaves were in Rome. Yet I was not discouraged, for another of HaShem's names overcame my sorrow: *El Gmulot,* the God of Recompense.

Justice might not be meted out in this life, but gentle Sabina would not be forgotten, and her death would not be unavenged.

Chapter Twenty-Four

During the summer of my fifth year in Rome, Dominus married Scribonia, a dignified, serious woman. The lady was several years older than Octavian, but she had powerful connections that would be useful to him. The wedding was a simple affair, yet the house flooded with highborn people ranging from senators to foreign kings.

I had been anxious as the day approached, afraid that Mark Antony and Cleopatra might appear, but they did not. Later I learned that Antony had been in Sicyon with his wife, Fulvia. The woman had fallen ill and eventually died, but Antony left her without even saying good-bye. He and Octavian were at odds over some issue regarding troop movements, and war between them seemed inevitable. But their legionaries, reluctant to fight fellow Romans, compelled the two men to make peace.

One of the wedding guests did cause my heart to beat faster — Herod of Judea had come to Rome and visited Palatine Hill to congratulate Octavian on his marriage. From a safe distance, I studied the Judean ruler and eavesdropped on as many of his conversations as possible. I could not forget that Asher and Yosef had fled to Judea, so they might be affected by anything this Herod might do.

During my eavesdropping I learned that Antigonus, a son of the high priest, had offered to pay the Parthian army if they would help him recapture his lands from the Romans. A battle ensued, Jerusalem was captured, and Antigonus named as king of Judea. The battle forced Herod and his brother Phasael out of power, and they had been named as tetrarchs by Mark Antony. So after Phasael was captured by the Parthians, Herod fled to Rome to ask for help.

"You see why I had to come," Herod told one of the wedding guests. "My family has been destroyed. Rather than be tortured and disfigured, my brother Phasael took his own life by smashing his head against a wall."

"A bloody land, Judea," the guest replied.

Herod offered a vague smile. "Is Rome any less bloody? Your Julius Caesar was stabbed numerous times by his friends, was he not?"

The guest's face deepened to the color of the wine in his glass, then he muttered something and wandered away.

I held a pitcher of wine and lingered near the doorway, studying the man who desired to be king over Judea. Was he the sort of leader Asher would support? Or would my brother be fighting for Antigonus and the opposition? I knew little about Judean politics, and in that moment I yearned for my father. Though any of these Roman men might be able to explain what had happened in Judea, only Father would understand which king was devoted to Adonai . . . or if any of them were.

Later that night, after I had been summoned to Agrippa's room, I sat on the edge of his couch as he attempted to explain what was happening in Judea, still home to thousands of Jews.

"To understand Judea," he said, pushing a stray hank of hair away from my eyes, "you cannot ask about what happened last year. You have to ask about what happened a hundred years ago, or even five hundred. Those people have long memories."

I smiled, knowing I had a far deeper knowledge of Judea than Agrippa realized. "I know a few things," I admitted, "but I am confused about this Herod and his brother. Are they good men? Are they righteous?"

Agrippa shrugged. "Who is truly righteous? And who can judge? Shouldn't we leave that to the gods?"

"Absolutely." I smiled. "Though I am sure my master believes he has the right to judge men."

Agrippa grinned, conceding my point. He reached for my hand and tenderly pressed his lips to the scar across my palm. "You do not really want to discuss Judea, do you?"

The touch of his lips sent an unwelcome surge of excitement through me. "I do."

"We could do other things to pass the time."

I gave him a reproachful look. In truth, I had grown fond of Agrippa and looked forward to our time together. When we were alone, he treated me like the gentle lady I had been reared to be, and I felt like myself again. He never forced himself on me, and even in public he never ordered me about.

But what could become of this friendship? As Octavian's second in command, Agrippa had risen to the pinnacle of social status, so he could never marry a slave, or even a free woman. Such things simply were not done. So I could become his mistress, yet . . . I could not.

Esther and Bathsheba had no choice when taken to their kings' bedchambers, and Samson had visited prostitutes, as had Judah, one of the twelve patriarchs. But Samson and Judah suffered consequences for those visits, and Solomon, the wisest man on earth, advised his son to flee the wanton woman.

I did not want to be the wanton woman in Agrippa's life. I cared too much for him.

Just when I made up my mind to be no more than a friend to Agrippa, I could hear Urbi calling me a fool. "Why do you deprive yourself of pleasure?" she would say. "Give yourself to him! What difference would it make?"

What difference, indeed?

Living among Gentiles had proved my father right — the Gentile world *did* operate by different principles than we who followed Adonai. The Egyptians, Greeks, and Romans considered sensual pleasure nothing more than an enjoyable act, and I had heard some Romans encourage prostitution, calling it a useful deterrent to adultery. The concept of loving one's wife was considered quaint, and kissing one's wife in public was apt to produce a scandal. But a man could regularly visit brothels with no repercussions. So long as an adulterer or fornicator restricted his attentions to the proper classes, no one cared. Free boys and free women were out of bounds, but any noncitizen or slave could be taken for a man's pleasure without guilt or shame.

Marriage had more to do with celebrating Roman ideals than love. Only citizens could marry citizens, and to wed a foreigner was unthinkable. A union between a Roman citizen and a foreigner — like Julius Caesar and Cleopatra — would never be accepted by Roman society. Marriage was designed to produce Roman families and sturdy Roman children, a guarantee for Rome's future success.

I knew I could never marry Agrippa, but something in me hungered for his touch. I looked at him, stretched out on the couch, handsome and smiling and waiting for me to come into his arms. I *wanted* to go to him . . . but surrendering would cost me dearly. I would forfeit a measure of self-control and self-respect. Before HaShem, who saw everything, I would demonstrate that I cared more about my personal desires than obedience to Him.

And that I could not do.

"Agrippa." I whispered his name, enjoying the feel of it on my tongue. "I do not know if I can make you understand, but I choose to live a holy life before my God."

"I know about the Jews and their law," he said. "And I know it is impossible for you to follow that law here. You cannot rest on the seventh day, you cannot keep kosher because you must eat what is set before you."

"It is true that I cannot do all I want to do," I said, "but when given a choice, I try to make the righteous choice."

A muscle clenched in his jaw. "Then I must leave you for a while," he said, rising from the couch. "I am not a eunuch, Chava. And when you are near me, I —"

I lifted my hand, cutting him off, and moved away from the doorway so he could pass. I would not embarrass us both by having him tell me where he was going; I knew the weaknesses of Roman men.

I stepped aside as he draped his toga over his shoulder, then he walked swiftly past me and left me alone.

After he had gone, I lifted my gaze and wondered if I was being unfair. By allowing myself to love him, by indulging in this pleasurable friendship, was I doing him a disservice?

"Am I, Adonai?"

I heard no answer in the quiet night, only

the unexpectedly swift beating of my heart.

A few weeks after Octavian's marriage, his sister Octavia, now mother to two daughters and an infant son, lost her elderly husband Marcellus. Seeking a genuine peace with his co-ruler, Octavian approached Antony about marriage to Octavia. If Antony married Octavia, Octavian proposed, they would renew the Triumvirate for another five years, cutting the empire in half: Octavian would rule over the west, including Gaul, and Antony would oversee the east. Lepidus, whose role had shrunk until it was nearly insignificant, would retain control of Africa.

At Brundisium, a city in southern Italy, Octavian and Antony entertained each other by giving banquets. Octavian's banquet featured the best in Roman fashion, and Antony played the host in Egyptian style, complete with painted eyes. The party then moved on to Rome, where Antony and Octavia were wed. They rode into the city on garlanded horses as if they were celebrating a military Triumph — which, I suppose, they were. The union resulted in peace.

I watched the newly married couple with a sense of impending doom. I genuinely liked Octavia because she was a good mother and a kind person, but the reports about Antony had not impressed me. The gossips insisted that Cleopatra was madly in love with Antony, but I knew better. Urbi loved Egypt more than anything. I believed she had been catering to Antony, doing whatever she must to keep him interested, to keep him on her side. Because he could take her kingdom away with a word.

Even Agrippa admitted that something sinister hid beneath Antony's affability and his love for fun and games — a cold and ruthless will, coupled with an inability to empathize with others. "I have seen his ruthlessness," he told me one night. "He can be cold and utterly without feeling when he is pressured."

Knowing Urbi's skill at reading people, I was sure she had sensed this about Antony. In light of his recent marriage, she would redouble her efforts to charm him, please him, and turn her kingdom on its head for him, because in a single moment he might take it all for himself.

And she possessed a ruthlessness that more than matched his.

Those few months of peace brought another respite of a different sort — Agrippa left Rome to mount a campaign in Gaul. A couple of the other girls teased me because

Agrippa was not around to single me out for attention, but I ignored their teasing and thanked Adonai that I was no longer tormented by desires I could not righteously fulfill. I missed him, but slept easier at night.

And I had something else to focus on. Barely two months after Octavian's marriage to Scribonia, our dominus had made an announcement: his bride was expecting a baby. I celebrated with the rest of the household but felt as if a coil in the pit of my stomach had begun to tighten. Octavian would expect me to deliver the child of his older bride, and nothing, absolutely nothing, could go wrong.

Summer had just yielded to autumn when we slaves became aware that our dominus was not himself. He had taken to smiling for no reason, and one of the housemaids reported that he had been singing in the bath.

I overheard several of the slaves talking in the kitchen.

"Has he come into money?"

"Bah! He has more than enough."

"Perhaps he is excited by the idea of becoming a father."

"He was not excited at the beginning of the pregnancy — why now?"

"Perhaps he is in love."
"Who is the lucky lady?"
I poured myself a cup of honey water and considered the question. Octavian often entertained visitors at the house, but the only guests who had appeared more than once were Tiberius Claudius Nero and his wife, Livia Drusilla. Nero was arrogant and unpleasant, but his young and very pregnant wife seemed intelligent and cheerful.

The couple had dined with Octavian and Scribonia several times over the past weeks. The women had shared stories about their pregnancies while the men talked about matters before the Senate . . . or so I had assumed. I searched my memory, trying to recall if Dominus had engaged Livia in conversation alone. Doubtful, especially with the other two spouses present.

In early September, Dominus announced that he would sponsor a public festival. At twenty-four, the fair-haired man was finally ready to experience his first shave. The Romans made a ceremony of nearly every "first," and the first shave was no exception. The *depositio barbae* was usually celebrated when a boy was in his late teens, but our master, who had accomplished so many things while young, was determined to let the world know that his body had finally caught up to his mind.

I had never seen Dominus so excited about a party. He fussed over the menu, got Amphion out of bed when inspiration struck at midnight, and modeled three different togas before settling on the one he would wear. The festival was to be held on his birthday, the twenty-third of the month, and as the day approached and our master grew more restive, I wondered at his motivation. Clearly he was trying to impress someone. The public? He cared little for what they thought. Mark Antony? No, Antony was in Egypt. His wife? Scribonia did little but complain about her pregnancy. Octavian's mother was deceased, his sister newly married and more concerned about her marriage than a party, so who did he wish to impress?

On the day of the festival, I joined the serving women and carried pitchers of honey water throughout the crowd. Octavian stood in a shaded corner, under an elegant canopy with two women at his side — Scribonia and Livia, with Livia's small son, Tiberius, standing in her shadow. Scribonia, who looked uncomfortable and tired, spoke little and wore a frown, but Livia sparkled under our master's attention.

Later, I asked Amphion for his impression

of the event. "You mean the party for Livia?" One of his brows arched. "It is a good match. Though he is the most powerful man in Rome, the aristocrats see him as a provincial upstart. Livia, however, is from an old and noble family, the Claudii. If they marry, each will help the other — he will be supported by her noble forefathers, and she and her family will have access to his power."

"But . . ." I drew a curved belly over my tunic, reminding him that both women were pregnant.

"Oh, that." He laughed. "Only a small impediment, dear. Wait and see."

Amphion knew his master well. On the day Scribonia gave birth to Julia, a beautiful little girl, Octavian divorced her.

A few weeks after the *depositio barbae,* our master became engaged to Livia. A grand betrothal banquet was held at the house, and all the fashionable people of Rome attended. Livia owned little slave boys known as *deliciae,* or darlings, and they scampered throughout the crowd, entertaining the guests and behaving like typical children. At one point I was offering our master a platter of pigeon eggs when one of the little darlings noticed that Octavian and Livia reclined on one dining couch while Livia's husband and another woman took their ease on another. "What are you doing here, mistress?" he asked, his high voice easily carrying over the rumble of the other guests. "Your husband is over there."

I froze, my back bent, the tray in my hand as the room went silent. Horror flickered in Livia's eyes, and Octavian paled.

Obeying an impulse, I dropped my supporting hand and allowed the tray to flip and rattle onto the floor, scattering pigeon eggs in every direction.

The guests gasped, and ladies moved out of the way lest they soil their gowns, but Dominus bent to help me pick up the mess at his feet. "Clever girl," he murmured, his gaze catching mine as he handed me an egg. "Very clever indeed."

I suppressed a smile and nodded, then heaped the rest of the food onto my tray and left them alone.

"Chava?"

I paused in the doorway to Livia's room, my basket of birthing supplies in hand. "Domina?"

"We are expecting a guest later in the day. Do you think you will be back in time to help serve? I know there are other girls, but this guest seems to have a particular fondness for you."

I felt an icy finger touch the base of my spine. Could it be — ?

"So will you be back?"

"I cannot say, Domina. As you know, some babies take their time."

"Indeed they do." Livia's youngest had come quickly, and with so little suffering that the new bride felt obliged to wail and scream, *after* the child's birth, as if the process had nearly killed her. Upon seeing the result — a healthy son and a happy wife — Dominus had been extremely complimentary of my midwifery skills.

Livia propped herself up on pillows and yawned. "If your dominus asks where I am, tell him I have decided to sleep a little longer."

I nodded and hurried out of the room.

Livia had made herself at home in our master's house, quickly eliminating every trace of Scribonia. Livia's two sons would remain under the authority of their father until they were of age, so Tiberius and baby Drusus lived with Tiberius Nero, though they visited often. Scribonia's daughter Julia lived in our household and rarely visited her mother.

I nodded to the doorman and stepped onto the street, where the wind had picked up. I lowered my head and walked toward the Aventine at a brisk pace, my feet keeping time to the heartbeat that had quickened when Livia mentioned their guest.

Could it be Agrippa? He had been away for nearly two years, and during that time I had heard many stories of his outstanding accomplishments, among them securing the frontier on the Rhine and founding a city he called *Colonia Agrippinensis.* He had recently come home to aid Octavian, who was facing a challenge from Sextus Pompeius, son of Pompey the Great. Sextus had bedeviled Octavian since the time of Julius Caesar, and Octavian was determined to remove him. But Sextus had become a man of the sea, and Octavian was far less sure of his navy than his army.

I paused as a man with an overloaded wagon cursed his mule for being unable to budge the load. Voices from a nearby insulae called down to insult the man who had dared to disturb the quiet of early morning.

I shook my head and walked on.

The delivery was another breech birth, one that required slippery fingers and all my concentration. But the mother was ecstatic when I placed a living son in her arms, and the father slipped me two sestertii for my trouble. "Your fee," he assured me, "has already been paid."

Of course it had. But I'd never see a copper of it.

I gathered my supplies, gave the mother a few final instructions, and left the house.

The sun was sinking behind the western hills as I approached the Palatine. I considered using one of my coins to buy a drink at a tavern, where I could wait until Octavian and his guests had finished dinner. But anyone who saw my slave's tunic would know I was out of place. Word might reach the Octavii house before I'd even finished my drink.

I trudged on.

I greeted the doorkeeper and dropped my basket on a bench. "Is Dominus having dinner?"

"Yes. Dinner was served in the peristylium."

"How nice." I smiled in relief — I could walk around the atrium and enter the kitchen. If Agrippa was in the garden, I wouldn't have to see him. But I couldn't resist knowing for certain. "The master's guests? Who is here?"

The doorman's smile broadened. "Master Agrippa, of course, and Caecilia Attica."

I blinked at the unfamiliar name. "Who?"

"Agrippa's betrothed. The marriage," the

doorkeeper glibly went on, "was negotiated by Mark Antony and will take place in this house. Exciting developments!"

I knew it wasn't reasonable, but the news stole my breath away. For some reason I had imagined that Agrippa would remain unmarried, but why should he? He was twenty-four, strong and virile, and he undoubtedly wished to have children. He and Octavian were close, and as Octavian rejoiced in his young bride, perhaps something had made Agrippa long for a wife of his own.

I gave the doorkeeper a false smile and walked through the atrium, then slipped through the shadows and went to the back of the house.

The cooks greeted me with absent nods and said nothing when I picked up a small loaf of bread. I'd eaten nothing all day, and the bread would keep my stomach from rumbling while I slept. I walked out to the veranda and hid myself behind a pillar, wondering if I could hear the diners at the center of the garden. . . .

I heard Octavian's bold laughter, followed by the soft murmurs of the women. Then Agrippa said something, and Octavian responded by standing — I saw the shimmer of his hair in the torchlight. "To marriage!" he said, holding his cup aloft. "And may the gods bless you with fruitfulness!"

I looked down and blinked tears out of my eyes. I was exhausted. I wasn't crying; my tears were simply an overflow of feeling, an excess of emotion after a long day.

"Chava!" I looked up, surprised to hear Dominus call my name. "Come at once."

Again I blinked the tears from my eyes and, with nowhere else to put it, tossed the bread over my shoulder. I walked toward the two dining couches at the center of the garden and resolutely refused to look at the seat where Agrippa and his betrothed reclined. "Dominus?"

"I thought that was you," Octavian said, smiling. "Our Agrippa is going to be married to this lovely young lady. And because Agrippa is my dearest friend on earth, I am giving him a most valuable wedding present: you."

A ripple of shock spread throughout my body, tingling my toes and leaving me lightheaded. Unable to believe what I'd heard, I broke my own resolution and looked at Agrippa, who appeared as shocked and horrified as I felt. "Octavian, you mustn't —"

"Indeed I must, for what better gift could I give? I know you have a fondness for the girl, and her income will provide tunics and stolas for your new bride. I'll have her delivered after the wedding."

My gaze shifted to the bride-to-be, and astonishment smote me again. This Caecilia was no woman — she was a child in her early teens, at best. Flat-chested and thin, and her cheeks still retained the plump curves of childhood —

He was marrying a baby.

Somehow I remained on my feet, then I murmured something — I cannot remember what — and backed away, disappearing into the palms surrounding the garden. I made it to the basement room where the women slept, then fell on my bed, too weary to weep.

How could I live with a man I loved while he was married to another? I would have to quell my feelings for him; I would have to crush them, turn them to hate. For although the Romans thought nothing of loving their slaves and tolerating their spouses, I would never be able to do it.

I closed my eyes and tried to summon up Yosef's image, but it had been too long. The nose kept elongating, the eyes brightened, and the chin and jawline insisted on being clean-shaven. Every face belonged to Agrippa.

"Adonai?" I mumbled the holy name into

my pillow, closed my eyes, and searched my memory in desperation. Was there a name for God that meant *door*? Because more than ever, I needed HaShem to provide me with a way of escape.

On the morning of Agrippa's wedding, I rose early and packed my few possessions into a basket, then slipped into a clean tunic. After the ceremony, I would walk with the wedding party to Agrippa's home, and there I would somehow find a way to fit into a new family and a new set of slaves.

The groom arrived first and remained with Octavian while slaves served guests lemon water and wine. Finally the bride appeared at the door, accompanied by her father, Titus Pompons Atticus. The young woman had gathered her hair into a crimson net and put on a long tunic, secured at the waist by a belt tied with the traditional Hercules knot, to be untied only by her husband. An orange veil, worn over a wreath of verbena and sweet marjoram, covered most of her face but revealed her excited smile.

Since I would be leaving with the bride and groom, I was not expected to serve at the wedding. I should have gone for a walk, but I couldn't help myself — I had to watch.

So I picked up a tray of sweets from the kitchen and mingled among the guests, keeping an ear open for gossip.

As soon as everyone had arrived, a priest of Isis walked to an altar in the garden and sacrificed a ewe lamb. The guests cheered when the blood splashed on the stones beneath the altar, then the couple turned to each other.

Caecilia Attica placed her hands in Agrippa's and said, *"Ubi tu es Gaius, ego Gaia."* Where you are Gaius, I am Gaia.

I closed my eyes as a sudden pang struck my heart. How often had I found myself wishing I could say those words to him! But it was not meant to be — not ever.

The guests shouted *"Feliciter!"* — Congratulations! — as the crowd poured out of the house and entered the street. The distance between Octavian's house and Agrippa's was not great, so I remained in the back of the throng as they escorted the couple to their new home. Flute players led the procession, followed by torchbearers, even in the bright light of day. Two young boys held Caecilia's hands and led her to Agrippa's doorstep.

Through watery eyes I studied Agrippa's home. The bright blue door had been garlanded with flowers, and Caecilia paused before entering. As part of a traditional ritual, she knelt to wind wool around the two doorposts, then coated them with lard, a symbol of plenty. Laughing, Agrippa lifted his bride and carried her over the threshold, for a bride's stumble would have begun the marriage under a bad omen. They were followed by Caecilia's three bridesmaids, who carried symbols of domestic tranquility: a distaff, a spindle, and a ball of yarn.

As the wedding guests followed the bride and groom into the house, I remained in the outer courtyard. I knew what would happen next. After singing a chorus of crude songs, the bride would be led to the bridal bed, where Agrippa would take off his bride's cloak and untie the Hercules knot. That would be the guests' cue to leave and close the door behind them.

I sat on a stone bench and crossed my arms, refusing to shed another tear. How could I rail against the inevitable? How could I allow myself to become so distracted from my goals? Every minute spent thinking or dreaming about Agrippa was a moment I was not thinking about midwifery or returning to Alexandria.

More than ever, I yearned to go home. I wanted my father, if he still lived. I needed him.

The events of the day had forcefully reminded me that I would never feel at home in Rome.

Chapter Twenty-Five

The ancient Egyptians buried their dead with hundreds of *ushabti,* small clay figurines depicting servants who raked, planted, baked, hoed, cooked, shopped, and any other kind of work imaginable. The Egyptians called them "answerers," because they would answer the deceased's call in the afterlife and do whatever had to be done. The ushabti had no feelings, thoughts, or lives of their own, but existed only to serve.

I worked for Agrippa and Caecilia as best I could, though I often felt like a ushabti.

Months after I went to Agrippa's house, I realized Octavian had inadvertently done me a great disservice: my wages as a midwife should have gone with me to my new master's house. But Octavian, who had no need of money, had forgotten about my wages, which meant I had accumulated nothing to earn my freedom while in his service. I could have asked Agrippa to remind him, but I knew he wouldn't want to appear petty in Octavian's eyes.

So I remained silent.

The year after Agrippa's wedding, the Roman popular assembly voted to buy Octavian a house. With a grant from the Senate, Octavian and Livia left Atia's home and purchased a group of houses near a hut said to be the former dwelling place of Romulus, one of Rome's founders. While Octavian met with architects to turn the houses into one large household, Livia worked tirelessly to ensure their new home reflected her husband's greatness and power.

I toiled quietly at Agrippa's house, tending to his wife when he was away on military missions, pretending not to care for him when he was in Rome. And hurrying out to deliver babies whenever someone sent for me.

Once I was amazed to discover I was delivering the child of a Jewish family. They had come from Judea, and while the mother labored, the pregnant woman's sister told me why they had moved to Rome.

"We had to leave," she said, holding her sister's hand as the pregnant woman panted. "The man on the throne is not even a Jew. He is descended from Esau, not Israel, and pretends to keep our laws and talks of rebuilding our Temple. But no one is fooled; he cares only for power and riches."

"I have a brother and a friend in Judea." I lowered my voice. "I have not heard from either of them in years, but I pray for their safety."

The woman lifted a brow. "Their names?"

"Asher, son of Daniel of Alexandria," I said. "And Yosef, son of Avraham the butcher. I do not know where they are living."

She shook her head. "Asher is a common name, as is Yosef. But if they worship HaShem, they are bound to be heartbroken by the current state of Jerusalem."

"Why?"

The woman shook her head. "We had hope, until recently. Aristobulus, a true son of Israel, was appointed high priest. Our hearts were cheered to think that a man from a proper priestly family would finally represent us before HaShem, but our acclamations and approval only made Herod jealous. A few days later, Aristobulus was drowned in the king's fish ponds. Herod claimed it was an accident, but we all knew Aristobulus was murdered. The priest's mother even prevailed upon Cleopatra, asking her to speak to Mark Antony —"

"Cleopatra is involved with Judea?"

"Mark Antony is," the woman said, her brows knitting. "She begged Antony to punish Herod for the high priest's murder, yet I do not believe anything will happen. Herod will offer bribes to clear his name."

As another pain subsided and the laboring mother relaxed, I motioned to a slave — time to record the reading on the water clock. The pains were coming faster now. Still, the baby would not come for some time yet.

I returned my attention to the sister. "I am sorry things are so bad in Judea. My father was always eager to hear tidings of Jerusalem — he kept waiting for news of the Messiah."

"I do not see how Messiah can come," the woman said, her eyes watering as her gaze drifted to some vision I could not see. "He has to come through the royal line of David, but how can He when sons of Esau occupy the throne? If He does not come, who will deliver us?" A tear slipped from her lower lashes and fell on her cheek. "And that is why my family came to Rome. HaShem will send His Messiah, but He will not come any time soon. Not in our lifetime. Not now."

I had no answer for her, and no hope to give. Once again I thought of my father and wanted to weep.

I often found it incredible that the people we Jews lived among — Egyptians and Greeks and Romans — had considered themselves kings of the earth, when everyone who followed HaShem knew that Adonai ruled over the affairs of men. He had shown the prophet Daniel a vision of a statue representing the world's kingdoms. Daniel had written that a great stone not cut by human hands would strike the statue and fill the entire earth.

In their debates about the meaning of Daniel's vision, my father and his students had agreed on one precept: one day HaShem would destroy the kingdoms of the world and replace them with His own.

When I walked through the Palatine, I would occasionally stop by the Octavii estate to visit with friends and see what had been done to the house. From Amphion I learned that Agrippa had taken charge of Octavian's navy and helped defeat Sextus Pompeius at sea.

"He built a secret harbor," Amphion explained, "by digging a canal that led to a lake on one end and the sea on the other. He also invented a weapon that sailors could use to hook a nearby ship, then draw it close for boarding." He tilted his head and gave me a curious look. "Do you not know this? Do you not talk to your master?"

I looked away to hide the telltale blush burning my cheek. "Agrippa does not talk about his work. And when he talks, he talks to his wife."

Amphion shrugged. "In any case, Dominus is doing well. He was involved in wars up until late, but he has finally defeated Pompeius. It appears that peace has come to Rome. Long may it last."

"By the way," I asked, "what news have you of Mark Antony and Cleopatra?"

The old man lifted a brow. "Antony has been away fighting the Parthians," he said, "so he left the queen and her twins for the battlefield."

I gaped at him. "Cleopatra has twins?"

"Aye. Alexander Helios, the Sun, and Cleopatra Selene, the Moon. They're apt to be toddling age by now. But now that Antony is done with Parthia, we expect him to return to Cleopatra."

"Not to his wife?" I thought of Octavia, patiently waiting for a husband who might not return to Rome. "Octavian cannot be happy about that."

"He is not. Nor is he happy about Cleopatra's oldest son, Ptolemy XV Caesar. The boy is near eleven years old and could cause trouble before long."

Amphion did not need to explain. Octavian had built his power base on the fact that he was Julius Caesar's adopted son, yet a biological son of Caesar lived in Egypt.

Experience had already taught me that two heads could not wear one crown.

After defeating Sextus Pompeius, Octavian and Agrippa came home and shifted their focus from war to improving Rome. Octavian named Agrippa to the post of aedile, a position that allowed Agrippa to apply his genius to the city's infrastructure. My conversation with Amphion had convinced me I should pay more attention to my master's work. But since Agrippa never talked about it, I had to learn by questioning others. Fortunately, Amphion was a walking reporter. Often I would ask him to join me for a walk. I would point to reports painted on building walls as we strolled, and Amphion would explain everything that was fit for a woman's ears. When the city artists only gave me hints of a story, Amphion was able to fill in details.

I learned that Agrippa had not only reorganized and refurbished the water system, he had also commissioned a new aqueduct to bring more water to a thirsty city. He built five hundred fountains, along with luxurious public baths. He distributed olive oil and salt to the poor and arranged for Rome's baths to open free of charge to everyone, slaves and free men, several days during the year. Unemployment had been a severe problem among the poor, but Agrippa's building programs provided jobs and public works that benefited the entire city.

Learning of Agrippa's success brought me great pleasure. During the years I worked in his house, my feelings for him calmed — partly because he was rarely in Rome, and partly because I had become fond of his wife. Caecilia had been sheltered as a child, and she continued to be pampered and shielded in her husband's household. I liked her, much as I might like a charming puppy, but I also worried about her. How would she survive if for some reason her life were upended? I thought of the proscription, when the political winds changed overnight and many comfortable noble families found themselves homeless, impoverished, and marked for murder. Could Caecilia Attica survive something like that?

In the fourth year of their marriage, Caecilia Attica became pregnant. Agrippa asked me to oversee his wife's pregnancy. So I did, spending time with her every day to evaluate her health and mental well-being. To my surprise I found Caecilia to be a highly literate and educated young woman. She had read widely and shared several of her favorite scrolls with me. Touched that Domina would think of me as a person and not merely a slave, my heart softened toward her.

One morning I went to see her as she was breaking her fast. She was heavily pregnant, and though I did not participate in her rituals to determine the sex of the child, she told me she was carrying a daughter. "I will name her Vipsania," she said. "Vipsania Agrippina. I think it has a melodic sound — do you agree?"

"I do." I gave her a sincere smile. "And how are you feeling? Any pains in the lower back? Any bleeding?"

"No and no," she said lightly. "And I am so glad you stopped by. I have something for you. A gift."

I blinked, stunned beyond speech. A *gift*? For a slave?

"I asked Agrippa if I should follow my impulse, and he encouraged me," she said, pulling an oblong object from beneath her couch. "Of course, when I saw this, I thought of you."

She handed me the object and smiled as I

slowly lifted the wool wrapping and let it fall away. A scroll.

"Thank you. I love reading. I am sure I will enjoy the writing, no matter who —"

"Look again," she said, her youthful voice softening. "Please."

I opened the scroll and read the first line. *The Septuagint.* The Writings. The holy Word of HaShem. For years I had been living on memories, but here was the Word for me to breathe in whenever I wanted.

"Thank you," I whispered, nearly overcome with gratitude. Blinking tears away, I looked up and saw sweet concern shining from her oval face.

"I know you are Jewish," she said, offering a shy smile. "I know you must be homesick. So I asked myself what might give you comfort in the way you have comforted me."

"Domina, I am only doing what a midwife should —"

"You must know how terrified I am of having a baby. Though I pretend to be brave for my husband's sake, sometimes I wonder if I am strong enough to do this. I find myself worrying, but whenever I do, you are always there to tell me I am doing well. I have taken such strength from that . . . I wanted you to know."

She stood and swayed slightly as she

reached for the table.

"Domina, are you all right?"

"Just a bit dizzy." She tried to smile but ended up grimacing as her hand moved to her lower back. "That hurts. My back. Does that mean anything?"

"It could." I gripped her arm and held her steady as we moved away from the couch. "Let me take you to your bed, and we'll see if the baby is coming."

I smiled, but my smile faded when I glanced down and saw blood on the front of her tunic.

After one look between my mistress's legs, I realized she was not in labor. Something had happened, something serious, but the entrance to her womb had not begun to open and her pain was not sporadic, but continual.

The blood kept coming. And life is in the blood, so the more she lost, the more of her life ebbed away.

I told her I needed clean water, then slipped out of the room and called for the vilicus, a slave called Lucius. He must have heard the urgency in my voice, for he appeared almost at once, his eyes wide and his brows lifted. "You called?"

"Do you know how to find Dominus?"

Lucius frowned. "He is away with Octavian."

"Can we send a messenger?" I lowered my voice. "The mistress is gravely ill. I am afraid she will die."

Lucius's jaws wobbled. "I will send a messenger to Octavian's house. I will —"

My mistress's agonized scream cut off his words, and Lucius pointed to the lady's bedchamber. "Go to her! I will find the master."

I turned back to my mistress's room, then hesitated. "Adonai." I breathed His name as a prayer, for I had no one else to turn to. "Show me what to do."

I searched my memory for any reference to profuse bleeding from the womb, but my mind returned instead to a Shabbat dinner, when Father lifted his copy of the Septuagint and read a psalm: *"Into your hand I commit my spirit. You have redeemed me, Adonai, God of truth."*

HaShem honored truthfulness, so that was what I would give Domina. I straightened my shoulders and returned to my mistress, ready to give her the hard news.

"Chava?" Despite her fear, her voice remained gentle.

I sat by the side of her bed and took her hand. "I believe your womb has torn. Your baby will die unless it is brought out, but your body is not ready to let the baby pass."

Caecilia's wide eyes went wider at this news, and her slick hand tightened on my fingers. "You must save my daughter."

"Domina" — I covered her hand with mine — "I cannot promise this child will live. And you have already lost a great deal of blood."

She shook her head. "This child will be the daughter of Agrippa and related to the great Cicero. Her life is more valuable than mine."

"Mistress . . ." I strengthened my voice. "Pliny the Elder says I can save the child if I cut your belly and quickly lift the baby out. But the technique is only used on women who have already died."

She lifted her head, her eyes blazing with ferocity. "Am I going to die?"

I could not lie. "Adonai may yet have mercy —" my voice broke — "but yes, you are."

She sighed and lifted her tunic, exposing the rounded mound of her womb. "Then cut my belly. Save my baby."

I stared, amazed at her courage. I had not yet met a Roman mother who would give her life for her child's. In a society where children were frequently abandoned because they were inconvenient, red-haired, female, or afflicted with some other undesired quality, babies' lives held little value.

"Listen to me." Caecilia clenched her jaw and forced words through her teeth. "Cut the child free! Do not think of me, think of my daughter. Tell Agrippa this was my decision, and mine alone."

Fear lodged in my throat, making it impossible to speak. I met Domina's gaze and pulled out the short blade I ordinarily used to cut the cord. I held it over the mound of bare belly, tested the tautness of her skin with my fingers, and then carefully inserted the tip of the blade into the apex of the rounded flesh. Caecilia's hands fisted in the linen sheets beneath her, and her clenched jaw imprisoned a scream.

The blade was not terribly sharp and did not move easily through the layers of skin, fat, and muscle. I had no time to send a slave for a sharper knife, so I worked it, moving it back and forth, until I had created an opening the width of my hand. I thrust two fingers inside to be sure I had pierced the womb. When I felt a tiny limb through the sac that held the infant, I knew the job was nearly done.

I picked up the blade again and gave my mistress an apologetic look. "I am so sorry,"

I said, dipping the blade into the cut to pierce the bag of waters. "Just a little farther."

A quick thrust resulted in fluid running over my fingers. I drew a deep breath, braced myself for my mistress's scream, and slipped my fingers inside the cut and pulled outward, enlarging the opening. I thrust in my right hand and felt for the baby's head, then scooped up the torso and lifted the baby out.

The pale child inside the punctured sac was swimming in blood-tinged fluid. Holding the infant in both hands, I bit the birth sac to rip it open and tore the membrane away. I brought the child to the light streaming through the doorway, hoping to see the baby's first breath.

"Is she — is she — ?"

I swiped mucus from the child's face and nose. Then, just as Elisha breathed life into the son of the Shunammite woman, I pressed my mouth over the nose and lips. I blew gently and felt the little chest rise. When I lifted my head, the child screwed up its face and cried.

Somehow Caecilia Attica found the strength to hold out her arms. I placed the little girl, still attached to the birth sac, in my mistress's hands. Her face paled as she gazed upon her baby, and after a moment she lay back upon her pillow and asked me to place her daughter at Agrippa's feet. "I know . . . I can trust you," she said, her voice fainter than a breeze. "And . . . tell Agrippa good-bye."

She took her last breath as I cleaned and swaddled the infant girl. I gave the tiny baby to Caecilia's weeping handmaid and told her to find a wet nurse straightaway. Then I closed Domina's eyes and asked another servant to find the vilicus. I had a baby to look after, and he had a funeral to arrange.

Sometimes, as I looked at my master, I wondered if his broad shoulders ever tired of the burdens he carried. He had been shaken by his young wife's death, but like the soldier he was, he did not weep. I feared he would blame me. Instead he marveled that his tiny daughter had survived such a violent birth. "She could fit into my hand," he said when I laid her at his feet, "and I would not have her if you had not been here."

I swallowed to ease the lump in my throat. "Your wife wanted to name her Vipsania Agrippina," I said as he picked her up and officially recognized her as his own. "I know it is customary to wait until the eighth day for naming a girl —"

"Whatever Caecilia wanted." Agrippa peered into the tiny bundle with a perplexed expression on his face. "Do you think she has my nose?"

I had moved closer and smiled. "I would say she does. But time will tell."

Now Agrippina was ten days old, growing stronger by the minute. Her father purchased a Greek slave to care for the child, and though the woman was already devoted to the baby, I still felt a certain responsibility for the infant. But if anything happened to me, I was certain the nurse would remain by Agrippina's side until she was grown. I had met many slaves who were as devoted to their master's children as they would have been to their own.

I was pacing in the peristyle, the mewling baby on my shoulder, when Agrippa entered the garden. "Octavian is on his way," he said, his expression grim. "He is upset."

I stopped pacing. "Something in his household, or something in Rome?"

"Rome. Give the baby to the wet nurse," Agrippa said. "Then prepare wine, so you can be nearby as we talk. You know Cleopatra, so it will be useful to have your input."

"What has she done?"

Agrippa did not answer, but at the sound

of someone arriving, he spun on the ball of his foot and strode to the front of the house.

I took the baby to the nurse, then went to the kitchen to prepare a tray. By the time I returned to the peristyle, Agrippa had taken a seat on a dining couch while Octavian was pacing with a scroll in his hand.

"And the Alexandrians thronged to the festival," he read,
"Full of enthusiasm, and shouted acclamations,
In Greek, and Egyptian, and some in Hebrew,
Charmed by the lovely spectacle —
Though they knew of course what all this was worth,
What empty words they really were, these kingships."

"Ha!" Octavian lowered the scroll and glared hotly at Agrippa. "The poet has named it exactly — empty words! But by all the gods, they are words too far! This time Antony and his lover have surpassed my patience."

I set the tray on the table and proceeded to pour the wine.

Agrippa cleared his throat. "So what did they call this ceremony?"

"The Donations of Alexandria," Octavian replied, his voice hoarse. "Held in the city's great gymnasium, no less. A silver dais with two golden thrones, one for Antony, dressed as Dionysius, and one for Cleopatra, dressed as Isis. The bastard was there, too — Caesarion, now a thirteen-year-old co-ruler with Cleopatra. And let us not forget the three little ones — Antony's spawn were on the dais, too, sitting at their parents' feet."

"I am sure," Agrippa said, "it was a glittering display."

"You can bet it was," Octavian answered, "given that woman's penchant for extravagance. But after a series of rituals, Antony proclaimed that Caesarion was Julius Caesar's legitimate son, for Cleopatra had married Caesar. He did not mention the fact that no Roman would ever marry a foreigner."

"So what was the purpose of this event?" Agrippa, ever practical, cut to the heart of the matter. "What was Antony thinking?"

"He showered Cleopatra and the children with territories — Roman territories, mind you. Alexander was given Armenia, Media, and all the land east as far as India. Ptolemy Philadelphius, the latest brat, was named king of all the Syrian territories and overlord of the client kingdoms of Asia Minor.

Cleopatra Selene received Cyrenaica and the island of Crete. Antony then declared Caesarion king of kings and Cleopatra queen of kings."

Agrippa lifted both brows and glanced at me. After looking to make sure Octavian's attention was directed elsewhere, I placed two cups of wine on the table and stepped back into the shadows.

"So what," Agrippa repeated, "was Antony thinking? Did he really intend to give those territories to children?"

"Of course not." Octavian stopped pacing and braced himself on the back of a chair. "Could he be so bold as to hope to overthrow us? Perhaps he would establish himself as emperor and Cleopatra as empress . . ."

"I think not," Agrippa said. "If that had been his aim, he might have given one of the children claim to Rome itself."

"Isn't that what he did when he called Caesarion the legitimate heir of Caesar?"

"Perhaps," Agrippa said, watching me, "the ceremony was merely a symbolic gesture, a way of uniting the people behind him and Cleopatra. As your poet said, the titles were only empty words."

I nodded, affirming Agrippa's theory. Of course Cleopatra was constructing an illusion. She wanted to obtain the support and approval of her people, and what better way to do that than to demonstrate that the dynasty would continue for years?

Octavian hung his head and sighed. "They are empty words *now.* Yet this enmity between me and Antony grows stronger every year. He knows how to undermine my credibility. He is a serpent, dangerous and subtle."

"Not always subtle," Agrippa reminded him. "Antony is also full of bluster, especially when he drinks. He is liable to make a mistake."

On cue, Octavian spied his cup and lifted it, quenching his thirst in one long swallow. "He sends me letters," he said, forgetting himself as he wiped his mouth on his sleeve. "I wrote and admonished him for being unfaithful to Octavia. He wrote back and asked if I had ever been unfaithful to Livia."

Agrippa lifted a brow, but did not speak. I did not need an explanation; I knew that few Roman men were faithful to their wives.

"You know," Agrippa murmured, "the people are not yet recovered from the last civil war."

"I know." Octavian sank onto his couch. "I do not want war, but I cannot let this stalemate continue. Already Antony and

Cleopatra have moved legions to Greece. They will soon strike."

"When they do, we will defend," Agrippa answered. "But we cannot make war on Antony. He is a hero to many, and he is Roman. If you go to war against him, the people will see it as Caesar versus Pompey all over again."

Octavian hung his head for a long moment, then looked up and smiled. "You are right, as always. So we will not make war on Antony. We will make war on Cleopatra."

The next day Octavian went to the Temple of Bellona, goddess of war. In front of the temple lay a strip of land officially designated as foreign territory. On that land stood a small *columna bellica* or column of war. Bellona's priests sacrificed a pig, collected the blood, and poured it over several spears. These were then thrown into the foreign soil.

When the ceremony had been completed, Octavian walked away, officially at war with Egypt.

Chapter Twenty-Six

Actium, a promontory on Greece's western coast, was a common stop for travelers by sea. A five-hundred-year-old sacred grove dedicated to Apollo stood on its shore, and the area was known for skilled pearl divers.

For several months, the Egyptian navy had been transporting legionaries to a base camp Antony had established there. According to reports, Cleopatra and Antony were encamped there, as well.

On the first day of the new year, Octavian entered his third term as a consul of Rome. He commanded Agrippa to take charge of the Roman fleet, and before leaving the city, Agrippa asked me to travel with him.

My first reaction was gratitude that he had asked and not commanded, which he had every right to do. But even though I felt grateful, I balked for several reasons. The first was obvious — if Romans despised Antony's relationship with a foreign woman, how could they approve of Agrippa's friendship with a foreign slave?

The second reason was more personal — I had managed to discipline my heart since coming to work in Agrippa's household, and I did not want to stir embers that could easily be rekindled.

I did not speak of my second reason, of course, and after hearing my first, Agrippa only shook his head. "Commanders frequently travel with their slaves," he said, "and you will not sleep in my cabin. I will find a safe place for you, but I want you nearby. You have insight and knowledge that may prove useful for Octavian."

So in March I found myself on a ship, sailing southward, toward Egypt. My heart lifted at the thought of Alexandria, but I had no assurance I would ever reach it.

In swift order, the Roman forces captured the fort of Methone, in the south of Greece, and a string of garrisons along the coast. Soon we had established a camp on high ground at Actium. Octavian drew up his fleet and offered battle . . . but nothing happened. Rumors of sickness, high-level deserters, and desperation in Antony's camp painted a bleak picture of the opposition, and I couldn't help but wonder what Cleopatra was doing in the thick of it. Why hadn't she remained in Alexandria with her children?

One afternoon in late summer, we looked across the sea and saw smoke. Our scouts went out and returned with reports that Antony was dangerously shorthanded. He was preparing to engage us, but because he did not want his unmanned ships to fall into our hands, he set them ablaze.

I was serving wine in Octavian's cabin as he and Agrippa pored over a map with tiny wooden ships riding a paper sea. "Antony had five hundred ships when we arrived," Agrippa said, "but from what we've heard, I doubt he's able to man more than two hundred thirty now."

"And here are our four hundred." Octavian moved the red ships closer to Actium. "If we load our ships with eight legions —"

"Ninety men per galley." Agrippa drummed his fingers on the map. "We will deploy near Actium and wait to see what Antony will do."

With Agrippa, I boarded one of those galleys and stood on deck as we stared across the sea. Antony had divided his fleet into four squadrons. One of them was Cleopatra's ship, the *Antonias,* and I knew her vessel would be loaded with gold and silver, all her treasures. She would remain in the rear, keeping herself and the royal treasury safe.

Agrippa walked over to join me — not so near it would appear we were standing together, but close enough for me to hear him. "We have heard that Antony gave an order to have the ships take their sails with them," he said. "His men have to be wondering if the man is capable of winning this fight."

I cast him a quick glance. "I do not understand."

"Ships never carry their sails in battle," Agrippa explained. "The canvas takes up too much room and makes a ship difficult to maneuver if the sails are raised. But if Antony told his captains to carry the sails, he is anticipating a need to escape. He is not as confident as he seems."

I gripped the rail more tightly.

As we watched, Antony's ships emerged from the narrow channel, rowing in unwavering lines, deploying in parallel columns that stretched between promontories. Squinting, I could see Cleopatra's ship behind the front lines, as if she planned to observe the battle from the deck.

We waited . . . and nothing happened. On both sides of the conflict, hundreds of men sat at benches beneath the deck, their ears tuned for the drum, their callused hands on the oars, their backs bent, ready to row.

Our ships sat motionless as the sun rose to its zenith. Finally, Antony divided his boats into two groups. The groups moved toward each other, and we could barely discern what was happening. I saw Octavian's ships surround Antony's, and I glimpsed men fighting with shields, spears, and flaming missiles. Antony's sailors launched flaming rocks from catapults while Octavian's ships struggled to get close enough to board the enemy's vessels.

For two hours the fighting raged, then the wind shifted as it always did at that time of day. Without warning, Cleopatra's ship unfurled its purple sails and moved steadily through the center of the fighting. Men on both sides of the fray stopped beating each other and watched as the *Antonias* moved brazenly through the battle toward the open sea.

Agrippa pointed to Antony's flagship. Unable to move due to the heavy fighting, Antony leapt from his vessel to a smaller boat and screamed at the rowers, determined to sail after the queen.

Agrippa muttered a curse and slammed the rail. "What?" I cried, confused. "What's happening?"

"I should have known." Agrippa gripped

the rail so hard his knuckles whitened. "*They took their sails* — he did not think he *might* need to flee; he intended this move all along. Cleopatra waited until the wind changed, then she barreled through the opening we left for her. I should have kept our ships in a line. We could have captured Antony's war chest."

Agrippa cursed again, then went below decks to share his frustrations with Octavian.

The next morning, sunrise allowed us to see the aftermath of the battle more clearly. We saw that Antony had lost between thirty and forty ships. Of the one hundred thirty or so remaining vessels, none was willing or able to continue fighting. Octavian had won the day, but we did not know if Antony and Cleopatra were aware of the outcome . . . or if they even cared.

Agrippa sent for me as we sailed back to Rome. When I entered his cabin, I found him standing behind Octavian, who sat at the desk.

"Chava." Octavian gave me an unusually bright smile. "Agrippa tells me you have been useful to him in this matter with Cleopatra and Antony. He also tells me that you come from Alexandria and are well-acquainted with Cleopatra."

I bowed my head. "Dominus speaks truthfully, as always. But I have not spoken with the queen in many years."

"I have a proposition for you." Octavian picked up a statue of Mars on his desk and idly spun it on the wooden surface. "We will go back to Rome and plan our invasion of Alexandria — it is the next logical step, and it is necessary. We must conclude what we have begun."

I nodded, not willing to speak until he had finished.

"When we leave for Egypt, which will probably be in the spring, we would like you to accompany us. We will take you to Alexandria, where we will send you to parley with Cleopatra on our behalf."

I blinked in utter astonishment.

"If you do this for us," Octavian went on, "Agrippa is prepared to offer you manumission, effective immediately. You have served both of us well — as a servant, a midwife, and as a trusted . . ." He looked at Agrippa. "What is she, exactly? Not a spy. Not an informant."

Agrippa turned to me. "I think *friend* is the word you are searching for."

Octavian slowly nodded. "Friend. Very well." He smiled. "We will always be grateful to you."

For a long moment, my head swarmed with words. Finally my mind cleared enough for me to ask, "What is it you want me to do for you? Do you simply want me to *talk* to the queen?"

Octavian smiled again, his face remarkably boyish. "I will give you terms you will communicate to her. It is my hope that she will respond more favorably to the words of a friend than an adversary. Your assistance will be invaluable."

I drew a deep breath as a dozen different emotions tore at my heart. Despite the pain she had inflicted on me and many others, I could not hate Urbi. I could not stand before her as Octavian's emissary if he wanted me to deliver her to death. I could not cooperate if he wanted to humiliate a woman who had sprung from generations of kings, a woman who had been my closest friend.

"I do not hate her," I said, that realization becoming clearer by the minute. "And I cannot tell her that you want her dead."

Octavian smiled. "I assure you, Chava, I do not want her dead. I am prepared to offer her generous terms. If she will surrender Antony, I will preserve her life and her children's lives. Is that not generous?"

What could I do? I looked from one man to the other, then burst into tears. My hope — my dream — had not been accomplished through years of hard work, but in one miraculous moment. HaShem's promise was being fulfilled, and I had done nothing to bring it about.

Octavian extended his hand to me. "So, do you agree to this plan?"

"I do. And thank you."

"Then go, get some rest. You will continue to live at Agrippa's home until we depart for Alexandria. After that, you may go or stay as you desire. That is all."

Dismissed as abruptly as I had been summoned, I staggered from the cabin and walked to the railing where I clung to the wood and tried to maintain my balance. I was free. I was going home.

I did not know what I would find in Alexandria after so many years away, but since HaShem had brought me back, I would trust Him. With a shiver of vivid recollection, I thought of a passage I had recently read in the Septuagint: *"Trust in ADONAI with all your heart, lean not on your own understanding. In all your ways acknowledge Him, and He will make your paths straight."*

He had prepared a path, and I was ready to walk on it.

■ ■ ■ ■

"The latest report from Egypt," Agrippa explained over dinner, "is that Cleopatra and Antony have dissolved their Society of Inimitable Livers and established what they call the Order of the Inseparable in Death. The premise seems to be that they will end their lives together. Until then, they will fill their days with a succession of exquisite dinner parties."

I stared at Agrippa, unable to believe my ears. "Do you jest?"

"Does that not sound like Cleopatra?"

"It does," I admitted, "but surely she won't surrender so easily. She is nothing if not resourceful."

"They know we are coming," Agrippa said, "and the time for negotiation has long passed, though every week Octavian receives envoys from Alexandria with new proposals."

"What does Octavian want? If she can remain on the throne, Cleopatra will give him almost anything. The throne is what she cares about. Being queen. Leading her people."

"Octavian wants Egypt and her treasures — for himself, and for Rome. He will be satisfied with nothing less. The question is this: Can Cleopatra be a queen in name only?"

I fell silent and nibbled at a bread loaf. I was still uncomfortable dining with Agrippa; the urge to stand in the shadows and pour his wine had not evaporated. Though we did not share a dining couch, I would be glad when my time in his house came to an end. The gulf between dominus and slave had kept us apart, and I did not trust myself now that it was gone.

"We sail next week," Agrippa said, rising. Perhaps he felt as awkward as I did. "Are you looking forward to going home?"

"Yes," I answered without hesitation. And I meant it.

Three weeks later, we were at anchor in Alexandria's harbor. Antony made a token attempt at defending the city when Octavian's forces landed, but within days our legionaries were encamped near the hippodrome, just outside the city walls. While we waited in the harbor, messages continued to fly between Octavian and Antony. Antony suggested that the two men settle their differences through one-on-one combat, commander against commander. Octavian dryly replied that there were many different ways by which Antony could die, implying that such a combat would not be one of them.

The next night, Octavian had his men conduct an *evocatio,* a ceremony in which participants called on the gods of an enemy city to switch sides. Since Antony and the Ptolemy kings had identified Alexandria with Dionysus, the men called on that god to change his allegiance. Thousands of Octavian's legionaries shouted and sang the gods' praises at the stroke of midnight. Later we learned that Antony had heard the sound of music and concluded Dionysus had abandoned him.

While I did not believe in Dionysus or any carved god, I pitied Mark Antony, understanding that in those moments he must have realized how worthless and empty his worship had always been.

Soon after sunrise on the first of August, Antony sent his fleet to meet Octavian's ship, stationing his remaining warriors on the high ground between the city walls and the hippodrome. But as soon as Antony's ships came within sight of Octavian's, they raised their oars and surrendered. Outside the city walls, the cavalry deserted and the remaining foot soldiers ran away.

Antony reportedly went back to Alexandria, stunned, bewildered, and furious. At some point he received word that Cleopatra was dead, so he staggered through the streets shouting that Cleopatra had betrayed him by dying first.

Though I did not witness these events, by the time I entered Alexandria, the story had spread throughout the city. Apparently the distraught Antony had gone to his chamber in the palace, taken off his armor, and commanded his slave to run him through. Terrified, the man turned away and fell on his own sword. Antony then stabbed himself in the gut and collapsed on his bed. The wound, while grievous, was not immediately fatal. In terrible pain, he begged other servants to end his misery, but they fled like frightened rabbits.

Some of them found Cleopatra in the tomb she was building for herself. Antony's servants told her what had happened, so she arranged to have Antony brought to her mausoleum where she had barricaded herself with her maids and her stores of gold, precious stones, and other priceless treasures. Half complete, the structure stood near a temple of Isis on a sandy strip of land with a commanding view of the sea. Rather than unseal the ground-level doors, she and two of her servants hoisted a litter bearing the dying Antony, then pulled him into the tomb through a high window.

Face-to-face with the man she loved, Cleopatra beat her breast and smeared her face with blood from Antony's wound. He did his best to calm her, they exchanged tender words, he drank a cup of wine . . . and then took his last breath.

I have often wondered if Cleopatra slipped a potion into his wine, something to alleviate Antony's pain and ease his journey into death. I suppose we will never know.

I was a witness to the aftermath of those events. After Antony's death, one of his bodyguards delivered Antony's bloodstained sword to Octavian aboard ship. The most powerful man in Rome stared at it for a long moment, gazed at the dried blood on the sharpened edges, and abruptly withdrew into his cabin. Those of us who stood outside heard him weeping.

"See how he mourns the man," one of his advisors remarked. But I knew him better. Antony and Octavian had barely tolerated each other, for they could not be more different.

I believe Octavian wept because the struggle was finally over. For years his leadership and authority had been balanced with Antony's on an unsteady scale, and the weight could have shifted at any moment.

With Antony gone, Octavian found himself free to solidify his role as the sole leader of Rome.

Shortly after that, Octavian made arrangements for us to go ashore.

As we entered the city through the Gate of the Sun, I realized that Octavian had never seen anything like Alexandria. Rome boasted of the same number of inhabitants as the Egyptian city, but Roman people and buildings were jammed together like teetering bricks forced into unreliable positions. Alexandria, on the other hand, had been thoughtfully designed by Alexander the Great. Its gleaming marble buildings occupied wide streets with room for vehicles and people alike. Life was more elegant in Alexandria, freer and far more luxurious.

Crowds had gathered to meet the conqueror, and Octavian walked at the head of his entourage with Areius, an Alexandrian citizen and well-known philosopher. Clearly, the Roman wanted to win the people of Alexandria to his side.

Many noteworthy events filled the following days, and I beheld them at a distance. I will not detail all of them, for my heart and mind were occupied with three things: Urbi, whom I had yet to meet; my father, who might still be alive in the city; and Agrippa.

After Octavian's tour of the city, he turned his attention to Cleopatra, as I knew he would. Before dying, Antony had reportedly told Cleopatra to trust a man called Gaius Proculeius, who served on Octavian's staff. She sent for him, and Octavian allowed Proculeius to go to the mausoleum and stand in front of the barred door where he talked to the queen through a grating.

After Proculeius reported back, I asked for an audience with Octavian. "Why not send me to the queen?" I asked, trying not to sound demanding. "I am ready to talk to her."

"Thank you for your willingness," Octavian said, his tone chillier than it had been when he first broached the idea of my visiting Cleopatra. "But at the moment I want her to feel that she controls the situation, and she has not asked for you."

"She does not know I am here," I pointed out. "If she did —"

"She has threatened to set fire to her treasure," Octavian countered. "So before anything else, I want her removed from that tomb. After that, we shall see."

The next day, Gaius Proculeius visited Cleopatra again in the company of Cornelius Gallus. This time Gallus stood outside the door and spoke to the queen while Proculeius mounted a ladder and climbed through the upper window. With a surprised queen and her treasure in his custody, Proculeius proclaimed Cleopatra Octavian's prisoner and remained with her, her servants, and Antony's body.

The next day, with Octavian's permission, Cleopatra left the mausoleum in order to arrange for Antony's embalming and burial. After she had done so, Octavian had Cleopatra moved to her quarters in the palace. Due to her broken spirit and the wounds she had inflicted upon herself in her mourning, she had grown physically weak.

Octavian charged a freedman, Epaphroditus, with guarding the queen. If he learned that she had plans to commit suicide, he was not to interfere.

On the twelfth day of the eighth month, Octavian summoned me just after sunrise and said his other messengers had failed, so the time had come for me to reunite with the queen. While he met with the citizens of Alexandria in the city gymnasium, I was to go to the palace and obtain an audience with Cleopatra — alone, if I could manage it. I was to offer her safe passage to Rome and assure her of Octavian's commitment to her happiness. Then I was to report back with her response.

I struggled to sort through my swirling emotions as I went to my tent and selected my finest tunic and himation. How should I address her after so many years? Should I be angry with her for the wrongs done to me and my family? Should I demand some sort of restitution? With Cleopatra defeated and broken, I might actually receive some sort of reparation. . . .

I searched my soul for the fury I had harbored for so many years, but little of it remained. Too much time had passed and I had changed too much. I was no longer the girl who had been sold into slavery — I was a free woman, a midwife, and a confidante of powerful people. I would be none of those things if Cleopatra had not betrayed me.

I stood in front of a polished bronze and stared at my reflection. Without a maid to help me, my hair hung long and straight and I wore no jewelry. My features remained pleasing, I supposed, but I looked like a mature woman who had actually *lived* in the world. Nothing of the sheltered girl remained.

I smoothed my hair, adjusted my sandals, and stepped out to greet the guards who would be my escorts. We entered through the Canopic Gate, then turned at the Jewish Quarter, where my heart lurched to see so many familiar sights. People stopped and stared as I passed with my Roman guards, yet no one seemed to recognize me, nor did any faces look familiar.

While Octavian and his party walked to the gymnasium, my guards led me to the harbor, where we took a boat and rowed to Cleopatra's palace on Antirhodos Island. We walked up the dock, moving beneath the impassive gazes of the red-granite sphinxes until we reached the main entrance. A flock of ibises strutted over a patch of grass, their long beaks persistently probing for bugs.

I glanced around, looking for new buildings, and saw several. But one was only half completed and stood on the beach next to the Temple of Isis. That had to be Cleopatra's tomb, emptied now of its queen and its treasures.

I walked to the palace, following the path I had taken so many times before. I led the guards as far as the main entrance, then stopped them outside the building. "Please — wait here."

"We have been ordered to escort you to the queen."

"This is her home," I said, keeping my voice low. "Everyone has deserted her and gone to the gymnasium. I will be perfectly safe."

The captain of my guard considered this, then nodded in agreement.

The marble hallways shone as they had in my childhood, but the place seemed smaller than I recalled. I walked to the grand hall where I had attended banquets and watched Urbi contend with her brother and his ambitious advisors, but the cavernous space was empty. Though the floor was littered with dried rose petals and the detritus of a party, an air of isolation hung over the place.

I left the room and moved to the north wing of the palace, home to Cleopatra's private chambers. Epaphroditus stood outside, and his eyes narrowed when he saw me. "I am Chava, daughter of Daniel the scholar," I said simply. "I would speak to the queen."

He nodded. "I will ask her." He disappeared, and a moment later he opened the door.

The anteroom was empty. I paused before walking into the inner chamber. I had crossed these tiles a hundred times before, but always as the weaker friend, the supplicant, the servant. Things had changed, and this time I held power in my hands — the power to forgive or not, and the power to make things easier for her with Octavian.

But I had never wanted power. All I ever wanted was to be her friend.

I moved ahead into the queen's chamber. Behind the sheer curtains I saw a woman on the bed. Little about her reminded me of my childhood playmate. Her chest was bright and livid with suppurating sores. Her hair, unwashed and undressed. Her eyes, sunken, and her skin as pale as parchment.

But she sat up when I entered, her eyes widening before they settled into a net of smile lines. "It *is* you." Her lips parted, and the ghost of a smile touched her mouth. "My old friend, come to haunt me at the end."

I sank to the floor and bowed — years of respect for her royal position did not vanish in a mere fifteen years. And when I rose, Cleopatra the queen stood before me, her arm extended and quivering as though she would like to embrace me, but feared I might vanish at her touch.

I broke through the awkwardness by lifting my hand and pointing to the straight white line across my palm. "Blood of my blood."

"Heart of my heart," she whispered. "I

have often wondered about you."

We stared at each other across a ringing silence. I breathed in the sweet fragrance of kyphi and was instantly swept back to the day when Urbi and I had taken that vow as girls. How I had loved her! I had been her shadow, longing for nothing more than a lifetime at her side. HaShem had promised that I would bless her, and then He had wrenched me away from her and everything I held dear. . . .

I rose and stood before her. "My queen, I have come here to represent Octavian and his commander Agrippa. They want me to assure you that all will be well if you go with them to Rome."

She searched my eyes for a moment, then her mouth curved in an endearing smile. "Oh, Chava, look at you! Your loveliness has opened doors to the most powerful men in the world, yet you remain completely naïve."

"I am not —"

"If you have been living in Rome," she said, "you cannot believe that they intend me no harm. They will mock me, privately and publicly. They will imprison me as they did Arsinoe. They will put me on public display in one of their gaudy triumphs. And they will murder my innocent children."

"As you murdered Sefu?" The words

slipped from my tongue, but Cleopatra seemed not to hear me. She only looked away and shook her head as if I would never understand.

"Octavian has given me his promise," I said. "If you surrender, he will not harm your loved ones."

She smiled, then pulled the braided cord by her bed. "Are you still so gullible?"

"No," I admitted. "Not everyone is worthy of my trust. I learned that lesson from you."

Two familiar faces appeared from behind a curtain: Charmion and Iras, her handmaids from long ago. The women were older now, with silver strands rippling through their hair, but they had not otherwise changed. Iras greeted me with a surprised smile, but Charmion stared as though she were seeing a ghost.

"Bring food for our guest," Cleopatra told Iras. "Anything but swine."

"I am not hungry . . . and I have come for yet another reason." I lowered my head in an attempt to meet the queen's gaze. "For fifteen years I have dreamed of seeing you again. In the beginning, when anger filled my heart, I planned to storm in here and confront you for the terrible wrong you committed against my family."

Slowly, Cleopatra averted her eyes. "You

have come all the way from Rome to berate me?"

"Not to berate you. To confront you." I raised my chin. "To show you that I could survive without you."

The royal lips trembled. "You left Alexandria," she said, rubbing her arms. "After I returned from Rome I sent a message to the prison, commanding you to come to the palace. You were gone."

The words struck like an unexpected blow. "Why?" I rasped. "After destroying my family, why would you send for me?"

A flush enlivened her pale face. "I did not intend for you to disappear." She put her hand to her forehead. "Yes, I had them take you to prison, but I was upset, pregnant, and worried. You were always so frivolous, always wanting to chatter. If you had not been so carefree, so everlastingly dainty and beautiful, I wouldn't have found it necessary. But he noticed you, of course. And Caesar did not know how to be loyal to only one woman."

I stared at her in a paralysis of astonishment. For a moment I could not speak, then: "You sent me to prison because of *Caesar*?"

Cleopatra's face bore an inward look of deep abstraction — whatever she had felt in those days, she was feeling it again.

"We had just returned from our trip through Egypt," she said, absently stroking her ravaged chest. "I was carrying his son. I thought he loved me. But at dinner, when I told him how you spurned my offer of citizenship, his face brightened like a lantern. 'I remember her,' he said. 'She safeguarded you in the carpet. A man would have to be insentient to forget that exquisite face.' "

Cleopatra blinked, then narrowed her eyes and looked at me. "In all my life, no one has ever called me *exquisite.*"

"My queen —"

"That is when I knew you had to go — and not only you, but your family. If I imprisoned you alone, your father would make trouble at court. So I had to keep all of you away from the palace, away from Caesar." She lifted one shoulder in a shrug. "I did not enjoy issuing the order. But by all the gods, I wanted you out of Caesar's sight."

I pinched the bridge of my nose, feeling as though the earth had shifted beneath my feet. Over the years I had imagined a half-dozen reasons why Urbi sent us to prison, but I had never come close to the truth. How could she be so cruel? So petty? How could she destroy my family when we had never done anything but support her?

I had defied my father to remain by Urbi's side. I had sacrificed the love of a good man, a home, children, everything a Jewish girl should want. I had ignored opportunities and wise counsel from my elders, all so I could remain close to my best friend and somehow be a blessing to her.

"And here you are again," Cleopatra said, her voice as light as a whisper. "And you probably despise me. Have you come for vengeance? Because though I cannot imagine where you have been living, I am certain your life outside Alexandria was not very pleasant."

I stifled the scream that threatened to claw its way out of my throat. How could she sit there and calmly admit what she had done? How could she look at me, once her dearest friend, and admit that she had acted out of simple jealousy? Why didn't she look for me after Caesar died? Why didn't she search for my father?

I realized the answers when I met her gaze. She didn't look for me because there would be other men and other alliances. If I were one of her ladies, I would always be a threat. And while she might have occasionally missed my company, she was far too pragmatic to risk her goals.

I should be grateful she did not choose to scar my face instead.

I drew a deep breath, reluctant to speak of a still-painful memory. "My life has not been especially pleasant. After you left for Rome —" my voice broke, but I gathered my courage and continued — "by Caesar's order, my father and I were sold at auction."

Cleopatra sank to her bed, wrapped her thin arms around herself, and looked up through the wispy hair on her forehead. "You have been a *slave*?"

"Fifteen years."

She looked away and released a sharp laugh. "I have been a slave, too. To Caesar. Antony. Egypt. And, if Octavian has his way, to Rome."

I struggled to restrain an outraged cry as indignation murmured in my ear. How could she compare her situation with mine? She had lived a life of fabled extravagance, and her so-called sufferings were the stuff of other people's fantasies.

I closed my eyes as memories played on the backs of my eyelids — the torture of the slave ship, the indignity of farm labor, the horror of that bloody attack. I saw Sefu, whom Cleopatra had murdered, and Arsinoe, who had been executed at her command. Urbi had been a bright and spirited child, but Cleopatra the queen would calmly murder anyone who stood in her way.

As girls we had been as close as two bees in a hive, but the passing years had hardened and hammered us until we had little in common. How was I supposed to bless the proud, defeated woman who sat before me?

From the corner of my eye, I saw Charmion pick up a feathered fan. She gripped the gold-covered handle and waved it gently toward her mistress, sending a puff of air toward my face. I felt the refreshing cool breath of the breeze, and in that instant I heard the voice I had heard so long ago during that Shabbat prayer: *Your friendship with the queen lies in my hands. You will be with her on her happiest day and her last. And you, daughter of Israel, will know yourself, and you will bless her.*

HaShem was speaking, repeating words that had long been carved upon my heart, but in their familiarity I had grown lazy with them, and I had neglected to remember and consider every word, and no word of HaShem's is ever wasted: ***You will know yourself.***

By the time Charmion lifted the fan again, I understood. Though I had suffered as a slave, HaShem sustained me. Though I was ill-used, HaShem gave me the strength to avoid bitterness. Though I was tempted, HaShem gave me the strength to remain strong. Adonai went with me through the valleys; He was my light on a dark path. He stripped away the indulgences I adored as a child, then He led me through trials that forced me to develop wisdom and maturity. And now that I knew myself and my God, He had brought me home to Urbi.

Because He meant to fulfill His promise.

A flash of wild grief rippled over me when I realized the significance of this meeting. I had been with Urbi on many happy days, but I doubted I would ever be with her again. So this was her last day, and I needed to bless her.

How? I would offer the most valuable gift I could give. A gift that would cost more than Cleopatra would realize.

I would not curse her for her cruelty. I would not burden her with the hard truths of my history. I would not speak of loneliness or pain or sacrifice.

I placed my arms on the queen's shoulders and helped her stand. As her confused, wary gaze moved into mine, I drew her into an embrace. "I forgive you, heart of my heart," I whispered in her ear. "And I thank you for sending me away. I would not be the woman

I am if you had not allowed HaShem to work through you."

Cleopatra did not put her arms around me or respond to my words. When I released her, she tilted her head and gave me a melancholy smile. "The years have changed you."

"They have."

"You seem . . . quite formidable."

"Truly?" I laughed. "No one has ever said that before."

Her eyes rested on me, alight with speculation, then she smiled. "I have not forgotten."

"Not forgotten what?"

"What your God told you."

I wanted to protest, to say anything that would ease her pain, but I could not deny what I knew to be true.

Cleopatra lowered her head, and for the second time in my life I saw her chin tremble as tears welled in her eyes. "But before you go, promise me one thing," she said, her voice in tatters. "Charge Octavian with the care of my children. They have done nothing wrong and they are no threat to him. Despite all of this" — she lifted her hand, indicating the costly furnishings around us — "my children are my only real joys, my only true treasures." Her gaze moved into mine. "I should have asked — do you have children?"

"No, but I have become a good midwife."

Her eyes widened. "I never would have thought so."

I laughed softly. "Nor I."

"I always wanted to be more like you." She smiled and pressed her palm to my cheek. "I am weary and heartsore, my friend."

"Then I will go so you can rest." Before leaving, I took her hand and squeezed it. "Rest well, Cleopatra. You are loved."

Chapter Twenty-Seven

I gave Octavian and Agrippa the truth — I found the palace nearly deserted, Cleopatra was resigned to defeat, and she completely distrusted Octavian.

He waved me away with a twitch of his fingers, then bent over his maps. But I did not go.

"Before I leave you," I said, crossing my arms, "I require one thing."

Octavian looked up, a frown line between his brows. "And that is?"

"Her children," I said. "I promised I would charge you with taking good care of them. They are innocents."

Octavian glanced at Agrippa, who folded his hands. "When we find them, I will entrust them to your care until we are ready to leave. But in Rome, I will have Octavia rear them."

I nodded, knowing Octavia would make a good mother. The children would have the best in all things, as befitted their station, and Octavia would love them as if they had been born to her.

I smiled my thanks and left the men to their plans.

Standing in the middle of the wide Canopic Way, I spread my arms and lifted my face to the sun, celebrating my status as a free woman.

"Crazy as a bedbug," I heard one man say as he walked by with his companion.

"Roman," another said derisively. "What can you expect?"

I ignored them.

I had done what Octavian asked, I had settled things with my former master, and I had come home. I was free to do anything I wanted . . . and I wanted to find my father.

I went first to the Jewish Quarter where I turned a corner and stared, openmouthed, at a new synagogue where a row of homes had once stood. The building was beautiful, gleaming in the sun, and a stela proclaimed in Greek, Egyptian, and Hebrew that the building had been sponsored by Cleopatra VII.

I smiled as happiness bubbled up inside me. Perhaps . . .

An older woman stopped to peer at me.

"Can I help you?"

I gave the commemorative marker an affectionate pat and faced the woman. "I am searching for a man known as Daniel the scholar. He used to tutor the royal children. Have you heard of him?"

The woman turned and squinted toward the horizon. "Heard of him? Yes."

"Good. Do you know where I could find him?"

"No." She lifted her hand and turned away.

"Please — do you know anyone who might know of him?"

I asked several people the same question. Several nodded, but when I asked if they knew where he was, they backed away as if I had leprosy. In a moment of shock I realized they did not trust me. How could they when they no longer knew who I was?

I searched for a familiar face, hoping someone would recognize me, but only strangers passed before me. I blew out a breath and left the synagogue, walking the streets until I found myself in front of our home. The front steps had been swept clean, so someone lived in the house.

Gathering my courage, I went to the door and knocked.

A slave in a white tunic answered. "Yes?"

"I am searching —" I swallowed to overcome the sudden rise of emotion — "for Daniel the scholar, who used to live here."

"Never heard of him." The man attempted to close the door, but I stepped forward, leaning my weight against it. "Please — is your master home? I would speak to him."

The slave chuffed in exasperation, then invited me into the vestibule. "Wait here."

Soon an aged man shuffled toward me, his white beard long and untrimmed. When he lifted his gaze to mine, I realized who he was. "Avraham! You came to the slave auction to tell us about Asher and Yosef."

He squinted. "I am sorry, but . . . Chava? Can that be you?"

I sighed and gave him a relieved smile. "Am I so changed?"

"No. But I never expected to see you again."

I caught his sleeve. "Tell me, do you know where my father is?"

"Daniel?"

"Yes! What happened to him?"

"A miracle that you should come here today." Avraham took my arm and pulled me toward a couch in the atrium. "How did you get here? Where have you been?"

"I have been in Rome," I said, impatient

for news of my family. "I am a free woman now."

Avraham sat and gestured for me to do the same. "Did you travel alone?"

"I sailed with Octavian's forces."

Avraham blanched at the mention of the Roman's name. "Are you a Roman now?"

"Not at all." I squeezed the old man's arm, eager to bring the conversation back around to my family. "I am looking for my father. Is he . . . dead?"

A tremor passed over Avraham's face. "Dead? No, child, not at all. He is here, working."

"Here?" I stood. "Where?"

"Let me have a moment. I will . . . prepare him for you."

Avraham stood slowly and walked away, his hips rocking as he entered the peristyle and headed toward the rooms beyond.

I paced before the reflecting pool, my thoughts racing. Why would Father need to be *prepared* to see me? Was he ill? Was Avraham keeping him as a slave?

My questions were answered a few moments later. Leaning heavily on his cane, Avraham returned, followed by my father, who walked between two slaves. He held his head erect, but his wide eyes were unfocused, and his step was deliberate and even slower than Avraham's.

"Why?" Father asked, irritation in his voice. "Why did you bring me out here? I was working on that passage in Dani'el . . ."

Blind. All those years of reading by candlelight, all the writing and work. He probably had someone read to him now, and perhaps he had an amanuensis to write his thoughts.

I looked at Avraham, who smiled with approval, then I ran to my father. The slaves obediently backed away, leaving him alone in the open space, reaching for support —

I caught his hands and fell on my knees in front of him. "Adonai has brought me home, Father."

His hands trembled in mine. Lowering himself to the sound of my voice, he placed his fingertips on the top of my head, then sank downward until we were face-to-face. "Chava?" His voice broke as his fingers brushed my forehead, my ears, my nose and mouth. "Can it really be you?"

I pulled his palms to my cheeks and let him feel the contours of my face. "HaShem has proven himself faithful. He restored my freedom and brought me back to you."

"Oh, my dear daughter," Father whispered. "Blessed be Adonai. Blessed be the name of the Lord."

We bowed our heads, forehead against

forehead. Tears ran over our cheeks, as warm and healing as summer rain.

"Why are you here?" Father finally asked. "Where have you been?"

"Time enough to explain later," I said, helping him stand. "But have you heard from Asher or Yosef? And how did you escape slavery?"

Father opened his mouth and closed it, unable to speak. Seeing his difficulty, Avraham spoke for him. "Asher sent a letter to this house, and I received it. He is living in Jerusalem, but I will write to him at once and tell him you are home."

"And Father? How did he escape slavery?"

Avraham helped guide my father to a couch. "After Daniel was sold at the auction, some of us combined our resources and redeemed him. The buyer could not resist an offer that doubled his investment."

"These friends wanted me to work for them," Father said, laughing. "Such stern masters!"

A grin flashed in and out of Avraham's beard. "We gave him his freedom at once," he said, "but we wanted him to continue his work on the testaments of the patriarchs. And because I did not think he'd want to live here without you and Asher, I moved in and brought my servants. We've been here ever since."

"But the man who answered the door said he'd never heard of Daniel the scholar. I thought —"

"We have lived quietly and discreetly," Father said, "since we did not know if the queen would continue to look for your brother. We advised Asher and Yosef to remain in Judea, and everyone thinks this house now belongs to Avraham. All the while, Chava, we prayed that HaShem would bring you back to us."

"He did." I paused, letting the words echo in the room. "I have spoken to the queen — Asher is no longer in danger."

Father lifted his head. "He can come home?"

I sank to the edge of his couch and caressed a few stray hairs from his forehead. "Yes," I said. "He and Yosef, too."

"My son will be happy to hear that," Avraham said, slapping his legs. "He has waited years for this day."

I looked at him, a question on my lips. "Has Yosef — ?"

"Has he married?" Avraham said, a smile beaming through his beard. "How could he when he was waiting for you?"

I woke to the sound of grim blasts of rams'

horns, a sound I had not heard since the death of King Auletes. After a moment of confusion, I understood their significance — Cleopatra had joined her father.

I dressed quickly, told a servant where I was going, and reached for a himation to wrap my hair. When the servant protested that a lady should not be on the street alone, I laughed, for I had faced far worse dangers and survived.

I walked to the Canopic Way, heading toward the harbor and the Royal Quarter. A double row of guards stood outside the entrance to the palace. If I wanted to see Cleopatra, I'd have to go through Octavian.

I doubled back and hurried in the direction of the camp outside the city walls. I was flushed and perspiring by the time I arrived, but the guards recognized me and allowed me through the gate. I paused outside the officers' tents and asked for Octavian or Agrippa.

Agrippa must have heard my voice, as he stepped out to greet me.

"How?" I asked, meeting his sober gaze.

He pressed his lips together, then slowly shook his head. "We aren't sure. Some say an asp; others say she took poison. But we found no snake and no bottle, just her and the two slaves."

"Iras and Charmion? What did they say?"

"They were dead, too." He looked at me and nodded. "Come. I'll take you, and I'll tell you everything I know on the way."

Fortunately, Agrippa did not make me walk. He mounted a horse, pulled me up behind him, and we set out. He let the horse walk, which allowed him to turn his head and share the story.

"Last night," he began, "Cleopatra asked the guard to carry a letter to Octavian. When Octavian received it, he read her request that she be buried beside Antony, so we knew she had ended her life. We rode over at once and found her lying on a couch. She was dead already, with one of the slaves lying dead at her feet. Another slave was adjusting the diadem on Cleopatra's brow. A guard asked, 'Was this right, Charmion?' And the slave replied, 'It is entirely right and fitting for a queen descended from so many kings.' "

Clinging to Agrippa, I turned my head so he could not see my tears. The Romans were undoubtedly asking why she would do such a thing, but I understood. Urbi had been raised to be a queen, and bear kings and queens for Egypt. If she could not do those things, she had no purpose for living. She could not imagine being anything or anyone else.

And Octavian could not let her keep the rich and fertile land he coveted.

"Octavian sent for snake charmers," Agrippa went on, letting the horse pick its way through the street traffic. "They tried to suck the poison from the wound, but it did not help."

"Wound?" I forced the word through my tight throat. "She had a wound?"

"Two tiny scratches on her arm," Agrippa said. "Some suggested she had pricked herself with a poisoned pin, the marks were so small."

I nodded and forbade myself to weep. "Go on."

"There is nothing else," Agrippa said, his voice heavy with compassion. "Octavian has given orders that her tomb be finished, that she be allowed to rest there beside Antony. The two handmaids will also be interred there."

We had reached the harbor. Agrippa dismounted, then helped me off the horse. We got into one of the small boats and rowed silently across the gleaming silver waters. We tied up at the royal dock and walked beneath the steady gaze of the red sphinxes, who appeared to have been shocked into wide-eyed silence by the fate of their queen.

Only two guards stood at the entrance to the palace, and they let us pass without a word. Epaphroditus remained at the door to the queen's chambers. He saluted as we entered.

I was about to cross the anteroom on my way to the bedchamber, but Cleopatra lay in the front room on a gold couch, reclining as casually as if she had decided to nap after dinner. Charmion and Iras were with her, Iras at Urbi's feet and Charmion at her side.

I stepped closer. Cleopatra wore the Egyptian-style gown she favored for official occasions, and in her hands she held the ceremonial crook and flail. Beside her, on the couch, lay a stack of letters. After picking them up, I saw all of them were from Julius Caesar.

I placed them back at Cleopatra's side. I did not know if she wanted to be close to them or perhaps remind those who would find her that she had once been precious to Caesar and a valued ally of Rome. In any case, I was glad Octavian had agreed to let her have the royal burial she wanted. He had won, and he would suffer disgrace in the eyes of the Alexandrians if he did not treat her with the respect she deserved.

I turned and tugged on Agrippa's sleeve.

"Let us go."

"So soon?" he asked.

I glanced back at the golden couch. "My friend is gone. Nothing remains here but her memory . . . and I cannot yet bear the weight of it."

I did not weep for Cleopatra as her body left the palace and rode in a gilded wagon to her tomb. I walked with the mourners who tore their hair and split the heavy air with ululations, but I did not shed a tear for the woman whose stone sarcophagus was nearly hidden by the many flowers thrown upon it during its short journey to the grave.

I stood like a statue as the white-robed priests recited passages from the Egyptian *Book of the Dead* and spoke about the afterlife in Greek. When slaves placed Mark Antony's sarcophagus on a stone table next to the queen and prepared to seal the huge double doors, I did not cry.

When Octavian, who stood with Agrippa and other Romans, lifted his hand to the people of Alexandria, I watched with indifference.

My eyes remained dry as I walked away from the tomb. I had not known the woman who loved Mark Antony and bore him three children.

But before going home, I went to the dock, the gateway to Antirhodos Island. I walked over the uneven planks, my ears filling with the hollow sound of sandals upon wood, and settled myself into one of the small rowboats. I reached for the oars, gripped them, and felt a splinter slide into the soft side of my thumb.

And I heard Urbi laughing.

I looked at the bow of the boat, where she had leaned back so many times, legs crossed at the ankles, curls blowing softly in the wind, dark eyes snapping with mischief. For an instant, her image was as clear as spring water, then it faded and all I saw was a weathered boat.

Loving Urbi . . . had been a blessing and a curse. So had Adonai's promise.

"Why?" I looked up to the sky. "Why did you let me know how it would end?"

I heard no answers on the wind, but an ibis that had been strutting over the dock hopped onto the edge of the boat. He tilted his head toward me, then stretched his wings and tucked them again as if settling into a comfortable position.

"Did you know her?" I asked. "Did she ever feed you from this dock?"

The bird danced on the edge of the boat, two steps toward me, two steps back.

Surrendering to my grief, through tears I told the ibis about the most remarkable woman I had ever known.

Rome officially annexed Egypt on the thirty-first day of the eighth month. A week later, I stood by the harbor and watched Octavian's ships sail away. Octavian, Agrippa, and Cleopatra's children by Mark Antony were aboard, and I doubted I would see any of them ever again.

Egypt would never be the same. With Cleopatra's death and Caesarion missing, Egypt had ceased to be an independent kingdom. It was now a province of Rome and would be governed by a Roman representative who reported directly to Octavian, soon to be named *Augustus*.

Would the new *praefectus* appreciate the rich history of the land he administrated? As he walked the halls of Cleopatra's palace, would he respect the genius that had fashioned Alexandria and built the wealthiest kingdom in the world?

I felt the wind blow my himation, flattening it against the side of my face as the sea breeze teased the fabric. The same wind blew the Roman ships farther out to sea, taking Agrippa with them . . . and a little piece of my heart.

"Chava?" Father's voice called to me. I turned and saw him waiting with Avraham.

"Coming."

The city had been overtaken by mourning. Women sat in the streets, beating their breast and grieving for their queen. Cleopatra's reign might have had a difficult beginning, but her people had loved her through feast and famine. Not once had her kingdom been rocked by revolt.

A few weeks later I was blowing out the lamps when I heard a knock at our door. A servant went to answer it and approached me soon after. "Mistress," he said, "a man asked me to give you this."

He placed a scroll in my hand, and my pulse skittered when I recognized the seal: Agrippa's. I took the scroll to a still-burning lamp and unfurled it.

Chava, do not hesitate to listen to the messenger I have sent to you. — A.

I wondered if Agrippa meant to pursue me now that we were no longer slave and master, but then I realized Agrippa was far too honorable to court me when he knew we could never marry. He was also in Rome, so this message had come a great distance.

Curious, I went to the vestibule, where the messenger waited. "Yes?" I asked.

"Mistress." He bowed his head. "Commander Agrippa has asked me to speak to you about a matter of vital importance."

I gave him a polite smile. "You may speak freely."

The man glanced right and left, then lowered his voice. "You may not be aware, lady, of all that is happening in Rome and Alexandria. The Senate has decreed the names Mark and Antony must never again be conjoined. His birthday has been proclaimed an unfortunate day on which no public business can be enacted. Several of Antony's close associates have been sentenced to death, including the Roman senator who supervised the queen's textile mills. People who were among those close to Antony and the queen have been quietly murdered."

Thoughts I dared not verbalize buzzed in some dark place, an ugly swarm. "What has this to do with — ?"

"Anyone who might be respected enough to rally the people to Antony's or Cleopatra's memory must disappear. That includes anyone who was close to the queen." A warning flickered in the depths of his eyes. "Do you understand what I am saying?"

"You think I am in danger? My family too?"

He nodded. "My master dared not put

these thoughts to parchment lest the scroll fall into the wrong hands. So he sent me."

"But I helped Octavian with Cleopatra. Agrippa would never let Octavian send someone to —"

"Octavian does not tell Agrippa everything." The messenger's mouth twisted into something that could not be called a smile.

"What should we do?"

"Leave Alexandria. Go anywhere but Rome. Live quietly. And depart as quickly as you can."

I crossed my arms and tried not to shiver as an evening breeze blew through the open door. An inner voice warned I could be leading my father into a trap. But Agrippa would never betray me, and the handwriting on the message had definitely been his.

"We'll leave soon," I told the messenger. "Though I still believe Octavian would not harm me."

"My master said you might be hard to convince, so he told me to ask you this — did Octavian not promise to keep Cleopatra's children safe?"

"He did."

"Then you should know that Caesarion has been murdered. And Antyllus, Antony's firstborn, was beheaded even as he begged for mercy."

I felt a cold hand slide down my spine. Those two boys were barely men. . . .

"I will not argue," I said, gripping the doorframe for support. "We will leave tomorrow."

We left our home and stayed with a friend of Avraham's as he arranged for our passage to Judea. Two days later, we walked to the harbor, where we boarded a ship destined for a port near Ashkelon, the city that had sheltered Urbi when she ran from her brother at the beginning of her reign.

So long ago . . . and now it was my turn to flee.

"Chava?"

I turned and found Father standing with Avraham on the deck. "Coming."

He smiled as I took his arm. "You are different now, daughter."

"I am?"

"In the best way."

I was not certain what he meant but decided not to question him.

Before I led him to our cabin, he lifted his sightless eyes toward heaven. " 'This sentence is by the decree of the watchers,' " he recited, his voice booming over the sounds of the sea, " 'this verdict by the command of the holy ones, so that the living may know the Most High is sovereign over the realm of man and bestows it to whomever He wishes, and may set over them even the lowliest of men.' "

I looked at Avraham. "Ezekiel?"

"The prophet Dani'el."

The prophet was right, of course. Though I could not understand what HaShem was doing in Egypt and Rome, I knew I could trust Him with the fate of the world.

"The time is near," Father said, turning to me. "The appointed time of *Mashiach,* the Prince spoken of by Dani'el the prophet. He is coming."

I nodded. We were going to find Asher and Yosef, then we would look for the coming ruler in Jerusalem.

It was time to begin another new chapter in our lives, and in the story HaShem had written for the world.

AUTHOR'S NOTE

Egypt's Sister is one of the most difficult books I have ever written, not because I lacked material, but because I had so much. Volumes have been written about the ancient Romans, ancient Greeks, and Cleopatra. I had to sort through many books, choose the most pertinent (and accurate) materials, and work them into my story about Chava, a fictional woman who would have lived in the century before Christ.

I chose to set this series in "the silent years" of the Intertestamental Period because I knew so little about it. I have always wondered how the Hebrew believers of the Old Testament became the Pharisees and Sadducees of the New Testament. How did the Old Testament Jews — who had trouble keeping God's laws — become such over-the-top law-keepers in the New Testament? How did Herod — who wasn't Jewish by birth — come to be their king? How did

Rome become involved in the mix? What Bible were they using? What Scriptures did they have access to? And where does the Talmud fit, if it fits into the timeline at all?

Some days I spent hours trying to track down some fascinating fact about Jewish history, only to realize it had nothing to do with my story.

But though Chava and her family are fictional, I have done my best to make sure the historical characters — Cleopatra, Caesar, Mark Antony, Octavian (who became Caesar Augustus), and Agrippa are represented accurately, along with the culture, geography, and history of that part of the world.

In the paragraphs below, I have addressed some particular areas you might wonder about:

- How do you pronounce *Chava*? The *C* is silent, so it is pronounced hah-vah with that slight throat-clearing sound before the *H.* (Hear it online: http://www.pronouncenames.com/pronounce/chava). Or just say Hah-vah.
- Was Urbi really Cleopatra's name? I doubt it. Many princes and princesses went by pet names within the family and took a traditional name when they

ascended to the throne. Since Cleopatra was an inherited family name (our Cleopatra was at least the seventh of that name), I gave her the pet name *Urbi.* Likewise, I gave the younger brothers the names *Omari* and *Sefu.*

- Some sources state that Auletes had six children, including a firstborn daughter who ruled briefly as Queen Cleopatra Tryphaena. Since not all sources mention this daughter, I omitted her.
- Some sources record that Caesar was divorced from Calpurnia when he met Cleopatra in Egypt; others maintain that he was still married. I mention both possibilities in the text.
- Did Daniel really write the Testaments of the Patriarchs? No, the Greek document actually exists, but the author is unknown. Debate rages over whether or not it was written before the time of Christ. If before, it contains clear Messianic prophecy. If after, the author may have inserted such prophecies.
- Was there really a Jewish Temple in Egypt? Yes. Based on a prophecy in Isaiah 19:18 ("In that day five cities in the land of Egypt will speak the language of Canaan, swearing allegiance

to Adonai-Tzva'ot. Once used to be called the City of the Sun"), a priest from the priestly line of Aaron wrote Ptolemy VI and asked for permission to build a Jewish Temple at Leontopolis. Leontopolis was located in the district of Heliopolis, "the city of the sun." Why? In short, because the Temple at Jerusalem had been desecrated by Gentile invaders. Most devout Jews still sent tithes to Jerusalem, but they could make sacrifices at the Temple in Leontopolis. The Egyptian temple stood until AD 73, when the Roman Emperor Vespasian ordered its destruction.

- Did Cleopatra really get pregnant with a second child from Caesar? Yes (even though it was not recorded in the movie with Elizabeth Taylor and Richard Burton). Stacy Schiff, who wrote a Pulitzer Prize–winning biography of Cleopatra, says that "all of Rome knew it [the second child] to be Caesar's. Either she miscarried or lost this child early, as it is never named."
- Do any of the practices described in Chava's midwifery scroll really work? According to at least one source, the "emmer/barley seed test" is fairly ac-

curate for predicting pregnancy.

- Did Cleopatra die from snakebite or poison? No one knows for certain, but all signs point to poison. The snake was never found, but assumed, as it was part of the Isis folklore. But it is doubtful that a snake could kill three women quickly and leave no physical sign.

  But when Octavian celebrated his Triumph over Egypt upon his return to Rome, the parade featured a figure of Cleopatra with a snake clinging to her.

- Has the tomb of Cleopatra and Antony been found? A lawyer from the Dominican Republic, Kathleen Martinez, believes she may have found the tomb of Cleopatra and Antony on a site known as Taposiris Magna, about twenty-five miles west of Alexandria. If authentic, the tomb would sit below a Temple of Osiris, but further excavations are necessary to confirm her theory.

  However, ancient historian Plutarch implies that Cleopatra's tomb was in the heart of Alexandria, near all the other Ptolemy kings' tombs. If that is where Cleopatra chose to build her tomb, it was likely destroyed and submerged when a tidal wave struck Alexandria on July 21, AD 365. Over the years, the buildings of the Royal Quarter submitted to damage from the wave and earthquakes. Temples, Cleopatra's palace, and other structures from the Ptolemaic Dynasty crumbled and fell into the sea. Not until 1995 were the ruins discovered and excavations begun.

DISCUSSION QUESTIONS

1. THE SILENT YEARS series will be set in the Intertestamental Period, the 400 years between the Old and New Testaments. How much do you know about this time period?

2. How much did you know about Cleopatra before reading this story? Did anything surprise you?

3. Chava's father tells her that God speaks to us in three ways: through the Scriptures, through the voices of our spiritual authorities, and through that "still, small voice." How often do you feel the Spirit of God speaking to you in these various ways?

4. Chava believes that she hears the voice of God. Do you believe she did, or was she only fooling herself?

5. Chava's faith is tested when she's taken from her home and thrust into a dangerously different environment. Have you ever been in a similar situation?

6. Compare the morality of ancient Rome to contemporary culture where you live. How are they similar? How are they different?

7. Can believers in God be close friends with nonbelievers? Should Chava have continued her friendship with Urbi? What were her options?

8. At the end, Chava feels that the promise she clung to for so long was both a blessing and a curse. How was it a blessing? How was it a curse?

9. Have you read any other novels in this time period? How does this one compare?

10. What other stories from the Intertestamental Period would you like to read?

REFERENCES

———. *The Age of God-Kings.* Alexandria, VA: Time-Life Books, 1987.

———. *Pompeii: The Vanished City.* Alexandria, VA: Time-Life Books, 1992.

———. *Egypt: Land of the Pharaohs.* Alexandria, VA: Time-Life Books, 1992.

———. *What Life Was Like on the Banks of the Nile.* Alexandria, VA: Time-Life Books, 1997.

———. *Everyday Life in Ancient Times.* National Geographic Society, 1951.

Achtemeier, Paul J. *Harper & Row and Society of Biblical Literature, Harper's Bible Dictionary.* 1st ed., 837. San Francisco: Harper & Row, 1985.

Beard, Mary. *SPQR: A History of Ancient Rome.* New York: Liveright Publishing Corporation, 2015.

Bianchi, Dr. Robert S. *Splendors of Ancient*

Egypt. London: Booth-Clibborn Editions, 1996.

Boucher, Francois. *20,000 Years of Fashion: The History of Costume and Personal Adornment.* New York: Harry N. Abrams, Inc., 1962.

Budge, Sir Wallis. *Egyptian Religion.* New York: Barnes & Noble Books, 1994.

Bunson, Margaret. *The Encyclopedia of Ancient Egypt.* New York: Facts on File, 1991.

Carroll, B. H. *Between the Testaments.* Walking through the Word, 2013.

Charles River Editors. *The Library of Alexandria and the Lighthouse of Alexandria: The Ancient Egyptian City's Most Famous Sites.* Charles River Editors, publisher, 2015.

Coleman, William. *Today's Handbook of Bible Times and Customs.* Minneapolis: Bethany House Publishers, 1984.

Coogan, Michael D., ed. *The Oxford History of the Biblical World.* New York: Oxford University Press, 1998.

Corbel, Anthony. *Nature Embodied: Gesture in Ancient Rome.* Princeton, NJ: Princeton University Press, 2004.

De Jonge, Marinus. "Patriarchs, Testaments of the Twelve." In *The Anchor Yale Bible*

Dictionary, 181–86. Edited by David Noel Freedman. New York: Doubleday, 1992.
Drazin, Israel. *Mysteries of Judaism.* New York: Gefen Publishing House, 2014.
Everett, Anthony. *Augustus: The Life of Rome's First Emperor.* New York: Random House, 2006.
Fox, Everett. *The Five Books of Moses.* New York: Schocken Books, 1995.
French, Valerie. "Midwives and Maternity Care in the Roman World," from "Rescuing Creusa: New Methodological Approaches to Women in Antiquity." *Helios,* New Series 13, no. 2 (1986): 69–84. Accessed at http://www.indiana.edu/~ancmed/midwife. HTM on April 2, 2016.
Gilbert, John. *Parallel Lives, Parallel Nations, Volume One: A Narrative History of Rome and the Jews, Their Relations and Their Worlds (161 BC–135 AD).* CreateSpace, 2015.
Goodman, Martin. *The Roman World: 44 BC–AD 180.* New York: Routledge, 1997.
Grant, Michael. *Cleopatra.* Edison, NJ: Castle Books, 2004.
Grower, Ralph. *The New Manners and Customs of Bible Times.* Chicago: Moody Press, 1987.

Halley, Henry H. *The Time Between the Old and New Testament.* Grand Rapids: Zondervan, 2000.

Hart, George. *Ancient Egypt.* New York: Alfred A. Knopf, 1990.

History.com staff. "Tsunami Hits Alexandria, Egypt." July 21, 2009. http://www.history.com/this-day-in-history/tsunami-hits-alexandria-egypt. Accessed July 29, 2016.

Ironside, H. A. *The 400 Silent Years.* CrossReach Publications, June 2015.

James, T. G. H. *Ancient Egypt: The Land and Its Legacy.* Austin, TX: University of Texas Press, 1988.

Jenkins, Simon. *Nelson's 3-D Bible Mapbook.* Nashville: Thomas Nelson Publishers, 1995.

Johnston, Harold Whitestone. *The Private Life of the Romans,* 103. New York: Scott, Foresman and Company, 1932. Accessed April 18, 2016. http://www.forumromanum.org/life/johnston_12.html.

Kaster, Joseph. *The Wisdom of Ancient Egypt.* New York: Barnes & Noble, 1993.

Kelpie, Lawrence. *The Making of the Roman Army: From Republic to Empire.* Norman, OK: University of Oklahoma Press, 1984.

La Riche, William. *Alexandria: The Sunken*

City. London: Weidenfeld & Nicolson, 1997.
Mackenzie, Donald A. *Egyptian Myths and Legends.* New York: Avenel Press, 1978.
Manniche, Lise. *An Ancient Egyptian Herbal.* Austin, TX: University of Texas Press, 1989.
McKenzie, Judith. *The Architecture of Alexandria and Egypt: 300 BC–AD 700.* New Haven and London: Yale University Press, 2007.
Metzger, Bruce M., and Michael D. Coogan, eds. *The Oxford Companion to the Bible.* New York: Oxford University Press, 1993.
Miller, Stephen R. Daniel. *The New American Commentary,* vol. 18. Nashville: Broadman & Holman Publishers, 1994.
Montet, Pierre. *Everyday Life in Egypt in the Days of Ramesses the Great.* Philadelphia: University of Pennsylvania Press, 1981.
Murray, Margaret. *The Splendour That Was Egypt.* London: Sidgwick and Jackson, 1949.
Myers, Allen C. *The Eerdmans Bible Dictionary,* 924. Grand Rapids, MI: Eerdmans, 1987.
Nicholas De Lange, ed. *The Illustrated History of the Jewish People.* New York: Har-

court Brace & Company, 1997.
Peters, Melvin K. H. "Septuagint." In *The Anchor Yale Bible Dictionary,* 1102. Edited by David Noel Freedman. New York: Doubleday, 1992.
Platt, Richard. *Roman Diary: The Journal of Iliona of Mytilini, Who Was Captured and Sold As a Slave in Rome, AD 107.* Somerville, MA: Candlewick Press, 2009.
Pollard, Justin, and Howard Reid. *The Rise and Fall of Alexandria: Birthplace of the Modern World.* New York: Penguin Books, 2006.
Pritchard, James, ed. *HarperCollins Atlas of the Bible.* London: HarperCollins Publishers, 1997.
Roberts, Alexander, James Donaldson, and A. Cleveland Cowe, eds. "The Testaments of the Twelve Patriarchs." Translated by R. Sinker. *Fathers of the Third and Fourth Centuries: The Twelve Patriarchs, Excerpts and Epistles, the Clementina, Apocrypha, Decretals, Memoirs of Edessa and Syriac Documents, Remains of the First Ages.* The Ante-Nicene Fathers. Buffalo, NY: Christian Literature Company, 1886.
Romer, John. *Valley of the Kings.* New York: Henry Holt and Company, 1981.
Russell, D. S. *Between the Testaments.*

Philadelphia: Fortress Press, 1960.
Schaff, Philip. *Through Bible Lands.* New York: Arno Press, 1977.
Schiff, Stacy. *Cleopatra.* New York: Little, Brown and Company, 2010.
Schnurnberger, Lynn. *Let There Be Clothes: 40,000 Years of Fashion.* New York: Workman Publishing, 1991.
Schulz, Regine and Matthias Seidel, eds. *Egypt: The World of the Pharaohs.* Cologne, Germany: Konemann, 1998.
Spencer, A. J. *Death in Ancient Egypt.* New York: Penguin Books, 1991.
Steindorff, George, and Keith C. Seele. *When Egypt Ruled the East.* Chicago: University of Chicago Press, 1957.
Stern, David H. *Complete Jewish Bible.* Clarksville, MD: Jewish New Testament Publications, Inc., 1998.
Surburg, Raymond. *Introduction to the Intertestamental Period.* St. Louis: Concordia Publishing, 1975.
Verne, Paul, ed. *A History of Private Life: From Pagan Rome to Byzantium.* Cambridge, MA: The Belknap Press of Harvard University Press, 1987.
Watson, G. R. *The Roman Soldier: Aspects of Greek and Roman Life.* Ithaca, NY: Cornell University Press, 1969.

Wilkinson, Richard H. *Reading Egyptian Art.* London: Thames and Hudson, 1992.

ABOUT THE AUTHOR

Angela Hunt has published more than one hundred books, with sales nearing five million copies worldwide. She's the *New York Times* bestselling author of *The Tale of Three Trees, The Note,* and *The Nativity Story.* Angela's novels have won or been nominated for several prestigious industry awards, such as the RITA Award, the Christy Award, the ECPA Christian Book Award, and the HOLT Medallion Award. Romantic Times Book Club presented her with a Lifetime Achievement Award in 2006. She holds both a doctorate in Biblical Studies and a Th.D. degree. Angela and her husband live in Florida, along with their mastiffs. For a complete list of the author's books, visit angelahuntbooks.com.

The employees of Thorndike Press hope you have enjoyed this Large Print book. All our Thorndike, Wheeler, and Kennebec Large Print titles are designed for easy reading, and all our books are made to last. Other Thorndike Press Large Print books are available at your library, through selected bookstores, or directly from us.

For information about titles, please call:
(800) 223-1244

or visit our website at:
gale.com/thorndike

To share your comments, please write:
Publisher
Thorndike Press
10 Water St., Suite 310
Waterville, ME 04901